Praise for *The Year of Soup*

"*The Year of Soup*, as with his first novel *A Family Institution*, clearly establishes Howard Reiss' credentials as an especially gifted storyteller with a knack for creating fully developed characters and original storylines that engage the readers complete attention from first page to last. *The Year of Soup* is highly recommended and thoroughly entertaining, making it an appropriate addition for community library contemporary fiction collections."

--The Midwest Book Review

"*The Year of Soup*, mixes a fine stew of intelligence and wisdom, while also at times stirring in a sharp wit and a pinch of genuine, heartfelt charm and humanity."

--IndieReader

The Year of Soup received the Silver Medal for Best Fiction in the North-East Region at the Independent Publisher Book Awards in 2013.

HOWARD REISS

Praise for *A Family Institution*

"By understanding our family history we can understand our future. A frank novel of family and what binds us all through our troubles, *A Family Institution* is a choice pick for general fiction collections."

--*The Midwest Book Review*

"The dialogue and the physical descriptions of characters ring with truth."
"If you liked *Where We Belong* [by Emily Giffin], you'll love.... *A Family Institution* by Howard Reiss."

--*IndieReader*

A Family Institution was a finalist in the 2012 IndieReader Discovery Awards.

The Laws of Attraction

Howard Reiss

Copyright © 2014 Howard R. Reiss

All rights reserved.

Published by Krance Publishing

Cover art by Michael Witte

ISBN: 0990806200
ISBN-13: 978-0-9908062-0-2

DEDICATION

To Ellen, my heart's affection, and to Shira, Erin, Lucy and Gus, my imagination.

Chapter 1 – The New Will

"All of my previous selves have their voices, echoes and promptings in me."
– Jack London

It seemed like a run of the mill case when it first came across my desk, a strictly civil matter.

About a year before Ben Everett's recent death, which was not, as the actuaries would have bet, the result of some opportunistic flu virus or too many eggs and fried foods—Ben was eighty-eight years old --but a tandem trailer that lost a tire which rolled a half of a mile down the highway and smashed into his windshield, Ben was befriended by and then betrothed to a twenty-four-year old young woman who now stood to inherit his considerable fortune.

Susannah McCreedy, even the name sounded made up, like the story I expected about love at first sight, and the irresistible, heart-tugging attraction of Ben's bald head, sunken eyes and wizened physique. "A love like the kind I found with Ben," I imagined her saying when I examined her under oath "is timeless, eternal and blind to age."

She wasn't going to sucker me. I don't care how many times she batted her big blue eyes in my direction. I'm immune to that kind of stuff, because I'm not a big believer in love, not that kind of love anyway, the love that overcomes all kinds of obstacles and sticks forever. I never saw it growing up and I never found it . . . not that I looked all that hard, but that's another story.

Of course, she'd be a real looker, Susannah McCreedy, one of those J.C. Penny models who stare back at single men like Ben and me from the breakfast table every weekend having tumbled out of the local newspaper with all the advertising supplements and looking like a long, cool drink of water.

I suppose by the time a man reaches eighty-eight his guard drops, leaving him as gullible as a newborn. So one thing led to another and before Ben knew it he was married and sitting in the attorney's office executing a new will. Some attorneys will do anything for a buck.

Anyway, you read about it all the time, homecare aide loots bank account forging her elderly charge's name or they marry and she gets her one-third spousal share or all of it if she's any good. The family objects, but they wind up settling for some large five or six figure sum to avoid the aggravation and publicity. Apparently, Susannah McCreedy was one of the very good ones since she was getting it all.

I can't deny that I took an immediate interest in the case having had my own experience with May-December marriages being born on my father's 64th birthday to a woman exactly half his age.

In a relationship divided by that many generations one party always dominates, and I mean completely. In Ben's case I had no doubt it was Susannah McCreedy, her bright eyes set on his fortune, who browbeat poor Ben into testamentary submission.

In my family it was the other way around. My father, known as Big Bart, because of his size, not his heart, was a railroad man who didn't stay in one place long enough to settle down, not until they turned him out to pasture at 62.

He wound up in the small upstate town of Cairo, New York where he met my mother, Mary, the Virgin Mary he used to call her on occasion when he'd had too much sacramental wine, who was plain and soft-spoken and still waitressing in her parents' diner.

Not surprisingly, Ben's three sons, Peter, Jeff and Mitch, supported by their 3 wives, 6 children and 8 grandchildren, were ready to declare war to prevent Susannah McCreedy from probating the new will, which Ben conveniently executed about a month before his death. With over $50 million at stake, they were ready to spend whatever was necessary for a total annihilating victory; a dream client and a dream case.

It sounded like an open and shut case. A sixty-four year gulf is an abyss in terms of the stages of life. It will terrify any jury forced to look down into it . . . if it ever gets that far. It'll bring up their own parents and their own children and fears of undue influence and overreaching, particularly since Ben had lost his wife of 45 years, Rose Everett, twenty-five years earlier and had never found anyone to replace her. In fact, according to his sons, he never even looked.

He was apparently one of those rare men satisfied with one great love, and, of course, lucky to have found it.

Indeed, Ben's sons were so incensed when they came to my office that they didn't just want to overturn the will, they wanted to charge Susannah McCreedy with a felony of some kind and put her behind bars for life.

They had almost convinced themselves that their father's death was part of Susannah's plan, as if she had figured out a way to loosen the truck tire, time it so it would come loose about ½ mile ahead of Ben's car and roll it at high speed down the highway, avoiding all the other cars on the road until it smashed into his windshield.

"Win the civil action first," I told them. And, I was sure we would, especially once I learned that Ben had only met Susannah about a month before they were married when she was sent over by Minute Maids to clean his house, replacing his long time Minute Maid who retired when her knees gave out.

"She was earning all of ten dollars an hour," Peter said. "Now she stands to win fifty million dollars. Not bad for ten months work . . . if you can call it that."

I'd undone more than my share of deathbed codicils and wills that radically changed family bequests where painkillers and anger were the motivating force, as opposed to a lovely, young body, although the mechanics and legal principles, I assured the three brothers, remained exactly the same.

In fact, I had prevailed before three juries where the revised wills were tossed aside and the original beneficiaries restored to their rightful place, although in two of the cases the witnesses to the revised wills turned out to be relatives of the new beneficiary and in the third the testator was lying almost comatose in a hospice when he supposedly had a change of heart.

I had also settled at least a half-dozen other cases on the eve of trial for terms quite favorable to my clients, so I assured Peter, Jeff and Mitch in no uncertain terms that the gold-digger would get exactly what she deserved . . . nothing.

"Not only did he redo his will," Peter said, "but a few months earlier he transferred his house to both their names and set her up with a big bank account."

"In lieu of a honeymoon, I suppose," Jeff said.

"How much did he give her?" I asked.

"A half million," Mitch said, "to help her with living expenses."

"She must have expensive tastes," I said.

"Now she does," Peter said.

"He never said a word about changing his will or the house and bank account," Mitch said. "Of course, the old man wasn't very talkative about his personal affairs."

"About anything really," Peter said.

"But he wasn't the type to give away money, not even to charity," Jeff said, while the other two sons nodded vigorously.

"What we have to do in the next ten days is file an objection to the probate proceeding," I said very confidently, the way you'd expect your lawyer to sound. "That will stop the process in its tracks and set it up for discovery and trial."

I told them that they were entitled to a jury trial, which I strongly recommended, although I doubted that it would get that far.

"Usually someone like that is looking for fifty or one hundred thousand to cut and run."

"She's not getting a dime," Jeff said, music to a litigator's ears.

"Can she get at anything in his brokerage account until then?" Mitch asked. "That's where the big money is."

"Not without a court order and then only if she can show compelling need. She'll never be able to do that, not with $500,000 sitting in the bank. I doubt her attorney will even try, since these Surrogate proceedings move pretty rapidly in Rockland County."

I assured them that there was no need to worry and that the $50 million was safe.

"She's a twenty-four-year old god-damn cleaning lady," Peter said, shaking his head and looking morose, as if she had died young, instead of striking it rich, or maybe that's just what he was wishing.

"She was probably living on $150 a week before she latched on to him." Jeff said and the three of their heads bounced up and down in unison, like a couple of bobble-head dolls on the dashboard of a car.

I really didn't care much for Ben's sons, but that's not a requirement for accepting a client under the Code of Professional Responsibility. It would put a lot of lawyers out of business if it was.

The possibility that Ben might have been happier those last ten months, and that perhaps she deserved something, albeit not $50 million, was not a thought any of My Three Sons were prepared to entertain. I think it was Jeff who suggested that she ought to be left out in the desert for the vultures to devour.

I looked at the three of them sitting across from me and imagined them foaming at the mouth and thought to myself the same thing I'd been thinking for the past couple of years-- it was time to quit and start taking those cooking and painting classes.

"Let's talk about your father," I said, flipping the page of my legal pad. "What was his mental state at the time of the marriage and the month before the accident when he did the new will? Would you say he was of sound mind?"

"He was eighty-eight-years old for Christ's sake," Jeff said.

"He fumbled around for words sometimes," Peter added, "repeated himself and forgetting things."

"A lot of old people are like that," I said. "I'm talking about his capacity to make up his mind, to weigh the facts in front of him and come up with a reasoned decision. What will his neighbors in Florida say if we ask them?"

Jeff and Peter folded their arms across their chests and stared straight ahead.

"The old man had all his marbles to the very end," Mitch said, staring down at his fingernails and looking none too happy. "I doubt any of his neighbors would say anything different."

Of course, that wasn't the end all I assured them since men that age can lose their minds in an instant or for an instant over the strangest things, a voluptuous young body for one thing. Besides, no jury in their right mind will believe that it was love at first sight, at least not for a 24-year old woman, except for his irresistible high net worth.

"What will his broker say?" I asked. "Did he actively manage his portfolio?"

"His broker will say that he was as sharp as a tack," Mitch said. "He called almost every day. He invested conservatively and didn't believe in mutual funds. He was strictly blue chip stocks and bonds."

"Finance is one thing, love is another," I said, sounding confident and reassuring--I could strike that tone if the building was on fire and collapsing around us.

"He was no dummy," Mitch added reluctantly, "and that's the whole damned truth."

Only people in denial damn the truth and the truth is never ever whole. It's fragmented like a puzzle with a thousand pieces that you can never quite fit together because the picture's always changing.

"When it comes to love," I said, "common sense is the first thing to go. Just think about all the stupid things it makes people do when they're in their twenties and thirties. Imagine what undue influence it's capable of by the time a man reaches eighty-eight."

That got My Three Son nodding again.

Of course, the only stupid thing it ever made me do was denigrate the intimate details revealed to me as I moved from one love to the next, certain that there was always another and better one around the corner. And there was, until time gradually reversed direction and no love ever seemed as good as the one before it. That's when I learned to love cooking, drawing, reading and keeping my own company.

"You'd think his pecker would have stopped caring at his age," Peter said.

"You never stop looking," Jeff said, "whether it still works or not."

"Would you guys stop it," Mitch said. "This is not about the old man's orgasms."

"I certainly hope not," Peter said.

Another thing I knew, which Jeff touched on, that had nothing to do with the practice of law was that while I once used to think about sex every few minutes or so, especially when I saw a pretty woman, the passing years had simply widened the gap, it hadn't eliminated it.

By the end of the meeting I got them to call me Joe instead of Mr. Clasen. I also had a signed retainer providing for them to pay me $350 an hour, which I recommended over some kind of modified contingency since Ben's estate was considerable and it didn't seem fair for me to have that big an upside for a case as simple as this.

Just before they left, Mitch mentioned that he flew down to Florida to see his father as soon as he heard about the marriage.

Mitch said he looked around the medicine cabinet for some Viagra but didn't find any.

"I haven't been with a woman since your mother died," Ben told him.

"You're eighty-eight, Dad," he said, "You sure this is the right time to change your mind?"

"All he did was look at me with this goofy little smile," Mitch said, "like he was some love struck teenager."

Chapter 2 – The Young Vixen

"I believe I shall, in some shape or other, always exist."
– Benjamin Franklin

"Do you both really want a jury on this?" Judge Shanawit asked in chambers when she met with me and Susannah's counsel, Bill Lustenberger, to set the date for the trial.

I had yet to meet the vixen, but I knew what a jury composed of sons and daughters would think when they imagined her in bed with their elderly fathers. Bill, on the other hand, pretended to be extremely confident that Susannah would play well before a jury.

The judge pushed us a little harder to waive the jury and accept a bench trial to expedite her calendar. She tried every which way, threatening to put us down for trial the next week or delaying it for six months, but neither one of us budged.

The judge set us down for trial in forty-five days, and warned us that there would be no extensions, jury or no jury. That didn't give us a lot of time for depositions, but I didn't need a lot of time. Susannah was first and last on my list. A little investigation into her sordid background–a criminal record is what I was expecting– along with her deposition was about all I figured I needed to send Susannah to the penniless widowhood that she deserved.

What happens when you practice law as long as I have is the exact opposite of what happens in real life. In real life expectations grow lower as you get older – a pretty girl who smiles at me or a train that runs on time is enough to make my day. In my law life, my expectations grow higher. So I was confident that if I gave Susannah enough rope at her deposition she would hang herself well before the trial.

"She's not who you think she is," Bill said on the way out of the courthouse.

"She's twenty-four-years old," I replied. "She's exactly who I think she is."

The next week Susannah McCreedy appeared at my office for her deposition.

My office is in an old building put up right before the Depression, the kind with heavy wooden doors with etched glass and painted lettering, marble floors that echo the steps taken down long hallways and large, tarnished light fixtures in every office that give off a soft dusk-like light which means you need lamps at every desk..

I knew something was odd when I heard her footsteps coming down the hall. They weren't the normal determined clicks of lawyers and businessmen. They were slow and heavy, heavy enough to make the glass in the door rattle a bit with each step.

I opened the door for her before Bill had a chance to.

She was nothing like I had imagined. She was short and fat–borderline obese--with closely cropped hair that made her ears protrude, as if they were trying to reach out to grab hold of something, and a nose that cast a shadow across half her face. Her mouth was the only thing attractive about her. It was big and wide with a perpetual, rather disarming smile.

She had a body like everyone else in the room, but it was hard to distinguish any of its features, certainly the ones below the neck. Her breasts hung down so low that it appeared as if they were in the process of being digested by her stomach and her backside loomed in the background like a large mountain range in the not so distant horizon. Tiny beads of sweat punctuated her forehead as she sat down at the conference room table and tried to catch her breath.

"That's a long hallway," she said, taking a napkin out of her purse to wipe her face.

She smiled up at me, reminding me for a moment of the way my grandmother used to look at me when I was small with a mixture of interest and awe.

Susannah didn't seem the least bit self-conscious about why she was here or the way she looked, certainly not in response to my shock, which must have flashed in neon across my face. She asked for a glass of water, which her attorney promptly poured for her, still smiling at me as he did so, enjoying my surprise.

"I've put on much too much weight over the last few months," Susannah said, taking her handbag off the table, an old-fashioned bag that she probably found somewhere in Ben's closet, and wiggling her bottom to fit better into the chair. It was an old chair made before people got as wide as a lot of people are now and couldn't be very comfortable.

She was at odds with the room, with the narrow windows, the thin crown molding that framed the ceiling, the old prints on the wall of fanciful barristers and English courtrooms and the worn wooden floor.

"All I've been doing is eating since Ben died. I feel as if my seams are about to give up the ghost as well." She laughed when she said that.

"Honey," the court reporter said, "you don't have to talk to me about stress eating. I stuff my face when the weather turns bad."

She clearly wasn't the seductress I had imagined, which meant that I would have to shift my strategy. I would have to argue that she played on every old man's desire for one final conquest, not that she offered Ben the opportunity for an up-close and personal look at what he'd only seen in gentlemen's magazines over the past twenty-five years. At eighty-eight, Ben was at a stage of life where a young, warm female body – no matter the size or shape – rising up to meet him had to be about the only real distraction from the emptiness, the longing and the silence he'd been keeping company with. What jury wouldn't sympathize with Ben? Words of love would have been as good as the real thing to an eighty-eight-year old man like Ben.

It didn't take long for me to realize that while Susannah may have been a high school dropout who looked like she grew up in a trailer park watching TV soap operas and eating stale potato chips out of large bags she was a quick study. She could see the shadows lurking around the corners of my questions sometimes before her counsel did and she refused to follow any of the confessional paths I tried to lead her down.

She wasn't bothered when I repeated the question a different way, because I didn't like the answer or my snide innuendos when I tried to shake her composure. She just answered my questions in her soft spoken and pleasant way with a smile that seemed so genuine it took an effort not to smile back.

She never rushed her answers and listened carefully to everything Bill and I had to say, as we spared with each other like a couple of young boys too afraid to actually throw a punch, without getting involved or appearing the least bit upset.

She didn't seem interested in explaining herself or asking for forgiveness.

In short, she was the consummate actress.

I tried making some of my questions more overtly accusatory to see if that might help me find her tipping point, since the goal of any deposition is to get the witness talking without thinking and the one surefire way to do that is to get the witness angry or agitated. Unfortunately, she wouldn't take the bait and the only ones who grew hot and agitated were Bill and I.

Susannah apologized on occasion for not being able to answer the question to my liking, but she never changed her answer. Susannah wasn't a fire-eater, willful and full of spirit, filled with ambition, instead she seemed more like the grieving widow Rose would have been if she'd outlived Ben.

"There was nothing cuter," Susannah said, "than the way Ben used to look up at the first evening star he saw and stop to make a wish . . . the same wish every night."

"And what was that?" I asked.

"For there to be a place to go when he was through."

"You mean heaven?" I asked.

"Exactly."

I cleared my throat and rolled my eyes. Susannah just smiled back at me. But I was still sure that the pressure would eventually get to her and I expected Susannah to eventually play right into my hands, as soon as I got to the heart of the matter, which was when I asked her to describe how she first fell in love with Ben. I expected her to say it was while she was mopping his kitchen floor and looked up to watch Ben carefully tucking his handkerchief into his pocket.

"I didn't fall in love with Ben while cleaning his house," she said sweetly, as if I was not a litigator set on ruining her reputation, but a casual friend who just didn't seem to get it. "And he didn't fall in love with me while I was scrubbing his floor, which I assume is your next question."

"Love at first sight?" I asked which I didn't believe in any more than I believed in God or heaven and hell.

I remember asking my mother once when she first knew that she loved my father. I had to have been very young, since later after taking notice of the way he treated her I knew better than to ask a question like that. She didn't answer right away. She was standing at the sink doing something, probably plucking the chicken that my father insisted on having every Sunday for dinner. She didn't turn around. All she said was, "When I decided I'd had enough of the diner."

"No," Susannah said, "It wasn't love at first sight."

"Are you saying that neither of you fell in love?"

"I'm saying that I arrived that first day already loving Ben, although I didn't know how or why, not until I came to understand."

"Understand what?" I asked impatient for an answer that I was certain would blow her case out of the water.

"Something that had been bothering me my whole life."

I had to bite my lip to keep from laughing and shouting out a dozen questions. I had to let the rope out slowly.

"What was that?" I asked quietly to nudge her a bit when she just sat there with her eyes closed and a hand over her mouth, as if she were reliving that very moment.

"I've always had this feeling," she said, "Ever since I was a little girl that it wasn't just me in here." She touched her breast or at least the mound of flesh that sat right below her heart. "That there was someone else."

"Another person," I said, dumbfounded by how easy this was getting. Was she going to pretend to be schizophrenic? I looked over at Bill expecting him to be squirming in his seat, but he just sat there doodling.

"No," Susannah said, "not another person, more like another memory and a different lifetime . . . like I'd been here before . . . and not too long ago."

"Déjà vu?" I said more a reflex than anything else, like it was a game of charades and I finally had the answer. It's important for an attorney to control the pace of a deposition and to keep the witness off-balance, but if anyone was off-balance at the moment it was me.

"That's close," she said, "but not the way you're using the word or most people do. It's not a coincidence or a simple matter of familiarity. Déjà vu is much more than that. It's based on an experience, an actual presence and memory that originated somewhere else, someplace deep inside. We all experience that feeling from time to time because we're all . . . ."

She hesitated here, like she wanted to give me a chance to catch up.

"We're all what?"

"Reincarnates, you see when I saw Ben I didn't see an eighty-eight-year old stranger. I saw him, for a moment, the way he was as a young man, the way he was when I first met him, and fell in love with him."

The stenographer nearly knocked over her machine and I wondered for an instant if I had heard correctly. I asked the stenographer to read back the answer, which she did.

"Do you mean to say you saw what he probably looked like as a young man?"

She shook her head slowly from side to side.

"No, that's not what I mean."

"Wasn't that the first time the two of you met, when Minute Maid sent you over to clean his house?"

Susannah sat back in her chair, a little half-smile on her face, as she thought it over.

"No, Mr. Clasen," she finally said, leaning forward in her seat, "that was not the first time. Déjà vu is a very real feeling, because it's based on an actual memory, even if it's one we can't readily identify. It's because we have all lived before, we are . . . ."

"Reincarnates, yes I got that," I said, interrupting her answer, which a lawyer should never do, "but what does that have to do with you and Mr. Everett. Can you expand on that?"

"Certainly, we are all souls traveling from one life here on earth to another until we have reached a level of understanding and purpose that permits us to spend the rest of eternity in God's presence."

I inhaled deeply and leaned back. Then relief washed over me and I covered my mouth to hide what I feared might be a smirk. If I couldn't have the unlikable vixen, the Playboy centerfold with a greedy heart, at least I could have a crackpot, some spiritual fanatic whose cruel trick on Ben would seem even more outrageous considering that she took aim at the weakest spot in his heart, the empty place left by his beloved wife Rose.

"Aren't we always in God's presence?" I was just trying to keep the ball rolling since I was completely off my outline.

"God's immediate presence."

Susannah sat there completely relaxed, her hands folded neatly in her lap.

"Are you saying," I said, trying to figure out the best way to phrase it so I could read it back to a jury if she changed her mind, "Are you saying Ms. McCreedy that you are the reincarnation of Ben's wife Rose?"

She looked up at me, her eyes focused on mine, and put her hands flat on the table.

"Yes I am," she said.

"Who died before you were born?"

"That's the only way to be a reincarnate."

Susannah smiled after saying that, not a big smile, just a little one, with her lips closed, not like she was laughing at me or fighting to keep her jaw from coming unhinged, but more like she was relieved to have finally let her secret out.

"Perhaps I should start calling you Rose?" I said which got a quick objection from her attorney on the grounds that I was badgering the witness, along with an instruction not to answer.

"That's OK," Susannah said. "The answer is no – a soul does not have a name. It only does during its life here on earth and in this life my name is Susannah."

She looked across the table at me, her eyes clear, her lips pursed together and her head shaking, as if she were feeling more pity than anything else. There wasn't the least bit of tension evident in her neck or shoulders, which is always the first place I can spot it in a witness worried about keeping a story straight.

"You're not a believer are you?" she asked.

"I've never given reincarnation any thought." I said.

"Do you believe in God?" she asked.

"I appreciate your interest Ms. McCreedy, but I ask the questions here, I don't answer them."

"I understand," she said. "But assuming you do believe in God and the eternal soul then what I'm saying shouldn't seem all that improbable."

She held my gaze waiting, I suppose, for a nod or some kind of admission on my part, but I just looked down at my legal pad. Now I know what I'd like to believe – that my mother who died when I was ten sits high above the clouds watching me trudge through life, avoiding the big mistake she made–but wishing hardly passes as faith, especially since what I've come to believe, as surely as I believe in the rule of law, is that it's lights out at the end.

My mother's death has always been a mystery to me. I came home one day in fifth grade and she was gone.

"Taken by the Lord," my father said.

He performed whatever ritual he believed was required that night in the living room. It was just the two of us and since my father didn't believe in emotions, I didn't show any of mine. He said displaying emotion was like questioning the will of God.

I thought this might be an exception since I couldn't imagine that the Lord would be upset by a little sadness, but there were no exceptions for my father. No one came to the house to pay a visit or to drop off a casserole the way they did for the neighbors, and my mother wasn't buried in the church cemetery along with her parents, but in the town cemetery next to the dump.

He never said a word about how she died, although after I became old enough to leave and run as far away as I could it dawned on me that it was might have been by her own hand, which would explain why she wasn't buried beside her parents and my father removed any trace of her from our house, refusing to ever say her name again.

I guess he felt that by performing some of his homemade Catholic rites during a makeshift service, attended by the two of us and two big men with shovels, he'd compromised as much as he could in terms of his God and rejecting her after she was gone was the best way to make amends.

"Just to be clear," I said, looking up from my notes, "You are swearing under oath unequivocally and without any doubt whatsoever that you are the reincarnation of Ben's late wife Rose."

"Reincarnate, yes, I am the same soul."

"And you married him because . . . because, in effect, you were already in love . . . already his wife."

"At one time, most souls spend many lifetimes together in one form or another. Ben and I have probably been together on and off for a thousand years."

"In one form or another?" I repeated.

"Yes."

"Can you elaborate on that?"

"I'm sure we weren't always husband and wife, although that is the only relationship I've been privileged enough to see. We could have been brother and sister, or father and son, or just good friends, any combination really."

"Could you have come back as Ben's pet?"

I meant it as a joke, but Susannah answered despite her attorney's objection.

"There are some sects in India that believe you can come back as an animal. They revere animals and treat them with great respect. However, I believe it's always a human form."

"You don't know for sure?"

Susannah smiled.

"I don't know any more than you do about God's ways. I only knew about my last life as Rose, because I was given this rare gift of second sight. It was as if someone suddenly turned on a light in a pitch black room."

I took a deep breath.

"So you're telling me that Ben fell in love with you and gave you all his assets, his worldly assets, because he believed you were his reincarnated wife?"

I raised my voice a bit for emphasis, as if I were already standing in front of a jury. Bill Lustenberger didn't object to this question, although he reminded me that it was a small room, and that I did not need to raise my voice.

"The answer is yes," she said, "which shouldn't be at all surprising since I am the same soul that he loved his whole adult life and shared for many others before that."

It sounded so bizarre, but she said it so softly and with such conviction that it seemed as if she really believed it. It was clear to me that Susannah McCreedy was either an Oscar caliber actress or certifiable, although I suspected the former.

"But if you are a reincarnate, if we all are, how is it you know your past life and the rest of us don't?" I asked. "What makes you so special?"

"That's two questions," Bill said.

"Answer the first one," I said.

Susannah looked up at the ceiling for a moment. Her eyes were a bit teary when she looked down, as if I'd finally asked a question that had somehow disturbed her peace.

Oh, she is good, I thought, probably too good for her own good. A jury is going to see right through that pretend look of longing, empty one moment and full the next.

"I don't know," she said very slowly and deliberately. "I wish I did. There is a door that closes one life off from another, except after death when it opens and you can know them all. For some reason, Rose's life never completely closed; as if the door was left open a crack.

"It was something I could feel as a child in bits and pieces, like there was a light shining in from the other side and if I pressed my eye hard enough against it I could catch glimpses of something, another world, which I eventually realized was the sixty-three year old me."

It was so quiet in the room it seemed as if all of us, except for Susannah, were holding our breaths.

"When I saw Ben it all flooded back, as if the door opened wide for a moment."

"How convenient for you," I said.

"Objection," Bill said, "argumentative, move to strike."

"I'll withdraw it."

"It was a good feeling, but a strange one," she said, as if she hadn't heard a word of our colloquy. "My whole body started to tingle, but I felt this enormous peace and relief. It was like a question that had been bothering me my whole life had been answered."

"What question was that?" I asked.

She looked over at me and sighed, as if she were feeling sorry for me.

"What happens after we die?"

With that I took a short bathroom break to compose my thoughts. Bill and I met at the urinals.

"I'm sure you were as surprised as me by this . . . story . . . when you first heard it," I said.

Bill didn't answer.

"You may want to consider a quick settlement," I said, "before she winds up with a quick commitment and becomes the laughing stock of the media . . . if this ever gets out."

Bill finished up his business before responding.

"How are you going to disprove it?" he said.

"She'll trip up over something," I said, "Con artists like that always do."

"I'll be interested to see that happen, because I haven't been able to shake her."

Of course, there are bound to be some questions about Rose's life that Susannah will think she knows the answer to, that she ought to know the answer to if she's channeling Rose, but she won't. Some misstep will cause her to stutter and blush; once a lie like that begins to crack the pieces fall away quickly enough.

"The burden of disproving it may be on me as a matter of law," I said, since we were the ones challenging the will, "but for all practical purposes it's going to be your burden to get a jury to believe a story as preposterous as that."

"You never know with juries," Bill said with a shrug.

"She's going to sound like just another one of those false prophets predicting the Rapture, another self-proclaimed Messiah, this time with the answer to the afterlife, but really just looking for a beach house."

"She doesn't sound that way to me," Bill said. "She sounds pretty sincere. She's a remarkable young woman, mature way beyond her age."

"A twenty-four year old cleaning lady who comes back from the dead to remarry her eight-eight year old husband who happens to be worth fifty million dollars – how sincere is that going to sound to a panel of our local suburban housewives, husbands and children?"

"I don't know," Bill replied, walking over to the sink, "I guess it all depends on what they think of her. But the world is a strange place and there's a lot we don't know."

"And she does?"

"She sincerely believes it and that's got to count for something, particularly if Ben did as well. It may be a tough sell . . . but so are a lot of things the priests and ministers tell us. It's probably not any tougher than believing in any of those May - December romances."

Particularly the way she looks, I thought to myself.

"An eternal soul – that's been drummed into most of us since childhood," Bill continued as he dried his hands. "It's got to go somewhere, why not come back. Over half the world believes it . . . that's going to give the jurors some pause."

I chuckled, my lawyer's chuckle, high performance art; I could do it staring down the barrel of a gun if I had to.

"Always the zealous advocate," I said.

Bill shrugged again.

"In any event," he said, stepping aside so I could reach for a paper towel, "It's going to be up to the jury, because I've been told in no uncertain terms no settlement no matter what the amount. She says Ben wouldn't have wanted it any other way."

"He wanted to disinherit his sons and grandchildren?" I said.

"He wanted to leave his money to his wife."

"His wife of 45 years," I said, "Not 45 weeks."

"And his wife will in the normal course leave it to the children and grandchildren," Bill said.

"What are you saying?"

"She executed a will the other day in my office leaving most everything to Ben's three sons."

"That's very thoughtful considering that she probably has a life expectancy of 60 years. Ben's three sons will have died long before her, assuming she hasn't spent it all by then or changed the will a dozen times."

Bill held the door open for me.

"I don't believe she thinks like that," he said. "She also intends to give a lot of it to them over the next few years."

"A real philanthropist."

"Hey, that's her position . . . if your clients are interested."

"So you are suggesting that they withdraw their challenge to the will and hope for the best?" I said. "Hope that she'll start acting like their real mother, instead of some con artist who claims to be possessed?"

"I'm not suggesting anything," Bill said, as we started walking back to the conference room. "Take it for what it's worth."

"If I can get her fifty thousand," I said, "and I'm not sure the family will go that high, I'm sure she'll take the money and run."

Bill stopped and looked me in the eye.

"I might recommend she consider it," he said and knowing Bill I had no doubt that he would, "but she's made it clear that she won't settle. She may be the weirdest client I've ever had, the only one I can remember who isn't all about the money, but she's damn clear about what she believes and what she wants."

"I suppose it's all the prior lives," I said with a smile, "the centuries of experience add up."

Bill smiled.

"Apparently it hasn't worked all that well with us," he said.

"You can say that again."

I paused before opening the conference room door.

"She's going to lose it all, you know," I said, using my confident litigator's voice, deep and unwavering. "No jury is going to buy that reincarnated first wife crap, even if they're all Hindus. They'll be scratching their heads at why God decided that Susannah McCreedy should be the one to prove to the world that there's life after death and in the process receive a 50 million dollar payout for her efforts. It seems like God could come up with a better and cheaper way of relieving the world's anxiety."

"You're probably right," Bill said with a little smile of his own, "but we all know that both God and juries work in mysterious ways."

With that we both entered the examination room and Susannah smiled.

"Are we almost done?" she asked.

"Far from it," I answered, as a matter of principle, although I hadn't come prepared with secrets from Rose's past life to trip her up with. What I did instead was ask her for as many Rose memories as she could recall so I could get them down on the record.

"Rose liked her hair short, I remember that.

"She liked to knit.

"I remember one vacation we took with the boys to the Adirondacks. We stayed in a cabin on the lake . . . I think it was called Schroon Lake."

When I pressed for more details and more memories she apologized saying that a reincarnate's view of the past is limited.

"It's like looking down from a mountain into a deep valley," she said. "I can see the big picture a lot better than the small details."

"That's very convenient," I said.

"Objection, that's not a question," Bill said.

"Withdrawn."

"Sometimes my Rose memories are clearer than other times. Past life memories come and go," she added, "Much like the sun on a partly cloudy day."

"And they're not that clear right now I take it?"

"No."

"But they were clear enough," I said, "When you first met Ben?"

"Yes, they were very clear the first few times we were together, most of the time actually. From what I've read past life memories can become a lot more focused when you're someplace you've lived before or with a person you once shared a life. I guess that's the spark behind déjà vu."

"I've never been so lucky," I said.

"Objection," Bill said.

"Perhaps one day you will be," Susannah said.

"So the memories were sharper when you were with Ben?"

"Yes."

"So they should come in loud and clear when you're with Rose's three sons as well, shouldn't they?"

"It could if they're open to it, at least with respect to their Rose moments."

"And if it doesn't? If their presence doesn't bring anything from Rose's past life into focus, what does that mean?"

"It doesn't mean anything. It could simply mean that we don't have a long history together . . . as souls. The past life recollections were strong when I was with Ben, because we shared so many other lives together. That might not be the case with Pete, Jeff or Mitch."

Their names slipped easily from her tongue, as if she'd said them a thousand times before. I wondered how many times she'd practiced that.

"Sitting in a conference room with two lawyers and a court reporter isn't conducive to seeing Rose's soul?"

"Oh I can feel it, my soul is always there," Susannah said, touching a spot between her breasts but a bit lower toward her stomach. "It's just that the past memories aren't clear . . . certainly not like they were when I was with Ben."

I was impressed by how well she'd thought this out and how well she delivered her lines, but I knew she would eventually falter. "How about if you close your eyes and pretend that I'm Ben," I said.

Bill objected and instructed her not to do that or respond.

"I'm sorry," she said, ignoring Bill's instruction, "It doesn't work that way. You can't pretend something like that. It depends on a very real spiritual connection, not imagination. Besides, you can't control the way past life memories come and go – I wish I could. I like it when I can see some of life through Rose's eyes. She learned a lot in her sixty-three years."

"Her eyes?"

"Her experiences."

"Have you seen any other past lives in there?" I asked.

"No, I know they're there, I can feel them sometimes, but I can't see them, not like with Rose."

"How about something during the Civil War?"

"I can't see beyond Rose."

"How about the Revolutionary War?"

"I'm sorry."

"Why just Rose's life?"

"I don't know, I suppose because it's the most recent."

"Can you see any future lives?"

"Of course not," she responded.

It was a question intended to annoy her and make her lose her patience. "Just the one past life as Ben's wife, Rose?"

"Yes."

Bill may be the settling type, I thought, looking through my notes for some more questions, but you can't settle unless you can convince your client to accept the offer and it was clear to me that Bill was unlikely to have any real control or influence over Susannah. I suspected that nobody did, except perhaps for her imaginary Rose.

I managed to stretch the examination out for another hour, but nothing really important came out. Susannah explained how after a few cleaning visits she told Ben what she was feeling and what she saw. He was less surprised than she had imagined he would be.

"He sensed something himself," she said, "because he hadn't found a woman this easy to talk to in twenty-five years."

"He said that?"

"Yes."

They spent the afternoon talking about their early years together and some of the more memorable moments from their marriage.

"Like what?" I asked.

"Like the time we sat by that lake in Bear Mountain and watched this tremendous thunderstorm coming. That was the night we got engaged. The lightning and thunder were spectacular, like 4th of July fireworks, but we didn't budge and did we ever get soaked."

Susannah smiled.

"Not a smart thing to do I know, but the war was over and we sort of felt like nothing bad could happen again, at least not for a while."

"What war?"

She looked across at me like a disappointed teacher.

"World War II."

"What else do you remember talking about?" I asked.

"The costume party we went to dressed as Ben Franklin and his kite. I was the kite."

"I wasn't wrong about anything," Susannah said. "I knew all the dates and places, which amazed Ben, as well as me. It was a little scary."

Child's play on the internet, I thought, or for a good carnival card reader able to draw out her customer and pick up on his subtle cues, mention a few moments and let him draw them out so it actually seems as if she's the one remembering, not him.

"This was strange, new territory for both of us," she added.

"Did Ben ever doubt what you were telling him?" I asked.

I was hoping the answer was no, because that would suggest Ben didn't have all his faculties.

"Of course he did. Ben's mind was sharp. His eyes might have appeared a bit cloudy, but they could see right through me; they always could. You should have seen them when he was a young man; they were like lasers. And to tell you the truth I doubted it almost as much as he did.

"I was trying to prove it to myself, as much as I was trying to prove it to him. It was hard for me to believe. To believe you've lived before is one thing, to find the soul you actually lived with, well, that's a whole other thing. So we just talked and talked, and after a while it was as if our souls recognized each other."

I looked up at the old fixture overhead which suddenly seemed much too bright for the room and stared a moment at the dust motes that circled around it.

I didn't have much left to ask at this point, but I wasn't ready to end it on that note.

"Are you a Scientologist?" I asked.

I had read recently in the paper in an article about Tom Cruise that Scientology believes each of us have had many lives.

"No, I'm a Christian."

"But the church doesn't believe in reincarnation."

I knew that from growing up. My father liked to discuss his Church dogma with me every night at dinner, particularly after my mother died.

"The original Christians did," she said.

I had to look that one up and it turned out she was right.

"When did you and Ben decide to get married?" I asked.

"I didn't feel it was necessary. I felt as if we were already married."

"Are you suggesting that Ben was the one who forced the issue?"

"He insisted that we get married, it didn't matter to me."

"You know," I said, "he could have left you all his money without marrying you, all he had to do was change his will."

"I didn't ask for that either," she said.

"However, the marriage did assure that he couldn't completely disinherit you, that you would get one-third as a matter of law . . . unless there was a prenuptial agreement or a waiver. Did you ever discuss a prenuptial agreement or waiver?"

I expected the answer to be no, I wanted the answer to be no, but again I underestimated her.

"Yes, I signed one."

"A prenuptial agreement or a waiver?"

"The second one," she said.

"A waiver of your one-third spousal inheritance?"

"Yes, that one."

"I demand its production," I said to Bill, "because it's not in any of the papers you've produced so far."

"You have everything," Bill said. "Ms. McCreedy has looked for it, but hasn't been able to find it."

"So you were aware," I said, turning back to Susannah, "that under Florida law you would be entitled to one-third of his estate upon getting married unless you signed a waiver?"

"I was not, but Ben was and he explained it to me. It was never about the money so I didn't care."

She had to have help, I thought, to be this well prepared.

"So you signed the waiver and married Ben knowing you would not be entitled to anything from his estate."

"That's right I didn't want anything from Ben."

"Is it your testimony that you didn't want Ben to change his will?"

"He suggested it and I told him I wasn't interested. I liked this new life fine enough the way it was. I liked the freedom of putting everything I owned into the back of a car and driving off to my next adventure. But he had a new one drafted up anyway without telling me, because he said it was what he wanted to do. When Ben made up his mind there was no changing it."

I leaned back on my chair. I liked her testimony here. She was trying to sound a little too disinterested in the fortune she was now fighting so hard to retain.

"One thing we did discuss," Susannah went on without waiting for another question, "was Ben's concern about what would happen to me after he died. He didn't want me being kicked out into the street and cleaning houses again, so he said he was putting the house in our name as a married couple, so I'd get it when he died, and setting up an account for me at the bank with enough money to cover my living expenses."

"You didn't object to that?"

"No."

"That account for your living expenses has $500,000 in it, isn't that right?"

"I didn't know the amount back then, I didn't ask, but I do now. Yes, it was $500,000."

A house and a half million to cover living expenses – that merited a place in any con artist's hall of fame.

"But he did more than that," I said, "he subsequently decided to change his will to give you everything . . . almost $50 million."

"He did," Susannah said, "but as I said I never asked him to. I tried to discourage him from doing it, but he insisted."

"Even though you would have gotten a third anyway?"

It was a trick question.

"But I had signed a waiver so I wouldn't have."

Bill, who had been ready to object, just sat back his arms folded over his chest.

"But you can't find this so-called waiver?" I asked.

"Objection."

"I'll rephrase it – You haven't been able to find the waiver that you say you signed?"

"No."

"What have you done to look for it?"

"I've searched the house from top to bottom," she said.

"And you have no idea where Ben would have put it - the same Ben you'd spent a whole prior lifetime with?" I asked, pretending to be incredibly shocked.

"Counsel," Bill said, "enough with the theatrics."

"No, Ben was never very organized. I was . . . Rose was always the organized one, the keeper of the records, I'm still the same way now, but I'll keep looking."

Clearly, she was setting herself up for a win-win situation considering that I was 100% convinced that Ben had not asked her to sign a waiver before they got married. But by claiming that he did, she was suggesting to the jury that Ben was careful and cautious when they first married, the opposite of a man subject to undue influence, and thus equally deliberate and competent when he decided to change his will.

Of course, on the remote chance that she had signed a waiver, she could have thrown it away without Ben's knowledge so she could still claim her one-third spousal share in the event she couldn't convince him to change his existing will, which left everything to his three sons.

The flaw in her plan was that if she lost in court and the jury decided that the new will was not valid, she couldn't fall back on her one-third share having sworn under oath that she had signed a waiver.

A gutsy call, I thought, going for broke like that.

"If he was so careful to make sure to get the waiver before marrying you and equally careful to make sure you had the house and a large bank account to live on after he was gone, what made him change his mind and decide to give you everything?"

She looked down at her hands, which she was rubbing together as if they were bothering her.

"I think that after a while any doubt he might have had . . . we both might have had . . . about who I was disappeared. Most everything he had was what we accumulated together during our marriage, which had grown significantly of course over the past twenty-five years – Ben was very good with investments - so I think he came to believe that it was mine or should be mine to do the right thing with, which he knew I would do."

"You being Rose?"

"Me being Susannah McCreedy with the same soul as Rose, he knew that I'd do the right thing with the money, because they were my children and grandchildren as well. It was something we discussed before the will was signed . . . and after."

I stared intently at her for any indication that she was bluffing or pretending - a self-conscious glance away, the slight biting of a lower lip, a nervous tapping of the finger or a bouncing leg, but I saw nothing, nothing but stillness.

"But you weren't close to his sons during your short marriage, were you?"

"No, I regret that, but it was awkward."

"In fact, you hardly spoke to them at all."

"It was clear they didn't want to speak to me, but I understood completely. I knew how it must have looked."

"Did Ben think you would become closer after he passed away?"

"He wasn't planning on the accident. He planned on living a long time, we both did. I think he thought that the boys would come around after we were together a while and that they'd eventually be able to see what he saw."

"Rose?"

"Her soul," Susannah said.

"Why didn't the two of you ever tell them about Rose and your prior life while he was alive?"

"We talked about it. Ben used to joke that they'd probably have him committed and me arrested."

"You would agree that reincarnation is not mainstream, wouldn't you?"

"Not here, though it is in much of the world. Ben felt they weren't ready and I agreed. The age difference was hard enough to accept. I'm sure we would have told them after a while."

Susannah took out a tissue and wiped her eyes.

"Of course, we didn't see the tire coming."

Bill asked for a few moments while he refilled Susannah's water and got her another tissue.

"Why did he leave it all to you," I asked again, "if he wanted most of it to wind up eventually with his children and grandchildren? Why not just leave a significant portion directly to them?"

"I suppose it was his way of telling me . . . and them . . . that he believed in the truth of our love and marriage, that he saw my soul as I did and knew I'd do the right thing in terms of our children and grandchildren."

"I would caution the witness not to suppose or guess," Bill said, "and only testify to what she knows."

Susannah looked at Bill and nodded.

"Your children," I repeated in amazement, "are more than twice your age. They're not your sons any more than they're mine."

Bill objected and instructed Susannah not to respond; I would have done the same if I were in his shoes. Of course, she ignored him.

"Age is irrelevant when it comes to the soul. All of our souls are ancient and have traveled together for eons. I'm sure that this is not the first time that our lives on earth have come together," she said, pointing at me.

"Is that from memory or belief?"

"That's what reincarnation teaches," she said.

"That age difference you're so quick to dismiss," I said, "is significant in terms of our needs and desires down here on earth, wouldn't you agree?"

Bill looked up from his pad, but I think he was tired of wasting his objections at this point. Neither Susannah nor I seemed to be paying much attention to them.

"It certainly is."

"The sixty-plus age difference between you and Ben was significant with respect to a lot of things, wasn't it?"

Susannah sat back in her chair and sighed.

"Yes, certainly with respect to a great many things."

"Some important things, like stamina, appetite, sexual performance, reasoning, susceptibility and memory."

"Yes, that's true."

"It certainly affected the physical aspects of your relationship, didn't it?"

I looked over at Bill to see if he would object, but he just sat there doodling on his pad.

Susannah took a long drink of water.

"It did to the extent that Ben was not as frequent or active as he was when he was younger, but the physical love and affection was still there, making up in quality what it lacked in quantity and energy, because the spiritual connection was just as strong. That kind of love never succumbs to age."

"If souls travel together," I said, "Why aren't there more cases of love at first sight? It seems to me that should be happening all the time."

"Objection," Bill said without looking up from his pad.

"That's OK," Susannah said, "I know what Mr. Clasen is getting at. I think it takes time for reincarnated souls to recognize one another, considering the barriers our bodies and minds put up . . . as well as society. If I hadn't spent all that time cleaning Ben's house, it might not have happened, although I'd like to think that a brief encounter in our case would have been enough."

"Why aren't there more May-December marriages?"

Bill put down his pencil and tried to hide his smile.

"Perhaps because society seems so intent on segregating people according to their ages. Maybe if we didn't and spent more time together with people of different ages there would be more."

"And how do you explain gay marriage?" I asked, throwing out a ridiculous question just to see how she would handle herself when the subject wasn't Ben or Rose.

"Souls have no genders. Why should love?"

"And divorce?"

"I don't know, not every marriage is between two perfectly matched souls. I suppose that's all part of the learning process."

I ended the examination at that point. Susannah wasn't cracking. The only one getting irritable and tired was me. What I needed for this trial were facts; hard, stubborn facts, not about reincarnation, but about Rose and Ben, as well as Susannah.

Since there was barely sixty days until trial, I would have to get my clients' permission to hire a private investigator to find out everything there was to know about Susannah. I wanted to know about her parents, what she liked to do when she was growing up, how she dressed, where she went to church, who she hung around with, her grades in school and what kind of trouble she got into. I suspected that there had to be a few run-ins with the law out there somewhere.

And when the PI was done with her I needed him to examine Rose's life, to look for those memories Ben hadn't gotten around to telling Susannah or perhaps forgot. If I was going to discredit her before a jury, I needed to focus on Rose and Susannah's lives, not on the existence of Rose's eternal soul.

I couldn't very well ask a jury to reject God and eternity. I wasn't that good.

Chapter 3 – Pre-Trial Prep

"I know I am deathless. No doubt I have died myself ten thousand times before. I laugh at what you call dissolution, and I know the amplitude of time."
– Walt Whitman

"And I'm Mussolini," Peter cried out when I filled Ben's three sons in on Susannah's creative defense.

"I think I'd have preferred love," Mitch muttered.

"They're soul mates," Jeff said sitting up and clapping his hands together.

"Religion can be tricky," Mitch announced. "It's harder to dismiss than love . . . at least publicly."

"You're as nutty as she is," Peter whispered.

"If that were the case," Jeff said, "Why didn't she ever mention it before he died? We spoke to her often enough on the telephone since you couldn't get through to him without going through her. She could have said, 'Oh by the way, I'm really your mother in a new body.' You don't forget to mention something like that."

"And why didn't dad say anything?" Peter asked.

"Because love always needs to hold on to a few secrets," I said, "At least for a little while."

"What?"

"I asked her the same question at the deposition and that was part of her answer."

I told them about the other part, their alleged plan to wait a year.

"She also said that you wouldn't have believed either of them if they had."

"Damn straight," Peter exclaimed. "I would have had him committed."

"And her arrested," Jeff added.

Ben's sons authorized me to spend whatever I needed to on a private investigator and gave me contact information for one of Rose's high school friends, Maxine, who was almost ninety and still going strong. But, when I pulled up to her assisted living center near Camden, New Jersey, a squat, brick building with barred windows and dead plantings in front that looked as if it might have once been a prison it turned out that I was an hour too late.

The first thing Maxine told me when she opened the door to her room, after inviting me to sit down at the small table by the window, was that I had just missed her.

"She left an hour ago." Maxine said.

"Who?" I asked.

She smiled at me like she thought I was joking.

"Susannah."

I could feel my heart beating in my throat and I stared out the dirty, rain streaked window at the cars and trucks racing by on the interstate.

I was going to ask Maxine not to speak to Susannah or her attorney, I was going to tell her that it was very important to Ben and Rose's children that she not, but Susannah was a step ahead of me and must have already pumped Maxine for those memories I might have been able to use to discredit her.

"Was she alone?" I asked.

"Yes," Maxine said, as she put down two cups of tea. She looked thin and frail, but her voice was strong.

"I told her she could stay, but she thought you'd prefer talking with me alone."

Maxine sat down and stared up at me with the same look of patience and calm that I had seen in Susannah. I wondered if I would ever look and feel that content.

"What did you tell her?"

Maxine tilted her head and raised one finger so that it rested across her nose and lips.

"Nothing much," she said, "I'm not sure what you're getting at. It was just a social visit."

Social my ass, I thought to myself.

"The poor girl," Maxine continued.

"Because her husband died?"

"Heavens no," Maxine said with a light laugh, "because of her weight. That's not easy to carry around, you know?"

"Did she know when I was coming?" I asked.

"I don't see how unless you told her . . . she just popped in to surprise me."

"Did she say how she found you?"

"She knew all about me."

"I'm sure Ben spoke about you, she must have asked him all kinds of questions about Rose's past."

Maxine didn't respond, she just looked closely at me then added a third spoonful of sugar to her tea.

"You get to eat whatever you want at my age," she said when she noticed me watching. "There's not enough time left for anything slow to kill you."

"Did she tell you that she claims to be a reincarnation of Rose?"

"She said they were the same soul," Maxine said, reaching for her tea, the cup clattering against the saucer as she wrapped her fingers around the handle.

"Did you believe it?"

"It made me laugh at first. I suppose that wasn't very polite, but it didn't seem to bother her. She just looked at me with her lips closed, with this mysterious, little smile, the pupils of her eyes so big that the whites seemed to disappear, almost like Rose when she was younger, before the cataracts. Rose had the biggest eyes. That was a little eerie I have to tell you that."

"Coincidence," I said and Maxine nodded, closing her eyes as she sipped her tea.

"I see people from my past everywhere I look," Maxine said, carefully placing her cup back down on the saucer. "Wait until you get to be my age. Sometimes it seems as if the memories are real and what's in front of you isn't."

Maxine examined me for a moment.

"What did she want?" I asked.

"She didn't want anything in particular. She said she just wanted to visit and see me again, as if she were the one about to depart soon, not me."

Maxine took another sip of tea. It was a slow process because it took a lot of concentration for her to hold the cup steady.

"She said she was hoping that her visit would somehow put me at ease . . . the eternal soul and all that."

"That was kind of her," I said not bothering to mask the bite in my tone.

Maxine snapped her lips shut like the clasp of an old-fashion purse. "I told her that I appreciated her concern, but I had no illusions about any of that, you know, about what's waiting on the other side."

Maxine stared into her teacup for a moment.

"But if she really was Rose reincarnated I certainly would have been a little disappointed."

"Why?"

"Because if it was true, I would have expected she'd have earned her eternity in the Lord's presence; I really wouldn't want to go through this all over again, at least not so soon."

"Did you say that to her?"

Maxine nodded slowly.

"How did she respond?"

"That she understood how I felt, but that it would be better the next time around because I had lived such a good life . . . and suffered as well, which made me wonder even more."

"Why?"

"Rose was as good a soul as the Lord has ever put down here and she died so young, relatively speaking of course, and this young woman, what was her name again?"

"Susannah."

"Her life didn't look all that easy, overweight and alone. She said she had no siblings. I would have thought Rose deserved better. She must have sensed what was on my mind, because she said that she was making up for something Rose didn't do that she should have.

"I asked her what that was because I had no idea, but she didn't answer. She just said that she was very happy with who she was now, especially since she got to spend some time with Ben again and was given this great gift of knowing her past life."

"Did she say she knew any other past lives?"

"We didn't really get into that."

"You weren't curious?" I asked.

"I must say I found her charming, not like the other young people that come in here."

I sipped some of the tea to give myself a little time to think about what to say next.

"You know, Ben left all his money to her," I said, "well over $50 million."

"She didn't say. That can't sit well with the boys."

"They are challenging the will in court."

Maxine stretched out her arm to touch mine.

"Tell them I send my best," she said.

"I will. Did she talk about the lawsuit?"

"What lawsuit?"

"The fight over the will," I said.

Maxine picked up her tea, pinky out, as if that might help her keep it better balanced.

"Funny she didn't mention it," Maxine said, "but I guess she didn't want to shock me any more than she already had. People are always tiptoeing around me these days, as if I might scatter like a dandelion with the slightest breeze. I suppose I did act pretty surprised when she told me about the marriage."

"What did she say?"

"That she and Ben had gotten married about a year earlier. I haven't blushed for years, but I'm sure my jaw fell open."

"What did you think?"

"Who am I to judge? I've seen too much of that over my life."

I nodded as if I agreed.

"She talked mostly about old times, when we were young girls growing up on College Avenue."

"Her Rose memories?"

"Yes."

"That must have seemed strange."

"It did at first, especially when I was looking at her. But when I turned away or unfocused my eyes and just listened it didn't seem all that strange. You can believe anything when your eyes aren't always in charge. I always say you shouldn't believe 75% of the things you hear and 50% of the things you see."

Maxine chuckled at her own joke and I smiled as well to be polite.

"Do you believe her . . . that she has Rose's soul?"

Maxine thought it over. I could see her gaze drift off behind me.

"No, I suppose not," she said. "I don't believe in miracles. Too many wasted opportunities in my lifetime when a miracle would have come in handy. Why would God waste a miracle on something like this?"

Maxine shut her eyes and remained silent for a moment. Her breathing was the only sound in the room.

"But I do believe that there's more to us than just a body," she said, opening her eyes which suddenly looked more severe and demanding, as if she had just decided she would accept no less out of the end of life, "I have to, I don't see any point to it otherwise, so I suppose it's possible."

Maxine picked up her tea and breathed it in. Her eyes softened as she did and she smiled at me.

"She did know an awful lot about what we did when we were young," she added, "and what we were like."

"Things she probably got from Ben . . . and possibly by picking up on a few cues from you. We telegraph a lot when we reminisce."

"Maybe," Maxine said, "but wouldn't it be nice if it were true. That would silence all the doubts."

Of course, I didn't have any doubts to silence. I was sure that it all went dark in the end and that there was nothing more to me than what I saw in the mirror.

I stood up. My back was tight. I didn't like the fact that Susannah seemed to be a step ahead of me. And I didn't like the idea of wrestling with a jury over the eternal soul.

"Mr. Clasen," Maxine called to me, "Are you all right?"

"Sorry, just stretching."

"You know," she said, "She did remember about Taft High School and some of the teachers."

"She could have looked that up on the internet," I said, "or found an old yearbook that Rose kept around the house."

Maxine shook her head slowly, sometimes up and down, sometimes side to side.

"How about something that only you and Rose would know – but something that you didn't discuss with her?"

Maxine looked up at the ceiling.

The smell in the room, a slight odor refusing to be overwhelmed by the disinfectant, urine and stale food, reminded me of visiting my father in the hospital as he lay there dying, gangrene climbing up both his legs, listening to him curse with his last breath those earlier years when he had turned away from God. I wondered if it wasn't the scent of decaying matter, a body that has already begun to decompose and turn to dust.

"Something only the two of you would know . . . something that happened to one of you or perhaps both of you? Something you promised each other never to mention to anyone else."

That must have rung a bell, because Maxine started nodding. She moved her chair forward and leaned closer to me.

"Rose's father died when she was 16," she said. "He had a heart attack at work. An acid heart attack they called it back then . . . quick and to the point."

"What did he do?"

"Salesman of some sort, he was young, early-forties, and hadn't been the least bit sick. Rose said the telephone rang after she got home from school. She was the only one around, but when she went to pick it up she suddenly stopped. She was afraid to answer it."

"Why?"

""She swore she knew it was from his office calling to say that he was dead. It wouldn't stop ringing and she finally picked it up and that's what it was. I told her it was her imagination, because she was upset but she said - and I'll never forget this - that while the phone was ringing she suddenly had this picture in her head of him laid out in his coffin, as sure as if it was already a memory."

"She told you that?" I said, as I wrote it word down on my legal pad.

"Word for word, you don't forget something like that. And she never told anyone else about it, not even her mother. She thought they'd think she was crazy."

"That's good," I said and Maxine raised her thin eyebrows. "I meant that she kept it to herself . . . and you. Do you know if she ever discussed it with Ben or any of her children?"

"I doubt it knowing Rose. It gives me the willies just to think about it."

"How about after Rose died, did you mention it to Ben?"

"I've never discussed it with anyone, not even Rose, not since the day he was buried. I think the thought frightened both of us. It's funny, now that I think about it I find it reassuring."

"And you're sure you didn't discuss it with Susannah."

"Most certainly not."

"She never mentioned the lawsuit?" I asked one more time before leaving in case something we talked about might have jogged her memory. I found it hard to believe Susannah wouldn't mention it.

"No, she said she just came by to see me one last time. I know I'm old – and I'm not afraid, I mean there's not much I can do about it and if there is something on the other side, I've got a lot of people I want to see. She said she came to make me feel better."

Maxine's eyes narrowed when she said that.

"I don't know what to believe Mr. Clasen," she said, opening the door, "but there is one thing I've come to realize."

"What's that?"

"That I don't know what happens next, nobody does, and one story is as plausible as another."

"That may be, but that doesn't mean Susannah has the answer or that she's telling the truth about Rose. If you ask me, she's just another clever con artist trying to get at Ben's money. A lot of people try to take advantage of the elderly."

Maxine nodded and shrugged at the same time.

"I suppose so, because Rose would never have cared about the money."

"Why do you say that?"

"Because she never did, she never talked about it like everyone else did when we were first married and she wasn't full of herself when Ben made it big."

"Well, the soul must be dramatically transformed with each new life," I said, "because Susannah surely wants to hold on to the money this time around and she doesn't care how much dissension she sows in the process."

Maxine didn't respond, but she confirmed that she would come to testify at trial about the telephone call provided I sent a car for her, although she couldn't understand why it would matter.

We shook hands as we said goodbye and Maxine stood there with her face wiped clean of expression, as if she were unwilling or perhaps unable to take a firm position as to whether or not Susannah was the genuine article, particularly in light of her current circumstance.

Chapter 4 – The Private Investigator

"Just because they don't remember, it doesn't mean they haven't done it."
– J.D. Salinger

I couldn't use one of the regular PI's I used for my run-of-the-mill personal injury actions, who were good at taking photographs of intersections at different angles and finding the witness that the police had overlooked. I needed someone a lot more creative and relentless. I needed someone who refused to come away empty-handed.

So I called Murray Cadwalader, a semi-retired old-timer whose specialty was the undercover operation. I had worked with him once before when I needed some dirt on a local politician trying to use eminent domain to seize a client's property so his friends could make money as part of a state funded revitalization program. Murray found a mistress and a gambling habit and the whole thing went away.

"Reincarnation," he roared through the phone. "Once around ought to be enough for anyone. It certainly has been for me." He laughed when he said that, but he agreed to see me that afternoon.

Murray was a lot heavier than when I had last worked with him and he was suffering from a recurrence of gout that kept him from getting up to greet me.

"A fucking rich man's disease," he said, looking down at his leg as if he would just as soon throw it away if it wasn't so attached to him.

Still, he sat there with his shoulders square and his handshake firm. He stared back at me with this killer look, like he was prepared to fight me tooth and nail if I made a wrong move.

"She won't know what hit her," he said, his pupils swelling at the thought of what he could do to Ms. McGreedy, as he started calling her.

"So you don't believe in the eternal soul?" I asked, thinking that it would be a better fit to have someone on the same page as me.

Murray stared back at me with the intensity of a man who had just found a good reason to live, "I don't believe in the eternal anything. I believe in the here and now, and doing the fucking right thing, not because of some great eye in the sky, but because of what's in here." He beat his chest when he said that and I nodded in agreement.

I hated the fact that Murray had a red drinker's nose that had a visible pulse if you looked closely enough, as if it had a life of its own, but since he wouldn't be testifying it didn't much matter.

He went on railing against religion for which I offered my sincerest and repeated nods. Murray opened his desk drawer to look for something and then slammed it shut when he couldn't find it.

"And if I'm wrong about what's upstairs," Murray said, "I'm prepared to pay the price. The heat down there will be good for my arthritis."

I figured I'd get Murray back on track by talking about Susannah McCreedy.

"She's twenty-four," I said, "But she's not what you'd expect; she's no model; she's fat and not the least bit attractive."

Murray scratched at what little hair he had left on the top of his head.

"What are you," he asked me, "About fifty-eight?"

"Sixty."

Murray chuckled.

"Give it another ten years counselor. You think your expectations are low now, you don't know what low is. It's more like falling off a fuckin cliff. What do you think that old man was like at eighty-eight? I'll bet she's stacked and damn fucking smart so she knows how to push the right buttons."

I nodded.

"That kind always is; never underestimate the mind of a swindler. The smartest man I ever met was a pyramid schemer who got ten to twenty."

"She doesn't seem like the kind to crack on the stand," I said.

"They're tough too," Murray said. "Besides, why should she worry? This is civil, not criminal, so what's she got to lose? She's had a damn-good run whatever happens."

She did and even if the will was voided Susannah would still have the house which automatically became hers upon Ben's death and the account he set up for her living expenses. It wasn't much compared to the $50 million at the end of the Surrogate Court's rainbow, but not a bad score for any con artist.

"I suppose I should go easy on her at first," I said, thinking out loud. "Lull her into a false sense of confidence. I don't want to jump on her right off the bat and risk getting some of the jurors feeling sorry for her. There are going to be people on that panel who will believe somewhere deep down that it's possible . . . they're going to want it to be true."

"Bullshit," Murray said, hitting his desk hard enough for the force of the slap to reverberate all the way up to the skin hanging down from his chin.

"Not that I want to tell you how to conduct your trial counselor, but you have to come out swinging with a scoundrel like that. Let the jury know what you think of her right up front and let her know she's in for a knockdown-drag-out fight. It's like a fucking boxing match, you keep jabbing and pounding the belly from round one until she drops her hands. Then you let her have it right in the kisser."

"That's where you come in," I said, "I'm going to need facts to hit her with."

Murray nodded and leaned back in his chair, which screamed in pain, and made him smile.

"Sixty days is not a helluvalot of time counselor," he said.

"That's all we got. Can you do it?"

"I'm the only one around here who can, but it's going to cost your clients. What did you call them . . . My Three Sons?" Murray laughed and almost choked on his own saliva.

"They're prepared to pay whatever it takes."

Murray continued coughing while he strained to cross one leg over the other so he could wipe something off his shoe.

"I'll need a twenty-five thousand dollar retainer," Murray said after giving his throat one final clearing. "Wait, I'm going to have to do a shit load of traveling, Florida, Minnesota, so you'd better make that fifty."

I nodded as I crossed out the first figure and wrote down the second.

Murray walked me to the door. He shuffled along pretty quickly for a man with gout.

"I'll find the warts on her ass," he said, "just don't tell me how to go about doing it. I don't need a leash and I need every bill I send you – and they're not all going to be for me - paid right away and without any questions. Is that understood?"

We shook on it.

I decided to sit down separately with each of the sons. It became too much of a pissing contest when they were all together. I started with Mitch since he seemed the least hotheaded. He arrived at my office in his expensive pin-striped suit and his shiny new shoes that reverberated through the hallway as if they had taps on the bottom of them.

I told Mitch about Maxine's telephone story just to make sure it wasn't public knowledge. He had never heard it before, but it didn't surprise him that Rose had never mentioned it.

"My mother never talked much about growing up," he said, "and it's not like we didn't ask, like every kid. While my father could talk about his childhood for hours, working in his father's hardware store, the trips to Coney Island, and North Africa during the war, my mother would always change the subject when it was her turn."

"Any idea why?"

He sat back as if he had to think about it.

"My mother didn't have an easy time of it as a child. They never had much money. Apparently, her father never lasted too long in any job. They always had to live on the top of these 6th floor walkups, because it was cheaper and they used to move every year for the free month's rent. All her clothes were hand-me-downs. And it got worse after her father died."

I wondered if Ben had talked to Susannah about any of that.

"And then there was her sister."

"Rebecca," I said, referring to the older sister who had died about 10 years earlier.

"No, there was another sister," Mitch said, "Eva."

"That's the first I've heard of her."

"Like most everyone else," he said.

"A secret?"

"Sort of."

"When did she die?"

"About thirty-five years ago, when I was twenty-two, I didn't even know she existed until I saw her headstone at my grandmother's funeral."

Every family has a skeleton or two in the closet. As an attorney, I'm used to opening closets and you'd be surprised at all the dirt I've uncovered over the years-- from drug addiction and prison to adultery and incest.

"So what happened with Eva?" I asked, "Why the big secret?"

"Eva had problems."

"What kind of problems?"

"I'm not sure exactly, neither my mother nor Rebecca would ever talk about her. As far as I could figure out Eva had behavior problems, but more than just acting out and temper tantrums. I think she was a little violent, maybe even self-destructive, because they wouldn't let her go to school, although apparently she was well enough to take care of my mother for years."

"Plenty of families had problems like that back then," I said, "so why keep it a big secret so long after her death."

"Secret is an understatement," Mitch said, staring down at his hands. "I couldn't get anything out of my mother or my aunt, not one word, other than that she'd been institutionalized and lived most of her life there.

"Apparently once she got in they couldn't get her out, or maybe she didn't want to leave. Anyway, my mother got so upset whenever I brought it up that I stopped. I did some research on my own and discovered that Eva was committed to Pilgrim State Hospital when she was eighteen. My mother was all of eleven. Not many people knew about Eva because they used to move around a lot back then. I doubt Maxine even knew about her since they met when my mother was twelve."

"Your father must have known," I said.

"He wouldn't talk either, even after Mom died. He said she made him promise when they first got married and my father was a stickler about keeping his promises."

"Which might mean it was a promise he kept even with Susannah," I said, although it might not count if he believed that she was Rose come back to him.

Mitch shrugged.

"Just before my mother died, after they'd given up on her treatment, we would sit around the living room after dinner. She got tired easily and there were long periods of silence when she leaned her head back and closed her eyes. So I wasn't always sure whether or not she was always awake.

"I was sitting alone with her one night, right near the end, when out of the blue she looks up at me and says that she's getting exactly what she deserves. What are you talking about? I said. What could you have done to deserve an illness like this?"

Mitch was quiet for a moment while he closed his eyes and waited for the memory to come into focus.

"I had never seen her like this, feeling so guilty over something, and certainly not talking about it. She always kept everything bad inside, like she had to keep it from spilling over into our lives."

Mitch sighed.

"It was different back then," I said, "The world wasn't all about talking things out and closure. You ignored what you could and what you couldn't you stayed quiet about."

"I couldn't imagine what it could be," Mitch said, "My mother was the most ethical, honest person I've ever met. She hated to lie and she hated to disappoint anyone. I begged her to tell me.

"She looked up at me. I remember how shocked I was by her eyes. They were cloudy and dark, as if she could no longer see out."

A shiver ran down Mitch's spine.

"I kept asking what was bothering her. Then she put her hand on my arm to silence me, the way she used to when I was little and nodded slowly. What kind of sister was I, she said barely above a whisper. What are you talking about, I said, Rebecca loves you. She shook her head and it kept shaking, like it was coming loose. Eva, she said. I was a terrible sister to Eva. God notices these things."

Mitch slumped back against the chair.

"I hated to see her in pain like that, but there was nothing I could say."

"Did she say anything else?"

"I don't know if she was talking to me at that point or to Eva or maybe God. It was like I was listening in on her thoughts."

Mitch paused and I sat very still with my pen poised over my legal pad.

"Eva used to take care of me, she said. She watched me when I was little because everyone else was at school or work, and when I started school she was there when I came home for lunch and at the end of the day. It was just me and her for a long time."

"Then she couldn't have been that bad," I said and Mitch nodded, "Something must have happened."

"After the funeral, my aunt said that Eva was very fragile and something inside her shattered. It sounded to me like maybe she tried to kill herself."

Mitch clasped his hands together.

"She said that her mother signed some kind of commitment paper. She thought it was for a couple of days or a week, but it left it up to the doctors and Eva never got out. This was back in the 30's when they got paid by the patient."

I wrote it all down, although I wasn't sure how, or if, I could use it. I couldn't be sure what Ben did or did not mention to Susannah, especially if he thought he was talking to Rose reincarnated.

"She had a lobotomy a few years later," Mitch said, "that much I got out of my Aunt Rebecca. I'm sure there's a lot more to it that I'll never know."

"Why do you think your mother felt so guilty at the end?" I asked. "Was she there when they came to take her away?"

"That wasn't it," Mitch said. "She told me why the day before she died. It was because she never went to visit her after, not once. They took her away when she was eleven and my mother never saw or spoke to her again. She was in Pilgrim State for thirty years and she never visited her."

If I believed in reincarnation, I thought to myself that might explain why her soul returned in the body of someone like Susannah.

"You were all of eleven, I reminded her," Mitch said. "But I grew up, she said, and I still didn't go. I said anything I could to make her feel better, but she just stared up at me her skin so pale and her eyes so dark and distant. She already looked like a ghost.

"That was all my mother could think about at the end."

"Did you ever find out why she didn't visit?"

"No, my aunt wouldn't talk about it, but if I had to guess I would say that my grandmother stopped her. I wouldn't put it past my grandmother to say that Eva didn't want to see her.

"My grandmother was a very opinionated woman and had her own old country logic. She knocked on wood and spit on the ground when she heard bad news and believed that if you ignored something long enough it would eventually go away. I'm sure she didn't want Eva to be my mother's burden. I'm sure she thought she was doing the right thing keeping Eva out of Rose's life."

By the time Mitch left it looked as if he'd been wearing the same suit for a week.

If Rose's soul was inside Susannah with her past life an open door then there was no way she wouldn't know about Eva and her guilt. That had to be something no soul could ever forget, no matter how many lifetimes pass.

I called up Murray after Mitch left and told him the story. Pilgrim State Hospital closed about twenty years earlier, Murray said, but he could find out where the records were stored and try to get access to them.

"Privacy always yields to the almighty dollar," he said.

I thought it over and decided it would be a waste of time. What I really needed, I explained, was to find out what, if anything, Susannah knew about Eva.

I could hear Murray's heavy breathing over the telephone.

"Well, I can't ask her," Murray said, "and she doesn't have any friends that I know of so you may just have to wing it."

"I can't take a chance like that at trial," I said.

"You litigators are scared of your own fucking shadows," Murray said, his sharp laugh turning into a coughing fit.

"I can bug her attorney's office," he said after clearing his throat. "They're bound to discuss what she knows about Rose's life."

I considered it for just an instant. I like to win, but I play by the rules.

"I'm not interested," I said.

"Not interested in what she knows," Murray asked, "or not interested in knowing how I find out?"

"I don't want you to bug an attorney's office. I don't want to violate the attorney client privilege."

"That's the last time I'm going to ask," Murray said before hanging up.

While I waited for Murray's first report, I looked around for an expert witness, a geriatric psychologist who could opine about Ben's inability to make a sound decision

The nearest one I could find willing to testify was Dr. Stanley Seymour who agreed to testify for $300 an hour paid in advance. I went to visit Dr. Seymour in his office, which looked like any other psychiatrist's office, at least in my imagination, with a large, heavy desk with files neatly stacked in the corner, a wall behind it filled with laminated certificates and testimonials, across from a deep, worn leather couch pushed against a windowless wall besides which sat a big armchair and a small round table with a lamp.

He showed no reaction when I told him Ben's story, writing it down on his pad as if I were just another one of his patients.

"It will be difficult for anyone to honestly opine about the soundness of Ben's mind and his particular ability to make a decision like that under the circumstances," he said, "Not without having had an opportunity to interview him."

"I understand that, but since he's not around neither side has that option. From the neighbors and friends that I've spoken with – including his broker – he seems to have had all his marbles."

That got a little chuckle from the good doctor.

"Of course, there are all different kinds of marbles," he said, "There are money marbles and friendship marbles, and then there are love marbles. They're not the same things."

"Generally speaking?"

Dr. Seymour nodded professorially. Most experts will offer you whatever you need if you pay them well enough, particularly when it comes to grey areas like psychology. The first attorney I worked for after law school called it the voodoo science.

"How would you explain it to a jury?" I asked.

"How a man that old appears when he talks to a neighbor or his broker, things he's done pretty much the same way for fifty years, doesn't mean he's going to be on the same sound footing when it comes to something out of the ordinary, something completely different, like fending off an aggressive, twenty-four year old seductress, sixty-four years his junior."

"She's overweight," I said, "and anything but attractive."

"That's not the point," Dr. Seymour said, "She's twenty-four and that's a ripe age in terms of memories. It can be like a blinding light to an eighty-eight year old man."

I knew I had a convert to my cause.

"Could you expand on that?" I asked, suggesting that he pretend for the moment that he was testifying in front of the jury.

He put down his notebook and looked at me, the imaginary juror, his eyes moist and earnest and his delivery slow and thoughtful - a testament to his compassion and integrity. Then he put his hands together as if in prayer and raised them to his chin.

Don't overdo it I thought.

"The elderly are disproportionately underserved by general psychiatry," he said, "particularly since we tend to focus only on the cognitively impaired – those individuals that have been significantly slowed by their deteriorating skills and misconceptions. We expect a certain amount of that in the elderly and as long as it doesn't pervade too much of their day to day existence we tend to overlook it and leave them alone."

He sounded a little too professorial, but I could work with him to tone that down.

"Which is why for a long time the elderly weren't studied the way they should have been, but that's begun to change, and what the studies are beginning to show is that delirium and dementia in the elderly, which would encompass the inability to make a sound decision under a circumstance such as the one you described, even to recognize a compromising situation like that, tends to be transient, ubiquitous and fluctuating in nature."

It sounded like he'd given this lecture before.

"Give it to me in layman's terms Doc."

"It comes and goes, but it's always there somewhere--the forgetfulness, the uncertainty, the confusion, the gullibility. It may not manifest itself all the time, but certain situations will bring it to the surface. That's why the elderly are such easy targets for con men."

He took in a breath expanding his chest and straightening his posture.

"At eighty-eight, I can say with almost one hundred percent certainty that Ben would have some very real indications of dementia, whether they were moments where he'd repeat himself or forget what it was he wanted to do . . . or limited to specific areas of thought and social interaction. He couldn't avoid it, not at that age.

"Conversations with neighbors, taking out the garbage, talking to his broker, things he'd been doing forever are the last places that dementia was likely to manifest itself. However, an offer of a young love or the promise of his wife reaching out to him from the hereafter would offer the kind of profound shock to a man that age that would undoubtedly trigger a transient episode."

"How undoubtedly," I said, writing down his words as fast I could.

"Ninety-five percent certain, however sound he may have appeared when it came to his neighbors his mind would have had enormous difficulty reacting to this new reality that this young woman was creating."

Dr. Seymour sat back smugly and folded his hands on his stomach.

He would need a little work so as not to sound too pompous, but I liked what he was saying. It had the ring of common sense and would allow the jury to toss the will without having to decide the truth about eternal recurrence.

Chapter 5 – Murray's Report

"I am confident that there truly is such a thing as living again, that the living spring from the dead, and that the souls of the dead are in existence."
– Socrates

Murray kept me appraised every few days about what he was finding out. I wasn't surprised to learn that Susannah came from a dirt poor family in Bemidji, Minnesota, the only daughter of an old farmer turned preacher and his third, much-younger wife, both of whom were killed about eight years earlier in a fire.

The head of the volunteer department told Murray that he always thought that the fire was suspicious because it burned so fast, although it was a lot easier just to label it as an accident.

"Insurance," I said.

"Nope and mortgaged up the wazoo."

Her father, Reverend John, wasn't too popular in town. Apparently, his wasn't a regular church. He also had his own collection of handy farm accelerants behind the barn, like he was preparing to bring the Armageddon on himself if it didn't come soon enough. Who knows, maybe Messiahs need to set up their own martyrdom. Maybe that's the way it works.

Susannah managed to escape by not being home.

"Where was she?" I asked, thinking that suspicions of patricide and matricide would certainly hurt her credibility with the jury.

"Drug rehab," Murray said.

"That's not bad," I told Murray.

"Don't get too excited counselor, it's not what you think."

Apparently, Susannah got hooked on painkillers when she fell off the roof of the barn a year earlier and broke her back. She was clearing off snow and was relatively thin before that.

"What did her father preach," I asked less than enthusiastic about the news so far.

"He was a part of the Cathars Unity Church."

"Never heard of it."

Murray said it was one of those New Age Christian sects.

"And get this," he said, "His church preached that reincarnation was part of Jesus' originally teachings."

"What else have you got?"

I could hear Murray over the telephone unfolding something. He'd found an old ad in the local paper for one of his services. It quoted Mathew 11:10-14 and 17:10-13 where Jesus said that John the Baptist was the prophet Elijah who had lived centuries before. It said that every soul was a fallen angel born again and again until they got it right and that the Cathars Unity Church could help you do that by guiding you through your past lives and their mistakes.

"Susannah never made it to public school," Murray said. "She was home schooled, and I couldn't find anyone in Bemidji who knew much of anything about her. Every response was pretty much the same – a strange girl from a strange family."

This was looking better, I thought. Most everyone on the jury would be from a mainstream religion and the Cathars Unity Church would explain a lot; brainwashed as a child and schooled in the tools of brainwashing, not that it took a lot of elbow grease when it came to a lonely eighty-eight-year old man.

The apple doesn't fall very far from the family tree, one nutty father and now a nutty, conniving daughter.

"One odd thing," Murray said.

What could be odder than that ad, I wondered.

"I found a story in the local paper about a year before the fire. They sent a reporter out to the farm to attend one of Reverend John's services. First line reads 'is it any more surprising to be born twice than once' not according to Reverend John McCreedy who preaches from the pulpit of his barn every Sunday, the odor of manure mingling with the fragrance of incense."

"What's the odd part?"

"Hold your damn horses," Murray said, "I'm getting to it."

Murray serenaded me with his heavy breathing for a while before saying another word.

Apparently there were about a dozen people at the service all from out of town and according to the reporter most of the service was bullshit fire and brimstone, hallelujahs and pass the hat type of stuff, but at the end of the service it was apparently customary for someone to come up front so Reverend John could try to open that locked door of ancient memories and set a past life free.

"Sounds a little like squeezing a pimple to me," Murray said.

Reverend John explained to the reporter before the service that he had to walk around whoever was called to testify three times in one direction and three times in the other before he called for the soul to reveal itself. The reporter called it a past life exorcism. Reverend John told him that no sinner ever stands closer to God than at the moment that door opens.

I liked the reference to exorcism. I had to figure out a way to get the article into evidence.

"Thanks," I said, thinking that was all there was.

"I'm not done yet counselor."

On this particular day it was the Reverend's daughter, Susannah McCreedy, who did the testifying. According to the article she walked slowly up to the front of the barn. Beads of sweat running down her forehead as Reverend John circled around her. Even with the barn doors open, it was as hot as hell . . . the reporter's word, not Murray's. She was standing so still it almost seemed as if she'd stopped breathing.

I could hear the paper crinkling in Murray's hand.

"She'd probably done it a hundred times before," I said.

I held my own breath since I was sure that Murray had found the smoking gun and that Susannah would talk about her most recent prior life as Abigail Adams, wife of the second President, or an Indian princess in a small village a thousand years earlier. Under those circumstances, I don't think my clients would offer $5 to be rid of her and the civil suit for the house and trust account would be a slam-dunk.

Murray went on reading the article.

Nothing much was happening and Reverend John told the congregation that this was Susannah's first time testifying so it was natural for her soul to resist. It looked as if the good Reverend was about to give up – he said sometimes it just didn't work, particularly with someone so young, but at that moment Susannah cried out that she could see a sliver of light, like the crack of an open door. Reverend John threw up his hands and cried hallelujah.

The reporter said it was quite a show, a cross between a revival meeting and a carnival sideshow. Reverend John got down on one knee and asked his daughter to tell the congregation what she'd seen. Tell us who you were in your prior life, he said, and open your soul to the faithful standing before you. She let out a sob and looked out at the congregation saying one word before she collapsed into her father's arms.

Murray waited for me to ask.

"What word?"

"Rose, all she said was Rose. That was it, end of service."

I started coughing as my saliva took a detour down the wrong pipe.

"You're joking."

"Wouldn't be much of a joke. Fucking Rose is all she said."

"You're not going to tell me now that you believe that crap," I said.

"Don't be a fucking idiot," Murray said, "She picked a name out of thin air. I'm sure she wanted to cry out Cleopatra or Joan of Arc, but daddy said to keep it simple . . . pick a God-damn flower."

"So what are you thinking?" I asked him.

"I'm thinking that she saved the fucking article," Murray said. "What kid wouldn't cut her name out of the newspaper? She's probably been carrying it for years in her little purse, right behind her phony ID, just waiting for the right mark to come along, some old man with a long wilted Rose, so she got lucky, sometimes that happens even to the scum in life."

I was thinking the same thing.

"Maybe it was more than a stroke of luck," I said. "Maybe she got hold of a list of old men in the area, men in their late 80's, maybe from a friend with access to Medicare information, maybe from the maid service and run them through the internet until she found one with a dead Rose in his past . . . twenty-five years in his past."

"It would be a lot easier than that," Murray said, "if she had access to social security records. She'd have found their records together, husband and wife, with DOD written across her file in large black letters."

I had to figure that Susannah intended to hand the article to her attorney on the eve of trial, like it was something she just found in some old papers and catch us by surprise. Some of the jurors are going to feel their hearts skip a beat when they hear that. Who wouldn't want something to take to bed on those long dark nights when it feels impossible to believe in anything?"

"If she searched social security records or anywhere else," Murray said, "she might have left a footprint out there and if she did I'll find it. Maybe she tried something like this before."

"That would be nice."

"I need to check out her computer."

"The judge will never let me do that."

"I'll get back to you," he said before hanging up.

I thought about it afterwards, about the different scenarios at trial. I wouldn't be much of an attorney if I didn't consider all the possibilities. Of course, the last one that crossed my mind being what if it was true.

Chapter 6 – Trial Prep

"Nobody in his right mind can visualize his own existence without assuming that he has always lived and will live hereafter."
– Erik Erikson

Bill Lustenberger took the depositions of Ben's three sons, but they were a complete waste of time. They knew almost nothing about Susannah and absolutely nothing about her claim to be their mother's reincarnate, since the first time they heard about it was in this lawsuit.

They tried to dance around Ben's apparent soundness of mind and the fact that he lived alone, drove a car, managed his own investments, paid his bills and never forgot a birthday or anniversary by swearing under oath that he seemed more and more confused over the past few years and that when it came to aggressive, young women he was out of practice and completely helpless.

It was an approach we had worked out based on our expert, and I'm sure Bill expected no less.

However, in anticipation of my case at trial, Bill did run through all the things Susannah had said about Rose during her deposition, including the foods she liked, bologna, shrimp and pistachio ice cream, the music she listened to, Herb Albert and the Tijuana Brass, Frank Sinatra and Mel Torme, the clothes she favored, long, dark-colored skirts with high-collared blouses, white cardigans with buttons, never zippers and black handbags with clasps, where she liked to eat on her birthday, the Nanuet Hotel, and how her hearing had been affected by a bout with the German measles that she'd caught from Peter when he was a little boy.

Susannah was right about everything. She had gone to school on Rose with Ben for ten months and studied hard.

"High pitch hearing loss," Peter said to me after his deposition was over. "She had trouble hearing you on the telephone if the TV was on in the background. She couldn't understand what anyone said in a noisy restaurant and forget about it when the three of us were fighting."

But those weren't really secrets, I told them, when we went for coffee after their depositions. They sat, heads hanging, like three forlorn puppies because they had validated all of Susannah's Rose memories.

"It's OK," I said. "You have to tell the truth and we're going to let her have the easy ones."

What she had was information you could get from a photograph album, from old records gathering dust below the ancient hifi in Ben's house, from old letters in the shoebox at the bottom of a closet, as well as from stories she wheedled out of him.

And there had to be quite a few more, I assured them, since her attorney certainly had her save a few for trial so she could remember things that she forgot at her depositions; stories that Ben may have told her about each one of them, their first stumbles and first loves, personal stories designed to make their jaws drop at trial.

"Which is why," I said, "You can never show any surprise in the courtroom. You have to keep a poker face and we have to be very careful about the theme we pick for the trial."

I had to explain that one to them.

Every trial has to have a theme, a main idea that runs in a circle starting at the opening continuing through the direct and cross-examination and meeting up again at the summation. I knew we couldn't let the theme be: "Look at what I know about Rose," particularly if Susannah's rate of Rose knowledge was a passing seventy percent. And it certainly couldn't be a simple test of faith either. I didn't want the trial to be about God and the hereafter. It had to focus on the present, the vulnerability of our senior citizens and the familiar theme of the doddering old fool taken advantage of by the sharp, desperately poor young vixen.

The theme had to be greed and deception against the backdrop of advanced age and gullibility.

"She's had almost a year to prepare for this," I said. "She knew it would be coming sooner or later, so she's well-schooled about your mother, but we'll find the loose ends. They're always a few when you try to knit together too many lies."

But, no matter how many strategy meetings we had, My Three Sons always left my office muttering to themselves, surprised at how picayune and nonsensical the legal system could be. I told them not to worry—I'd have to be about the worst lawyer in the world to lose a case like this.

Murray called me a couple of days later. He had left Bemidji and traveled to Florida to speak to Ben's neighbors. They all liked Ben and swore that they knew right away that Susannah would be trouble – just by looking at her- although not one of them said a word to Ben. They couldn't because she was always with him. When he walked outside in the morning to pick up the paper she was standing at the door. When he went for a walk after eating, she walked alongside him. When he drove to the food store or the pharmacy, she was sitting in the passenger seat.

As soon as she came on the scene, they told Murray, Ben stopped coming to the pool and clubhouse, and if anyone called she was always the one to answer. She was not very social, one of the neighbors said, although neither was Rose, according to Mitch, outside of her family and her small circle of close friends.

Still, the neighbors confirmed that Ben seemed happy enough. He did wave and call out a greeting when they passed by and he always smiled when they waved back. He still took his weekend walks around the lake, although with Susannah now.

"What did they say about his mental state?" I asked.

"That he was the smartest one around. He was the one they went to when they had questions about their retirement funds or were thinking about reverse mortgages. He sounded like he had more on the goddamn ball than me. I still keep every cent in a savings account in the bank. I missed the entire fucking mutual fund revolution."

"At his age that can change very quickly," I said.

"Yeah, well, spying on neighbors is a favorite pastime down here and the general consensus was that the two of them were like a couple of love birds and shopaholics, always going out to dinner and taking trips to the mall. According to one neighbor, Susannah's wardrobe changed a helluva lot after she met Ben.

"She went from cleaning lady casual to retiree chic," he said, "everything loose and baggy, lots of gold and black with sequins and shiny fabrics, nothing cheap for our Ms. McGreedy."

"She certainly didn't dress like your average 24-year old at the deposition," I said.

"Big and flowing is the way to go down here," Murray said, "particularly for our grande girls."

"Anything else?"

"I did get into the house," Murray said.

"You broke in?"

"They didn't ask who the fuck I was working for. I got a key from one of the neighbors. They all exchange keys down here, because they're afraid of dying with the door locked."

Before I could object Murray added that it was a waste of time.

"A big fucking zero," he said. "The black widow didn't have a computer, even if she had a laptop there'd be some evidence of it in the house. But she does keep the place damn clean . . . a real professional when it comes to dust."

"So we're still nowhere," I said, "just another crime of opportunity."

"Calm down counselor, I'm not sitting around with a thumb up my ass. I've got some ideas."

"Talk to me."

Murray cleared his throat and took a drink of something.

"She had an old car when she first arrived here that had a Nevada plate. I got the number from Minute Maid, so I traced her old address," Murray said "and I'm off to Vegas."

I wondered if he'd lose interest in the case surrounded by all that booze and blackjack.

"You think it's worth the trip?" I asked.

"She had to start somewhere," he said, "Practice her skills on someone. Once a con artist like that finds a group to scam she tends to stick with'em and move around the country, at least until she can reel in the big fish and retire to the good life."

"Any police record?"

"Not even a traffic ticket," Murray said. "But I did speak to Alma Brown."

"Who is she?"

"The Minute Maid Susannah replaced. She worked for Ben for about ten years before her knees gave out."

"What did she say?"

"Jealous as all hell and I don't blame her, wondered why he never got around to punching her meal ticket."

Murray coughed and took what sounded like a drag on a cigarette.

"She said Ben was a real talker, liked to follow her around while she worked and chew her ear. Said she didn't mind because he was the only one of her clients who always offered her something to drink. He also gave her a tip – a small one- which was against Minute Maid policy. She pretty much knew his life story and Rose's by the time she quit."

"Bingo," I said, sighing into the telephone, "There's our informant."

I could hear Murray exhale.

"You know that stuff will kill you," I said.

"That's what I'm hoping. Otherwise I'm going to run out of money first."

"So what else did Alma say?"

"That she spent an afternoon with our siren going through her book of clients. She said Old Susannah asked a ton of questions, some of the typical ones like how particular this person was about what gets dusted, what they didn't want her to touch, who looked under the rugs and who counted the silverware. Some of her clients, she said, treated their dogs better."

"And?"

"And our girl had a lot more questions about the widowers and their dearly departed. Alma thought it was odd, but she said you get a lot of crazies in that line of work."

"Cleaning?"

"They don't run background checks," Murray said. "If you can get down on your knees you're hired."

"She said that?"

"Nope, I did."

"How old is Alma Brown?"

"Late-sixties," Murray said, "Looks a lot older. McCreedy probably heard the bell ring in her head as soon as she found out that Ben's wife was named Rose and she'd been dead for over twenty-five years."

"Is she willing to come up to New York to testify?"

"She'll do anything if you pay her for it. She's a bit of a flake if you ask me, has a real burn on for McCreedy; said she didn't like her from day one. Said she was too fat to get down and scrub a floor the way it needed to be done, the way she did it. If she comes up maybe I'll ask her to do my place."

Murray coughed into the telephone.

"But you can clean her up and she'll follow orders. She's looking for the notebook she kept with the information about her clients. She says she went through it with McCreedy and it had a lot of info about Rose. If she finds that," Murray said, "You may have something."

That kind of fact witness – the one motivated by money and filled with envy always scares me. They need a lot of prep and handholding. They're a real crapshoot before a jury. Jurors don't like testimony if it's too canned or too expensive, except from experts. They'll give an expert the benefit of the doubt no matter how many times he says the same thing and no matter how much he gets paid, so long as he comes across sounding more like a professor lecturing to his students than a cheerleader supporting his team.

What if Susannah is really off her rocker, I wondered? What if she hides it well, disguising her quirks so no one notices, except for this one glaring oddity? What if she's not a con artist as much as a psychotic, a multiple personality who upon hearing the name Rose returned to the person she was at age 16 under the influence of her father and his barnyard church? Perhaps Alma's description of Ben and Rose didn't unlock a plan as much as unleash a fantasy that she'd been carrying around since she was a young girl.

What if I had to concede at trial that Susannah was not malicious or evil, not the scammer or psychological pickpocket, but had to prove instead that she was mentally ill, arguing that while she might really believe what she says - a convincing, articulate, idiot savant when it comes to recreating the past – she's still just a schizophrenic unable to distinguish the truth from fantasy?

And Ben buying it--a lonely old man who expected to join his wife shortly in the great unknown--would put him in the same boat. That meant they were both delusional. That wasn't a battle I'd relish. Evil is a lot easier to accept and dismiss than illness. Besides, I'd need to have her examined by an expert psychologist if I were going to fall back on a theme like that, which was not possible in the short time remaining before the trial.

Of course, I didn't believe any of that. I believed that Susannah knew exactly what she was doing and that she was the best damn liar I'd ever come across.

Chapter 7 – The Cat Gets Out of the Bag

"I have been born more times than anybody except Krishna."
— Mark Twain

Justice Shanawit required both sides to file pre-trial memoranda outlining the issues, identifying the tentative witnesses and listing the exhibits ten days before the trial, and when you file something in Surrogate's Court it is open to the general public, the public in this case being a stringer for the local paper who routinely checks new filings to see if there might be anything of interest.

Two days later the story appeared in the top right column of the front page of the *Journal-News* with a banner headline: "Local Widow Claims to be Reincarnation of First Wife."

It's no surprise that readers everywhere can't get enough of life and death, particularly the womb and the tomb, so I suppose it should not have come as a big shock that the entire nation would get excited about another debate over the hereafter. A purported reincarnate's right to the love and money from her prior life was a new twist that engaged everyone--from the creationists to the psychics.

I declined to take the first few calls, hoping that it might blow over, but within twenty-four hours I had to leave the phone off the hook and rely on my cell phone to conduct business. I couldn't leave the office without being chased by reporters camped out in the parking lot across the street and jeered by a gathering storm of demonstrators for challenging Susannah's great revelation. The doubters, of course, who considered Susannah a blasphemer held their own demonstrations in front of Bill Lustenberger's office.

It wasn't much different for Peter, Jeff and Mitch, although they were more than happy at first to speak to anyone about the fraud that the evil Ms. McCreedy had perpetrated on their "elderly, almost senile father." Of course, they were a religious family, they assured the television audience, but how many wrongs have been committed over the course of human history by phony faith healers and saintly pretenders, as well as thousands of others who fraudulently claimed to have an open line to God in order to collect their personal tithes, using the money instead for fast cars and fast women. In short, Susannah was a liar, pure and simple, and this trial was nothing more than a run of the mill con, albeit with a religious angle.

What they said, of course, was the real theme of our case, but My Three Sons sounded shrill and angry as they stood in front of their palatial homes.

I give credit to Bill Lustenberger for remaining above the fray, as did I, unwilling to have this matter tried in the court of public opinion. Ms. McCreedy, on the other hand, was just as willing as My Three Sons to talk to the press.

However, unlike the three men, Susannah came across as very mature and thoughtful, almost likeable. She didn't focus on the money or the legal issues, no matter what the question, talking instead about reincarnation and Rose and Ben, and how happy she was to have had the opportunity to be with him again.

"And to know for certain," she told the television audience, "that our lives are not extinguished like the flame of a candle."

She had clearly learned some tricks from her father.

She told the press that she had no idea why she had been blessed with this open door to her soul. Ultimately, she told the reporters she suspected that she was some sort of messenger sent to make people feel good about themselves and what lay ahead. Of course, there was a method to her madness. She was clearly intent on turning the trial into a referendum on the soul and the afterlife.

"The more she talks," I said to Murray when he called from Las Vegas, "The less she sounds like a scammer and the more she sounds like a TV evangelist."

"A popular profession," he said, "for the better scammers."

"Could she actually believe what she's saying?"

"The mind can convince itself of anything, and in a lot of people it doesn't take much convincing."

"If she believes it," I said, thinking out loud, "How can anyone really fault Ben for believing it as well? You can't take away an old man's hope and if that's the case what's wrong with him changing his will on a prayer or a belief, however misguided. It's only money. You can't disprove what she believes any more than she can prove it?"

"Aren't you the gloomy doom today," Murray said.

"I've got to consider all the angles."

"It's not about the fucking truth in this business," Murray said, "It never is. It's about perception and possibility. Take a good look at her. Does she look like goddamn saint material?"

Of course, who knew what a saint was supposed to look like.

"In the end," Murray said, "it's all a fucking game to you guys anyway – the truth doesn't matter as much as winning . . . and the fee."

I was too preoccupied with my own thoughts to try to defend my profession. I wasn't even sure that I could. I was thinking about what Job had cried out thousands of years earlier.

"If a man dies, shall he live again?"

God's answer my father would repeat without the least bit of hesitation was a resounding yes. But, of course, he believed that man would live again in heaven or hell. He wasn't coming back to earth for a do-over.

One day when I came home after school my father was on his knees praying. He prayed at numerous times throughout the day and always on his knees, because he didn't believe God would listen otherwise. But this afternoon he didn't pull me down to join him. Instead, he stood right up as if God was expecting the interruption and ordered me into the room behind the kitchen. It was a small pantry really, but he kept it empty and it was his place for solitary prayer and instruction for me when he wanted to make sure I had time alone, without any distractions, to think about whatever it was he wanted me to think about.

"I heard from your Sunday school teacher," he said, his jaw shaking the way it did when he was angry.

"I heard you rejected what happened to Jonah."

"That's not true," I said.

"That you didn't believe he was swallowed by the whale and spent three days in its belly until he repented and God set him free."

I must have been about fifteen and he couldn't entirely shut out the influences of public school. "I just said . . . ."

He raised his hand to silence me. He had an enormous hand that could cover me like a mask.

"I know exactly what you said," his hands now balled into fists. "That it was made up, like it was just some kind of magazine story."

"I didn't say made up."

He started pacing back and forth and I backed into the corner.

"I said it teaches that God will take pity on you . . . and forgive you if you repent, wherever you are."

"Are you calling Mr. Barish a liar?"

"No."

"He told me you said it was made-up."

Of course, he'd heard it right, I did say made up. How could anyone survive three days in the stomach of a fish?

"So you doubt that the Lord could save Jonah like that?"

"No sir," I said.

"Do you doubt that these are the words of the Lord?"

"No sir."

The next thing I felt was a smack to my ear that left my head ringing for hours. "Whoever knows that there are sins in his conscience let him repent them and he will be pitied before the Lord," he said. "You think about that the next time you doubt the truth of the scriptures."

With that he shoved me into the kitchen closet and locked the door. He shut off the light and I settled in for a night of confinement. It wasn't the first time. The dark didn't bother me, not as much as the thirst. I remember wondering whether if I truly repented God would set me free from the closet. Of course, I wasn't prepared to try it at the moment.

"You still there," Murray asked, "I'm billing by the hour too you know."

"I was just thinking."

"I knew an attorney who used to bill for thinking in the shower. I guess that's called multi-tasking."

I couldn't help but chuckle.

"So what's your trial strategy now, counselor?"

"Focus on Ben," I said. "And perhaps catch her in a bunch of inconsistencies on Rose."

You don't get coincidence without exactitude.

"And focus on her. She wasn't born this way. She's more a creation of her father than God. Get the jury to dislike what this does to Ben's children and grandchildren."

"It doesn't sound very sexy," Murray said.

"I don't want sexy, I want matter of fact. Focusing on who's going to get the money will play a lot better in the suburbs than a question of faith."

"Maybe," Murray said, "but they like their religion here too, provided it's like the mall, easy to park, nice on the eyes and easy to just browse ... and it has to offer some quick Bromo Seltzer relief when they get too fucking bloated."

"Where did you grow up?" I asked

"The Bowery," he said, "no miracles there, just hellfire and damnation."

Murray started coughing and I waited for him to stop before continuing.

"Ok, what did you find out in Vegas?"

I could hear Murray flipping through his notepad.

"She came here right after her parents were killed in the fire and worked in one of those one-hour wedding places. The Honey Bell Chapel," Murray said, "Just like the Florida orange."

"She didn't perform weddings, did she?"

"No, but that would have been nice; she filled out forms and was one of the professional witnesses." Murray paused for a moment. "And get this . . . she was also one of the customers."

That got my heart thumping.

"What does that mean?"

"That she took advantage of the employee benefits plan, one free ceremony per year."

"Bingo," I said, "a bigamist."

Unfortunately, it didn't turn out as easy as that. While her first husband turned out to be a much younger man in his mid-seventies, he was not in nearly as good shape as Ben. He was stuck in a wheelchair with a smoker's cough that could rattle the stain-glass windows.

"Her first sucker," I said, equally satisfied with all the new possibilities this opened up. We now had a modus operandi. "How much did she roll him for?"

Another dead end since Rudolph, husband number 1, came over from Denmark after the war and lived from paycheck to paycheck. He was another one of the professional witnesses and Murray said he was terminally ill when she married him and he died about a month later.

"No social security, no money," he said, "All she got was the old car she drove to Florida."

It didn't much matter if her first mark was a bust. What mattered was that she liked to marry old men for whatever she could get, even if it was just a car.

"Maybe she'll claim to be his lover during the Middle Ages," I said.

Not quite, since the minister of the Honey Bell told Murray that Rudy had asked Susannah to do him a favor. Apparently, he was illegal and had been for fifty years, always working off the books, so he had no medicare and he was desperate for some painkillers. He figured that if Susannah married him he could cash in on some government program. Unfortunately, the marriage didn't even last thirty days.

"Lucky him," Murray said.

I'm sure he could hear the sound of my hopes deflating.

"According to Reverend Honey Bell," Murray said, "Susannah figured that Rudy was the reason she was drawn to Las Vegas."

"Another connected soul."

Murray coughed in response. It didn't rattle my windows, but it certainly hurt my ears.

"She was talking about moving to Los Angeles after he died, because it was closer and the car was a piece of junk, but then she heard a voice that said Florida."

She called it a voice, Murray said, but our Pastor of the Honey Bells said it was probably a dream, which wasn't so strange considering that Florida was in the news at the time back then because of all the hurricanes.

Susannah never discussed reincarnation with him.

"Of course, the Honey Bell wasn't the holiest of holies," Murray said with a chuckle. "Hell, the vicar had a ponytail and dressed a little like Liberace."

I took in a deep breath and in the quiet I heard slow, heavy footsteps in the hall. With all that was going on with the reporters and the demonstrators I listened to make sure whoever it was passed by my door, which I was keeping locked. I'd gotten a little paranoid since someone egged the windshield of my car.

The footsteps stopped and I listened for someone trying the doorknob, but I couldn't hear anything. Then the steps receded down the hall.

"I'll keep at it," Murray said, "These creeps always forget something."

I listened for a few moments to Murray's heavy breathing while I glanced down at the book on Reincarnation I had opened in front of me. I had been looking through it when Murray called. I had stopped on a passage about William James, another believer.

The body, he said, either produces light or reflects it. A candle produces light. If you put out the candle, the light goes out. A mirror reflects light. If the mirror shatters, the light continues. So why is it so hard, he concluded, to suppose that the body reflects the soul like a mirror, rather than producing life like a candle?

For someone like me, who had every drop of religion and spirituality wrung out of him as a child, who turned to math and science instead, and became a fervent believer in the rule of law, whether written by man or promulgated by nature - one of my favorites being that the sum total of energy and matter is always constant – there was no room for an eternal soul and the continued consciousness and memory that it presupposes, a thread that would defy the laws of nature by refusing to ever break.

I wouldn't be human if I didn't want to believe in what Susannah was saying, even though I could never believe in what she was doing.

"We're running out of time," I said, tiring of my own thoughts.

"We all are."

"Fine," I said, "Just keep me posted."

"I will," Murray said, obviously a little annoyed at the sarcasm in my voice, "And try to calm your damn clients down a bit so they don't always come across the idiot box like they miss their millions more than their father."

I haven't lost too many cases at trial, two actually if you counted, because the ones I'm not confident about winning I make sure to settle. It's something I learned at my first job. I started working after law school with this wizened old personal injury attorney, Charlie Messner, famous around town for his bow ties and contrariness.

He was a damn good attorney, even if his suits were always rumpled and he wore as much of his meal as he ate, because he had a great intuitive sense of people, spoke to the jury like they were all friends sitting around the dining room table and he had this disarming, deceptive intelligence that lulled many an opponent to sleep. He always said that only a fool rolls the dice.

I knew that Bill Lustenberger practiced the same way. No one likes to have a jury call your client, and by extension you, a liar. I could see it in his eyes when we ran into each other in the courthouse on other matters. He knew that all he had to do was raise the subject of settlement and the dialogue would begin. I would make sure of it. I had yet to have a client that I couldn't convince to settle for something when the time was right.

Meanwhile, the press sought permission from Judge Shanawit to televise the trial on CourtTV. I objected strenuously. But the judge agreed provided the camera's presence was not too prominent since she didn't want the jurors staring at the lens, instead of the witnesses.

Once it was clear that I couldn't get the judge to change her mind I requested that the cameras not be allowed to show any of the jurors' faces and requested that they remain unidentified to the press until after the completion of the trial. I didn't want them or their families feeling pressure from any of the religious fanatics.

I don't think Judge Shanawit had any real idea of the intensity of the emotions unleashed by putting the afterlife on trial, as some of the papers put it, because she seemed hesitant until I told her about the threatening call I had received the night before on my home number from a woman who said she had a message from God which was to "let the will go." She delivered the line like she meant to say "let my people go."

Judge Shanawit agreed to maintain their anonymity after that.

I also requested that the jurors be sequestered for the duration of the trial, since they would likely ignore the court's instructions not to watch the reruns on TV after they got home, or the news, or talk to anyone who did.

While juries in the county were routinely sequestered during murder trials, no jury had ever been sequestered in Surrogate's Court. Still, Judge Shanawit agreed since the news coverage was growing more and more intense as the trial approached and the Court Deputy told her that they were expecting a spectacle outside the courthouse.

The judge decided that the jurors would board a minibus behind the courthouse after each day of trial and be whisked away to an unknown destination with all the exits from the courthouse, as well as some of the local roads temporarily closed. An undercover police escort in front and behind would keep the press from following.

I met with My Three Sons over the weekend to prepare them for the trial. They already knew what they would testify to since it wasn't a whole lot and they knew my philosophy, which I had borrowed long ago from Mark Twain, that if you always tell the truth you never have to remember anything.

What they needed was some basic hand holding since they had no idea what to expect, notwithstanding all the courtroom dramas they'd watched on television. The real thing is always different, particularly when you're not watching it with a drink in one hand and some potato chips in the other, and have a big personal stake in the outcome.

"Get a good night's sleep," I said, "because you will never feel as tired as you will after sitting in a courtroom all day with the jurors watching your every reaction. At the end of the day, it's going to feel as if you've just finished running a marathon."

I told them not to speak to the press during the trial and not to react to anyone's testimony, particularly Susannah's, which I guaranteed them would make them want to puke.

"Keep a poker face," I said, "because the jurors will keep a straight face." They always seem to do that naturally enough, except for laughing at the judge's jokes. "And they'll resent it if you can't. You may think Susannah's full of crap, but they'll want you to respect the court and the process.

"Besides, the press will be watching and they'll read into your expressions the exact opposite of what you intend, they'll see fear and concern when you mean disgust, and that's not taking into account that the judge will jump all over you.

"If you have anything to say to me, write me a note. I won't be able to follow what's going on with you whispering into my ear at the same time. And if you try the jury will wonder whether or not something is going wrong. Just write it down, the jurors will be a lot less curious about that."

My Three Sons all nodded quietly.

We talked a little about settlement in case it came up and they were moving away from their refrain of millions for defense not one cent for tribute. It was clear to me that they'd jump at a five figure number, and I could probably get them to one or even two hundred thousand if I really pressed.

"How did Dad put us in this position?" Jeff said. "What could he have been thinking?"

"He wasn't thinking," Peter responded. "It was his dick's last gasp."

"He always said that we had to make our own way in the world and shouldn't count on his money," Mitch added.

"Then he should have given it away to charity, for Christ's sake. I could have lived with that."

"Bullshit."

"And watch your language in the courthouse," I reminded them. "The walls there really do have ears. Outside as well, there will be press everywhere."

What I did tell them to make them less anxious was that unlike most of the personal injury and commercial disputes I've handled their testimony would not make or break their case. It was all about what the jury thought of Susannah. All I expected them to do was shed some light on Rose and Ben and confirm just how different Susannah the reincarnate was from Rose. Indeed, I told them that I'd been toying with the idea of putting just one of them on the stand, Mitchell, the least hot-headed of the brothers, so as to reduce their exposure and not be too repetitious.

"It'll be a last minute decision," I said.

Peter and Jeff looked relieved by the prospect.

I sat down with Murray over the weekend to see what else he had uncovered. He'd been back to Bemidji and found out that

Susannah was adopted and that her father, the Reverend of Reincarnation, was once accused of molesting one of his congregants by having her remove her shoes and socks so he could fondle her feet, a foot fetish that he probably practiced on Susannah as well. Unfortunately, I couldn't use it. The last thing I wanted was to have the judge, the jury and the television audience feeling sorry for her.

"What about Rose?" I asked.

"Quiet, unassuming, liked to play canasta."

"I know all that."

"Broke her toe once when she went to kick one of the boys and hit the wall."

"So she had a bit of a temper?"

"Only time it ever happened as far as I can tell. Everyone has a boiling point."

Even Susannah, I thought, writing it all down. Susannah hadn't mentioned it and if I got desperate or needed to fill some time it might be useful.

Murray flipped some more pages of his little notepad.

"She loved to read, but never bought a book. She got everything out of the library. She traded recommendations with friends."

Susannah had mentioned during the deposition that Rose loved to read books, but that she was making up for it now by sticking to magazines. It was an attempt at a joke, I believe, but it fell flat with me. Of course, that was something she could have easily learned from Ben.

"Didn't like shopping," Murray said, "not many rich broads like that."

"A product of the depression," I said, thinking how glad I was that Murray wasn't taking the stand.

"Good cook."

I put my pencil down and leaned back on my chair.

"You know about Eva," Murray said. "She had a lobotomy, got raped and pregnant and had an abortion . . . and she didn't die of natural causes."

"What do you mean, she was murdered?"

"Come on counselor, what do you think this is fucking CSI New York? I think she killed herself, it was way too sudden."

"How could you know that?"

"I have sources."

"You saw her file?"

"They don't put shit like that in files."

I couldn't use any of that at the trial.

"Anything about what Rose might have known?" I asked.

"Nope, only her mother and sister ever visited," he said, "Sounds to me like they kept her away because she was the baby in the family."

"I suppose if I get desperate," I said, thinking out loud.

"There's something else I'm working on that might be useful," Murray said.

"What's that?"

"You know, I went down to interview that attorney who drafted up the new will," Murray said.

I nodded. I had asked Murray to do that after I spoke to the attorney on the telephone and he was pretty curt. Lawyers get very defensive, particularly with other lawyers, and he didn't like the idea that I was questioning anything that he had drafted.

People down here are always changing their wills, he said, disinheriting children and paying off new love interests. It wasn't his job, he explained, to question or challenge motives or reasons, nor was he required to do a psychiatric evaluation. He just followed his client's instructions. He prepared the will and sent it along with instructions on how to execute it.

I thought that was a little odd since most New York wills are executed in an attorney's office. Or course, we don't have quite the same population of housebound elderly.

Murray said that the attorney tried to give him the bum's rush, but once he sat down he wasn't easy to get back up. The attorney said he never met with Ben about the changes in his will, but only spoke to him over the telephone. He said he recognized Ben's voice because he'd come into the office not too long before that to add Susannah's name to the deed and to set up a separate account for her.

He had never met Susannah and he just stuck the new will in the mail.

Ben executed the will without a notary, allowed in Florida, with two witnesses who turned out to be a very old, sickly couple who lived around the corner and who both, conveniently, kicked the bucket shortly afterward. Murray spoke to their daughter who said she couldn't be sure whether it was their signatures since they were both nearly deaf and blind and their hands shook from Parkinson's, so their handwriting had really deteriorated over the last few years.

"I'll tell you what I think," Murray said. "I think Ben had no intention of changing his will which is why he transferred the property and set up the account for her expenses. Why do that if you're planning on giving her everything anyway?"

"But he did the new will three months later," I said, "maybe his feelings changed."

"I say she nagged him until he called the attorney," Murray said, "or she got him a little soused first."

"You'd think an attorney would notice that, even over the phone."

"Not this ambulance chaser with his bus stop ads and flyers on cars. He's like the Burger King of wills and trusts. I'm betting that if Ben was humoring her when he called, trying to get her off his back, and had no intention of signing it, which is why she picked an old sickly couple around the block instead of one of the neighbors as a witness."

"What difference would that make?" I said. "A witness is a witness."

"Come on counselor, use your fucking imagination. Because he didn't sign it in front of them or maybe she forged his signature and wanted a couple of witnesses who wouldn't know what the hell they were signing. Maybe she hired some stooge to pretend to be Ben. They were practically deaf and blind so how would they know . . . and they'd be dead soon enough anyway?"

"But the handwriting expert confirmed it was Ben's signature."

"How certain?"

"Pretty certain."

"So she copied it. You don't think McCreedy is good enough to copy the signature of an eighty-eight -year old man? Shit, did you see his signature - a 6-year old could copy that scribble."

I'd used handwriting experts before and they weren't shy about raising any doubts based on the slightest tilt of a t or a bigger swirl on the top of the e. I'd used this guy before and he seemed pretty certain that the signature was genuine, too certain to ever consider using at trial.

"OK, then what if he signed it without the witnesses, thinking that it wouldn't be any good," Murray said, looking down at his nails which were chewed down to the cuticles."

"Not believable," I said.

"Or signed the signature page thinking it had to do with a new car for his beloved or the special account? She could have told him anything. If he bought what she was selling with Rose that would have been a piece of cake."

That I might be able to sell.

I looked at my copy of the will again. There was a boilerplate paragraph above his signature and nothing else. I could tell it was the last page of a will, but if you didn't know what you were looking at, or glanced too quickly at it, you could mistake it for something else, some other kind of legal document. Ben could have believed it was some kind of tax form that his young wife needed to file for access to his social security benefits down the road.

I swiveled my chair to the side and stared out the window at the media trucks gathered across the street.

"Got anything else?" I asked.

"That's it for now." And probably forever, I thought. Murray hadn't found a smoking gun and wasn't likely to at this late date, although I couldn't blame him, a lot of cases just don't have one.

"I'm going to speak again with the daughter of the witnesses to the will," he said. "She might be worth using."

Murray closed his notepad.

"I do have one idea I wanted to bounce off you," I said.

"I charge extra for legal advice."

"Pretend you're a juror."

"Who would seat me? I'd have my mind made up before the opening," Murray said. "All I'd need is one look."

"Hear me out," I said, "I've done a lot of reading about reincarnation and all the others in history who claimed to be reincarnated and gave names and places to prove it. Not one I read about ever tried to reclaim anything from a prior life. I mean how could they since most of their prior lives were a century or two earlier."

"So what's your point counselor?"

"Reincarnation is supposed to allow for a new life in a new body to compensate for something in the past and to help elevate the soul to a higher plane."

"You sound like a fucking convert," Murray said.

"A true reincarnate, according to the books I've read, would never have married Ben since he was about to leave his earthly body. She wouldn't want to interfere with the past or the life she'd left."

"Is this the hereafter according to Joe Clasen?"

"No, according to the expert on reincarnation I found."

With that I handed Murray the CV for Mithalal Somnigupta, a professor in Far Eastern religions at the University of Vermont.

"Oh I like this," he said, "the trial isn't already going to be enough of a circus, you're going to treat her like reincarnation is fucking real and she's the queen, only she's a bad queen for breaking the rules."

"It's just a 'what if' argument. I argue that she's a liar and a thief, not a reincarnate, but even if you believe in reincarnation and accept its precepts, she's not a true reincarnate, not according to Dr. Somnigupta, a world renowned expert . . . first, because she would never have come back so soon, and second, because she would never have married Ben or allowed him to disinherit his children."

"Robert's Rules of Reincarnation," Murray said while looking at the resume. "No sleeping with past lives and no handouts."

"He's a full professor of Far Eastern religion and has written two books about it."

Murray continued to study the resume.

"You're a juror now," I said, "not a cynical private dick."

"What the fuck," he said, "I'd use it assuming the guy doesn't come across like he's a Hari Krishna or selling time shares. It just gives me another reason to ding her even if I still want to believe in heaven and hell."

"That was my thinking as well, but I'll have to be careful. I didn't want this to turn into a trial about the eternal soul and reincarnation. It's got to be about her."

"What do you got to lose?" Murray said, handing me back the resume along with his bill. "It's not your money."

I'd been thinking seriously about it since I met Dr. Somnigupta last week, because I thought he'd make a good witness. Although he was short and thin and reminded me a little of Alfred E. Newman from Mad Magazine, he spoke very well, very professorially, and with absolute conviction.

Besides, I was beginning to think I didn't have much of a choice.

Chapter 8 – The Trial Begins

"As far back as I can remember I have unconsciously referred to the experiences of a previous state of existence."
– Henry David Thoreau

The clients were not present for the jury selection on Monday, but the press was out in force along with hundreds of spectators and demonstrators.

The crowds were herded behind ropes and sawhorses set up on either side of the small park across the street from the courthouse. To the right were demonstrators holding signs heralding Susannah's revelation as a gift from God, along with scattered signs denouncing abortion and euthanasia. To the left there was an interesting mix of agnostics and atheists, the AARP crowd and the heaven and hell contingent.

Of course, a nice day in June will tend to bring out the nuts, which included a few men dressed in biblical costumes, long flowing robes and long staffs, and two others wearing old-fashioned sandwich board signs with the usual dire threats and warnings about the apocalypse. There were even six people dressed like gypsies, who wandered from side to side like a band of troubadours offering to help anyone who wished to look beyond their present life. One carried a sign that said Susannah was not only the reincarnation of Rose, but of Krishna himself – brought back as a sign that God would soon reveal himself to everyone.

Thankfully, the state police had been brought in to keep order.

I had the local paper with me and the headline read, "God Takes the Stand."

The first question for the jury, according to the reporter, based on his interview with Bill Lustenberger, was whether they believed there was an eternal soul. If the answer was yes, then the next question was whether that soul could return to earth from time to time. If so, the final question was whether Susannah had the same soul that once belonged to Ben Everett's wife or at least she believed that she did, which meant that Ben could have come to believe it as well, so that their marriage was based on a common belief, as opposed to fraud or senility.

"People have used their fortunes to build churches and to help homeless animals," Bill Lustenberger was quoted as saying, "so why should Ben's freedom of choice be any more limited."

Every attorney tries to define the playing field. Bill could try to do that in the papers, but I wasn't going to let him do it at trial. The trial issues, as I intended to present them, were much more mundane: was Ben of sound mind when he married Susannah and executed a new will, or was he unduly influenced by the story this young woman told him and, even if he wasn't, was the new will properly signed and executed. My analysis of the trial issues, which was stated in my pre-trial memorandum, much less sensational than my adversary's, was buried at the end of the article.

In light of the article and the number of reporters, I asked the judge to reconsider her decision about the cameras, but she declined. Judge Shanawit did not like to second guess herself and I suspect she didn't mind the public exposure.

Of course, the reporters and spectators were excluded for the jury selection process and since the clients were not in attendance it was just Bill, me, the judge, her law clerk, the courtroom deputy, and the largest panel of prospective jurors I had ever seen, well over 50.

Bill and I each got twice the normal number of automatic rejections, 6 each, for which no reason need be given to exclude them. We could object to other prospective jurors for cause if we had some good reason to believe that they might be prejudiced – whether for religious reasons or simply because they hated May/December weddings - and so would be unable to keep an open mind.

With Judge Shanawit denying most of our requests to excuse jurors for cause and limiting the lunch break to 30 minutes Bill and I had our 6 jurors and 4 alternates picked by 4pm.

I can't say that I was jumping for joy, but that's rare, and I was satisfied that I'd gotten a pretty good jury under the circumstances, one that would be skeptical of the claims of a 24-year old woman to the estate of an eighty-eight-year old man, whatever the reason, and be more inclined to protect his children and grandchildren.

The judge sent the jurors home for the night instructing them not to speak about the case, even among themselves, or the fact that they had been selected as jurors, except to their immediate families, and to avoid watching the television news or reading the newspapers. They were directed to return at 9 am sharp with their bags packed for what she anticipated would be a three to four-day trial.

They left with the entire pool of jurors, those already rejected and those not yet called, who were still being held in the jury assembly room downstairs so that there would be a mass exodus at the end of the day and the press would have no idea who had been picked. The police were stationed in all the parking lots to make sure no one tried to talk to anyone from the prospective jury pool before they got into their cars. To prevent them from being followed all the exits from the courthouse were blocked for 30 minutes, except for the juror's parking lot.

Both Bill and I were besieged when we left the courthouse, but we could only describe the make-up of the jury, which they would find out tomorrow when spectators would be allowed into the courtroom.

I called Mitch, Jeff and Peter to give them my take on the jury.

"It's a pretty good panel," I said, reading them the descriptions from my notes. "What's important is that I think we avoided any real killer jurors."

And believe me, I told them, a few of those managed to get called to the box; jurors with personalities so strong and compelling that they could steal your breath away, like a frigid winter wind; who could take hold of a jury and bend it to their will; narcissists who would eagerly disregard the evidence and testimony for their own sense of right and wrong; contrarians who lived to shock society and convention and would have loved to announce to the world that a court of the great state of New York has found for reincarnation or determined that man was without a soul.

The problem with juries – as with people – is that while you can always spot the loud and obvious problems, the quiet ones, the ones capable of subtle control, who seethe below the surface with some sort of secret vendetta or hidden agenda, are much more difficult to identify. Those are the ones you really worry about when picking a panel, because they can easily slip by and change everything.

There were three on the jury who worried me a bit. There was Matt the musician who seemed harmless enough, but was probably hoping to find some kind of creative muse in the trial process. What's more, artists as jurors, at least in my experience were prone to embracing the romantic, miraculous side of any story.

Then there was Ira, the dandy, who wanted to appear richer and more successful than he was and probably carried around a short-changed chip on his shoulder. He might like the power to make some poor farm girl from Minnesota rich, while at the same time penalizing a family that had had too much for way too long.

Finally, there was Frank, the postal worker, who was angry at something. It was obvious by the way he sat there like he was wearing a military brace, by his short answers, zippered mouth and the stony looks he gave to both Bill and me. The problem with anger, any kind of anger, is that you can't always tell who it will be aimed at or when, not until it's too late, and it can make people do strange, unpredictable things.

The three other regular jurors – Millie, late 50s, 2 years of college, 3 daughters in the area, two married, corporate husband, nicely dressed, Ellen, elementary school teacher, colorful clothes, husband dentist, two teenage boys, widowed father who remarried an old high school friend's widowed mother, and Lauren, owner of a small promotion business, amused by the intensity of our questions – all seemed standard fare and not likely to take a leap into the unknown.

The 4 alternates were a mixed bag – number 1 was my favorite, Rose, 74, widow, 12 grandchildren, quiet determination, kind who could move a panel if it drifted too far away from family, Karen, 35, dental hygienist, husband attorney, two children, son autistic, Banerlee, 40, programmer from India, wife, four children, raised in a family that believed in reincarnation, but hasn't given it much thought for many years, and Jesse, overweight insurance agent, unmarried mid-20s, awkward, nervous energy, legs bouncing up and down and way too eager to get on the jury if you ask me.

Chapter 9 – The Trial

> *"Europe is that part of the world which is haunted by the incredible delusion that man was created out of nothing, and that his present birth is his first entrance into life."*
> *– Arthur Schopenhauer*

The next morning the jurors drove to a special parking lot in the back of the courthouse where the judges and court personnel parked. Only Bill and I, and our clients, had to pass through the phalanx of reporters and demonstrators being held back by police barricades.

My Three Sons and I waited for Bill and Susannah to go up the courthouse steps first. She waved and nodded like she was on stage, drawing strength from the cheers to her left and oblivious to the hisses and boos to her right.

She was not dressed in a manner that I imagined Rose would have approved of. Instead of something plain and simple, she had on a long white silk pants suit with a gold belt. It made her look like the high priestess of some religious order.

We walked up the courthouse steps, four blue suits and red ties, without acknowledging the roiling crowd.

Inside the courtroom the cameras had been set up and the reporters scattered among the spectators per the judge's instructions like dandelions in a field of green. But, there was no mistaking them as they sat there with their notebooks out and pens poised.

"Before I bring in the jury are there any preliminaries we need to address?" Judge Shanawit asked.

I had none, but Bill had one.

"My client has a request she would like to personally make before we begin."

"Go ahead Ms. McCreedy," the judge said.

Susannah stood up from her seat at the counsel table next to Bill and brushed some invisible lint off her blouse. Then she looked over at Mitch, Peter and Jeff with a kind smile, a motherly smile, which the three of them met with exaggerated looks of disgust. I leaned over to remind them what I said about making faces.

"Your Honor, I appreciate this opportunity to address the court," she said, speaking very slowly and very clearly, traces of her preacher father in her voice, which started off simple like a single chord, but quickly expanded to a more complex, orchestral sound.

She didn't sound anything like she looked, although I already knew that. Judge Shanawit however sat back and covered her mouth with her hand.

She was too good a speaker for this neighborhood if you asked me, too polished not to be a conartist. I hoped the jury would take note of that when they got to hear her; more than just words and documents go into a decision like the one they had to make.

"I would like to deliver the opening statement on my own behalf," she said.

My pen slipped right from my hands and clattered on the floor. Clearly, Bill had no control over her.

I could hear the sound of pen hitting paper behind me as the reporters furiously wrote it all down.

"I have no objection," I said, quickly jumping up after retrieving my pen.

"That is why you have counsel, Ms. McCreedy."

"He will handle the rest of the hearing."

"This is a trial, Ms. McCreedy, not a hearing. You will have an opportunity to address the jury when you take the stand to testify. Unless you are prepared to discharge your counsel and proceed on your own, I won't allow it. Are you prepared to discharge your counsel?"

I looked over at Bill and from the look in his eyes I could swear that he wasn't sure what she would do.

Bill reached over and touched her sleeve and she sighed. I wished the jury was here to see this show, I thought, because it was already over the top.

"No, Your Honor."

"It's all or nothing in my part there's no double teaming," the judge said, looking up at the cameras. "I have no doubt that your counsel will do a fine job representing you in all aspects of the trial."

Susannah looked like she was about to argue and I saw Bill give her a little tug back down to her seat.

"Are we ready to begin?" Judge Shanawit asked.

Both Bill and I stood up and responded yes.

The jurors filed in. We waited for them to settle in their seats, leaning forward as they always do in anticipation of the opening.

Bill stood up slowly and nodded at Susannah, me and the judge.

"May I proceed Your Honor?" he asked.

The judge nodded and Bill approached the jury box. The jury can sense concern and doubt, so it's always important to appear calm and deliberate.

"Ladies and Gentlemen of the jury, this is an unusual case, there's no getting around it." Bill slipped his hands out of his pocket and leaned on the railing of the jury box, his eyes traveling from juror to juror, lingering long enough to make eye contact, exactly the way it's supposed to be done.

It's what people do when they are telling the truth; they look you in the eye. He waited a little bit too long for my taste to start speaking again, the silence becoming a little awkward as the jurors started fidgeting in their seats, but attorneys are creatures of habit and religiously follow the style that has served them best in the past.

"My client, Susannah McCreedy, is young. She's only twenty-four years old, yet she stands before this Court, before you, ready to inherit fifty million dollars from her late husband's will.

It's an awesome responsibility that she doesn't take lightly, you'll see that when she takes the stand.

"She comes before you because her late husband Ben Everett, who was eighty-eight, changed his will to make her his sole heir. It was a serious thing for him to do, we would be the first to admit that, but that doesn't mean it wasn't intended, and that he didn't have his reasons and beliefs; and that he wasn't entitled to do with it what he wanted."

Bill took a breath and walked slowly away from the jury box to the lectern where he stopped and turned back to the jury. He stared at them for a moment and nodded slowly.

"You are not here to judge Ben's reasons or decide whether or not it's something that you would have done under the circumstances," he said his voice raised a bit, not a shout but something more emphatic than a normal speaking voice.

He looked over at Susannah and then back at the jury.

"You are here to decide two simple questions. Did Ben marry Susannah of his own free will or was he somehow tricked, and did Ben know what he was doing when he decided to change his will – it's what the law calls being of sound mind. We will argue that the answer to the first question is yes, Susannah did not trick Ben into marriage, she believes in what she will say here every bit as much as Ben came to believe it too.

"People marry for all sorts of reasons and having a common spiritual and religious experience and belief is one of them. The answer to the second question follows from the first and that answer is also yes. Ben had the right to decide what to do with his money, he was intelligent and aware, and he decided to give it to his young wife. My opponent, of course, will argue the opposite on both questions."

Bill walked over to counsel's table and stood next to Susannah. She looked over at the jury with a warm, welcoming smile, a grandmotherly smile that she must have practiced for weeks.

"Let's discuss the first question for a moment, did Susannah trick Ben into marrying her or did he marry her of his own free will. Now if I were you sitting there I'd be asking myself - how can I answer that question without Ben being here?

"Of course, we wouldn't need a trial if he was here, because he could speak for himself. We wouldn't be here if that was the case, but he's not. It's a difficult question to answer under the best of circumstances, love is never easy to define or understand, but you will have to do that, and you'll have to base your decision on the testimony and evidence that you hear and see. You have to leave your own feelings and beliefs in the jury room."

Bill looked over at My Three Sons and the jury followed his gaze, then he looked back at Susannah.

"Now you will hear from some of Ben's family and friends," he said, raising one hand to his chin and rubbing it, like a college professor in front of his class. "They will tell you that he may have been eighty-eight, but he hardly seemed it. He read, he exercised, handled his own financial investments and was as sharp as a tack.

"In fact, he was the one neighbors went to when they needed financial advice. You'll hear how happy Ben seemed after he met Susannah and how he laughed at the age difference, always himself, always in control, a man who knew what he wanted – a marriage to a much younger woman with a secret, something somewhat unconventional, I grant you that, but one they had both come to believe, along with half the world I might add.

"Whatever Ben's reason for marrying Susannah, however he found that comfort and connection we call love, it was something he was certainly entitled to do after so many years of loneliness."

I thought about objecting since there was no way anyone could testify about Bill's loneliness, but I hate objecting during an opening. Judges don't like it and I didn't want to risk bringing more attention to Bill's remark and giving the jury the impression that I was somehow concerned about it. He should have said many years of being alone instead, which was an objective fact.

"You will hear Susannah testify how she resisted at first, but how lonely she was herself, her parents having died when she was young in a terrible fire. Of course, she needed a father figure, what young girl doesn't. Is that any less of a reason to marry than some of the others we hear about and accept every day? Is a need for companionship any less a kind of love? I don't think so, even though the reason here, you will learn, goes well beyond that."

Bill sighed and put his hands together as if in prayer. I wondered how long he could avoid the R-word.

"In any event that's not for you or me to judge, decide or measure, the differences or similarities for that matter between two people who marry is not what's at issue here. The question is whether Ben married of his own free will, believing, as did Susannah that they had found in each other something that they both needed and wanted . . . something spiritual, something that transcended time and life. That's the first question you have to decide.

"Let's jump to the second question for a moment – Did Ben appreciate and understand what he was doing when he changed his will? I think that's the easier of the two questions. Unless my adversary can convince you that Ben had suddenly lost his mind and was no longer capable of making a decision about what to do with his savings – perhaps measuring in his mind what more it could do for Susannah who had so little compared to his three sons who had so much - then the answer is yes, he knew exactly what he was doing.

"Of course, I'm just speculating as to what Ben's reason was, because there's no way of knowing that, but it's not the reason that matters with respect to the second question, the only thing that matters is that Ben was of sound mind when he made the change . . . and that is really the crux of what you have to decide.

"With respect to that issue, you have to look at the things we can know, like the circumstances of the will's execution and the people who knew Ben. That would be his neighbors, his stockbroker, Susannah, and even Ben's sons. No one who knew Ben ever doubted his mental capacity right up to the moment he died in a very unfortunate accident when he was driving alone on the highway and a tire came loose from a truck ahead of him and slammed into his windshield."

Bill placed a hand lightly on Susannah's shoulder.

"As we discussed when you were being interviewed for the jury, all Susannah asks of you during the trial is that you keep an open mind and accept that many of us have different beliefs, no less sincere and no less true than any others, since at the end of the day there is no definitive answer to that one question that is always in all our hearts and minds."

Bill took a breath and looked carefully at the jury, narrowing his eyes and lowering his voice so that they had to lean forward to hear him.

Here it comes, I thought, time for the afterlife and the one that follows that - the R-word - clever to save it to the end.

"Susannah grew up as an active member of a small Christian church, the Cather's Unity Church, where her father was a preacher. It's a very small denomination that believes not only in Jesus as the savior, and the eternal rewards he offers to all of mankind, but in reincarnation as well.

"Now you and I may not believe that every soul comes back, rising from the ashes like the Phoenix to live again, but many people do, billions of people actually, followers of the Buddhist and Hindu religions, the Mormon religion, and many others. Many great men--from Henry Ford and Charlie Chaplin to Walt Whitman and Mark Twain--have believed in reincarnation."

Bill straightened up, removed his hand from Susannah's shoulder, and started walking toward the jury box.

"Susannah felt a connection to Ben that very first day she showed up to clean his house and he felt it as well; the beginning of a friendship perhaps, or a sense of companionship or love, or perhaps the continuation of feelings from another perspective and another life – déjà vu, if you'd like. It all depends on what you believe.

"If you believe in reincarnation, as you will see Susannah most certainly does . . . and Ben came to as well as he got to know her; if it can be true for you and comforting in terms of answering that great unknown question we must all answer in our own way, than Ben and Susannah's feelings for each other are no less real than anything else you or I may carry in our hearts.

'It certainly is no great leap to go from belief in the hereafter and the eternal soul to the belief that that eternal soul may return from time to time. Indeed, you will hear how mention of reincarnation can even be found in the bible."

Bill looked like he was about to sit down, as if he were finished, but I've used that same technique before. The jurors lean back as if they've got it, they let down their guard, and then you hit them with another blast.

"We're not here to judge my client's or her husband's beliefs. It's enough for them to hold that belief in their heart, to be motivated by that belief, as both Ben and Susannah were. But we must never forget that beliefs have an origin . . . that they grow from events, kernels of truth, such as the crucifixion and the resurrection, that serve as their foundation."

I started rising up from my seat to object, but sat back down. It was already out and too late to take back. If Bill was trying to make this all about God and religion, I would have to add a few things in my opening to deal with it.

"There's an interesting kernel of truth here, a moment – perhaps some might even call it a small miracle, it's certainly a moment that will make you pause and think hard in terms of what you believe. It will get you right here," Bill said, lightly touching his heart, "As well as here," he said, this time patting the side of his head.

I knew what was coming next. He thought it would be a big surprise to me. I could tell when he glanced over to take the measure of my suspense. All he and the jury saw was my completely non-plus, poker face.

"When Susannah was younger--about sixteen--participating in a Sunday service, she will tell you how she stood in front of the congregation to give testimony, their services being more like a spirited revival than a Latin mass, when suddenly she felt a door to her heart open, and she saw into her soul – a kind of religious experience some of us have had in one form or another and all of us wish for.

"She felt as if she could feel the infinite and her own eternity and for a moment she knew another life, a past life, another existence that had recently been completed. And before that door closed she stood before the congregation and cried out one word, a name, Rose, she cried out Rose, the name of Ben's wife who died two years before she was born."

Bill let out a loud sigh, as if he were relieved to get it off his chest.

"Of course, I know what you are thinking. How do you know this isn't something Susannah just made up for this trial or one of the witnesses did? That's a very fair question."

Bill reached into his pile of documents and pulled out an old newspaper clipping.

"Because there happened to be a reporter there that day from the local newspaper who wrote a story about what he saw and it's right here. The young girl was asked to reach back into her past life, but nothing happened, and just as it seemed the preacher – her father - was about to give up she began to shake and called out the name Rose before collapsing into his arms. You'll get to see the article, clearly written by someone who did not believe in reincarnation, but who reported accurately nonetheless what happened that day."

Of course, I could have objected to the reference to an article not yet in evidence, and the judge would have slammed him for referring to it in his opening, but I didn't want the jury to think I was surprised or concerned.

Bill put the article back into his folder of exhibits and stood silent for a moment, his eyes on his client.

"Life is strange, death is stranger, and what we don't know . . . is so much more than what we do. All that I ask is that you take this journey through Ben and Rose's life, through Susannah's life and the last year she spent with Ben with an open mind. Listen closely to the testimony, be critical, of course, but at the end when it comes time to deliberate don't let the beliefs that you have brought into this courtroom interfere with how you judge the sincerity and truth of what Susannah and Ben believed, and what they did in response to those beliefs. Try to see things through their eyes. Love whether it's through the years or through many lifetimes trumps money. It always does."

With that, Bill sat down and I popped right up. I never like to give my opponent's words too much time to hang up there, like a brilliant full moon. I don't want the jurors basking in their reflection or having too much time to think. I want to replace those words as quickly as I can with my own.

"May I, Your Honor?"

The judge nodded.

"Good morning ladies and gentlemen of the jury," I said, before I even had a chance to walk around counsel's table and take my place at the railing of the jury box to make the same sweeping eye contact with each of the jurors. I wanted them to switch their focus to me and my words before too much of what Bill had said could soak in.

"You are ultimately going to be asked to determine whether the life savings of Ben Everett, accumulated during his long marriage to Rose, and carefully preserved over the remainder of his life after Rose passed away – a very significant sum, $50 million – should go to his three boys and his grandchildren, or to Susannah, a 24-year old woman, who he married less than a year before he was tragically killed in a highway accident.

"That's the overview and I am willing to adopt the two principal questions that my colleague put before you, although I would say that they are both equally important and, despite what he just suggested to you, both deserve an unequivocal no."

I stopped and rubbed my chin as if I were thinking how best to proceed. I didn't want the jury to think my opening was too rehearsed and I wanted to wait for each of them to look up at me expectantly. I wasn't going to proceed until I knew that I had their attention, each and every one of them.

Alternate juror number 1, my own Rose, held my eyes the longest and I could swear that I saw an almost imperceptible nod.

"Let's look at the first question. Did Susannah trick Ben into marrying her or did he marry her of his own free will? Since Ben is no longer alive, you will have to determine that by applying your own common sense and your own experience to the evidence you will hear, judging both the credibility of the source and his or her self-interest. Let's look first at what you will hear from the witnesses that are disinterested and have nothing to gain by lying."

I looked at Susannah as I said that, then I moved closer to Ben's three sons, Mitch at counsel's table and Peter and Jeff right behind him, looking down at them for a moment and giving the jurors time to imagine them as little boys, as their own little boys. When the silence became a bit uncomfortable, I turned toward the jury box.

"Rose, Ben's beloved wife of almost forty-five years, died after a long, lingering illness," I said using my soft voice. "Ben, as devoted a husband and father as anyone could wish for, did not have so much as a girlfriend or companion over the next twenty-five years, other than his sons and his grandchildren."

I smiled.

"One great love like that in a lifetime is a great stroke of luck, as much as anyone can ask for."

I took a breath and moved closer to the jury box, raising my voice slightly.

"He had his sons and daughters-in-law, and he had his grandchildren. He had friends and neighbors. He wasn't alone. He never complained about being lonely, despite what my colleague has suggested. He enjoyed walking and swimming. He read voraciously. He went to the clubhouse. He managed his own finances, keeping his money in conservative, stable bonds and CDs so he'd have a legacy to leave to his sons and grandchildren to help pay their way through college and through life. It was by any measure a full and satisfying life, minus of course the love of his life who still filled his heart with warm memories.

"Plenty of older women in the community befriended Ben, but he wasn't interested. He was self-sufficient and content on his own. He used the services of Minute Maid who sent someone over once a week to clean his house. You will hear about Alma Brown, who started working for Ben almost eighteen years earlier when she was in her mid-forties, a single mother who came by once a week and befriended Ben, getting to know all about Ben and Rose, because he talked about her all the time, until she had to leave for knee surgery and was replaced by a recent hire from Las Vegas."

I moved up to the railing around the jury box and rested my hands on it.

"Alma Brown started when Ben was in his 70's. A lot happens to a man that age over eighteen years. By the time he reaches eighty-eight he slows down and a lot of things seem less clear and certain. We lose some of those natural instincts, those barriers of skepticism and caution that are so important for our safety and protection wear away over time. Still, Ben's life hadn't changed much for twenty-five years, until Ms. Susannah McCreedy was sent over as Alma's replacement."

I walked toward Susannah, looking at her, but not getting too close.

"Ms. McCreedy had just arrived a week earlier from Las Vegas, where she had worked at one of those instant wedding chapels – the Honey Bell Chapel – as a professional witness and where she had married another older man, a terminally ill gentleman who also worked there as a witness. He also died shortly after they were married and from him she inherited the car that she used to drive east to Florida."

I stopped talking for a moment. I looked for a reaction in the faces of any of the jurors and saw nothing, except perhaps for Rose whose bit down on her lower lip. I wasn't surprised, it was too early. They were still blank slates, still mindful of the judge's admonition to keep their minds open and their thoughts to themselves.

"Within a month of cleaning Ben's house, after four Wednesdays of work, Ms. McCreedy was married to Ben. How that happened, and whether it happened fairly, whether Ben's resistance and judgment was unduly influenced by a fantastic story will be for you to determine, but I'm going to suggest a possible explanation that I will ask you to consider as you hear the evidence to see whether you agree that it has the ring of truth to it."

I walked back to counsel's table and shuffled around some papers and folders as if to suggest that there was documentary evidence backing up my theory. I picked up one of the folders, held it for a moment and then put it down.

"Ms. McCreedy grew up as a member of the Cathars Church, which was run by her father out of a small barn on their farm, where he preached that each of us was reincarnated many times over, our souls repeatedly being brought back to this world until we got things right and if you looked hard enough, with his help, you could see those past lives.

"Now you heard my opponent refer to this newspaper article in which Ms. McCreedy, all of sixteen, cried out the name Rose at a service in which her father brought her up front and called for God to reveal her prior life so he could announce it to the congregation – which I might add from the article - was about a dozen people."

I turned to Bill after saying that and nodded ever so slightly to let him know that I had known all about the article.

"Is it any surprise," I said, "That in response to her father's call she screamed out a name, whatever name came to mind, a flower, the name of a grandmother, Rose, and then collapsed into his arms. It sounds more like one of those old fashioned revival meetings where the traveling preacher pretended to heal a blind boy–usually his son–before passing around the hat."

"Objection," Bill said, jumping to his feet.

"Obviously," Judge Shanawit said, addressing the jury, "What either counsel say in their opening is not evidence, it is just argument. The evidence comes from the mouths of the witnesses and any documents that are admitted for your review."

The judge nodded for me to go on.

"Ask yourself whether what really happened is not that Ms. McCreedy suddenly discovered that her prior life was as Rose, Ben's late wife, but that once she heard the name of Ben's late wife from Alma Brown and realized that she had died shortly before she was born; once she learned from Alma Brown that Ben was well off, as opposed to her first elderly husband, and lived far away from his children and grandchildren; once she learned from Alma Brown that Ben was getting along in years and perhaps not as sharp as he once was, she realized she had the perfect mark, and that the chill her counsel referred to when she realized she had called out the name Rose nine years earlier was the chill that ran up and down Ms. McCreedy's spine once she realized the opportunity that presented itself for a big score."

I leaned back for a moment on counsel's table to catch my breath, as well as to let the words reverberate around the room. Out of the corner of my eye I caught sight of the camera. I had completely forgotten it was there and I immediately tried to forget about it.

"Now that's only the first question, and if you find, as Ben's children and grandchildren hope you will, that Ms. McCreedy tricked Ben into marrying her by pretending to be his wife back from the dead, then your deliberations will end there, where it should.

"But even if Ms. McCreedy truly believed that she was Rose reincarnated," I said that with as much irony as I could muster, looking dismissively in Susannah's direction. "Or even if it were somehow incredibly true," I smiled at that line, "you will still have to decide the second question. Was Ben of sound mind when he changed his will?

"Did he know what he was doing when he disinherited his children and grandchildren giving everything to a twenty-four year old drifter with nothing but an old car she inherited from her last elderly husband? Is that what the real Rose, his wife of nearly forty-five years, and the mother of his children would have wanted? Let's take a look at this question for a moment and see what the evidence will show."

I could see a couple of the jurors beginning to fidget in their seats; I knew I couldn't go on much longer.

"You will hear how almost immediately after they were married, Ben arranged for his home in Florida to pass to Ms. McCreedy upon his death – by putting it in her name as well as his, a gift that was irrevocable . . . that he could not change, and then made sure that she'd have enough money to live there after he was gone by setting up an account for her with his broker into which he put 500,000 dollars.

"Now that would seem to be pretty generous by most anyone's standard. Yet strangely enough, you will hear how six months later Ben - supposedly of his own volition - called a lawyer to ask him for a revised will disinheriting his three boys and his grandchildren and leaving everything . . . and I mean everything, from the old family photograph albums and the watch that Ben's father had passed down to him to the silver candlesticks from Ben's mother, every scrap of furniture, every single memento, everything to Ms. McCreedy. If Ben knew what he was doing, if he wasn't under the influence of this woman, why wouldn't he have at least provided his children with their old photographs and the silver from their grandmother?"

I backed away from the jury box. I was sure they had gotten the point.

"The first time anyone one heard about Ms. McCreedy's claim to be Rose was when Ben's three sons objected to the petition she filed in this court to probate the new will. Until then, Ms. McCreedy didn't bother to reveal this momentous news to anyone . . . nor did Ben.

"And a curious thing about that will - most people go to their attorney's office to sign their will, because it requires witnesses and procedures that they are unfamiliar with. Yet Ben simply had the new will mailed to his home – so he never actually had to see the lawyer.

"He had it mailed to the home he was now sharing with Ms. McCreedy. Perhaps he did it because Ms. McCreedy had been asking him to do it, nagging him, perhaps she forced him to make the call at a weak moment, a disoriented moment, or maybe she made the call and pretended to be him. We will never know for sure.

"What we do know for sure is that this new will was sent home, not executed under the watchful eye of an attorney, but executed in the presence of Ms. McCreedy, who picked an elderly couple as witnesses, both very ill, not immediate neighbors as you might expect, but a couple that lived around the corner and who, not unexpectedly, died shortly thereafter, leaving no one except Ms. McCreedy around to talk about Ben's state of mind when he signed the new will, and, more importantly, whether he actually knew that what he was signing was a new will disinheriting his children and grandchildren, as opposed to something else that Ms. McCreedy might have told him she needed witnessed, something perhaps having to do with the death of her first elderly husband in Las Vegas."

I walked over to counsel's table and stood beside Mitch, the son I picked to sit beside me, since all three would have made it seem as if we were triple-teaming Susannah. I stood there shuffling papers to give my words a few moments of silence so they could sink in.

"At the end of the day, there is no evidence whatsoever, other than from Ms. McCreedy, that Ben knew what he was signing, and that he really wanted to leave everything he had to Susannah McCreedy – including all the personal keepsakes that he and his late wife Rose had accumulated over the years along with the fifty million he had saved."

I turned to stare at Susannah as I spoke and she smiled weakly back.

"The answer to the second question I put to you is also a resounding no. Do not let Ms. McCreedy get away with pretending to be the reincarnated soul of Rose, a blessed memory, a wife and mother, and then manipulating Ben into marrying her, giving her his house and a significant bank account, and then when she decided that wasn't enough and she had more time to work on him, having a new will prepared to take away everything Ben had worked a lifetime to secure.

"It goes way beyond the bounds of credibility and decency. All Ben's sons can ask is that you listen to the witnesses and apply your own experience and common sense in determining their credibility, especially Ms. McCreedy's credibility. We ask you for nothing more than that."

With that I sat down and glanced at the camera imagining that when they replayed it later that night this would be the spot to break for a commercial.

"Ladies and gentlemen of the jury," Judge Shanawit said, "you have just heard the openings. I remind you again that the openings are just argument and nothing either counsel has just said is evidence. The evidence will come now from the witnesses and the documents. Mr. Lustenberger, please call your first witness."

I didn't expect Bill to lead with Susannah—a trial is a little like a musical. You need an overture first and perhaps a few early scenes to warm up the audience before the star takes center stage.

Bill didn't disappoint me. He started with Mrs. Shirley Alito, one of Ben's neighbors, and Mr. Michael Milstein, his stockbroker. I had spoken to both and nothing they said surprised me. Mrs. Alito testified that Ben hadn't slowed much, certainly not mentally, over the ten years that she had known him.

"He was as sharp as a tack," she said, waving her finger in the air as if to punctuate her remarks. "If I had a money question he would be the one I'd ask."

"And did you ever ask him any money questions?" I asked at the beginning of my cross-examination.

She had to think about it, which she did by covering her mouth with her hand.

"I'm sure I must have."

"Do you remember any of the questions?"

"No, not really."

"If it was something important, you'd remember it wouldn't you?"

"Oh yes," she said, turning to the judge. "I'm pretty sharp myself."

That got a little titter from a couple of the spectators in the back of the courtroom.

I did get her to confirm on cross-examination that some things changed after Ben married Ms. McCreedy.

"We used to chat sometimes in the morning in front of the house when we both went out to pick up the paper."

"How did that change?" I asked.

"She got the paper. She waved, but she wasn't much of a talker, not when it comes to old people, like a lot of the young people these days."

"Any other changes?"

"She and Ben were always getting in the car and driving off," Mrs. Alito said, "Coming back with packages . . . buying her things I suppose."

She also said that he stopped visiting the clubhouse and attending the community functions like he used to.

"Did Ben attend them regularly before marrying Ms. McCreedy?"

"Not as regular as some, the single women used to chew his ear off, but he'd show up pretty often. He liked to talk finances and sports with the other men. He was a big Yankee fan."

I looked down at my outline.

"But when I did talk to him he sounded pretty much the same," Mrs. Alito volunteered without a question.

"When did you last talk to him?"

"I bumped into him about a week before the accident at the mailboxes. We don't get delivery to the house. You have to pick up your mail at the clubhouse. It's the one thing I don't like about Florida."

"What did you talk about?"

"The usual things, the weather up north, someone we knew who just had a bypass."

"How long did the conversation last?"

"I don't know."

"Less than a minute?"

"Probably."

"And Ben seemed pretty normal that day when you talked to him about the weather and someone's recent operation?"

"Sharp as a tack."

"Mrs. Alito, let me ask you this question. How did you find out about the marriage?"

"I noticed she had moved in," Mrs. Alito said, pointing over at Susannah, "And when I asked Ben if she was one of his grand-daughters he said no she was his wife."

"Just like that?"

"Ben didn't beat around the bush. He was always a plain talker."

"That must have come as quite a surprise," I said.

"I'll say."

"What did you think of it?" I asked.

"Objection," Bill said, springing to his feet.

"Sustained," the judge responded.

I knew it was an improper question, but her disapproving facial expression and closed body language gave her feelings away.

"Did he mention anything about reincarnation?"

"Oh no," Mrs. Alito said very seriously, "I would have remembered that."

"Did you have any opportunities to speak with Ms. McCreedy after she moved in?"

"Not much more than hello."

"So she didn't go out of her way to make friends or to get to know any of the neighbors?"

"No, but in all fairness neither did we. We really didn't have very much in common," Mrs. Alito said, "If you know what I mean."

With that I sat down having made the only points I could that after the marriage Ben kept away or was kept away from his old haunts and neither he nor Susannah ever said a word about Susannah being a reincarnate. I planned to argue on summation that there could only be one real reason for that.

Bill had a few questions on redirect.

"What was it like when you did speak to Ms. McCreedy?" Bill asked.

"She was very pleasant. She seemed very mature for her age."

"Did you ever get the sense that she was keeping Ben away from the clubhouse or any of the community activities."

"Objection," I said.

"Sustained."

"Did they hide in the house?"

"Oh no, they were always out and about, and Ben usually did the driving. Men are men whatever their age."

That got a laugh.

"They went to dinner quite a lot and I saw them walking around the lake once."

"Did he seem happy?" Bill asked.

"He didn't seem unhappy," Mrs. Alito quickly answered before I had a chance to stand up.

"Objection," I said.

"Strike the last answer," the judge said. "Ladies and gentlemen of the jury please ignore the witness' speculation about the deceased's state of mind. Go on counselor."

"Did Ben appear sickly to you or under the weather in any way?" Bill asked.

"No, he looked about the same."

"Did he walk slower than before?"

"We all walk slow down there."

That got a smile from some of the jurors.

"What I meant was did it seem like he was walking slower than he had before?"

"No."

"One last question Mrs. Alito," Bill said, "did you ever see them being affectionate."

"I saw the two of them holding hands and kissing when they got out of the car."

With that Mrs. Alito was excused.

Michael Milstein, Ben's broker, testified that Ben used to call almost every other day to discuss his account. He was very knowledgeable with respect to his investments and very conservative. He always had a stop order to sell anything he bought if it dropped too low, although he mostly stuck to bonds and treasury bills. In fact, he said, Ben had called the day before the accident to discuss moving some money into tax free municipal bonds.

"He usually talked about a trade for a week before he made it."

"So it all seemed fairly typical to you," Bill said, "Until the accident?"

"He called a little less frequently after the marriage, but otherwise yes."

"Did Ben call you to discuss setting up an account for Susannah in the event of his death to help her with living expenses?"

"Yes, we discussed that one for a couple of weeks before he pulled the trigger."

"What did you discuss?"

"Largely the amount which ranged at times from fifty thousand dollars to a million, ultimately he settled on $500,000. And then he wanted to make sure she kept it in a CD or a short term treasury bill, something safe."

"Cautious as always?" Bill asked.

"Yes sir."

The first question I asked when it came time for cross was whether he had been consulted about Ben's decision to revise his will.

"No, I was not."

"Do you think that was odd?"

"Objection," Bill said.

"Rephrase the question counselor," Judge Shanawit said.

"Would you normally have expected him to call you to discuss revising his will before he did it?"

"Yes."

"Why is that?"

"Because there are always tax implications when it comes to estate planning, it was something we had talked about in the past."

"Revising his will?"

"No, ways to reduce his estate taxes so as to maximize what he could leave to his children and grandchildren?"

"This was before he remarried?"

"Yes."

"You said that he called to talk to you before setting up that separate account in Ms. McCreedy's name?"

"Yes."

"Did he call as well to tell you that he had decided to transfer the house into Ms. McCreedy's name?"

"Yes."

"Did he ask your advice?"

"Not so much my advice as the best way to do it to and the legal ramifications."

"Such as?"

"Would it be better to transfer the property from him to him and her, as husband and wife, as opposed to just her? I told him it was better if he kept his name on the deed for now. This way she couldn't mortgage it or sell it."

"So you had concerns she might do something like that?"

"Anyone would have concerns when a man that age gets married. That's why he decided to put it in both their names as husband and wife. Either way I told him that he couldn't transfer the property back if the marriage didn't work out. Once it was transferred to both their names as husband and wife it would automatically become hers upon his death. He understood that."

"Were you surprised when he told you what he was planning to do?"

"Objection," Bill said.

"Rephrase it counselor," Judge Shanawit said.

"Did you raise any reservations or concerns with Ben when he told you what he was planning to do?"

"Other than the risk of putting the house in her name only while he was still living there. You have to understand that a lot of my clients find themselves near the end of their lives with more money than they need or their children need and they often set up trusts for people they care about or arrange for charitable donations."

"You wouldn't call Ben's 24-year old wife a charitable donation, would you?"

"Of course not, what I'm saying is that I was not shocked by what he wanted to do."

"He didn't talk about her being a reincarnate did he?"

"No."

"The first time you heard about that was in this probate proceeding?"

"Yes."

I walked back to my seat and turned back to the witness. You always save a few good questions for the end.

"So if Ben were planning to change his will, you would have expected him to bring it up during one of your frequent telephone calls?"

"I would have thought he'd ask about the tax implications. For example, we'd talked a number of times about the possibility of setting up separate trust accounts for each of his grandchildren."

Every so often you get a good answer that's a bit unexpected. It's like finding a twenty dollar bill on the street. It was hard for me to imagine why Ben would be talking about setting up trust accounts for his grandchildren if he was planning to give everything away to someone else. It also evidenced his concern for making sure that some of his money trickled down to his grandchildren. So I stepped away from my chair and walked back to the witness, my hands folded below my chin.

"When did you talk about the trust accounts for the grandchildren?"

"On and off over the past couple of years."

"When was the most recent conversation in terms of the date of the accident?"

"He raised it again maybe a month or two before the accident."

"Which would have been about when the new will was allegedly being signed?"

"I don't know."

I read him the date on the will.

"Yes, it was probably around that time."

Bill sat there rubbing his chin.

"When you talked to Ben was it always over the telephone?"

"Almost always."

"Had you seen him since he married Ms. McCreedy?"

"No."

"Did you ever talk about anything personal with Ben after the marriage, anything other than finances?" I asked.

"No, not really."

"How about before the marriage, did he ever talk about being lonely?"

"Not that I recall."

"Did he seem a bit more forgetful the last year or two?"

Milstein thought it over.

"I have a fairly old clientele and it's not unusual for them to forget things."

"You said that his mind was sharp when it came to investing and managing his money?"

"Yes, it was."

"Was his mind equally as sharp when it came to his personal affairs?"

"I couldn't say."

"You didn't really know him personally, did you?"

"No, it was a business relationship."

"Have you ever had any elderly clients, Mr. Milstein, or elderly family members who were sharp when it came to speaking over the telephone about their finances, but not so sharp when it came to other things such as driving or dealing with a home contractor, or the loss of a friend, or some other personal matter?"

The judge looked over at Bill, but he didn't object.

"Of course."

"Elderly people who pay their bills and review their checking accounts, but cry at the oddest times and seem forgetful when it comes to things they just did a few minutes before?"

Again no objection.

"I suppose."

"You have no idea do you, what Ben Everett was like when it came to matters of the heart and love?"

"No."

"You don't know whether he was lonely and afraid as he closed in on 90?"

"I do not."

"Whether he was having cognitive problems with respect to any other aspects of his life?"

"No."

"No further questions," I said, turning my back on the witness and walking to my seat at counsel's table. Mitch gave me a slight nod.

On redirect Bill had Mr. Milstein explain to the jury how changing his will to leave everything to his wife, Susannah McCreedy, did not in any way divest Ben of full control over all of his assets while he was alive.

"He could have set up trusts for his children or grandchildren or anyone else he wanted to at any time, couldn't he?" Bill asked.

"Of course."

"He could have given all his money to his sons or given it all away to charity so there would be nothing left to pass to Ms. McCreedy in the will, isn't that correct?"

"Yes sir."

"He could have spent it all?"

"It would have been out of character, but he certainly could have."

"The will didn't restrict him in any way, did it?"

"It only applied upon his death."

"And he could have changed it again at any time?"

"Yes."

"He could have done a new will whenever he wanted?"

"Yes."

"Unfortunately a highway accident prematurely ended any possibility of Mr. Everett setting up a trust or doing something else that he might have been thinking about doing?"

"That's correct."

"Would you say that Mr. Everett, as astute as he was with respect to his finances, understood that he could die at any moment and that anything he had been thinking about possibly doing before that might not get done?"

"Objection," I said.

"Sustained."

"Did Mr. Everett sound any different during your last conversation with him shortly before his death than he did when you first started working with him almost twenty years earlier?"

"Different? He certainly sounded older."

"Did he sound less in control of his faculties?"

"No."

With that Bill sat down. Mr. Milstein certainly seemed friendlier to Susannah's side than I would have expected, probably because he hoped to keep the money in his investment portfolio at the brokerage house if Susannah won.

I asked the judge for permission to ask a few additional questions on re-cross, which she reluctantly gave me.

"When he transferred title to his home from his name alone to his and Ms. McCreedy's name, as husband and wife, he could not undo that, could he?"

"No."

"There was nothing he could do to prevent her from taking title to his house after he died?"

"No."

"And nothing he could do to take it away from her while he was alive, if he changed his mind?"

"No."

"And when he opened an account in her name and put $500,000 into it to cover her expenses after he died, he couldn't take that back either, could he?"

"No."

"And he discussed that with you before he did it?"

"Yes."

"Did he ever discuss with you giving her anything in addition to that?"

"Not with me, no," Mr. Milstein said.

"He never said words to the effect that I don't think a half million dollars is enough, I should add more to the account?"

"No."

"He never said that he was thinking of changing his will to leave her something more?"

"No."

"You manage you client's money and avoid becoming involved with their personal affairs, would that be fair to say?"

"Yes."

"The fifty million in Ben's account is significant in relation to the other clients you have, isn't it?"

"Yes it is."

"In fact it's the largest account you have, isn't it?"

I was breaking a cardinal rule here asking a question that I didn't know the answer to. Ben could have been an average account for all I knew, but I didn't think so. He wouldn't be up here voluntarily trying to help Susannah if it wasn't so important to him. The subpoena power of this court doesn't reach outside of New York so she couldn't have forced him to come.

I got lucky, even though he could have lied and said that he had two dozen larger accounts and I would have had no way to disprove it. Of course, he didn't know that. He didn't know what was in the papers I had clutched in my hand.

"It is," he said.

"And you would like to have those funds remain under your management in Florida, wouldn't you?"

"Certainly."

"Has Ms. McCreedy indicated her desire to continue working with you if she prevails and the will is probated?"

Another blind question, although this time I was not so lucky.

"No, I haven't spoken to her at all about it."

"But that is what you expect will happen if she wins this lawsuit and continues living in the house, isn't that true Mr. Milstein?"

"What?"

"You hope to keep the account with you if she prevails."

"Of course, what broker wouldn't want an account like that?"

"No further questions," I said.

"One question, Your Honor," Bill said, standing up before I even got back to my seat.

"You will make the same pitch to Mr. Everett's three sons to keep the account if they prevail, won't you?"

"Of course, I have done very well by that account. The average annual return is well over 5% on very conservative investments. I think that's pretty impressive."

"And some of that is Ben's doing."

"Yes, certainly."

Bill sat down and I sprang up.

"But Ben's sons live in New York, not Florida, and it's likely they already have their own brokers, isn't that correct?"

"I would imagine so."

"And Ben's assets would be split three ways if the new will is rejected, it won't remain as one account?"

"Yes."

I sat down and Judge Shanawit quickly excused the witness before anyone stood up with another question, at which point she adjourned the trial for lunch. The jurors, of course, had to eat in the jury room, which meant that the county paid for their lunch to be brought in from one of the local delis. My Three Sons and I walked back to my office where my secretary had sandwiches ready. They already looked pale and worn out.

"I thought your opening was good," Mitch said.

"So was his," Peter said.

"Most openings are good," I said. "They're the easiest part of any trial."

The summation is much more important, I explained, since that's where the testimony and documentary evidence are all tied together. Few jurors remember much about the opening by the time they begin their deliberations and no one makes up their mind up based on what a couple of attorneys argue, at least not before they have a chance to get their bearings and hear one or two of the key witnesses.

"Try each case for summation," I said, "that's the cardinal rule."

The first two witnesses weren't bad for their side, but that's the nature of the game. This was their case and if they couldn't put on a few decent witnesses to start they'd have settled by now.

"Trials are a lot like football games." I explained. "Sometimes it seems as if one team has the upper hand, but then the momentum shifts and it's the other team that's moving the ball."

While Mitch, Peter and Jeff ate their lunch, I stared at mine.

Chapter 10 – Minute Maid to the Rescue

"Our soul is but a sleep and a forgetting; the soul that rises with us, our life's star, hath had elsewhere it's setting and cometh from afar."
– William Wordsworth

In the afternoon, Bill called two more witnesses and stretched them out a bit longer than necessary so he wouldn't have to call Susannah until the next morning when she and the jurors would all be fresh.

The first witness he called was the owner of the Minute Maid franchise, Alegre Norman, who said that she was initially reluctant to hire Susannah because she seemed so young and was so overweight, both violations of the anti-discrimination laws, but she was desperate for someone and got a good recommendation from Susannah's old job at the Honey Bell Chapel in Las Vegas. She couldn't remember who she spoke to, other than that it was a man who said she was always punctual, did her job and never caused any problems.

"That's a pretty good recommendation," she said, "at least for the kind of employee I need."

Susannah was pretty quiet, according to Ms. Norman, which wasn't surprising since she was "the new girl on the block." The one thing she said when someone asked her why she moved all the way to Florida - and she remembered it well because it seemed a bit strange - was that she was called there. She said she wasn't sure what the reason was yet, although she was sure it would reveal itself soon enough.

"I said it was probably to work for me and everyone laughed."

"Did her remark bother you?" Bill asked.

"Not really. There are all kinds of religious beliefs in Florida," she said, "I mean with so many people around from the islands."

"Had she started working for Mr. Everett at that point?"

"No, this was before that, the end of the first week I think. Hey, I don't care what my employees believe so long as they don't steal anything or try to take advantage of our elderly clients. I tell them all that the first day they show up for work."

"So what she said didn't bother you?"

"Not as long as she did her job. Besides, there was something very genuine about her."

I thought about objecting. The judge would have surely stricken the last part of her testimony as unresponsive. But, now that it was out, it would only highlight what she said and make it seem more important than it actually was.

"Did she bring up reincarnation during those first couple of weeks that she was working for you?" Bill asked.

"She did."

Mitch had his face on straight although he was squeezing the arm of his chair so hard that his knuckles turned white. The whole room had suddenly gotten very quiet. So quiet I could hear Peter and Jeff fidgeting behind me. I looked over at the jurors who looked nonplussed, except for Matt, the musician, and Frank, the postal worker who were both leaning so far forward it seemed as if they might fall off their chairs.

"What did she say? Bill asked.

"She said something that first week when I wasn't around, because one of the girls, Angelina, mentioned it to me the other day when I told her I was coming up here."

"Objection."

"Sustained," the judge said, "The witness' last answer is stricken, and the jury is directed to ignore it. What other people supposedly say to someone else is called hearsay and because of its inherent unreliability it is not allowed as evidence in any matter as a matter of law."

"Ms. Norman," Bill said, "You have to confine your answers to what you heard personally. You can't testify about what other people say they heard, do you understand?"

She nodded rapidly while glancing over at the jury. She had a comical look on her face, her eyebrows raised as if in a permanent state of surprise. She certainly didn't seem like someone with nothing at stake, which made me wonder if Susannah had promised her something or was paying for more than her time and expense.

"Did you personally have any discussions with Ms. McCreedy about reincarnation?"

"Yes."

"When was that?"

"About two or three weeks after she started working for Ben Everett."

"What did she say?"

"That she had been his wife in her prior life."

"How did you respond to that?" Bill asked.

"By choking on my coffee, but then she explained it to me about her father's church when she was growing up, and how she called out Rose's name. I suppose it's not that farfetched if you believe in the soul, which I do."

She directed her last remark to the jury. Otherwise, she either looked at Bill or Susannah the whole time.

"How often did she speak about reincarnation?"

"Just that one time, it wasn't too long after that she quit to get married."

"Did she seem sincere in her belief?" Bill asked.

The judge sustained my objection before I got to my feet.

"Did she show you anything to back up what she was saying?"

"Yes," Ms. Norman said, "she showed me that old article about her calling out Rose's name."

"Did you discuss anything else that day?"

"About what?"

"About reincarnation?" Bill asked.

"She offered to do a past life reading for me."

"Did you call Mr. Everett after she told you she was getting married?"

"Yes."

"Why was that?"

"To see how he was, you know, and wish him luck."

"And how did he seem to you?"

"Fine, he sounded the same as he always did, so I congratulated him, he thanked me and then said he wouldn't need our services anymore." Ms. Norman made a face at the jury. "Of course, I wasn't very happy about that. Ben Everett was one of my oldest customers."

I started my cross-examination with one of her most recent answers. I was particularly curious that Bill didn't follow up the question. It was almost as if the answer had caught him by surprise.

"Did she ever do that past life reading for you, Ms. Norman," I asked, "the one that she offered to do?"

"Yeah."

"How does she do it?"

"Based on the exact time and date of your birth, she fits them somehow into a star chart."

"The kind the astrologers use?"

"I suppose so."

"What did those charts tell her about your prior life?"

She looked a little sheepishly in Susannah's direction.

"That I had last lived during the Revolutionary War."

"That's quite a while ago," I said. "Where were you for the two hundred twenty-five years between then and now?"

"She said I was floating in the cosmos."

A couple of the jurors looked away in an effort to conceal their smile. She was too flaky a witness for Bill to have used, but he probably had no one else to corroborate the reincarnation story, or at least not someone willing to lie about it in exchange for a lifetime contract to clean Susannah's newly-inherited home.

"Who were you during the Revolutionary War?"

"I worked on the docks in New York City."

"A longshoreman?"

"That's right. I was paid to fight in the place of one of those rich gentlemen and got shot."

"Killed in action?"

She nodded.

"You can't nod," I said. "You have to give a verbal answer."

"Yes."

"Did she tell you where?"

"Shot right in the heart."

I saw a couple of jurors bite their lips.

"I meant where you were killed. What battle?"

"Somewhere in New Jersey, near the Delaware River," Ms. Norman said, turning to look at the jury. "Susannah said when you die like that you get a long chance to rest before you come back. Cleaning other people's messes now was my penance, because I shouldn't have been selling myself to fight like that for someone else."

"Ms. McCreedy told you that?"

"Yes."

"By the way, are you being paid for your testimony here Ms. Norman?"

"Only my expenses to get up here."

"Nothing else?"

"No."

"How about a promise to use your services to clean Ms. McCreedy's new home."

"No."

I started back toward counsel's table, but then stopped and turned around.

"What did you really think when Ms. McCreedy first told you that she was Mr. Everett's wife in a prior life?" I asked.

"I don't know."

"Did you believe her?"

"I've never known what to believe about that."

"About what?" I asked.

"About what happens after we die, it could be as true as anything else they say."

"Weren't you a little concerned that she might be trying to take advantage of Mr. Everett?"

"What do you mean?"

"You knew he was well off, didn't you?"

"He had a nice house, but I didn't know what he had in the bank."

"You weren't the least bit worried that she might be making up a story to get him to marry her so she could get at his money?"

"Not really."

"You mean to say, that thought never crossed your mind?"

"Maybe for a second, but Mr. Everett was clearly able to handle himself and make his own decision, and she didn't seem the type."

"Can you always spot a liar?"

"A mile away."

"Didn't you telephone Mr. Everett for another reason, besides what you told us to congratulate him?"

"What do you mean?"

"Didn't you also want to hear what he sounded like? To make sure he knew what he was doing. Things can change suddenly when you're that old, particularly when it comes to a younger woman. Didn't a part of you want to speak to Ben to see if Ms. McCreedy might be trying to take advantage of him?"

"No, not really, maybe just a little, mostly it was just to congratulate him . . . and he sounded exactly the way he always did."

She'd have been better off saying yes, I thought. She was swimming against the current of common sense.

"Didn't you have the telephone number for one of Mr. Everett's sons in case of an emergency?"

"Yes, we always get next-of-kin notification numbers. You never know what the girls will find when they get to the house."

"Did you think of calling one of his sons to let him know?"

"Let them know what?"

"About the marriage."

"I assumed they did. It wasn't my business."

"Were you worried about how that might affect business?"

"I don't know what you mean?"

"It can't look good if your employees start marrying their elderly clients."

"It didn't occur to me," she said, sitting up straight and looking directly at the Susannah.

"So you did nothing in response to Ms. McCreedy's announcement other than to call Ben on the telephone to congratulate him?"

"What was I supposed to do?" she said. "They're both consenting adults."

"But you were a little concerned?"

"A very little."

"By the way," I asked, "how often had you spoken with Mr. Everett over the past ten years?"

"At least once a year when it came time to renew our services."

"You called to ask him if he was interested in continuing as a customer."

"Yes."

"You didn't get into a lengthy conversation with him, did you?"

"I asked him if there was anything more we could do. We do laundry and even some cooking for clients. He just wanted cleaning."

"Would it be fair to say that those renewal calls were fairly short?"

"It depends how you define short."

"Under 5 minutes?"

"Probably."

"Did you speak to him after Alma gave him notice about her knee surgery?"

"Yes."

"How did he react to that news?"

"He was upset."

"Did he indicate why?"

"Alma had been working for him a long time and he was sorry to see her go."

"Ben didn't like change, did he?"

"None of them do."

"Them?"

"The old people."

"How long was your congratulatory call to Ben?"

"I don't recall."

"Under a minute?"

"Oh, longer than that."

"Under two minutes?"

"Maybe three."

"So based on a two or three minute conversation on the telephone in which you probably did at least half the talking you concluded that Mr. Everett had all his marbles when it came to marrying Ms. McCreedy?"

I expected Bill to jump up and object. The judge wouldn't have liked my choice of words either, but Bill just sat there. I suppose he had prepared her as well as he could and knew how she would answer.

"I speak to old people all the time and I can tell pretty quickly whether or not they're all there, and Mr. Everett had as many marbles as you and me, maybe more."

The spectators chuckled at that answer. The jury did not.

"By the way, when was the last time you saw Mr. Everett," I said, backing slowly toward my seat."

"I don't know."

"Is it fair to say that you hadn't seen him for many years?"

"Yes."

"Five years?"

"Could be."

"No further questions," I said, sitting down at counsel's table.

Bill had no redirect.

The last witness of the day was a throwaway witness, a time-filler, with very little real significance. Richie Sciaretta was the owner of Dee Maria's, a restaurant where Ben and Susannah used to eat every Wednesday night. He was a short, bald man with tufts of hair growing from his ears and neck like weeds. Ben and Susannah were one of his early-bird customers.

"When they first walked in I thought they were grandfather-granddaughter, but you learn in this business not to make any snap judgments because you can never be sure."

He said it didn't take long for him to figure out that they were married. He saw the rings and the way they sometimes held hands and whispered in each other's ear.

"They were very pleasant," he said, "And sounded sometimes like all the other old married couples."

"How did they do that?" Bill asked.

"You know," he said, rubbing his bald head like he expected the answer to pop out like some genie, "Like they knew what the other was going to say, finishing each other's sentences, things like that."

Bill sat down and my cross-examination was brief. It was too much of a set up to impress any jury. They seemed like an older couple? I couldn't resist smiling when he said that, which I had no doubt some of the jurors noticed. The script was hard to disguise and a bit over-rehearsed if you asked me.

"Is your restaurant successful, Mr. Sciaretta?" I asked.

"Yes sir, it's always very crowded."

"A lot of seniors come for the early bird special?"

"Tons."

"Not much time to talk with any of them?"

"I always find a few minutes for my regular customers."

"How many children did Mr. Everett have, do you know?"
"I don't, I think two or three."
"Did you know where Mr. and Mrs. McCreedy lived?"
"What do you mean?"
"What town did they live in?" I asked.
"I'm not sure. They come from all over to my restaurant."
"Do you know where Ms. McCreedy was originally from?"
"No," he said, "we didn't get that personal."
I walked back to my chair, but I didn't sit down.
"Ms. McCreedy paid your expenses to come up here."
"Yes sir."
"Nice hotel?"
"Very nice and dinner last night in Little Italy."
The judge and jury smiled, so did I as I leaned against counsel's table.
"One last question, Mr. Sciaretta, do you believe in reincarnation?"
"Objection," Bill said.
"I'll allow it," Judge Shanawit said.
"I haven't thought much about it, but my father did. He used to say that he was a soldier for the Medici Pope during the Reformation, Pope Leo X."
The spectators in the courtroom laughed. Even the jurors smiled and I hadn't seen alternate number 1, Rose, smile to this point.
"No further questions."
Bill had no redirect and with that we adjourned for the day. We all had to remain in the courtroom for 30 minutes, including the press and spectators, while the jurors went back to the jury room to get their stuff and were taken by the sheriff to an unknown destination for the night. The judge warned them before they left not to discuss the case with anyone, not even each other.
"Who is your next witness, Mr. Lustenberger?" Judge Shanawit asked after the jury was gone.
"Ms. McCreedy."
"And after that?"

"No one else, Your Honor."

"Mr. Clasen, you should be prepared with at least one witness for tomorrow in case we finish with Petitioner."

"I will Your Honor."

With that I went back to my office and My Three Sons went home for their shots of scotch, warm meals and king-sized beds.

I had a couple of energy bars for dinner that I found in my secretary's desk and was working again on my cross outline for Susannah when Murray called. He was still on the road looking for evidence, although he caught some of the proceedings on CourtTV.

"I have you ahead by a nose," he said.

I couldn't tell if he was being sarcastic.

"That's not so bad," I said, "considering that today was their day with their witnesses."

"I don't like it when things are that close," he said.

"Neither do I. What have you got?"

"I found a half-brother."

"Of Susannah?"

"Abel McCreedy, son of her father's first wife, twenty-five years older, a working stiff slob like me a real country hick."

"And?"

"Susannah stayed with him for a little while after the fire."

"And?"

I was tired and impatient. Murray either didn't notice or didn't care.

"He said that their father was an early follower of L. Ron Hubbard, you know, the Scientology guy."

"They're big believers in reincarnation," I said.

"Susannah's father called himself Pastor Jim Bartholomew, although his real name was Carl. He needed a young kid, like a trained monkey, to do his tricks, and had no luck the old fashioned way with his third wife, so he adopted Susannah, at least that's the word according to Abel."

Murray started laughing but it quickly turned into a cough. It sounded like he was about to spit out a lung.

"I hate these fucking filters," he said after the coughing fit ended. I could hear the click of him lighting another cigarette.

"Abel said that he probably picked Rose for her alter ego after his father's grandmother."

"Bingo."

"She was long dead before Susannah came into the picture."

That would make for good cross.

"He said his father was a natural born liar."

"It'll be a little risky," I said, "without some proof that Rose was in fact Susannah's great-grandmother's name. If she claims that she doesn't know her name or denies it then I look like an idiot. I need some proof."

"I'm working on it, but apparently Pastor Bartholomew's grandparents got off the boat without a trace and left the same way."

By the time Murray hung up I was exhausted and the building felt a little eerie with all the other offices quiet and dark.

The phone rang and I nearly fell off my chair.

I'd made it a habit these days of not answering my telephone after my secretary left, avoiding the harassment of the crazies, but I picked it up this time because the shrill ringing was more unsettling than whatever damnation the caller would promise awaited me.

"Mr. Clasen?"

"Yes."

"You don't know me; my name is Aurora, as in the aurora borealis."

"The northern lights."

"That's right," she said, as if I had just passed her first test.

I wanted to hang up and go home to bed, but I'm not good at being rude so I figured I'd let her tell me what God was going to do to me and then politely excuse myself.

"How can I help you?"

"Actually, I'm calling to help you. I know for certain that Susannah is not doing Rose's bidding and that she's really out for the money."

"Tell me something I don't already know."

"But I have something important to tell you to help make sure she doesn't win. I'm afraid you're about to make a big mistake."

I sighed and turned the desk light back on. At least, she wasn't one of those fire breathers. And I couldn't ignore the possibility, however slim, that Aurora might know something I didn't, and wasn't just another kook, although from her name and the tenor of our conversation so far I was leaning very strongly toward the latter, notwithstanding her soft and sweet voice. Something about it seemed very calming. Of course, in the state I was in just sitting still for a moment felt like a deep sleep.

"I'm listening," I said.

"May I call you Joe?"

"Certainly."

"I'm a spiritualist Joe," she said.

"Madame Aurora?"

"That's right, have you heard of me?"

"No, I thought all psychics called themselves Madame."

"I'm not a psychic, I'm a spiritualist."

"What's the difference?"

"A psychic has extrasensory perception and mental telepathy. A psychic can see around time and space, as if it weren't there. They can project themselves into another person's thoughts. It's a much broader power than I have. My talent is much more limited. My grandmother was a psychic."

Oh great, I thought to myself, a third generation palm reader.

"And a spiritualist?" I asked, too tired to get up now that I was slumped down in my chair. I was tempted to ask her to guess my weight over the telephone. Of course, she'd probably seen me on CourtTV so she could be right on the money.

"A spiritualist can do only one thing Joe--be an intermediary between the living and the dead."

I let out another long, tired sigh.

"I know it's late," she said, "and I know you don't believe in me anymore than you believe in Susannah McCreedy, but just hear me out."

"You've got about five minutes before I fall asleep."

"We're all reincarnates Joe. There are only so many souls in existence. God isn't creating new ones. All souls have all been here since creation and God is the first among all souls. Can you accept that Joe?"

"Probably not."

"It must be hard," she said, "going through life like that."

"The only faith I have is in the law."

"That's too bad."

I thanked her for her interest and tried to excuse myself.

"Just hear me out, Joe," she said. "What have you got to lose?"

"Go ahead."

"Despite what you believe, we are all God's angels, and we are born and reborn until we attain that state of perfect grace that allows us to remain forever by God's side."

"If there are only so many souls," I asked, "how did the earth's population grow to 5 billion. Someone's got to be making new ones somewhere."

I slid further down my chair and smiled at that bit of logic.

"Oh, there are trillions of souls with God, always have been, some who have been born to earth countless times, some who have not yet been born but will be, and some who never will."

"Because they're already perfect?" I asked.

"Because they're already close to God."

I was about to thank her again for the information and hang up when she added "but I didn't call to discuss souls, or to try to convert you, I called because I heard from Eva."

"Who?" I said, straightening up in my chair.

"Rose's sister."

"How do you know about Eva?"

"I don't know anything about Eva other than she was once Rose's sister, and a soul who has traveled with her for a thousand years."

As far as I knew, no one knew about Eva other than My Three Sons. The big question was whether Susannah did.

"How did you hear about her?" I asked again. "Do you know someone in the family?"

"Joe, I don't know anything about the family," she said. "All I know is what Eva's soul told me."

It felt as if her voice were coming from inside my head instead of over the phone.

"We are each born with free will Joe. The soul does not control the mind or the body. That's why it's not found in the head or the heart, but someplace deeper and more distant, a place closer to the stomach.

"We are not bound by our prior lives or prior attitudes. That's the purpose of each life Joe, to try again, to start fresh. We learn by making new mistakes, and repeating old ones if necessary. The soul doesn't interfere, nor do our prior lives."

"What's your point?"

"Eva spoke to Rose's soul before she was reborn."

"They talk up there?"

"Not like we talk, they communicate, communication doesn't require words. It doesn't even require words down here. Anyway, the two of them shared their thoughts about their prior life together as sisters. That dialogue afterwards is part of the learning process. Eva did not have to return right away. She may never have to. The last life she led was a very painful one. God holds close those who suffer."

I was listening, but still trying to figure out how she had found out about Eva. Maybe one of the sons talked, even though I had warned them not to. Or maybe she had a family member in the same institution. That wouldn't have surprised me. For a moment, I wondered if Aurora was going to try to shake me down for some money.

"Rose did not stand up for her sister during her life," Aurora said, "she was weak and afraid so she was sent back quickly into a new life, one that would be a lot more challenging. She knew that and she looked forward to it. Rose's soul is not in control now, any more than your soul and your prior life controls you - that's not the way it works.

"It's Susannah's mind and heart that's in control and she's taking advantage of her gift of sight for her own reasons. People do it all the time. That's free will, that's how we learn. She'll pay for it next time around, but that doesn't mean much to her now."

She was losing me.

"And how is this supposed to help me at the trial?" I asked

"She's a clever girl that one."

"No kidding."

"She's laying a trap for you. She knows everything that you know about Eva. She knows all about Rose's regrets at the end. She even knows about the call."

"What call?" I said, my heart beating in my ears.

"With the premonition about her father's death."

"Who's been talking to you? How do you know about that?"

"From Eva," she said, as if she were a bit surprised by the question at this point in our conversation. "Susannah knows all about Maxine. You have to believe me Joe. If you try to use any of this information to trick her it's going to backfire. It's going to make the jury's jaws drop and she just might win."

And make me look pretty foolish at the same time, I thought to myself.

"She wanted to warn you," Aurora said.

"Who?"

"Eva."

I wondered if Murray could be the leak. He's not what he once was.

"Do you know someone named Murray Cadwalder?" I asked.

"No, who is he?"

She sounded so believable.

"It's not important. So what are you and Eva suggesting that I do?"

"A past life doesn't control the present life," Aurora said, "focus on that. Don't try to disprove who she was, work on showing how bad she is behaving now. Susannah is using what she knows for her own end. She wants to bring her message to the world. It's not her soul doing this but her ego. She's not a messenger from God, she's a mistake. Focus on the now, be in the moment, don't test her with questions from the past."

She sounded like one of those new age prophets that advertise their life changing tapes on late night television. It was too much for me to swallow.

"Thank Eva for the advice," I said, before hanging up and heading home.

I used to have trouble sleeping sometimes when I was younger, even when I was exhausted, as I was now. My father used to say it was because I hadn't prayed hard enough. Before my mother died, she used to tell me it was because I was overtired. It never made much sense to me back then, but it did now as I lay in bed too tired to roll over and keep my eye shut because my mind, as tired as it was, couldn't let go.

Was the call a set up, I wondered, by someone trying to get me to doubt my cross-examination strategy at the very last moment? If so, who could be behind it, one of Ben's relatives who knew more than anyone suspected and carried some sort of secret grudge? A friend of one of his sons who was jealous and resented their inherited wealth? Or could it be a friend of Susannah trying to mess with my mind?

What if it's real? What if there really was a spiritual component to all this and I was just blind to it? What if I were fighting forces of the universe beyond my wildest imagination?

Well at least I had Eva on my side if that were the case, I thought.

Of course, I didn't believe any of it. What I did believe was that my secret information had somehow been compromised. Perhaps my secretary hadn't shredded all my notes or someone had broken into my office. Maybe my phone was tapped.

Whatever it was, I had to decide what to do and I had to decide tonight. Do I continue with my plan to challenge Susannah with her supposedly incomplete memories of Rose's life to make her story look like a big lie, or do I change direction and focus solely on how wrong this would be whether or not she's a reincarnate?

In light of Aurora's call, the latter approach seemed a whole lot safer. Susannah's claim was so ridiculous on its face in today's nano-explanation-for-everything world that I could make light of the whole reincarnation thing, relying instead on common sense, the geriatric psychologist and perhaps even my Hindu expert to make a farce of Susannah's assertions that Rose is in there somehow influencing her thoughts and actions, as she desperately tries to hold onto Ben's fortune for her new life.

I got up and turned on the computer to see if I could find Madame Aurora's name in the local Yellow Page listings. There was a Madame Estretta, an astrologer with a specialty in finances, a Madame Serafina, who could improve your love life, and a Madame Sophie, who could find whatever it was that was missing in your life, whether it was a lost necklace or a reason for living. There was no Madame Aurora. Of course, she could have been calling from Arizona. After all the trial was national news and I wouldn't think that a spiritualist would be limited by a soul's former earthly residence.

I felt a little better when I lay back down, because I had just about made up my mind. If Madame Aurora knew about Eva and Maxine, then others probably did as well. I couldn't take the risk that Susannah knew.

Instead, I had to fight it out on a field of battle that the jurors were familiar with--scamming an old man out of his life's savings.

In fact, I thought as I lay there listening to the sound of a big truck passing in the distance, I could argue that even if you accepted the ridiculous assumption that she is Rose reincarnated, it would still be unfair to deny Ben's children their due. If Rose's soul has been given the gift of a do-over, than isn't that exactly what Susannah McCreedy is supposed to do, start again from scratch, not steal from the life she left behind?

I hated having to make a "what if" argument because it gave her too much credibility. I could feel myself drifting off and for a moment I had this image of a trillion points of light up in the heavens all with their eyes looking down on me.

Chapter 11 – The Reincarnate Speaks

"It is the secret of the world that all things subsist and do not die, but only retire a little from sight and afterwards return again."
– Ralph Waldo Emerson

The crowds out front had grown overnight; they lined the sidewalks like it was the Memorial Day Parade. The spectators had taken over the entire town, filling every seat at Sean's Café and every metered spot on Main Street. Two news helicopters circled above and their noise, like a dense fog, wiped out just about everything else.

I couldn't hear what the reporters were saying into their microphones, but their eyes looked desperate for information. The police had cleared the steps of the courthouse so they couldn't reach us even with outstretched arms and My Three Sons and I marched up the steps like we owned the building.

We got a late start because one of the jurors, my favorite, the other Rose, alternate number 1, was late. She had to wait for her son to deliver some medication that she had forgotten to bring with her.

"I expect to finish with the petitioner today," the judge said, while we sat around waiting.

"I would hope so," Bill said, "but of course that depends on the cross."

"Mr. Clasen?"

"I'll do my best judge."

"Because I expect this to go to the jury before the end of the week, I want to avoid holding the jurors over the weekend."

The courtroom deputy led the jury into the courtroom and they already looked like a group of old friends whispering to each other and exchanging nods and little smiles. That happens to jurors, the strangeness wears off and they bond quickly, which is why there are so few hung juries.

You could hear the buzz from outside when Bill called Susannah McCreedy as his next witness. She was dressed in her best grieving widow's outfit, a loose all black dress with shirt sleeves, an ankle length skirt, and a high collar that made her look like a cross between a high priestess and a professional mourner.

Bill started off at birth and it quickly became clear that he wasn't going to hold anything back. I wasn't surprised. It's always a good idea to get as much of the bad stuff out as possible on direct, this way it doesn't appear so dramatic on cross.

"Tell me, Susannah," he said, "did you believe in your father's church – in what he preached about reincarnation - when you were a young girl?"

"No, not really," she said. "I mean I believed in God, I always have, and the eternal reward for a life lived well, but I wasn't so sure about the reincarnation stuff, it sounded so weird, like being possessed, at least not until I saw it with my own eyes."

"How old were you?"

"Almost sixteen."

"Tell the jury what happened."

"I'd seen people stand up and give witness to their prior lives. Sometimes they knew all the details and were so convincing that it was impossible to doubt them . . . and sometimes it seemed as if they were trying too hard, trying to please my father, and making things up."

"Can you give us some examples?" Bill asked.

"Sure, some people would stand up and swear that they used to be a king or a queen. I remember one saying she was Joan of Arc. We can't all be royalty, and I didn't believe a lot of those people, neither did my father. He could always tell who was making it up and who wasn't. He said the truth had a smell to it . . . a damp earthy smell."

That was probably the barn, I thought.

"But you are going to get people faking like that at most every service in any religion. They want to believe so badly sometimes."

Susannah took a sip of water and smiled at the jury. No one in the jury returned the smile, although Matt, the musician, and alternate juror number 4 appeared to nod.

"Go on," Bill said.

"There were people who you could tell right away felt something. They looked confused and lost, as if suddenly they could barely recognize their own thoughts. You just knew they weren't making it up. I remember someone who raised sheep three hundred years ago in Spain and knew the name of the town and the streets, and another woman I remember was a servant in an inn.

"They knew about places and people far away and long ago that turned out to be true, although there's no way they should have known it. My father would check during the week and would always tell the congregation what he found out."

Of course, he could have told them anything, after all he was preaching to the converted.

"Can you give us another example?" Bill asked, as he tugged at his collar like it was getting too tight.

Perhaps she had forgotten to mention the one they had discussed in preparing for her testimony. No attorney wants to look like he's prompting the witness.

"There was this woman who lived over the border in Canada who used to come to services a couple of times a year. She was a nice lady, probably in her 60s. She had a bakery and used to bring me the best chocolate chip cookies."

Susannah turned to the jury and smoothed down her dress.

"As you can see I'm a big cookie fan."

This time almost all the jurors responded with polite little nod.

"Anyway one day she stood up to testify and said that she liked to come down to church here because she grew up around

Bemidji in another life. She said she was a young Indian girl who died of smallpox five hundred years earlier and that her favorite thing to do was swim in Occum's Pond. Now no one had ever heard of such a pond and the next week my father went to the town library and pulled out some old maps and found something called Occalum's Pond that disappeared from the maps about two hundred years earlier, probably filled in or dried up. Things like that made me think . . . if there's a soul, and I know that there is, why wouldn't God send it back sometimes to try again?"

"Let's go back to what happened to you when you were about sixteen."

"Right," Susannah said with a little smile, "Sorry. I had never stood up to give witness before."

"Did your father ever ask you to?"

"He never pushed it. It has to happen on its own, he said. You have to feel it and on this Sunday I just felt it. I don't know how to describe it. It was almost like watching a fish swimming just below the surface. So I stood up and walked to the front. It took a while, and I was about to give up when I suddenly saw something . . . not really saw it . . . more like I sensed it, like a story book that had fallen opened to the first page."

She touched a place below her heart and above her stomach.

"I saw a kindly old woman with three sons living in New York. Her name was Rose and she moved to Florida just before she died. It was a long painful death and she had come back quicker than most because she had to make up for something that she didn't do in her life, as opposed to something that she did do."

A hint about Eva, I thought, trying to bait me into asking what that was. I thought of what Madame Aurora had told me last night.

"I could see her," Susannah said. "She was short and stocky with grey bobbed hair and tiny, but strong hands. She had deep-set dark eyes, a wide nose and a small, soft mouth, very fragile looking, but she wasn't, fragile I mean, she was tough . . . and wise and grandmotherly."

Of course, describing Rose after spending ten months looking through family albums was no big deal.

"I saw her life pass by me in a flash . . . for me there has never been any doubt since."

"Any doubt about what?" Bill asked.

"About our eternal reward . . . and that I had Rose's soul."

Bill walked back to counsel table and pulled out the newspaper article, which was now laminated.

"Let me show you this and ask you if you've seen it before."

"I have."

"What is it?"

"I didn't know it at the time, but there was a reporter there from the local paper, and he wrote this story afterward. They didn't much like us in town, I guess because we weren't mainstream Catholic, which you can tell when you read it, but I saved the article anyway because it mentioned me and how I called out Rose's name."

"I offer it into evidence," Bill said, handing it to me to look at.

"No objection, Your Honor," I said. I could have objected and probably convinced Judge Shanawit to keep it out, after all it was hearsay evidence from a reporter who was not here and might, if pressed under oath, admit that he didn't really hear the name clearly so he made one up.

I could have forced Bill to advise the Court what effort he made to get the reporter here to testify, which I knew was nothing. But it wasn't worth the fight in light of her testimony. It would look as if I were afraid for the jury to see it. And if the judge overruled the objection it would be even more damning.

"Claimant's Exhibit 2 is admitted into evidence," the judge said.

The courtroom deputy took it, stamped it and handed it back to Bill. Exhibit 1, the new will, was already accepted into evidence by mutual consent before the trial began.

"May I show it to the jury?" he asked.

The judge nodded and we sat quietly for a few moments while the jurors passed the article around.

"So at that service," Bill said, "You called out the name Rose?"

"Yes."

"Did you call out any other names?"

"No."

"Have you ever seen any other prior lives?"

"No, it's been a gift just to see this one."

"Why is that?"

"Because it brought me back to Ben for a little while," Susannah said. "We are two souls who have spent many lifetimes together."

Bill took the article back and handed it to the courtroom clerk. He resumed the background questions. Susannah confirmed that she was adopted, something her father told her around the same time as her revelation, although she never made any effort to find her real parents.

"I never had that burning desire to find them," she said. "Since we are all reincarnates why does it matter? We'll all get to meet again between lives and in new ones."

Bill let the answer sit out there awhile before asking Susannah what happened to her father. She told the jury about the fire that took the lives of both of her parents.

"I was in the hospital at the time," she said. "They were trying to get me off these painkillers the doctor had me taking after I fell off the barn roof and cracked some vertebrae in my spine."

"What were you doing on the barn roof?"

"I was helping my father shovel off some late winter snow. He didn't want me to, but I begged him. I was a lot thinner then, more athletic, and could talk my Dad into pretty much anything. He was a real pushover."

Murray described him as anything but a pushover, but I wasn't going to waste my time during cross going off on a tangent. I couldn't very well accuse her of lying about her father. The jury wouldn't look too kindly on that. It's one thing to call the daughter a crook it's another to impugn her father's love as well. In any event, I didn't have any proof to the contrary so why bother.

I had still had this nagging suspicion that perhaps Susannah was not in the hospital and was somehow responsible for her parents' death. Of course, litigators suspect the worst. It's an occupational hazard.

"It wasn't the same after they fused two of my vertebrae. I put on a lot of weight and got hooked on these pain killers."

"Did you eventually get off them?"

"I did, that's what the rehab was for."

She talked about how sad her life was after the fire, living with her older brother until she turned 18 and moved out to Las Vegas. If the jury was feeling sorry for her I couldn't tell from their faces, I know I was beginning to. If she was pretending here as well, she was damn good.

"Why Las Vegas?" Bill asked.

"The papers were always saying how it was the fastest growing area of the country, and I didn't have much of an education or any real trade, so I figured I'd have an easier time finding a job there."

She told the jury that she found two jobs, one as a professional marriage witness and another working with cancer patients in a hospice."

Murray hadn't warned me about that one.

"Why something like that for such a young women?" Bill asked.

"I don't know. I suppose subconsciously because Rose had died of cancer and spent her last week in a hospice. Besides, death doesn't bother me, not in light of what I know. It's just a stage, a passing from one state to another."

"And sometimes back again?" Bill said.

"Yes, and sometimes back again."

I suspected it was very short lived and probably volunteer. Another point I really couldn't cross her on; I didn't want to emphasize it or complain about it. I just wanted it to sink to the bottom of the jury's collective memory.

Susannah talked about the Honey Bell Chapel, including some funny wedding stories that brought another round of half-smiles to the jury; you know the kind about brides showing up half-drunk and getting married in a bathing suit.

Apparently, being of sound mind was not a requirement for marriage in Nevada. Fortunately, the laws in Florida and New York law are a little more stringent. She was certainly doing her best to make herself likeable– but that was the very nature of a scam artist.

"Were you ever married before?" Bill asked.

"I was."

"Tell us the circumstances."

"It was to another professional witness, you needed two in Nevada. His name was Rudolph, but we all called him Rudy. He was from Denmark, about seventy-five, he'd never tell me his real age. He was wheelchair-bound with this terrible cough. It felt like the roof was going to come down on our heads sometimes when he had one of his fits.

"It turned out to be lung cancer and Rudy had no insurance. He wasn't even a citizen. He came here after the war and just worked and drifted around. He asked me to marry him so he could get some health care from the state. Lord knows he couldn't afford anything on his own."

"And you did."

"I was happy to help him. We never consummated it or anything like that."

"And did he get some medical care?" Bill asked.

"He did, but it was too late. He died about two months after we were married."

"Did you love Rudy?"

"No and Rudy didn't love me. I liked Rudy and I'm sure that our souls had crossed paths in the past, and that was the reason I was called to Las Vegas, to help him out. But it was nothing like Ben."

"What did he leave you when he died?"

"Nothing really, all he had was his clothes, which I donated to the Salvation Army, and an old car which I used to drive to Florida."

"Did he do a will of any kind?"

Susannah shook her head from side to side.

"You can't shake your head, Ms. McCreedy, you have to answer verbally."

"No, he didn't have anything. He actually put the car in my name when he got too sick to drive and I had to take him to his doctor appointments. He figured it would be easier after he died. He was a very considerate man."

She tried to unobtrusively wipe away a tear. She didn't overdo it and kept her grief understated and subtle.

"What happened after he died?" Bill asked.

"I couldn't stay in Las Vegas anymore. It's a weird place to begin with. It never sits still; it's like a heart that can't stop racing. Besides, I think that's why I had come there in the first place – to help Rudy - and now that was done so it was time to move on."

"Why Florida?"

Susannah looked up at the ceiling like she was expecting help with the answer from some higher authority.

"It's a funny thing because I had my heart set on California. I'd never seen the ocean and it was close and Los Angeles sounded so . . . I don't know, romantic. I figured maybe I could get a job as a receptionist at a studio and meet all kinds of movie stars."

Susannah looked over at the jury. They were all listening intently, but still not giving anything away.

"Then they had those hurricanes in Florida, really bad ones, and something told me to go there. It felt as if something or someone was waiting for me there. I don't fight those feelings. You get them for a reason."

I looked at alternate number 1, my Rose, and I could see her jaw moving back and forth as if she were grinding her teeth. I bet that she wasn't buying any of this. If I was a religious man, I would have been praying hard for one of the first six jurors to take ill, nothing serious just enough for her to move up; an acute appendicitis for either Matt the musician or Ira the pretender would have been perfect.

"Tell us what happened when you got to Florida."

"I needed a place to live and a job. I had saved up a little money in Las Vegas, not very much, just enough to rent this studio apartment near Delray Beach for a couple of months."

"How long did it take you to find a job?"

"That was also fate if you ask me. The landlord told me about someone he knew who was working for Minute Maid but was going to quit for a knee operation. He said that they were looking for someone to replace her, so I called, went for an interview and got the job."

"How long did it take from the moment you arrived in Florida until you found your apartment and the job?"

"It was like bang bang," she said, "Within two days of arriving I had both. I was clearly on a mission of some kind."

Bill was trying to counter my suggestion during the opening that Susannah had her eye out for a widower with a wife named Rose who might have died long enough ago to qualify her as a possible reincarnate. From her direct, it certainly didn't sound like she was looking for anything more than a place to live and a job. My point, however, was not that she was looking, but that she was on the lookout and as luck would have it someone fell right into her lap.

Bill asked her about her first days working at Minute Maid and about taking over Alma's customers.

"I sat down with her to go through her book of business. I had to learn about each customer, what they liked her to do and not do. I remember one older man, I forgot his name, I think it was Sam, he was very particular about touching anything on his dresser, you couldn't even dust it . . . things like that."

"What about Ben Everett?"

"He was one of her long time regulars. I don't remember all that much about what she said. I was keeping notes in a little notebook to help me remember."

"What happened to that notebook?" Bill asked.

"I threw it out after I stopped working. I didn't think I'd need it."

"What did she say about Ben, as best as you can recollect?"

"That he was one of the watchers and talkers."

"What does that mean?" Bill asked.

"Some people disappear as soon as you show up, as if they're embarrassed by their own dirt, or think that you've got to be too stupid to bother with. They leave directions in notes on the kitchen counter and then get upset if you can't read their handwriting. They sit in their lanais pretending that you're not there.

"Others follow you around like puppies, yapping away a mile a minute; some because they want to play the big boss making sure you don't forget the corners or under the couch; others, like Ben, because they just like the company. I guess if you're home alone all the time it's nice to hear a human voice, your own as well as someone else's."

I wasn't certain but I could swear that juror number 4, Matt the musician, nodded ever so slightly. He looked like the type who hated television and might like Susannah because she believed in things that you couldn't see. Susannah turned to the judge.

"May I have a break to go to the ladies room?"

With that the judge declared a 5-minute recess. Of course, a 5-minute recess in trial terms never lasts less than 20 minutes.

I went back to the witness room we had been assigned to speak with My Three Sons.

"I think the jury already has her pegged as a nut," Jeff said.

"Jurors one and two maybe," Mitch said.

"Millie and Ellen," I said, "why do you think that?"

"They won't look her in the eye. When she looks at them they turn away."

That was a good sign.

"I don't think any of them are buying any of this sweetness and innocence crap," Jeff said.

"I'm not sure about the postman," Mitch said. "He spends more time watching us than her."

"So does that last guy, the one with all the jewelry," Peter added. "What's his name?"

"Ira." I looked at my watch. "That's what jury's do," I said, "they look for reactions, try to measure surprise and concern."

"How do you think she's doing?" Mitch asked.

"About what I'd have expected," I said. "But it's still her direct case this is when she's supposed to be at her best. He's lobbing in the fat pitches, she knows what's coming and she's hitting every one. It doesn't get any easier than that."

"She sounds a little believable if you ask me," Mitch said.

Jeff and Peter rolled their eyes at each other.

"As do all the crooks that sell those pyramid schemes, the can't-miss investments in the middle of the Arizona desert, and miracle creams that grow hair," I said. "She wouldn't have gotten this far if she wasn't believable."

"Five minutes counselor," the courtroom deputy called out knocking on the door.

"Listen," I said, "I've decided to stay away from quizzing her on your mother's life. I don't want to turn the trial into a final exam, I'm going to focus on Susannah and your father instead. What brought her to this point, what your father was thinking when he married her and changed his will? And the circumstances of the execution of that will. Those are the real questions for the jury."

With that I stood up and walked out of the room. I purposely raised it now so there wouldn't be time for discussion.

"All rise," the courtroom deputy called out, as the jury returned to the box.

They were all smiles coming out of the jury room. Bill and I looked at each other and nodded imperceptibly. These jurors might disagree and argue once they started their deliberations, the first vote might be even, but in the end they'd reach a verdict.

"Tell us what happened when you first met Ben," Bill said, after the judge gave him permission to resume.

The jurors sat back in their seats, glancing at one another, like they were at home in their living rooms getting ready to watch their favorite show on TV. The first attorney I ever worked for used to say that when jurors begin looking that comfortable you'd better be straight with them or they'll cut your client to ribbons.

"His place was pretty dirty, I remember that. Alma had missed the last two weeks, her knee was really bad so he was happy to see me. I mean he clearly missed Alma, Ben had a good heart, he sent her flowers after the surgery, only a handful of her clients even sent cards, but I think he was happy to get back to the routine. Ben liked routines . . . as much as I do."

"Objection," I said half-heartedly, as I rose to my feet.

"Sustained," Judge Shanawit said, equally as half-heartedly. "Strike the last sentence. Ms. McCreedy if you confine your answers to the questions this trial will move along a lot faster."

"Sorry judge."

"Tell us what happened that first day?" Bill quickly asked.

"Not much really. I cleaned. Ben hung around talking and asking questions. I didn't mind, it made the work move faster. I wasn't looking at him much because I was busy cleaning – you know I wanted to make a good first impression on all the clients, but there was something about his voice that seemed to reach right into me. It was so familiar. I thought at first he might have sounded a little like my father . . . voices are so hard to remember after a few years . . . but that wasn't it."

Susannah moved up in her seat and leaned against the railing, as if she were getting ready to tell everyone a big secret.

"I was just finishing up, getting ready to go, when I dusted a few of the photographs in the entrance hall. That's my late wife Rose, he told me, and as soon as I looked at her my knees began to buckle. For a moment it felt as if I were looking in a mirror. I saw everything again for an instant, her whole life."

Susannah sat back in the chair and Bill looked slowly from juror to juror. They were all wearing their poker faces.

"What did you do?" Bill asked.

"Nothing, I thanked him for the tip and got out of there as quick as I could. I don't mind telling you I was a little scared."

The courtroom was completely silent, except for the whir of the air-conditioner and this sound I couldn't quite make out that I could barely hear that seemed to come from nowhere and everywhere, which turned out to be my own breathing.

"Did you call him the next day or say anything to anyone?"

"No, I just kept working hoping the feeling would go away."

I made a note of that on my pad.

"When did you see or speak to Ben next?"

"The following week, my normal time, I was still a little freaked out about it, so I almost didn't go. I intended to keep quiet about it."

"Go on," Bill said.

"I was cleaning and Ben was talking, but I knew so much about him and Rose, so much more than he was saying that I could hardly breathe. I kept nodding, but I could hardly think. My thoughts were too cluttered to clean, and I know I was doing a bad job. Ben asked me if anything was wrong."

"What did you tell him?"

"Just a little indigestion so he made me tea."

"You didn't say a word about what you were really feeling that second week either, did you?" Bill asked.

"No."

"Why not?"

"I couldn't bring myself to. I wasn't sure what was right or why I was there. It was a prior life and it didn't have anything to do with this one, it shouldn't, and I just wanted to live the one I had now. That's the way it's supposed to be, the way I was taught, the way it's always been.

"I mean there have been exceptions over the years, people who knew something and went back to visit where they once lived to correct something that had gone horribly wrong, but I never thought it would happen to me, not like this. I just didn't know what to do. I wished my father was around to ask."

Bill nodded thoughtfully and rubbed his chin, a gesture calculated to make the jury think that her answers were spontaneous and unexpected, as if he wasn't sure what to ask next. "Did you tell anyone what you were experiencing?"

"I didn't know anyone well enough to tell," she said. "I might have mentioned something to my boss around that time . . . about reincarnation, nothing specific."

"Ms. Norman?"

"Yes."

"When was the next time you saw or spoke to Ben?"

"The next week, Wednesday morning, it was always Wednesday morning."

"What happened on that day?"

"I cleaned and Ben talked. I think he must have been feeling something as well, because he talked a lot about Rose."

"Hadn't he before?"

"Sure, some but not like he was now. It felt as if he was talking to a place deep inside me, almost to someone else, someone I couldn't see, but he could, and he wouldn't let me leave without having some of the tea that he said Rose always loved, which it turned out I loved as well."

"What kind of tea is that?"

"Chamomile."

That's all my mother ever drank Mitch wrote on the legal pad between us.

"Is that when you told him?"

Susannah nodded.

"You have to answer out loud," Bill said.

"Yes," Susannah said, closing her eyes as if she were fighting her way through some powerful memories. "He laughed at first, but sweetly. I knew there was something funny about you today, he said, almost like you were older and wiser. Maybe he was humoring me, I don't know, but then I started telling him things that I knew and his eyes opened wide."

There was a lot of hearsay in that answer, but I saw no way of challenging it now without looking bad.

"Ben wasn't one of those religious guys on the outside, the opposite I'd say, but it was different on the inside, there had always been plenty of room there for doubt. That's all believing ever really needs. He said he sometimes had the feeling that Rose was up there looking down on him, but never that she was sitting across from him, but if he could find her by looking in one direction, he said, why not the other."

"My father was an agnostic his whole life," Mitch said, leaning over and whispering in my ear.

I pointed down to the pad. I wanted things written down. I didn't want the jury or Susannah speculating about what we were discussing, or wondering whether she had hit a chord, or whether we were surprised, or upset. Besides, I wasn't going to argue Ben's religious inclinations with her. That was a no win situation. Certain ideas change as you get older and closer to the end, religion is often one of them.

"What happened next?" Bill asked.

"I couldn't talk, because I had another house to clean. Besides, both of us needed some time to digest what was happening, but I promised to call him."

"Did you?"

"Not that night."

Susannah looked like she was struggling to keep her composure, but it seemed like an act to me. Of course, I was prejudiced. I looked over at the jury and except for my Rose, Alternate 1, who was looking down at her through her bifocals like she was some traveling salesman who had just knocked on her door, I couldn't tell if any of the other jurors were buying it.

"I was still of two minds," she said slowly, hesitantly, as if she were holding her feelings and thoughts up to the light for the first time. "I was tempted to quit and drive across the country to

California so I could get on with this life, my own life. But then I started wondering if there wasn't a reason for all this. Surely it wasn't a coincidence or an accident, not something like this. I wondered if this wasn't just another step in the evolution of soul, according to God's plan, to finally start making the connections between one life and the next a little more visible, more a continuation, a learning process combining down here with up there. Maybe if people understood it more, understood what came after, there wouldn't be as much violence and war. If a path was being laid out for me, I thought, it must be because I am supposed to follow it."

Out of the corner of my eye I saw jurors 1 and 2, Millie and Ellen, shifting around in their seats, as if they couldn't find a comfortable position, which I liked. On the other hand, jurors 4 and 6, Matt and Ira, were riveted on Susannah's face, as if they had no idea how it would all turn out. Jurors 3 and 5, Frank the postal worker, and Lauren, with the small promotions business, looked a little bored as their eyes wandered around the room searching the spectators for their reactions, a sign perhaps that they already had made up their minds. If they had at this point, it would certainly be in my favor.

"What did you decide?" Bill asked.

"That there was a reason why this was all happening and I couldn't run away from it. So I called Ben and we spoke over the telephone a couple of times over the next week."

"Did he call you or did you call him?"

"Both, I called him the first time and then he called me the next day and the day after that."

"Did you discuss your belief that you were a reincarnation of his wife Rose?" Bill asked.

"Yes, of course, that was pretty much all we discussed. He was still skeptical, but who wouldn't be if you didn't grow up believing in reincarnation the way I did, the way billions do around the world. It's a basic part of all the Far Eastern religions."

"Objection," I said, forcefully.

"Sustained," the judge said. "The jury will disregard the witnesses' last remark concerning Far Eastern religions."

"Sorry," she said, looking up at the judge before turning to the jurors and shrugging her shoulders a bit.

"Go on," Bill said, "You were telling us about your telephone conversations with Ben."

"The more we talked, the more he realized – as did I-- just how much I knew about Rose and him, small, silly things that no one else would have known about."

"Can you give us some examples?"

Susannah put her hand to her mouth and blushed.

"Like the first time we did it on our wedding night. He couldn't believe that I knew it was on the couch, not the bed."

Jurors 4 and 6, Matt and Ira smiled. So did juror number 1, Millie, the late-50s homemaker with three daughters and my favorite alternate, Rose; maybe it struck a familiar chord.

"What else?"

"That Ben couldn't fall asleep without first laying on his back for at least 5 minutes with his hands under his head, that Rose loved Chanel No. 5 and hated wool. It made her itch, me too."

Susannah scratched her neck as if the very mention of the word brought it on.

"Anything else you can think of?" Bill asked.

Susannah looked up at the ceiling.

"A lot of things, I can't remember them all at the moment. I remember telling him that I knew about the small scar on Rose's left shin where she was hit by the swing as a young girl."

Did you know that, I wrote on the pad?

No, Mitch wrote back. He remembered the scar, but not the accident, and he never heard about the couch, although his mother did love Chanel No.5 and hated wool, and his father liked to lay on his back in bed with his hands folded behind his head.

"I also knew that tomatoes gave him gas."

That got a chuckle out of the whole room. Mitch wrote a check mark down on the pad. Of course, Ben wasn't around to verify whether or not she brought any of these things up with him or when. These were all things she could have learned from Ben after they were married and from photographs and old letters. She just moved the discussions back to the initial telephone call to make the seduction that much more believable.

"Rose and Ben also liked to dance alone sometimes before going to bed on Saturday nights . . . ."

Mitch drew a question mark on the pad.

"When did you see Ben next?"

"The following Wednesday when I came to clean."

"What happened," Bill asked.

"I cleaned. Ben wanted to talk, but I insisted on doing my job, so we talked as I dusted, vacuumed and mopped. His house was easy, one level, one person. Ben didn't make much of a mess. When I was done, Ben asked me out to dinner."

"Did you go?"

"Not that night, Wednesday was my big day, it was a long day, and I was always exhausted at the end so we went out the next night. He picked me up in that big Lincoln he had. It was the biggest car I'd ever been in."

"Where did you go?"

"He asked me what I'd like and I suggested seafood, which I'd never had, you know the ocean kind. All I'd had was lake fish, but I knew it was Ben and Rose's favorite."

True, Mitch wrote.

"We had a nice dinner at the Sea Shanty. I had lobster for the first time, which I loved. I loved everything he had me try, everything except for the clams."

"Too slimy," she said with a shudder, like she was remembering back to the moment she swallowed one.

That got a few more chuckles. Even Rose, alternate 1, smiled. I thought of standing up and applauding.

"Did you talk about reincarnation during dinner?" Bill asked.

"Sure, Ben was in pretty good spirits, he had his shot of scotch. He had that before every dinner since he was in his twenties."

Mitch checked the pad.

"He said it stimulated his appetite and helped his digestion. If you ask me, it was his way of unwinding from the day when he was working and he just kept it up after he retired."

Cute, I thought, weave in the past life knowledge without making it seem too obvious.

"Tell us what you discussed about reincarnation," Bill said to keep her on track.

"He was beginning to believe and it wasn't just because of what I knew about him and Rose. He said it was because of the way I spoke and the way I acted; the way I looked at him sometimes. He said I reminded him of Rose in a lot of ways."

"What ways?" Bill asked.

"He said my eyes were steady and calm like her. Reassuring, I remember he used that exact word . . . without all the demands he said he was used to seeing in so many of the older women in the neighborhood. And I didn't talk as much as they did. He said I wasn't all about words . . . just like Rose."

Mitch checked the pad.

"Rose had the same smile, I remember him saying that at dinner, not the first one, the second or third I think. He said it started small and always seemed to grow. Rose was quiet, but she was a very happy person . . . as am I, despite what I might look like and the hardships I've had so far in this life. I guess that's the nature of my soul."

Susannah smiled, starting small and letting it grow until her teeth practically shined at the jury. This was something she must have practiced for months in the mirror. It was different than the smile she'd flashed before. This one was more provocative and colorful. It was harder to ignore. It made it difficult not to smile back, as Matt, Ira and Fred did. Could the angry retired postman be cracking, I wondered.

"Ben said I was very patient and not the least bit self-conscious, also like Rose, and not pushy in terms of my beliefs. He said Rose was the same way, particularly since she was so much more religious than Ben."

Susannah stopped and turned her gaze toward the window, like she was overwhelmed for a moment by some revelation.

"I remember one particular discussion we had on the car ride back from one of our dinner's out. I was discussing with Ben how the same souls often stay together up in the cosmos, as well as down here, so that he and Rose could have been sisters at another time or even mother-daughter since souls have no gender.

"One thing for certain, we would always be together in one way or another, which is what it really means to be soul mates. Ben thought about it a while and asked if he could come back right after he died and somehow wind up back with me, me as Susannah. I told him I didn't think so. That what had happened here was very unusual.

"We would be together again either in the cosmos or in another earthly existence, but it wasn't up to us, and it might not be for another hundred years or even a thousand years. Souls usually don't come back that quickly. Ben was disappointed about that.

"When you have that long view time isn't that noticeable, I told him, not like it is down here, and when we next meet we'll hardly feel the absence. I think that's when he took my hand. Ben was a big hand-holder when he and Rose were first married."

Mitch checked the pad.

"Why was Rose reincarnated so quickly?" Bill asked, and it felt as if everyone in the courtroom leaned forward in their seat to hear the answer.

"That's exactly what Ben asked, and I have the same answer now as I did back then . . . I don't know. The reason for something like that is beyond a mere mortal's understanding or appreciation. My father once said that for a soul to be sent back so soon it had to be because they left their prior life in a very sudden or painful way or with a serious unresolved issue."

Was she baiting me, I wondered. Did she want me to jump in on cross and try to embarrass her about Eva.

"Anything else you remember discussing over that first dinner at the Sea Shanty or on the ride home, anything that you may have left out?"

Susannah thought about it a moment and then began to nod slowly.

"We also talked about what I wanted to do in this life, you know, where I was headed, what my plans were. And what Ben wanted. Just because you're old doesn't mean you don't dream."

Susannah took a deep breath.

"He was alone and had been without Rose for over twenty-five years. He was far away from his family. They had busy lives, he understood that, and they didn't have a lot of time for him."

I glanced over at Mitch to make sure he had no reaction. He didn't, I just hoped that Jeff and Peter showed as much restraint.

"Ben liked the community and clubhouse well enough, but he was missing someone who knew him so well he wouldn't have to explain anything. I knew the feeling. I'd been alone like that since my parents died."

"Was anything else discussed?" Bill asked.

"Like what?"

"Like marriage."

"Oh, no," Susannah said with a little chuckle. "Ben asked me what I thought we should do when he was dropping me off and I said nothing just enjoy it. My father always said that a reincarnate that can see into the past has a gift and a responsibility to honor what went before, to leave it intact and undisturbed.

"So I answered that we could be friends, I'll see you on Wednesdays. He asked if we could go out to dinner from time to time and I said I'd like that very much."

"So how did you leave it?"

"Just like that."

Bill took a little stroll around counsel's table, scratching his forehead like he was unsure where to go.

"When did the subject of marriage first come up?" he finally asked, after the judge impatiently cleared her throat.

"Three weeks later when I was at the house cleaning. Ben said he'd like me to move in with him and I said I wouldn't do that."

"Why not?"

"It made me feel uncomfortable. It's not the way I was raised. So he asked me to marry him and I also refused."

"Why?"

"For the reasons I just mentioned about not interfering with the past."

Susannah let out a little sigh and shook her head slowly.

"Plus there were about 64 years worth of other reasons I could think of."

"The age difference?"

"Yes sir."

"What did Ben say about that?"

"That it wouldn't be for long considering his age and that after making his last years more pleasant and comfortable I'd still be young enough to find someone else my own age."

"What did you think about that?"

"It was almost like Rudy again, except Ben wasn't dying of cancer, he was dying of old age and loneliness. I didn't see how I could say yes to one and no to the other, especially with the two of us soul mates. There had to be a reason I was here, just like Las Vegas, and this must be it. I figured I could stay out of the way of his family and interfere as little as possible, and that way wouldn't be disturbing much."

There was a chorus of forced coughs from Jeff and Peter. I pretended not to notice, but the jury and the judge certainly did. Judge Shanawit shot me a warning look that made it clear the next time she would give them an embarrassing warning to keep quiet or be removed from the courtroom. I turned around and glared at the two of them.

"Did he promise you anything in terms of money?" Bill asked.

"No, I didn't want any and I didn't ask. At some point, after we'd been married a few months he said he wanted me to have the house to live in after he was gone and enough money to cover my living expenses."

"What did you say to that?" Bill asked.

"I don't need it and I don't want it, I said. I've always had trouble sticking around after people die and I figured I'd just jump in the car and head to California. But he did it anyway without telling me. I found that out after he died."

"How did you find out?"

"From his broker, I forgot his name."

"Mr. Milstein?"

"Yes, he told me about the account and the house."

Bill stood there like he was waiting for her to continue.

"And I found this letter he wrote and at the bottom of one of his drawers. It said to open it after he was gone," Susannah said, wiping one of her eyes with the back of her hand, "But we never expected it to happen so soon, not in a freak accident like that."

Bill went back to counsel's table and picked up a single handwritten sheet of paper.

"This is dated before Ben decided to change the will?"

"Yes, way before that . . . maybe 6 months earlier."

"Is this the letter he left for you?" Bill said, walking over to handing her the letter to examine.

"Yes."

"Is that Ben's handwriting?"

"Yes."

"I offer it as plaintiff's exhibit 3."

"May I see it Your Honor?" I asked.

"Certainly," the judge said, "why don't we take another short break."

That was exactly what I hoped the judge would do, since this was the first I had heard of this letter, and I intended to object strenuously, although I preferred not to do it in the presence of the jury. I took the letter back with me to the jury room and read it out loud to Mitch, Jeff and Peter.

> *My Dear Susannah,*
> *Thank you for everything. I have deeded the house from me to you and me as husband and wife, which means if you are reading this letter it is yours now. I've also set up an account so you can afford the upkeep. Until our souls meet again.*
> *Ben*

"It's an odd letter for a dead husband to write to his wife," I said. "It doesn't sound very affectionate."

"When's it dated?" Mitch asked.

"February 9th."

"They'd only been married two months at that point," Mitch said.

"Why didn't he sign it love?" I asked.

"The old man hated that word," Peter said. "He complained that it was overused and meaningless. I never heard him say it. I suppose he did to my mother when they were alone."

Peter figured that she doped him up and told him what to write. Jeff said his father never did anything without discussing it a month in advance, particularly when it came to money, so she had to be lying when she said it was a big surprise. Mitch thought it looked like his father's handwriting, but said he wasn't hard to imitate since his letters were all pretty much the same, big and slanted to the left.

"He hated spending money," Mitch said.

"Or giving any of it way," Peter added.

"He had that Depression-era mentality, no matter how much he had he was always afraid of running out."

I picked up the letter.

"And why is it so short?" I asked, expecting that most husbands would have a lot more to say in a post-death farewell.

"He was a man of few words," Mitch said, "particularly when it came to writing them down. I don't think he ever wrote me a letter or a postcard when I was at college. My mother used to take care of that. After she was gone he'd send birthday cards with a check and sign his name, but that was about it."

The letter would suggest to the reader that Ben knew what he was doing when he married Susannah. It certainly sounded as if it was written by someone still of sound mind, which is probably why Susannah wrote it or had Ben write it and Bill wanted to introduce it.

Of course, if it was a forgery I had no time to retain a handwriting expert.

"Can they keep a letter like this a secret and then surprise us with it at trial?" Mitch asked.

"No, they were supposed to produce it in advance, and she certainly should have mentioned it in response to some of my questions at her deposition. He'll probably say she just found it."

When we went back into the courtroom I asked to speak with the judge before the jury was brought in. Normally, counsel would sit with the judge in the robing room with the court reporter called in if a ruling was necessary, but I suspect the judge didn't want to lose any televised airtime and she confirmed that by taking the bench to hear my objection.

"Your Honor," I said, standing up behind counsel's table, "we object to the introduction of this letter as an exhibit. It has never been produced, nor was its existence raised in response to any of the questions I asked during Ms. McCreedy's deposition. The rules of evidence do not look too kindly on trial by ambush."

"Your Honor," Bill said, standing up as well to address the court, "My client had no knowledge of the letter at the time of her deposition. She found it this past weekend when she went back to Florida. It's simply being introduced to confirm what my client has already testified to."

"Why wasn't counsel promptly given a copy as soon as it was found, if not over the weekend, than first thing Monday morning?" the judge asked.

"I apologize," Bill said, "She handed it to me along with a lot of other things on Monday and I didn't get a chance to focus on it until late last night."

"Let me see it," Judge Shanawit said.

I handed the letter to the courtroom deputy who brought it up to the bench.

"Put Ms. McCreedy back on the stand," the judge said.

"Should I bring the jury back in?" the bailiff asked.

"Not yet."

"Why don't you do some voir dire counselor," the judge said after Susannah had taken the stand.

I stepped around counsel table and approached the witness.

"Ms. McCreedy, when did you find this letter?"

"Over the weekend, I had returned to Florida to get some more clothing."

"How did you find it?"

"It was at the bottom of one of Ben's drawers. I was emptying them out to donate to the Salvation Army."

"He never mentioned the letter to you while he was alive?"

"I'm pretty sure he did mention that he had left a letter for me in the event something happened to him, but it was never discussed again and I'd completely forgotten about it."

"What made you decide to clean out his drawers the weekend before the trial?"

Susannah clearly didn't have a ready answer. She fumbled around for a moment until she finally explained that she couldn't sleep.

"I was lying in bed staring up at the ceiling and I decided I was better off doing something so I got up and started cleaning."

I was surprised that she didn't complain about how hard it was sometimes for old people to fall asleep with all that history on their minds.

"You didn't go through his drawers before that?"

"No, just the closets."

"You didn't go through any of his drawers after he died to check for important papers, insurance, things like that?"

"I went through the document drawer in his desk in the den. That's where he kept his important papers. I did open some of his clothing drawers, he kept some extra cash under his underwear, but I missed the letter. It was lying flat in the back under the socks."

"When did you give it to your counsel?"

"Sunday . . . late afternoon . . . after I returned to New York."

"Your Honor," I said, "I renew my objection to this last minute disclosure. We have no opportunity to have the note analyzed by a handwriting expert or even to prepare for cross. I wasn't even given the courtesy of a copy before we started this morning, let alone yesterday, and counsel has had it since Sunday. This should have been immediately produced. It was clearly not in this instance in order to preserve the element of surprise."

"What is there to prepare for," Bill said. "It's a two-line handwritten note. There is no dispute concerning the transfer of the house and the account set up to cover the expenses, neither is at issue in this trial. It simply confirms what she just testified to that she was unaware of what her husband had done and that she learned about it after his death. The note doesn't say anything that Ms. McCreedy hasn't already testified to."

"In which case," the judge said, "you don't really need it. You have her testimony on the subject and I'm going to exclude it."

Of course, she knew as well as I did that Bill wanted the jury to see the letter not for its substance with respect to the house and the account, but because the handwriting was strong and certain, the language sparse and clear, the sentiment reasoned and calm, and above all because it made Ben sound normal, nothing like an old man tricked by some clever young woman claiming to be his reincarnated wife.

The judge handed the letter back to the bailiff who returned it to Bill.

"Bring the jury back in," she said.

The jury came back looking relaxed and whispering to each other like classmates on an outing, all except Ira whose lips were shut so tight that his mouth looked almost like a scar below his nose. There's the problem I thought to myself, but as long as it's only him it's OK since civil matters only require a 5-1 vote.

"Ladies and gentlemen of the jury," the judge said, "I have decided for legal reasons not to admit the letter into evidence. Please don't speculate as to why. These things often happen during the course of a trial. Counselor, you may continue with your direct examination."

Bill stood up and walked around counsel's table and began by reminding the jury what Ms. McCreedy had testified to before the break, then he asked, "Did you discuss the transfer of the house with Ben a second time?"

"No, he knew it wasn't my intention to stay around after he was gone, but he did it anyway without telling me, which was just like Ben. When Ben made up his mind there was no stopping him."

"When did Ben first raise with you the possibility of changing his will? Withdraw that, who first raised the possibility of Ben changing his will?"

"Ben brought it up. It had never entered my mind."

"When did he bring it up?"

"On our six month anniversary."

"Can you tell the jury the circumstances?"

"Certainly, we went to the Sea Shanty to celebrate. That was our place. I couldn't get enough lobster."

Susannah looked at the jury and smiled, but the only response she got was from juror 6, Ira, who licked his lips.

"We were having dessert when Ben said that he'd been thinking of changing his will to make me the beneficiary. I didn't know what he had at that point. I mean I knew he was well off, but he never discussed the details with me. I told him I'd prefer he didn't do that since it belonged to the children."

"How did he respond?"

"He said it was his money and he could do what he wanted with it, and I got a little angry and told him that was not a good enough reason. Ben could be very obstinate. It was the same when he was young. Still, if you called him on it he would usually soften up and then we could talk more calmly about it."

"What happened next?"

"That night in bed he said he had some other reasons as well."

"What were they?"

Now I could have objected to all this. Anything Ben had to say would be hearsay, but it was too late now to start objecting and I didn't want it to look as if I was trying to prevent poor Susannah from getting her story out. Besides, I had decided that it was better to let her put words in Ben's mouth, because I was still convinced that she'd hang herself in the end if I gave her enough rope.

"First, he said the main reason was that it would save a lot of money in estate taxes if it came to me first. He said that there was no tax on what a husband left to his wife."

Bill waited for her to continue, but when she didn't he asked if he said anything else. Of course that kind of question meant that she'd forgotten to say something they'd gone over when preparing her testimony. Could it seem any more scripted, I wondered to myself, glancing over at the jury who were paying close attention and didn't look nearly as skeptical as I was.

"Oh yes," Susannah said, "he also said that since I was so young I could give $50,000 every year to the children and grandchildren tax free. Ben was big on avoiding taxes when he could. He said there was a lot of money, he wouldn't tell me how much, and I didn't ask, but he said there would be plenty left over for me to do some charitable things and live my own life."

"Did he give you any other reasons, aside from the taxes?"

Susannah rubbed her chin.

"He said his sons had more than enough money and he'd rather it didn't go to another house on the lake or something like that. He figured we could give more to the grandchildren as they got older, you know give them a real leg up in life."

She was careful not to say "his grandchildren" or "our grandchildren," using the more neutral "the grandchildren" instead, which could easily include her as the grandmother without appearing too shameless or obvious.

"And do some good in society. He said he knew the goodness of my soul – Rose's soul – and he was content that the money would be put to good use, charitable stuff and things like that."

My father never gave a dime away, Mitch wrote.

"What did you say in response?"

"I told him I didn't want the responsibility, but he said it would make him rest easier doing it that way and there was nothing much I could do about it since it was his decision and he was the one who had the last word on what he did with his money."

Bill walked toward the jury box.

"Was anything decided that night?"

"No, of course not, we talked about it for the next couple of months; Ben insisting and me resisting. It was the only real disagreement we ever had."

Susannah took a deep breath after she said that, as if she were trying not to cry. I had to remind myself of my own advice and not make a face.

"Did you know when you got married that under Florida law you would be entitled to $1/3^{rd}$ of his estate anyway, no matter what his will provided for, unless you signed a pre-marital waiver?"

Bill was doing a good job anticipating my cross-examination.

"I didn't, but Ben explained it to me before we got married and had me sign something that said I would waive that. Of course, I didn't care."

She was making Ben look like he was being cautious and thinking ahead, like a man who knew exactly what he was doing, who gave her the house and some money to make up for it after a few months of wedded bliss, an amount way less than one-third, but who eventually became convinced that he had found his soul mate and decided he wanted to go all the way.

"You remember signing that waiver."

"Absolutely."

"Did you look for it in your husband's papers?"

"I searched everywhere for it. I asked Ben's broker if he had a copy but he didn't."

"Did Ben have a safe deposit box?"

"No, I think he may have thrown it away once he signed the new will. I suppose it didn't matter anymore."

Unless, of course, Ben decided to change his will again – and write her out - in which case he needed the waiver to prevent her from taking one-third.

"Ben handled all the finances and important papers," she added. "He did it his whole life with Rose and it was no different with me."

Mitch made a check on his pad.

"What happened next with respect to the new will?"

"You mean after the month or two of discussions?"

"Yes."

"Ben said that he called the lawyer and about a few days later an envelope came for him with the new will in it."

"Did he show it to you?"

"I saw it. I didn't look through it. He told me what it said and what it did. He said that he was returning things to the way they were when Rose was alive with everything to his wife, and that it was his choice and his choice alone."

"Leaving it to Rose?" Bill asked.

"No, to me, he was leaving it to me, he knew the difference. I may have the same soul as Rose, but I'm not Rose. I never pretended to be. I'm me. He said his sons would just have to understand, and he had no doubt that I would give the tax free gifts to the children and grandchildren that we had discussed . . . once they reached twenty-one of course. He didn't want me to start before then."

"What did you say to that?"

"I couldn't control Ben any more than his sons could. I said fine and told him that I wouldn't be spending very much, because I didn't need very much to live, never have, and I'd make sure that the children and grandchildren got most of it and the rest to charity."

"Are you still planning to do that?"

"Yes, of course."

Her wide pale face filled with pride and love as she looked over at My Three Sons, a kindly, motherly expression in her eyes and mouth.

Bill walked back to counsel's table and shuffled a few papers around like he was looking for the next smoking gun. Sometimes an attorney does that to divert the jury's attention away from the witness so they don't look too hard or too long at her expression, so that the self-conscious cracks don't become too visible; sometimes an attorney does it to give the last answer time to sink in; sometimes an attorney just needs some time to think, no matter how detailed the outline.

"Do you know why he didn't go to the lawyer's office to execute the new will?" Bill asked.

"I don't think Ben was particularly fond of lawyers, and the lawyer told him he could do it on his own, as long as he had two witnesses."

"What happened next?"

"I called a couple of the neighbors, but no one was home. Most of the neighbors were singles so that wouldn't have helped us. And Bill didn't want to go over to the clubhouse. He didn't like everyone knowing his business. Then Ben remembered the old couple around the corner. They didn't move very well, he said, so they were always home. We went over there and they witnessed Ben's signature."

"Did Ben explain to them what they were witnessing?"

"No, I did. They were a little hard of hearing and I can be loud, a lot louder than Ben," Susannah said with a smile.

"What did you tell them?"

"That it was Ben's last will and testament. I read that from the top of the first page."

"Did you tell them what was in it, what it did?"

"No I didn't, was I supposed to?"

"No," Bill said, "I just wanted to clarify to the jury what it was that you did tell them."

"Just that it was Ben's last will."

There was no reaction from any of the jurors, although no one looked bored either, a sign perhaps that some of them were finding this more difficult than they thought. Even the spectators were quiet and still.

"Did Ben sign it in front of them?"

"Yes."

'Did they know Ben?"

"I think they recognized him from around the community, although they didn't know me. I think they thought I might be a daughter or something."

"Did you watch them sign on the witness lines?"

"I did. It was a slow process. They're hands were a bit shaky, which you can see from the signatures."

"What happened after they finished signing?"

"We sat around a bit and talked, mostly about their health problems. They didn't get too many visitors, other than their daughter, and I think they were a little lonely."

"What did Ben do with the will afterward?"

"He said he sent it back to the attorney because he said attorneys have safes and usually hold the wills."

Bill asked the courtroom deputy for Exhibit 1.

"Let me show you this document Ms. McCreedy and ask you if you recognize it?"

"Yes, that's the will."

"Do you recognize the signatures?"

"Yes, there's Ben's and below that is Mr. and Mrs. Burger. They couldn't press down very hard so they're a little lighter."

"It's the original, is that correct?"

"Yes, it looks like it."

"The stamp on top indicates it was filed in the court as part of the probate petition?"

"If you say so," she said.

"How did you get it after Ben died?"

"From his attorney in Florida."

"It has already been marked as Exhibit 1 Your Honor."

The judge nodded.

"One last question," Bill said. "As long as you knew Ben was he mentally sharp and aware of what he was doing?"

Susannah smiled.

"He was in great shape for a man his age, walking everywhere, driving on his own . . . until the accident."

"How about mentally?"

"Even better, Ben was one of the smartest men I'd ever met. He read constantly, followed the news, had opinions on everything . . . and more importantly, he knew his own nonsense."

Almost all of the jurors smiled. My Rose, alternate number 1, was the lone holdout.

"What does that mean Ms. McCreedy?"

"That he knew the difference between the truth and his own nonsense. My father used to tell me that if you wouldn't buy someone else's baloney, you shouldn't buy your own."

"I have no further questions," Bill said, walking back to counsel's table and slowly lowering himself down into his chair.

"We'll start with the cross," the judge said, "after the lunch break."

We all stood up while the judge and jury walked out.

I asked My Three Sons to have lunch without me, so I could gather my thoughts for the cross. I think of cross sort of like guerrilla warfare. You lie still and innocuous in the reeds, waiting until the enemy gets lulled into a false sense of security before jumping up for a surprise blow.

I was happy to skip lunch and happier still to avoid the crowds and press outside. It was beginning to resemble a carnival out there with vendors selling food and drink, as well as souvenirs from religious books and rosary beads to t-shirts and hats. The crowd was growing each day with extremists gathering like the trial was a call to arms.

I surveyed the crowd from time to time as I walked up the courthouse steps wondering who it was who egged my car and made the threatening phone calls. I wondered if it was one person or more than one. I also looked around from time to time for Aurora because I had this feeling she'd be easy to pick out.

When we resumed after lunch the air conditioning had stopped working and the heat in the courtroom was oppressive. The windows were all open, the noise that rose up from the street below was like a shadowy presence that darkened the room from time to time and made it feel as if there was more at stake here than just money.

The judge apologized to the jurors for the inconvenience, but insisted that we had to press on. "The wheels of justice," she said, "like the post office continue turning whatever the weather."

Of course, everyone laughed, as if it were the funniest joke they'd ever heard.

"Ms. McCreedy," I said, standing at counsel's table while I gathered my notes, "We have met before, haven't we?"

"Yes, we have."

"And that was at your deposition, your examination under oath about one month ago in preparation for this trial."

"Yes."

"And you testified under oath then, just as you are doing now?"

"I did."

I stepped away from the table with my pad in hand and flipped to the next page.

"How did you spend your first week on the job after you were hired by Minute Maid?"

"Mostly training, going out on some jobs with the other girls."

"And did you testify that you sat down with Alma Brown at some point to prepare to take over her customers?"

"I did."

"And she told you all about her clients, including Ben?"

"Yes."

Short answers, as I advise all my witnesses during cross. Don't elaborate, just answer what's asked. It's always easy to do in the beginning, before the exhaustion takes hold. I like cross-examination much better than direct, because I'm allowed to lead the witness and nothing is ever rehearsed. It's a little like a chess match.

"Did Ms. Brown keep a notebook with entries for each of her clients?"

"She did," Susannah said, maintaining her friendly and cooperative tone.

"In fact she showed it to you when you met with her, didn't she?"

"Yes, we went through it together."

I could feel Bill wince behind me, too much elaboration. She was showing me the way.

"So you spent a day going through the book with her?"

"Not the whole day, most of one afternoon."

"Was that in the Minute Maid office?"

"No, it was at her apartment. Her knee was pretty bad by then."

"Do you remember what the book said about Ben?"

"Not really, maybe a little bit."

Well prepared, "a bit" left a lot of room for I don't remember or I don't know.

"What do you remember it said about him?"

"That Ben was in his late eighties and a talker, liked to follow her around as she worked, not very demanding, place always pretty clean. It could have been from the book or what Alma told me, I'm not exactly sure which."

"Do you remember anything else that Ms. Brown may have told you or wrote in her notebook?"

Susannah put her index finger to her lips.

"Not at the moment," she said, hedging her bet.

"Did the book mention the name of Ben's late wife, Rose?"

"I'm sorry," she said, "there were so many names in the book I just don't remember."

Since Alma Brown was not listed as a witness, Susannah probably felt pretty confident about her answer. Of course, neither she nor Bill knew that I had the notebook. Murray had paid $500 for it. I took Alma's book from one of my folders and asked the court's permission to approach the witness.

Of course, unless Susannah authenticated it, it would be difficult getting the notebook into evidence without Ms. Brown's testimony, but Murray felt Brown was a loose cannon and not worth the risk. If I couldn't get it in I could at least use it to refresh Susannah's recollection and challenge her credibility.

"Let me show you this notebook."

"May I see it first?" Bill asked.

I gave it to him and he leafed through it. It wasn't on my exhibit list, but it didn't have to be since I didn't have to identify what I might use to refresh a witness' recollection or challenge her credibility.

Bill asked for a sidebar and we approached the bench.

"This hasn't been produced," Bill whispered.

"It wasn't a document in our possession, custody, or control," I whispered back. "Our investigator obtained it from Ms. Brown last night and brought it to me this morning. Whether it would be of any use or not wasn't clear until counsel finished his direct. This is rebuttal evidence and I intend to use it in the first instance to refresh her recollection."

"He can certainly refresh her recollection with it," the Judge said, "If counsel decides to offer it into evidence we'll deal with it at that time."

With that Bill went back to his seat and I handed the notebook to Susannah before walking back to the lectern.

"Ms. McCreedy," I asked, "That's Ms. Brown's notebook, isn't it?"

She flipped through it.

"It looks like it."

"It has her name on the inside cover."

She looked.

"Yes, it does."

"That's the book you went through with Alma Brown that you just told us about, isn't it."

She looked at it again.

"I think so."

I had planned to ask her to read the entries about Ben to see if it refreshed her recollection about the things Alma told her, but I changed my mind.

"I offer it as Respondents' Exhibit A."

I clearly didn't have enough to get it in at this point and I was hoping not to anger the judge, but I was betting Bill would be concerned about looking bad if he objected. Besides, if the judge sustained his objection I could still use it to refresh her recollection and challenge her memory, so I didn't have much to lose.

"May I see it again a moment," Bill said and I handed it to him.

He leafed through it.

"No objection."

"Exhibit A is admitted into evidence," the judge said, giving me a bit of the fish eye.

"Ms. McCreedy, please look at the page with the bookmark in it."

"Yes."

"Is that the entry for Ben Everett?"

"It is."

"Do you remember looking at it?"

"Vaguely, I remember looking through various parts of the book with Alma. I don't really have any specific recollection about this page as opposed to any other pages. At the time, Ben was just another customer. I had no idea who he would turn out to be."

Well coached, I thought.

"Do you see where she refers to his late wife Rose?"

"Yes."

"It says that she died over twenty-five years earlier, doesn't it?"

"Yes."

Here I was about to score some points for the home team and Susannah sat there smiling, answering each question with the same deliberateness and equanimity, almost as if we were sitting on someone's porch having a conversation over tea.

"And she writes how much Ben liked to talk about Rose?"

Susannah took some time to read the entry. She wiped her right eye in a dramatic gesture.

"Yes he does . . . I mean she does, she writes about how much he talked about her."

"Does that refresh your recollection about what you discussed with Ms. Brown when you were being prepared to take over for her?"

Susannah put her hand to her chin.

"Not really, I'm sure I saw it at some point or we discussed it, I just don't remember for sure. We went through all of her clients and she had over 75, not all were weekly like Ben. I do remember some of the things she said about Ben only because he was one of Alma's favorites. She said that he never complained or talked down to her, like some of the others. I noticed the same things about him as soon as I started working there."

"So is it fair to say that before you started working at Ben's home, you already knew that he had a wife named Rose who had died almost two years before you were born?"

"I suppose so, it's not something I would have noticed, I don't remember. I'm sorry."

She was much calmer than her attorney who was crossing and uncrossing his legs, like he was waiting his turn at the dentist's office.

"So you knew before appearing that first day to clean his house that Ben was still very attached to Rose and liked to talk about her, didn't you?"

"As I said, I don't remember. Although it's possible. In any event, I certainly knew after that first day cleaning for him."

"Why is that?"

"Because he talked about her as I was cleaning."

"Didn't the name Rose have a special meaning for you back then when you were sitting with Ms. Brown going over her clients?"

"What do you mean?"

I went over to the clerk's table and picked up Exhibit 2.

"Well, you testified on direct about that Sunday morning prayer service at your father's church in the barn where you came forward and gave testimony about your prior life, do you remember that?"

Susannah smiled, not a bead of perspiration despite the temperature.

"Of course, that was the first time I experienced my past life, and yes it was Rose. I wasn't sure what you were getting at."

"And the name Rose, the name you picked for your past life, it's mentioned right here in this article, isn't it?" I said, waving the exhibit in front of me.

"It's not a name I picked. It's who I once was, and yes the name I called out was Rose."

"And you kept this article and carried it with you all these years?"

"I saved it, what sixteen-year-old wouldn't."

"You kept it with you as you traveled across the country?"

"Yes, I kept it. It reminded me of my family and growing up."

I felt like admonishing her that I didn't ask why she kept it, only that she kept it, but I didn't want to come across as an ogre.

"And Alma Brown's notebook or Alma Brown herself made it clear that Ben's Rose died over twenty-five years earlier, almost two years before you were born."

"Yes," Susannah said, "Rose died before I was born, that's the only way you can be a reincarnate."

For the first time she sounded a little snippy, not upset, but a bit resentful of my tone of voice and the disrespect lurking behind each of my questions.

"Did you think when you heard about Ben's Rose that perhaps this was the same Rose you called out at sixteen?"

"I don't recall thinking that way, no."

This is the point where I drop down into the reeds again and move on, hoping that the jury can make the logical leap on its own. If not, I'll make sure to drive the point home during my summation.

"Ms. McCreedy, I think you said on direct that most souls are not reincarnated as quickly as Rose, unless they leave this life with something significant that's unresolved."

"That's what my father taught me."

"What king of things might cause a soul to be reincarnated so quickly?" I asked.

"A violent death or an early illness, some terrible guilt about something a person did or didn't do," Susannah said, perhaps trying to nudge me toward some questions about Eva.

I couldn't resist sticking my toe into the water just a bit to see what she actually knew.

"Since Rose allegedly came back so soon after her death, what was unresolved in her life? Did it have anything to do with Ben?"

"No, it wasn't Ben."

"How about her children?"

"No."

"Could it have been the cancer?"

"I suppose that could be true in some instances, it was long and painful in Rose's case, but that would be true of countless souls. I don't think it was the cancer in her case, although there aren't any hard or fast rules about these things."

"So what was left unresolved?"

"Her relationship with her sister."

"And that's something you talked about with Ben, isn't it?"

"Yes."

Right on the money, I thought. Perhaps Ben talked more than anyone thought. Anyway, that was about as far as I was prepared to go, I didn't want to make her look too knowledgeable. Let the jury just assume that Ben had told her everything.

"A bad relationship is enough to bring you back this soon?"

"Perhaps," she said. "I don't have the answer to that. The why is not for me to know."

I walked back to my desk and stared down at my outline.

"Why is it most people, just about everyone actually, are unaware of their prior lives?"

"Because a new life is meant to start fresh so the learning process can begin again."

"Why the exception in your case?"

"I don't know."

"I assume that there have been others throughout history like you?"

"The history books are full of them. My father used to mention them in his sermons . . . Henry Ford, Mark Twain, Ralph Waldo Emerson, Ben Franklin and Walt Whitman."

"They believed in reincarnation, Ms. McCreedy," I said, cutting off her obviously well-rehearsed answer, "they didn't profess to know about their past lives, did they?"

"No, you're right. I'm sorry, I misunderstood the question."

"What I was asking was whether there have been others like you who could see into their past lives."

"Of course."

"Can you name some of them?" I asked.

"Edgar Cayce," she said, "he wrote about his."

"Anyone else?"

"Not that comes to mind."

"So it's very, very rare, wouldn't you say?"

"Yes."

"Oh, Audie Murphy was another one."

"Two in one thousand years?"

"Objection," Bill said, "that's not a question."

"Sustained."

"Is it just a lucky accident, one of those one in a trillion things?"

"Nothing in this universe is an accident, Mr. Clasen, certainly nothing like this. Perhaps I was meant to make Ben's last year easier. Or perhaps I'm here to create doubt in some and certainty in others. Who can explain the ways of God?"

"Does what you're supposed to do depend on you having a lot of money?"

Susannah shook her head dismissively from side to side.

"Of course not, we're all here to learn and learning requires little more than observation and awareness. Money has nothing to do with it, although what you do with it can be an important measure of your life. At the end it's not what you take from life that matters, but what you give."

"That's a well-known phrase, Ms. McCreedy, isn't it? You didn't just make it up."

"My father used to say it all the time."

I wasn't getting anywhere, so I walked back to counsel's table to look at my notes before starting a new line of questioning.

"May I see Exhibit 1," I said, walking over to the clerk.

"I'd like to show you the original will again, Ms. McCreedy, and ask you if you handled it on the day that it was executed and witnessed?"

'Handled it?"

"Did you hold it in your hands at some point?"

"Yes, of course. Ben took it out of the envelope and signed it, and I gave it to the Burgers to sign. Then I took it back and put it in the envelope for Ben."

"Who mailed it to the attorney?"

"Ben did."

"Was that the first and only time you handled the new will?"

"Yes, the attorney sent it back to me after the accident."

"Look closely at the top left corner," I said, "where it's stapled."

"Yes."

"Do you see where it looks as if it was re-stapled, as if it was taken apart and put back together again."

Susannah looked closely at the top corner of the will.

"You can see that one of the holes is off, as if someone tried to line it up and didn't get it perfectly through the same staple hole."

"Yes, I can see that," Susannah said without any of the guile or resistance I would have expected from an adverse witness, particularly one faced with a possible flaw in her foolproof scheme.

"Do you have any idea how that might have happened?"

"Not really," she said, "Perhaps the attorney took it apart to make a copy of it."

"Attorney's know better than that Ms. McCreedy."

"Or one of his secretaries."

"They know better as well."

"Objection," Bill said rising to his feet.

"Sustained, the jury will ignore counsel's last two remarks."

Of course, I knew that what I said was objectionable, but once remarks like that get out they are difficult to erase. No attorney in his right mind would ever take apart a will and put it back together so it looks as if it were tampered with, neither would his secretary. If they had to copy it they would just fold the pages.

The judge nodded for me to resume.

"Maybe Ben took it apart to copy it," Susannah said, still examining the will, "before he sent it back to the attorney."

"Did you find a copy of it anywhere around the house?"

"No."

"Could it be Ms. McCreedy that you were the one who had the revised will prepared."

"No."

"That you called the attorney and asked for it?"

"No, that's not what happened."

"Could it be that Ben wasn't sure what he was signing or thought that he was signing something else, because he only signed the last page with the signature line with the other pages detached, and the Burgers did the same?"

"No, Mr. Clasen that's not what happened. I wish I could explain the staple hole, but I can't. All I can think of is that either Ben made a copy for himself or maybe the attorney's secretary took it apart to correct a page before sending it to him in the first place."

"You have no reason to believe that a secretary did that, do you?"

"No."

"And if Ben were to have made a copy, when would he have done that?"

"When he went to the library, which he did about once a week; they had one of those ten cent copying machines there or maybe when he went to the post office to mail it."

"Then you would have found a copy around the house, wouldn't you have?"

"I suppose, but I wasn't looking for one since I had the original from the attorney."

"So you're saying that it's possible he might have taken the will apart, copied it, re-stapled it, and hid the copy somewhere in the house, but that you just haven't found it yet?"

"Anything is possible. I certainly haven't turned the house inside out looking for a copy of his will, because up until now I never thought there was a copy or that I needed one."

I glanced at the jury. Most of them looked bored, they liked the theological questions better; all except jurors 4 and 5, Matt, the artist, and Ira, the pretender, who were both staring at me with cold, stony eyes.

"Do you remember whether Ben and the Burgers signed with the same pen?" I asked.

Susannah thought about it, as she glanced down at the will. Stupid mistake, I thought to myself, I should have taken it back first before asking the question so she couldn't look at it and see the obvious color difference.

"No, Ben always kept a pen in his breast pocket, one of those nice pens you find in the glass cases at the stationery store. He didn't like to lend it out. He'd had it for years, long before Rose died."

Another check on Mitch's pad.

"He was always afraid that if he lent it out he'd forget to get it back. The Burgers used their own pen. It looked like something they got for free at the supermarket from one of those politicians running for office."

I took the will back from her and put it on the clerk's desk.

"Ms. McCreedy, did Ben believe that you were a reincarnation of his late wife Rose?"

"I think he did. I certainly hope he did. Why else would he have wanted to marry me? I'm certainly not much to look at."

She didn't miss a trick.

"It's a yes or no question, Ms. McCreedy did he believe you?" I quickly asked to draw everyone's attention away from her little self-depreciating moment.

"Yes."

"And that was because of all the little facts you knew about his late wife's life, facts that you could have gotten from Alma Brown, picked up working around the house, or even from listening to Ben?"

"Objection," Bill said, "that's a compound question which assumes facts not in evidence."

"Sustained."

"I'm sorry, "I said. "Let me break it down."

"Was that because of all the little facts you knew about his late wife's life?"

"Certainly that got Ben's attention at first," Susannah said slowly and deliberately, "But you don't believe, truly believe, in something or someone based on a few parlor tricks. Belief is a connection that runs much deeper and is much more elemental. Ben believed once he got to know me and saw into my soul."

"And what he saw was his late wife Rose?" I asked.

"No, he saw the same soul."

"Do you think, Ms. McCreedy, that an eighty-eight-year old man near the end of his own life, who has pined for his late wife for over twenty-five years, might be a little susceptible to believing a story like that?"

"Ben wasn't your typical eighty-eight-year old man. He was skeptical and observant; sharp as a tack. Nothing got passed him and he made up his own mind based on his own observations and feelings . . . and belief is all about feelings. It's not about the things that you can see and touch, or know for certain. You don't need to believe in those things.

Belief is about the intangibles, the spiritual matters that can never be known for sure. I think he was more sensitive and aware at eighty-eight than he ever was. Sometimes it takes years of experience to appreciate what we don't know and embrace the doubt, to sense the things that aren't visible, which we tend to overlook when we're young."

My Rose, Alternate No. 1 was sitting up straight with her lips shut tight, in contrast to Matt the musician whose mouth was wide open.

"That wasn't my question Ms. McCreedy, my question was whether you thought that an eighty-eight-year old man near the end of his life might be more willing to believe that he was in the presence of his reincarnated wife than say a fifty-year-old man."

"I don't know how to answer that," she said, "except the way I did."

"OK, then let's start with that," I said leaving the lectern and walking slowly over to counsel's table. "Now I can appreciate the difference between belief and knowledge Ms. McCreedy as you explained it, and it's clear from what you have just testified to that you don't think there was anything wrong with Ben's intelligence. Is that a fair statement?"

"Yes, yes it is."

"Would you agree with me that intelligence is not the same as emotion, that the analytical mind is different from the heart, sort of the other side of the coin?"

"I guess so."

"And some judgments we make with our heads and some we make more instinctively and intuitively with our hearts?"

"Yes."

"Which is what you were just discussing before about the difference between what we know for certain and what we believe, isn't it, between intelligence and feelings, the mind and the heart?"

"I'd say that's right."

"However smart a person is in the world of finance or in dealing with current events and day to day chores and responsibilities, doesn't necessarily mean it's the same when it comes to love and intuition, does it?"

"There's a difference, of course," she said, "Although I think that there is some kind of symmetry between the two."

"Meaning if you make good analytical judgments based on weighing the facts, you should be able to make good intuitive and emotional judgments based on feelings?"

"Something like that yes."

"But that's not always the case, is it Ms. McCreedy?"

"Nothing is always the case Mr. Clasen, life is full of exceptions."

"You wouldn't deny that there are quite a few men who we read about and hear about, some we even know who are brilliant and make tons of money in business, but seem to make bad choices time and time again when it comes to companions."

"I suppose."

"They wind up marrying two or three different times, sometimes more - that's not all that uncommon, is it?"

"Unfortunately not, people these days are too quick to divorce. They're unwilling to do the hard work."

"So success in business is not always matched by success in love?"

"No."

"So you would agree that there is a difference," I said, "Between a person's state of mind when it comes to his financial intelligence and when it comes to his emotions."

"I would, except the extent of that difference varies greatly from individual to individual."

"Would you agree that at eighty-eight most men are nearing the end of their lives here on earth . . . at least actuarially speaking?"

"Yes."

"And would you agree with Alma Brown and everyone else who knew Ben, his friends and neighbors, his children and grandchildren, that he had a large open wound, let's call it a big space in his heart for his late wife Rose, one that never completely healed?"

"I would," Susannah said with an exaggerated nod, "Because I saw it the moment we met."

"For twenty-five years he carried that torch and never had another relationship with another woman, isn't that correct?"

"Yes."

"Not until you came along telling him that you were a reincarnation of Rose."

"My telling him wasn't what mattered. It was his feeling it and believing in what he himself saw and felt."

"Do you think it was something that he wanted to believe, regardless of what his intelligence might have told him?"

"We all want to believe," Susannah said, "But we don't unless we have a good enough reason."

"And you gave him that reason, didn't you?"

"Yes I did, just as what I saw and felt at 16 gave me a good enough reason?"

"And within a month you were married and shortly thereafter the owner of his house, and a bank account in your name, and a little while after that the sole beneficiary of his new will."

"Yes."

"Now does that seem like an exercise in intelligence to you or purely an emotional response?"

"They aren't mutually exclusive," she said, "both play a role in any decision like that."

"Do you consider the fact that Ben still talked so much about Rose twenty-five years later and was unable to establish a relationship with any other woman during that time an indication of his emotional inability to move on or perhaps instability on a certain level with respect to love?"

"I'm not sure that I follow you," Susannah said.

"You took advantage of an old man who had spent years fixated on his late wife by praying on his emotional weakness, didn't you Ms. McCreedy?"

"Objection."

"Sustained."

"Once you heard his wife's name from Alma Brown and how long she'd been dead, didn't that bring to your mind that old newspaper article you carried around with you?"

"I told you earlier I didn't recall thinking about that at the time or anything like that."

"It didn't start you thinking, before you'd even met Ben, that this was an opportunity to connect with this eighty-eight-year old man?"

"Objection."

"Overruled, you can answer."

"No, it did not," Susannah said as emphatically as she could without slamming her fist down on the railing.

"But you did discuss the article with him, didn't you?"

"Eventually, not right away."

"And you showed it to him?"

"Yes, maybe a month later."

"But before you married?"

"Yes."

I took a gamble there since I didn't know the answer, but it would have defied common sense if she had answered no.

"You didn't point that out on direct, did you?"

"I don't believe I was asked about it in that context."

I was not having much luck wearing her down. Getting a hostile witness tired or flustered is the best way to get them to make a mistake and blurt something out without thinking. I took a walk back to counsel's table to look at my notes and get my bearings.

"Ben was very vocal throughout his life that he didn't believe in God, wasn't he?"

"Not to me."

"How about when Rose was alive?"

"Yes."

"He never went to church?"

"No."

"He liked to say that the holidays were for family and for eating, didn't he?"

"He did," Susannah said, "But what people say and the doubts they feel deep inside are not necessarily one and the same."

"But Ben was pretty adamant in his belief or should I say disbelief about God and the afterlife, wasn't he?"

"Yes."

"And that all changed when he met you?"

"I'm not sure changed is the right word. I think that a lot of disbelievers are more agnostics. They're unsure. That's what Ben was if you ask me. He was one of those men uncomfortable with not being sure, like a lot of people he wanted to believe, he just needed a reason."

I walked slowly toward the jury.

"And you provided that reason?"

"In part."

"Ms. McCreedy, wasn't Rose the name of your grandmother, your father's mother?"

"Yes."

"And she died before you were born?"

"Many years before."

I was getting lucky again, so I pushed further.

"Didn't you and your father tell some of his congregants that you were a reincarnate of your grandmother?"

"I was sixteen and had caught just a glimpse of a life. When I first felt Rose that day I didn't see any of her past. I saw a short, gray-haired old woman. My father assumed it was my grandmother. I did too for a long time. It made sense to my father, because he said souls travel together."

"Is that unusual," I said, "That you couldn't tell the difference between your grandmother's past life and Ben's wife's past life?"

"I can't say, although a past life is not something that reveals itself all at once, certainly not to a sixteen-year old."

"So it wasn't until you met Ben that you finally figured out which Rose you were reincarnated from."

"I've never heard it put quite that way, but I guess the answer is yes."

I stood there a moment trying to decide if that was enough.

"Your Grandmother Rose died what – thirty years before Ben's Rose – yet you couldn't tell the difference?"

"Thirty years is an instant in God's time."

"Is it possible that you got your wires crossed again and that Ben's Rose was the wrong Rose as well?"

"No, that's not possible, because I saw everything at that point. It triggered the connection. I knew too much about Ben's Rose for it to be a mistake."

I wasn't going to accept her invitation to turn the cross into a quiz about Rose. She was clearly well prepared for that, so it was time to move on.

"You said on direct that when you got that Rose feeling the first time in Ben's house you were upset by it." I flipped through my notes. "Your exact words were –I was hoping that the feeling would go away."

"Do you remember that testimony?"

"Yes."

"Why is that? Here you had met the soul that you had shared you last life on earth with, learned who you had been, knowledge any one of us would be grateful to know. Why did you want it to go away?"

"I supposed because I was afraid of what might happen."

"What might happen?" I asked.

"That I'd somehow get my present life all mixed up with my past life."

"Isn't that what actually did happen?"

"Yes," Susannah said, "Even though I didn't want it to. I couldn't resist making Ben's last days as comfortable as possible."

"And in the process you stand to gain a great deal of money?"

"Objection," Bill said.

"Overruled," the judge said.

"That wasn't my goal. It was what Ben wanted and I feel that I owe him enough to grant him that wish."

"What is it he wanted?" I asked.

"For me to have the house to live in and the money for charity and he wanted me to give it to the children and grandchildren each year as they got older."

"Is there a provision in the will, a trust of any kind that requires you to distribute Ben's estate over time to his children and grandchildren?"

"No."

"So you could give them nothing?"

"I suppose that's true, but Ben knew I'd never do that."

"You said earlier that Ben was a careful man when it came to his finances, isn't that correct?"

"Yes."

"So why wouldn't he have put a provision in his new will to make sure that his wishes got done, it would have been easy enough for him to do?"

"I don't know, I suppose because this is how he wanted to show me and the world -the children as well-that in the end he really did believe."

"In you?"

"In me, in God and that the right thing would be done because it is the right thing to do, because of who I am . . . and was . . . and not because some line in a will said so."

"You said on direct that a reincarnate is supposed to live his or her present life and not interfere with the past ones."

"That's correct."

"Don't you think that inheriting all the family money and doling it out as you see fit is interfering with the past life Rose left behind?"

"It's not what I think that matters or what I was taught. God can make an exception to any general rule and I supposed he did in this case."

"There is nothing stopping you Ms. McCreedy from leaving this court if you win and going right out and buying a $5 million yacht, is there?"

"Just my heart and soul."

I glanced over at the jury to see if it sounded as strange to them as it did to me and I saw both Ira and Matt looking uncomfortably at their hands.

"A few more unrelated questions Ms. McCreedy," I said, walking back to counsel's table to flip through my notes. I decided to skip anything having to do with Rose's past life, as well as a few others subjects, like her first husband, Rudy, and the hospice, since I didn't want to make her seem too noble. The only thing I had left on my list was the waiver of her spousal interest in Ben's estate.

"Ms. McCreedy, you testified on direct that you were aware before you married Ben that Florida law provides that a wife is entitled to one-third of her husband's estate and that can't be changed once you're married?"

"Yes."

"How were you made aware of it?"

"Ben told me about it."

"But it can be avoided before you get married and that's why Ben had you sign a waiver giving up your one-third spousal interest in his estate, wasn't that your testimony on direct?"

"Yes, he had me sign a waiver the day before we got married."

"Did Ben discuss why he wanted you to sign the waiver?"

"He explained what it did and that he wanted to keep his options open. Of course, I didn't care. He knew that the money didn't matter to me."

"But it apparently did to Ben, enough for him to make you sign a waiver, didn't it?"

"At the time I suppose it did."

"This way there would be no effect on his existing will, which left everything to his three sons."

"That's what I understood."

"Why would he have you sign a waiver to protect his original will if he believed you were a reincarnation of his first wife?"

"I think at this point," Susannah said with a seemingly rehearsed hesitation, "Ben still had his doubts; after all it went against a lifetime of disbelief."

"About reincarnation?"

"About God and the soul."

"If he had his doubts," I said, "Why did he marry you? Why didn't he wait until his doubts were gone?"

"I don't know."

"Why was he so concerned about protecting his sons' inheritance at this point, yet willing to give it all away a few months later?"

"That would be something you would have to find in Ben's heart," she said, "but I would say it's because he came to believe, without doubt. There is nothing more powerful than belief."

I leaned back on counsel table. It wasn't a big point, but it was a nice little one. If he didn't believe she was a reincarnation of his wife he would never have married her, certainly not for her cleaning services and companionship which he could have had for a couple of seafood dinners a week, and if he did believe in reincarnation why bother with the waiver.

The answer I will argue to the jury is that there was no waiver, she made it up to give them the impression that Ben was still of sound mind–financially, as well as emotionally--as opposed to the real truth that Ben was besotted, confused and muddled, too far gone emotionally to deal with Susannah's carnival-like ability to make his stories about Rose seem as if they were coming from her.

"Do you have a copy of that waiver, Ms. McCreedy?"

"I haven't been able to find it."

I took a stroll around the room.

"Have you looked?"

"Yes, of course."

"Does that seem like something he'd throw away?"

"I wouldn't think so, but he became less of a saver as he got older."

I crossed one arm across my chest and rested my chin on the other as I strolled around the room making eye contact with my clients, the jurors and the judge. I stopped in front of Ms. McCreedy and very softly asked my next question.

"There was no waiver Ms. McCreedy, was there?"

"Objection."

"Overruled."

"I remember signing something that Ben called a waiver, although I didn't really read it, not closely."

"Why not?"

"Because I didn't care, I trusted Ben. For me it was all about the comfort of being with a soul that I'd spent many lifetimes with."

"Was the waiver one page or more than one page?"

"I'm not sure."

"Was it witnessed?"

"Yes, there was someone there. We didn't do it at home. It was in a store, maybe it was a bank."

"You don't remember where you signed it?"

"Not at home," she said. "I think it was in a drug store."

"Do you remember who witnessed it?"

"No."

"Was it a notary?"

"I don't recall."

"And you haven't been able to find it?"

"No."

"The attorney didn't have it, like he did the will?"

"No."

"There was no waiver, Ms. McCreedy, because Ben didn't really know what was happening when he married you, he was emotionally confused, wasn't he?"

"Objection."

"Sustained."

"No further questions," I said, turning my back on the witness and walking quickly to my seat.

"We'll take a short break here before redirect," the judge said and we all stood up while she and the jury filed out.

My Three Sons couldn't sit still when we got back to the witness room. They paced around like expectant fathers.

"That was great," Jeff said, slapping his hands together. "She was clearly lying about the waiver so the old man wouldn't sound like an incontinent old fool. He didn't know what he was doing when he married her, any more than he did when he changed the will."

"She's a cool cucumber that one," I said, slumping back on the chair. "She never lost her composure."

"How do you think it went?" Mitch asked me.

I nodded. I thought it had gone well, but not quite as well as Jeff did.

"No one's going to buy her bullshit," Jeff said.

"I'm still worried about jurors 4 and 6," I said.

"I've been watching them," Mitch said. "I think she's losing them. I'm more worried about 3 and 5."

Frank the postal worker and Lauren with the promotion business.

"Why?"

"He's been staring at the three of us way too much, like he's already decided we have enough money to last a lifetime."

"And her?"

"Single, older woman, I think she'd like to find her own rich, old man to marry. She's not going to like the idea that whatever he does with his money can be overturned by his family."

"All we need is a 5 to 1 vote," I reminded them after the clerk knocked on the door, "so we can afford to lose someone."

Of course, it's often the one you least expect, like jurors 1 and 2, Millie, my sweet homemaker, mother of 3, or Ellen, the diminutive elementary school teacher.

Bill's redirect was short. Susannah confirmed that she wasn't searching for a job on the "off chance" she'd find an older man with a wife named Rose who died before she was born.

"The job found me," she said, "Which I suppose was part of God's plan."

She confirmed that Ben's state of mind was "clear and true" until the day he died and she suddenly remembered that that idea for the pre-marriage waiver came from a dentist Ben knew who had recently remarried.

"Is it unusual that you can't find the waiver?" Bill asked.

"No, Ben was always misplacing things."

Susannah chuckled.

"That's why we kept a pair of his reading glasses in every room. It wasn't so much an old age thing, as a Ben thing. He'd been doing that since we first met."

"We?"

"Since he and Rose first met. That first summer after Rose and Ben moved to that split level in Rockland County Ben lost his front door key four times. Rose kept going to the hardware store to make copies. After a while, the locksmith thought Rose was involved in some sort of burglary ring."

True, Mitch wrote down on the pad.

On re-cross I simply asked her why she hadn't remembered that the waiver was the suggestion of a dentist friend when I asked her about it earlier.

"I don't remember you asking, but if you did, I'm sorry. You didn't give me a whole lot of time to think sometimes. I remembered it during the break and told my attorney."

She couldn't remember his name and I asked her twice.

"He wouldn't have thrown the waiver out, would he?" I asked.

"I don't think so."

"So if the waiver hasn't turned up yet, it's because you haven't looked in the right place?"

"That's right."

"Or it never existed."

"Objection."

"Overruled."

"It existed. I remember signing it. It's just lost."

"What did you do to look for it?" I asked.

"I went through all Ben's clothing drawers."

"Anything else?"

"All the boxes at the bottom of the closet, I went through his desk and the kitchen cabinets. I was looking for any important papers, not just the waiver."

"When did you do all that, was it shortly after he died?"

"Yes and last weekend when I went back down to Florida for more clothes."

"Any places you haven't searched?"

She put her finger to her lips.

"The garage, but I can't imagine he'd have put it there."

"So in all likelihood it's lost?"

"Unless he gave it to one of the boys to hold."

One question too many, I thought to myself. It's an occupational hazard.

To make up for it I turned to look at My Three Sons and when the silence got a little uncomfortable I slowly turned around to Susannah with as much of a look of disbelief as I thought the judge would allow.

"Ms. McCreedy, if one of Ben's sons had the waiver they would have been required to produce it to you before this trial, isn't that correct?"

"I don't know, I suppose so."

I walked back to counsel table and was about to sit down when I had a thought.

"Just a couple more, Ms. McCreedy," I said. "Why is it that you never discussed your reincarnation with Ben's sons until after they challenged the alleged new will?"

"Objection," Bill said, "beyond the scope of re-direct."

He hadn't asked her any questions about that subject, which technically meant I couldn't go into it again on re-cross.

"I'll allow a few questions," the Judge said. "You may answer."

"Ben and I discussed it. We wanted to wait a bit to give them time to accept me. We figured we'd tell them on our first anniversary. We both felt that once they got to know me – over time - they'd begin to sense their mother's soul as well, even if they couldn't see it the way Ben did."

"Apparently they have not, Ms. McCreedy, have they?"

"No, I suppose not."

"Is there anyone else you mentioned reincarnation to other than the owner of Minute Maid?"

Susannah thought it over.

"Not that I recall."

"Why was that?"

"I didn't really have any friends in Florida and it's not the kind of thing you go around broadcasting. Unfortunately, most people will think you're a little crazy, at least in this country. They feel the same way if you go around talking about God in general. Some things people just don't want to hear talked about in everyday conversation."

"You were married by a justice of the peace in a civil ceremony at town hall, is that correct?"

"Yes."

"No witnesses."

"There were some people there."

"No witnesses that either you or Ben knew."

"No."

"This was your choice?"

"Both of our choices, the ceremony itself wasn't important, what was important was that we had found each other."

"The service lasted about 5 minutes," I said, "it was a quick in and out?"

Susannah smiled.

"Not quite that quick. Not like Las Vegas."

That got a smile from juror number three, Frank, the mailman.

"Did Ben ever see a doctor from when you first met him until the accident?"

"You mean for a checkup?"

"For a checkup, for a cold, for any reason whatsoever."

Susannah looked up at the ceiling as if she were hoping that Ben would answer that one. The heat was finally getting to her and her temple was covered with little beads of sweat.

"Not that I can recall. He was very healthy for his age."

"So there is no doctor who you know of who can confirm Ben's soundness of mind either when he married you or supposedly changed his will. All I'm looking for is a yes or no."

I didn't want to give her the opportunity to ramble on. Susannah shook her head slowly from side to side.

"Not that I know of."

"No further questions."

With that Bill rested his case, and we adjourned for the night.

My Three Sons went home to their warm dinners and I sat in the office planning how to present our witnesses. Murray called as I was eating the turkey sandwich that my secretary had left for me.

"This may be a religious country," Murray said, "but they like their personal deities and afterlife kept in the closet . . . alongside their sex."

I chuckled to be polite.

He asked me who I had decided to call on our case and I told him Mitch, the geriatric expert and perhaps the reincarnation professor.

There was a long pause during which Murray cleared his throat at least 3 times.

"Ok, who else do you have in mind?" I said, knowing Murray didn't just call to just chew the fat.

"Mr. and Mrs. Burger's daughter."

"The dead witnesses to the will?"

"Yep."

"What's she going to say?"

"They were both blind as bats and almost as deaf. They didn't recognize her half the time. McCreedy could have hired a man dressed up as a clown to play Ben Everett and they wouldn't have known the difference. They couldn't have witnessed anything because they probably had no fucking idea why they were signing their names."

"But even Mitch says it looks like Ben's signature."

"Even I could copy that signature," Murray said. "Besides, it could have been signed before she brought it to the Burgers. For all we know, Ben thought he was signing a petition to resurrect Ronald Reagan."

"Your favorite President, no doubt."

"The last one I voted for," Murray said, "the last one who wasn't controlled by his pecker and his wallet."

I thought over Murray's suggestion. It would certainly raise some more doubts in the mind of the jury, particularly since Susannah hadn't deemed it worth mentioning the details of the Burgers' condition during her direct testimony. It wasn't a bad idea to spend a little time with the will execution front and center.

"How soon can you get her up here?"

"She's on her way."

I figured that I could slot her in right after senior shrink, as Murray called him.

I heard some footsteps walking down the marble hallway and held my breath until it passed by my door.

I gave the stranger 15 minutes to make his exit before I decided to go home and look at my notes in bed. As soon as I turned off my desk lamp the phone rang and I knew exactly who it was even though I am about as clairvoyant as a stone.

"Aurora?"

"Hi Joe," she said, "I caught most of the trial on TV."

"What do you think?"

"I'm glad you listened to Eva," she said.

"So you still think she's Rose reincarnated?"

"I don't think it, Joe, I know it."

"Well I'm glad you're not one of the jurors," I said with a chuckle.

"There's more to life than what we can see," Aurora added.

And less than we hope for, I thought to myself.

"You should come for a session," she said, "after this is all over."

"To speak to Eva?"

"To learn about those souls who watch over you," she said.

"I'm more concerned with the eyes that are watching me down here," I said, "Particularly those sitting on the jury."

"That's understandable, a bit limited in vision, but understandable."

"More advice tonight?" I asked, too tired for any more pleasantries.

"Yes."

"From Eva."

"Yes."

I sighed into the telephone.

"Go ahead."

"I'd prefer to tell you about it in person."

"I was just about to go home. It's been a long day."

"I'm in the lobby of your office building, if you'll buzz me up. It won't take long."

I don't know why, but I did. I suppose because it seemed like the path of least resistance. I opened the entrance to my office and shut the light in the waiting room. With my office door open I would be able to sit at my secretary's desk and see her before her eyes had a chance to adjust to see me.

I also moved the signed Mickey Mantle bat that a grateful client once gave me behind the desk so it was in easy reach; not that I was really concerned, but at my age you realize that precaution is always the better part of valor.

She appeared in the doorway suddenly, as if by magic. Shielding her eyes she asked, "Joe?"

"I'm here," I said, getting up from the desk, "Follow me."

She moved slowly through the waiting area and followed me to my office. She looked nothing like I had imagined. I pictured a carnival gypsy--short, top-heavy with a low cut peasant blouse that offered a glimpse of the deep and dark beyond. I imagined a long flowing skirt, a patchwork quilt of colors, long hair wrapped in a bright silk scarf and big dangling silver earrings that could have served as a perch for a canary.

Aurora, however, was tall and wispy, like white birch. She looked like a schoolteacher. Her hair was somewhere between short and long. It was blonde with streaks of grey and pulled back into a loose ponytail that looked good on her. She had to be about ten years younger than me. Her black wire rim glasses made her look literary and her features were petite, perfectly balanced and relaxed. In short, she was very attractive.

"Were you that afraid that you left me in the dark," she said with a chuckle, as she entered into my office. "Is there a bat behind your desk too?"

"No," I said, "My secretary has been a bit jumpy with all the demonstrators and crank calls."

Aurora closed her lips and nodded like I was just a kid telling a fib.

Instead of a carnival of colors, she was wearing a long black skirt, slit along the side to show some leg. She did have on the peasant blouse, although it was a soft pink, like a Brooks Brothers' shirt, with a higher neckline that only offered a glimpse of cleavage. There were no gold necklaces or big, dangling silver earrings just a string of pearls and small gold hoops.

She walked over to the desk and extended her hand. She had long, graceful fingers, like an El Greco painting.

"It's nice to finally meet you in person," she said, sitting down in the chair nearest the window, which forced me to turn my chair to face her.

She wore very little makeup, another surprise, and her smile, which appeared whenever our eyes met, was almost contagious. I actually had to hold myself in check to keep from smiling back.

"I'm sorry to bother you like this," she said, "I know it's late and you must be exhausted, but I don't like talking about these things over the telephone."

"What things?"

"These messages from beyond, they're meant to be discussed face to face . . . not broadcast over a wire."

"You did the other night."

"There was no time, I won't do it again. It's hard to judge someone's credibility over a telephone."

"Are you talking about yours or mine?"

She didn't smile this time, although our eyes touched for a moment before I looked down at my legal pad and picked up a pencil. I felt bad about sounding flippant. Although when I stared down at my notes on the pad what I really saw was her face. There was something very kind about her, very calm and accepting.

I looked back up and she hadn't moved. I liked the streak of grey hair around her temples. She couldn't have been very vain to allow that. I also liked the fact that she sat there very comfortable in the silence. I pretended to look past her out the window, but I guess I didn't do a very good job of it.

"You're staring," she said.

"I'm sorry. You're not what I expected."

"What did you expect?"

I didn't reply right away.

"Baubles, bangles and beads?" she said.

I couldn't help smiling.

"Sort of."

"You've been watching too many old movies. I'm not a gypsy, my mother was a librarian and my father was an accountant."

"How did you pick this line of work?" I asked.

"I didn't, it picked me."

"Is Aurora your real name?"

"No, it's my professional name. Betsy Rotelman wouldn't have the same panache."

I nodded.

"Any other questions," she said with a smile, "Because I'll answer them all."

"Does it pay?"

"Am I under oath," she said.

"I'm sorry you don't have to answer that."

She laughed.

"Just kidding, no, it's not very remunerative because I don't charge. I don't need the money. I'm an only child and my parents left me more than I could possibly need."

That eliminated the number one motive on my list. I looked at her hand again to make sure I hadn't missed a wedding ring or the outline of a ring, a darkness where the ring had once been. There was nothing.

I don't know if I was happy or annoyed that despite my exhaustion and my focus on the trial I couldn't help fantasizing about what she would look like undressed.

"Joe, are you still with me?"

"Sorry, I'm tired."

"I won't take up much of your time. I just wanted to introduce myself and tell you what I learned last night from Eva."

"That's one thing I don't get," I said.

"What's that?"

"Why should Eva want to help me? Wasn't Rose . . . Susannah, her sister, her kindred spirit? Not that I believe any of this, mind you."

"You have to remember Joe that a soul doesn't have any allegiance to the lives lived here on earth . . . that's all transitory. Living is about suffering, learning and moving on. It's not about accumulating money. It's not the comfort down here that matters. It's about taking chances and kindness."

"Which means?"

"She's not the least bit interested about who gets the money, Ben and Rose's children or Susannah McCreedy."

"A disinterested witness of sorts, that's nice to know."

Aurora made a face, a cute face, like a teacher who didn't have the heart to reprimand one of her favorite pupils."

"Sorry, go ahead."

"Eva says that Susannah is not controlled by Rose's soul. She makes her own decisions down here. That's how you learn."

"Which means?"

"She's not planning to save most of the money for the grandchildren. She's going to spend most of it on the Reincarnation Institute."

"I never heard of it."

"It was set up by Rose's father years ago to help people discover their past lives."

"Sort of like a cat scan of the soul?" I said.

Aurora laughed.

"He wanted to unlock the soul and bring about the end of the world so we could all return to God."

"Which makes Susannah what . . . the next messiah?"

"No, I think she's a mistake if you ask me, a freak of nature, not everything in the universe is planned or controlled, which is why I think Eva has reached out to me."

"How does Eva know all this . . . from Susannah's father?"

"Souls communicate Joe, even the ones down here. Eva says that Susannah wants to resurrect the Reincarnation Institute and make herself the head of it."

"Isn't that some kind of violation of the cosmic law?"

"It's free will Joe. Susannah controls the life down here. The soul doesn't control her. She believes that what she learned about her past life has a purpose, this purpose, and that it wasn't just an accident."

"A faulty lock on a loose spiritual door."

"Joe, I'm being serious. Rose's soul has a lot more to learn, more lives to live."

"The words of Eva?"

"Yes."

"It sounds to me," I said, struggling to keep my eyes from drifting down to her skirt, "like some souls carry their grudges to the hereafter. Maybe it's not all that different up there than it is down here."

Aurora sighed.

"That's why they return . . . all of us down here are far from perfect."

"Listen Aurora, or should I call you Betsy?"

"Whatever you're more comfortable with."

"Betsy," I said very lawyer-like, patronizing really, "You are a very charming woman and I have no doubt you believe what you say."

She cut me off with a look.

"I'm not here to convert you Joe, just to inform you of what I was told. It seemed important and there must be a reason why I'm being visited. Take it for what it's worth, isn't that what lawyers always say?"

"Thank you," I said politely, "I'm not ungrateful for your interest, but I need to get some rest."

At that point I put some files in my briefcase and we rode the elevator down together. She smelled nice as well, sort of like the beach after a warm summer day. The parking lot was deserted except for our two cars, the reporters and protesters probably assuming that I had snuck out earlier.

"Good luck tomorrow Joe."

"Thanks."

For a moment I thought about asking her out for drink. Perhaps our knees would have touched after a while and we'd forget our differences. Maybe we would drive over to my house after for some coffee. I had this feeling that we had a lot more in common than either of us realized.

It had been a long time.

But I knew I'd never ask. I'd surely regret it if it somehow made the papers that I was consulting a spiritualist or even sleeping with one in the middle of a trial like this. My practice would be destroyed. Besides, I already had more than enough regrets.

I also knew that she'd say no. She'd be sweet about it and say she'd be happy to another time and perhaps she'd really mean it.

"If I hear anything else Joe may I call you?"

"Sure."

She walked over to me and put her hand on my arm, and in a concerned tone said, "Sometimes it's hard Joe to tell the difference between what's real and what you believe."

I moved to open the car door and she stepped back.

"I know what I don't believe," I said, tossing my briefcase onto the passenger seat.

"Doubt is a very good thing sometimes Joe. Sometimes the hardest thing to do is to try to live without it."

I shrugged, she was probably right.

"I know we will speak again and I look forward to it," she said and walked to her car. It was a new red Acura so she wasn't lying about being well off.

She seemed so sweet and kind, I thought as I headed home that I'd have given anything at that moment to believe her.

Of course, I couldn't sleep. So I sat on the couch watching some mindless reality show about the CEO of Dunkin Donuts who pretends to be an hourly employee and plays Santa

Claus at the end when he takes off his uniform and reveals his Ralph Lauren three piece suit.

I called Murray and asked him to investigate the Reincarnation Institute and to see if Susannah had set up any non-profit corporations in Minnesota, Florida or New York. I could always call her back to the stand on my case to question her about it if she had.

"I'll check her bank account as well," he said, "and see what she's spending her money on other than her counsel."

"You can do that?"

"I can do anything provided I grease enough palms."

Murray promised me an answer during tomorrow's lunch break.

As I lay in bed replaying the day's cross-examination in my head, taking back questions I wish I hadn't asked and asking ones I wish I had, my thoughts kept drifting back to Aurora.

Mercifully, sleep finally overtook me.

Chapter 12 – The Opposition

"God generates beings, and sends them back over and over again, till they return to him."
— Koran

The crowd the next morning was restless. The press was bored by now with interviewing spectators and demonstrators, and the weather, even more unbearably hot and humid, was sapping everyone's energy.

Dr. Seymour was waiting in the witness room when I arrived. We had spent all day Saturday working together and I felt confident that I had polished down some of those pompous edges.

"Just remember," I said, "to look at the jury the whole time or the judge when she asks a question. Don't talk down to the jury, you'll lose them the first time you do, so try to put your answers in simple, layman's language."

"I'm ready," he said, adjusting the blue suit and red tie that I suggested he wear.

We started five minutes late because of a problem with one of the TV cameras. The courtroom felt like a sauna, and an expression of shock passed from face to face as the jurors walked in from the air-conditioned jury room.

The judge suggested that gentlemen remove their jackets because of the heat. Susannah, who was wearing a cream-colored, pants suit, took off her jacket as well. She was wearing a sleeveless blouse on top and you could see the sweat dripping off the folds of skin that hung down from her arms like hammocks.

"Counselor," Judge Shanawit said to me, "Please call your first witness."

"I call Dr. Winston Seymour to the stand."

The courtroom deputy went back to the witness room to get him.

Dr. Seymour was a small man, particularly in comparison to Susannah, but he made a tall entrance the way he strode past the spectators with long, deliberate steps, his back straight and his head held high, as he nodded at me, the judge and the jury.

The jury knew what was coming and they were clearly interested. It was the beginning of the day and they're minds were a clean slate.

We started with his credentials: Ph D in geriatric psychology from Columbia in 1980, over 30 years studying and writing about aging and the elderly and a thriving practice counseling seniors. He was an adjunct professor at Rutgers University and had so many memberships and certificates that I had to cut him off after 5 minutes.

"What inspired you to study the psychology of the elderly," I asked.

"My parents died in a car crash when I was eight and I grew up with my grandparents, so I spent a lot of time around old people."

"Your Honor," I said, "I would move Dr. Seymour as an expert on the psychology of the elderly."

"No objection," Bill said, although he requested permission to approach the bench for a sidebar.

During the whispered discussion with the judge, Bill explained that he had no problem with Dr. Seymour's qualifications as an expert, but he objected to his testimony on the ground that he had never examined Ben and therefore had no direct knowledge about his soundness of mind.

Dr. Seymour's testimony, I explained, would offer generic insights into the elderly that the jurors were free to accept or reject. Educating them about the elderly was a big part of our defense. The judge agreed and told Bill that he could raise his point during cross-examination.

The first thing I had Dr. Seymour confirm was that he had never spoken to or met with Ben Everett, his sons or Ms. McCreedy. Then I went right for the jugular.

"We have heard testimony during the course of this trial that Ben Everett, even at eighty-eight, was sharp and confident, and appeared perfectly normal when he went to restaurants, spoke to his neighbors and discussed his finances with his broker. How does that translate to other areas in an elderly person's life, if at all?"

I saw Bill itching to object and I had to be careful not to lead too much.

"How a man that old appears when dealing with the more routine aspects of life, such as talking to a neighbor, doing errands, going out to eat or even handling his own finances, which he has been doing the same way for most of his life, doesn't mean he will operate at the same high cognitive level, or anywhere near that when it comes to something unusual and more emotional."

He gave a few examples like reacting to a personal illness or a death.

"And romance, of course," Dr. Seymour said, "Certainly pursuing a romantic interest with a much younger woman would fall into what I call the moments of 'selective dementia'."

He explained that he was referring to those unusual, out of the ordinary moments where an older person's normal intelligence and caution may not work quite as well, if at all.

"And I use the term dementia in a much broader sense than the general public. It includes much more than the classic forgetfulness and temporal displacement; it also includes lack of control, excessive emotion, impulsiveness, poor decisions and poor judgment."

"Can you give the jury some examples?"

"Conversations with neighbors, talking to a broker, are all part of what I call the comfort zone. It's the last place that selective dementia usually manifests itself, at least when there isn't a physical cause. However, an offer of a miracle cure, or a winning lottery ticket, or the promise of a wife reaching out to someone from the hereafter could easily result in the kind of shock that will promote the manifestation of age-related dementia or, at minimum, a transient episode."

"Objection."

The judge thought it over.

"Overruled," she said before turning to the jury. "Ladies and gentlemen of the jury, let me remind you that what Dr. Seymour is doing is giving you his opinion as an expert with respect to the elderly in general. It is up to you to weigh the worth of his expert testimony and its applicability, if at all, to the situation here."

She looked back at me and nodded.

"The disruptive effect of love on our ability to make decisions isn't limited to the elderly, is it Dr. Seymour?"

For a fleeting instant I thought of Aurora. I wondered if she was watching.

Dr. Seymour let out one of those fake, professional laughs, too high in the throat and to even to be spontaneous and real.

"Of course not," he said, "all you have to do is read a book or watch a movie to see how foolish love often makes people act . . . at any age."

That got a flash of smiles from the jurors as well as the spectators.

"It's worse for the elderly. No one is ever the same person he was at sixty, or even seventy, particularly when it comes to a stressful or unusual situation. Appearances can be very misleading."

"Can you give me an example?"

"Sure, you read about it all the time in the newspapers; a seemingly healthy and normal woman in her late eighties, living alone, who suddenly starts loaning money to a friendly new neighbor who tells her some made-up tale of woe, while her family doesn't pick up on it despite calling a couple of times a week."

I glanced over at Bill who wanted to object, but didn't want to run the risk of being overruled. It was clear that the television camera was having an effect on Judge Shanawit.

"For many years," Dr. Seymour said without waiting for the next question, another thing I warned him against, "The elderly were not the subject of case studies the way they should have been, but that has changed over the past decade, and what the recent studies have shown is that delirium and dementia in the elderly, which encompasses the ability to make a sound decision under highly stressed or emotional circumstances, as well as the ability to recognize a compromising situation, tends to be transient, ubiquitous and fluctuating in nature."

I tried not to sigh or slap my forehead with the palm of my hand.

"Give it to me in layman's terms, Doc."

"It can be found in all of us once we get old enough and while it's somewhat unpredictable it's always lurking there. However sound an elderly person may appear when it comes to the more routine aspects of life his or her ability to process information and make a well-reasoned decision can change when it comes to a highly emotional situation; dementia can suddenly appear – flare up so to speak – and disappear just as suddenly. The death of a friend will do that or a sudden illness, certainly a romantic attachment with someone young enough to be your grandchild and who claims to be a reincarnation of your late wife could be expected to as well."

I looked over at Bill. If he didn't object now, he'd never object. It was out and impossible to undo.

I looked over at the jury. Their faces were expressionless and hot, except for juror number 6, Ira, who looked annoyed and unimpressed.

I ended with a few questions about how much Dr. Seymour was being paid for his testimony. I saw a few jurors raise their eyebrows when they heard his hourly rate.

Bill moved quickly around counsel's table as soon as I sat down. He wanted to avoid any possibility that the judge might call for a short break since he wanted to get him off the stand and out of the courtroom as quickly as possible.

"Good morning Dr. Seymour."

"Good morning counselor."

"We have never met before, have we?"

"Not that I recall."

"Have you ever testified before as an expert witness?"

"Yes, I have."

"On how many other occasions?"

"Four."

"Were they at trials like this or at depositions?"

"Two trials and two – I think they called them examinations before trial. Is that the same thing as a deposition?"

"Yes. Can you tell us about them? Let's start with the first time that you testified?"

"That was about 5 years ago."

"What was the case about?" Bill asked.

"An elderly woman had refinanced her home at what she thought was a much lower rate, but she didn't understand that the rate could jump each year and it did to the point where she quickly couldn't afford it. They were foreclosing on her home."

"What was the nature of your testimony?"

"I opined concerning her inability to fully understand the terms of the loan when she signed it, which she did through a broker . . . without an attorney."

"Did you testify at that trial?"

"Yes."

"And was your testimony based on an interview with the woman?"

"Yes, it was."

"In fact," Bill asked, "it was based on more than one interview, wasn't it?"

"Yes."

"You needed those personal interviews before you could give an opinion concerning her state of mind and the soundness of her decision, isn't that correct Dr. Seymour?"

"To give an opinion as to the soundness of her mind, yes, I needed to examine her, but not to give a general opinion concerning the ability of most women her age to fully understand the detailed documentation."

"But you didn't have to give a general opinion in that case because you actually interviewed her?"

"That's correct, because she was around to be interviewed."

Don't be too combative, I thought to myself, not right off the bat.

"How did it turn out?"

"It settled and she got to keep her house."

"How about the second time?"

"That was an examination before trial."

"How long ago?"

"About 4 years."

"What was that case about?"

"An elderly man had gifted a large sum of money to his caregiver, a nurse's aide, and the family sued to get it back."

"What was the nature of your testimony there Dr. Seymour?"

"The man's inability to make a sound decision with respect to the gift, in effect, to resist the entreaties of his caregiver, a person he'd come to depend on."

"Did you interview him at length?"

"Yes."

"More than once?"

"Yes."

"Was he on a number of different medications?"

"Yes."

"How did that case turn out?"

"Settled as well."

"By the way Dr. Seymour," Bill asked, and I always warn witnesses to be wary of questions that start out by the way, "did Ben Everett take any medications?"

"I don't know."

"Do you know if Ben Everett was under the treatment of a doctor or psychiatrist?"

"I'm not sure about a doctor, but I know he wasn't being seen by a psychiatrist."

"How do you know that?"

"From counsel," he said, gesturing in my direction.

"When you testified earlier about the elderly having these transient moments of dementia where they might have difficulty making a sound decision, is it fair to say that those moments generally pass?"

"Not in the way you are suggesting."

"I haven't suggested anything yet Dr. Seymour," Bill said. "All I'm asking is whether those transient moments of dementia pass."

"They can."

"Otherwise you wouldn't call them transient, would you? The very definition of transient is short-lived or passing quickly."

"That may be the dictionary definition, but it's not the psychological one. Transient moments of dementia are called transient because they don't pervade every waking moment, but are either limited in time or confined to a specific situation. Once an episode has occurred in a certain circumstance it tends to continue to manifest itself in that circumstance, sometimes in that circumstance only."

I liked the answer, even though he still sounded a little too argumentative.

"Once that moment passes Doctor - that transient moment - isn't that elderly individual capable of understanding what he's just done, and accepting or correcting it?"

"That's what I thought you were getting at earlier," Dr. Seymour said, "and the answer is on occasion, but not in most cases. A decision made or an action taken during a transient moment of dementia usually remains, in effect, unalterable in the mind of the elderly victim, if I may use that word.

"That impaired judgment will often remain as a sort of subconscious justification or rationalization. It's not easy for people half that age to understand and fully appreciate something foolish that they've done and to try to correct it. It's that much more difficult when you're eighty-eight."

"Often, but not always."

"Yes, not always."

"And you have no idea in this instance, assuming Ben Everett had a transient moment of dementia when he married Ms. McCreedy, whether he was able to fully appreciate what he had done and understand and accept it afterward."

"I don't."

"And that ability to recover or correct something foolish, as you put it, would vary from individual to individual."

"Yes, depending in part on one's age and how unusual the circumstance being presented."

Bill took a little stroll in front of the witness, rubbing his chin as he did so.

"You used the word foolish in your answer, the ability to fully appreciate that something you did was foolish, do you remember that?"

"Yes."

"It's the same word you used earlier on direct when you talked about how love makes all of us do foolish things, whatever the age, do you remember saying that Dr. Seymour?"

"I do."

"Love may make someone stand under an apartment window in the middle of the night singing a love song?"

"Exactly."

"Or walk ten miles in a blizzard?"

"Yes."

"Or spend more than he or she can afford on a birthday gift?"

"Of course."

"Or make someone your beneficiary in the event of your death, you'd call that a foolish thing to do for love as well, wouldn't you Doctor?"

"In some cases."

"The foolish things that we do for love doesn't cheapen or eliminate the sentiment and the truth of what motivates us to do it, does it Doctor?"

"I'm not sure I follow," Dr. Seymour said.

I could see him walking right into Bill's left hook.

"If we do it for love, Doctor, that doesn't mean we've lost our senses, it just means we're following our heart, doesn't it?"

"If we do it for love and not because we're confused or lost. Foolish was probably the wrong word to use in this context since it sounds too romantic . . . like a Hollywood movie. Perhaps a better word would be doing something stupid or regrettable because some form of dementia has the better of us, something we wouldn't do if we were able to think more soundly about it."

Bill put his pad down on the table and turned to look at Susannah. He looked pleased with himself; any backtracking is good. Attorneys on trial are very insecure people - they're satisfied with the flimsiest of promises, a small nod, a barely perceptible smile, even a witness who admits he used the wrong word. Bill knew it was time to move on.

"Tell me about the third time you testified, Dr. Seymour."

"It was another examination before trial. An elderly woman addicted to the Home Shopping Network."

"What happened there?"

"She bought much more than she could ever hope to pay for. Most of it sat unopened. She was being sued for the balances due."

"Did you interview her?"

"Yes."

"What did you conclude?" Bill asked.

"That she was normal in most everyday respects, at least that's how she appeared to her family and neighbors, but when it came to the late nights, when she felt the emptiness the most, she was unable to resist the TV solicitations."

"That case also settled," Dr. Seymour said, trying to anticipate Bill's next question.

"That interview was important, wasn't it?" Bill asked, "Because all people are different, with different abilities and problems, no matter what their age."

"Of course that's true," Dr. Seymour said, "But what we are talking about here is our diminishing ability to make sound judgments as we age, I'd say that happens to ninety-nine percent of us as we get older to one degree or another."

I tried not to wince when he said that. He'd never used a ninety-nine number like that in any of our prior conversations.

Bill stood still, his hand on his chin, his eyes focused on the witness.

"You wouldn't sit here Dr. Seymour and say that 99% of men over 85 are unable to make a sound decision?"

"No, of course not, how sound that decision is would vary greatly from individual to individual and from situation to situation."

"Exactly," Bill said, turning to the jury, "and you have no idea what kind of individual Ben was?"

"No," Dr. Seymour said, "but I know the unusual circumstance he faced."

Good answer I thought, praying that Dr. Seymour was finished.

"Of course, there are always exceptions," Dr. Seymour said, "even in emotional circumstances such as this, but they are few and far between at the age of eighty-eight."

It was all I could do to keep from banging my head on the table.

"Precisely my point Doctor Seymour," Bill said. "It is possible that Ben Everett was one of those exceptions, a man with a firm grip on his reasoning and reactions even in this unusual circumstance?"

"Anything is possible."

"And the fact that Ben was so capable in every other aspect of his life, wouldn't that suggest to you that he might have been one of those exceptions?"

"As I said earlier, how one handles the day to day routines is not necessarily indicative of how that same person will react when it comes to an unusual emotional event."

"But you don't know in this case because you never met Ben. You never took the time to speak to his wife, Susannah, or any of his children. You never tried to interview one of his neighbors."

"I did not, although I do know that a twenty-four year old professing to be in love with an eighty-eight year old is hard enough for a man that age to process, but add to it that she claims to be a reincarnation of the man's late wife and you have created a circumstance so unusual and so profoundly disturbing, particularly at Mr. Everett's end stage of life, that it's highly improbable in my opinion that he could make any decision in the same manner and with the same intelligence he might bring to bear when talking to his neighbor about whether or not he's planning to attend a clubhouse social or to his broker about whether or not to buy or sell a stock."

Redeemed, I thought, a bit pedantic, but a good answer. I looked at the jury for any reaction, a faint smile or slightly raised eyebrow, but there was none. They all looked like they were beginning to wilt. They clearly got the point of Dr. Seymour's testimony and had quite some time ago.

"Tell us about the last time that you testified as an expert."

"It was at a trial like this."

"What was it about?"

"The capacity of an elderly gentleman to execute a codicil to his will."

This was the one case I knew Bill would have a field day with. A 90-year old man had amended his will shortly before his death disinheriting one of his four children-his youngest son. Dr. Seymour testified on behalf of the disinherited son arguing that the codicil was the result of undue influence and an unsound mind.

"The jury disagreed with you in that case, Doctor, isn't that correct?" Bill asked.

"Yes."

"They found he was of sound mind when he made the change."

"Yes, because he was the wayward son who had borrowed a lot of money from his father over the years without ever paying any of it back. Since the loans were being forgiven in the new will, I guess the jury felt he wasn't being completely cut out."

"You're just speculating now doctor, you don't know what the jury was thinking, do you?"

"No, but that was what the other three sons argued, and it wasn't a radical change, not like the will at issue here."

"I didn't ask you that question Dr. Seymour. My question was that whether or not you knew what the jury was thinking. You weren't in there during their deliberations?"

"No, I was not."

"And you didn't question them after the verdict, did you?"

"No."

"You testified in that case – just as you did here - about the father's doubtful soundness of mind based on generalities and, in particular, his age, without having ever spoken with him?"

"That's always impossible to do when it comes to a will contest because the issue arises after the person has died. My testimony was based on scientific studies and thirty years of practice. I applied general principles of elder psychology."

"The same as you have here?"

"That's right."

Bill stood quietly a moment rubbing his chin. Then he walked back to his seat and stood there like he was done, although I knew he wasn't. He wanted to go out on a higher note than that.

"What was the emotional event you identified in that case that triggered the transient episode of dementia," Bill said with as much irony as he could muster, slowly and carefully pronouncing each of the last four words.

"I'm not sure I recall."

"It wasn't his failure to pay back the loans, because that took place over many years, was it?"

"That's not entirely correct . . . that was clearly a factor."

I bit the inside of my lip. I told him more than once not be too cagey. He knew the answer because he brought it up during our prep session, and I warned him that Bill will have done his homework and spoken to one of the attorneys on the case.

"It was because his youngest son had forgotten to call him on his ninetieth birthday, wasn't that it?"

Dr. Seymour shook his head slowly up and down.

"Right, I remember that now, but that was only part of it – the straw so to speak that broke the camel's back."

Bill looked over at the jury.

"His son forgot to call him on his ninetieth birthday," Bill repeated, "and you testified that was enough to trigger one of your episodes of transient dementia?"

"At that age we are like eggshells and crack much more easily than we do now. In that case we were talking about an emotional strain that was many years in the making. Ninety is a milestone birthday and has great significance to someone near the end of life. It carried a lot of emotional baggage with it, including years of disappointments."

Dr. Seymour went on before Bill had a chance to ask another question.

"Of course, in this case we have something much more significant, a marriage to a younger woman claiming to be a reincarnation of his late wife and the disinheritance of not one wayward son, but an entire family."

Bill walked back to his seat. He knew that he had asked one question too many.

"Is there anything short of ordering dinner at a restaurant, watching television or selling stocks and bonds," he asked, "that isn't in your opinion enough of an emotional event to affect the soundness of an elderly person's decision?"

I saw alternate number 1, Rose, out of the corner of my eye leaning forward in her seat.

"Of course there are many things. It's a fact specific analysis that varies from person to person and situation to situation, and depends as well on how significant the decision is."

I would have signaled to Dr. Seymour to stop there if I could have, perhaps by drawing my hand across my throat.

"In the case of the disinherited son," Dr. Seymour continued, "the jury undoubtedly came to believe that the father's decision was sound in large part because he'd given him more than enough money during his lifetime, by way of all the loans."

Bill nodded and couldn't help a little smile.

"So if Ben Everett came to believe in the eternal soul and reincarnation, a belief held by billions of people around the world, and came to believe that Susannah was connected to him in some way that was larger than this life, and decided to change his will in recognition of that belief, could it be that he also knew what he was doing when he decided that his sons already had more than enough?"

I thought about objecting since a statement like that belonged in summation, but I hadn't objected so far and I didn't want the jury to think that Bill was scoring any points.

"Not in my opinion, not under those extreme circumstances."

"Are you saying that any person who comes to believe late in life in the eternal soul and acts on that belief is incapable of making a sound decision?"

"I'm not saying that. I might feel differently in terms of the soundness of his belief if he had come to it after study and participation in some sort of religious activity and was able to talk about it to his family and friends."

"Do you believe in the eternal soul, Dr. Seymour?"

I stood up and objected. It was far too personal a question. Dr. Seymour's religion was not at issue here.

"I think I will allow it in the context of the witness' testimony."

"I do."

"Does that render you incompetent to make a decision about your assets?"

"It might if I believed that the woman who showed up to clean my house was an angel or had my mother's soul and therefore should get all my money, particularly if I was sick or elderly."

That got a few chuckles in the audience, but not one juror smiled. I think they'd had just about enough of Dr. Seymour.

"Would your answer be different Dr. Seymour if in fact it were true?"

"If what were true?"

"If reincarnation was true; if the eternal soul that you believe in was indeed returned to earth to live again?"

"This is way beyond my pay grade counselor."

Bill smiled and nodded.

"You don't know whether Ben was convinced in part by all the things Susannah knew about Rose and his life with Rose, private, personal things that she couldn't have found out from anyone else?"

"I do not, although I know that at his age she wouldn't have needed very much since people that old tend to be very gullible . . . hence the high incidence of fraud against the elderly."

Dr. Seymour was circling back well to our talking points.

"You're not saying that all religious beliefs, whether arrived at when younger or older are based on fraud, are you Dr. Seymour."

"No, of course not."

At this point, Bill asked for a short break to review his notes to see if he had any further questions.

My Three Sons and I adjourned to our witness room.

"Maybe it's time to make her an offer," Mitch said to his brothers. "We are rolling the dice here with a lot at stake."

"Over my dead body," Jeff said with Peter nodding rapidly in agreement.

"Bill said she's not interested in settling," I reminded Mitch.

"Because she hasn't heard the offer," he said. "I'm talking about offering something like a half-million dollars."

"You're fucking nuts," Peter said.

"Is there a chance she might win?" Mitch asked me.

"There's always a chance when you're before a jury."

"What are the odds? Give me a ballpark."

"Ten to twenty percent," I said.

It was probably lower than that but no litigator is going to give any guarantees when it comes to a jury.

Mitch looked at his brothers. "So you're willing to gamble fifty million on five to one odds?"

"You're damn straight," Peter said. "Eighty percent chance of winning, I like those odds. Besides, I'm not giving that crook a dime."

Mitch shrugged.

With that came the clerk's knock on the door and we went back into the courtroom to finish Dr. Seymour's testimony.

"Just a couple of more questions Dr. Seymour," Bill said, as soon as the jury took their seats, "If there was no claim of reincarnation here, just love, would your opinion be the same?"

"For an eighty-eight year old man like Ben, I would say yes."

"Is that because you believe that an eighty-eight-year old man can't be of sound mind if he falls in love with a younger woman?"

"I'd certainly have my concerns if she were in her mid-twenties."

"How about thirty?"

"Yes."

"Forty?"

"It depends on the circumstances."

"Does love play any role for you in defining those circumstances?"

"I suppose it could, yes."

"It could," Bill repeated, turning toward to the jury.

While I couldn't see his face I was fairly certain that his eyebrows were raised and his eyes wide open for the jury's benefit.

"Isn't it all about love?"

"What?"

"The decisions we make about who we want to be with and how we want to allocate what we have after we're gone."

"I suppose."

"And wouldn't you say Doctor that love is at best unpredictable?"

"I'm not sure I know what you're getting at."

"We don't always get to pick who we fall in love with, do we?"

"I suppose not."

"Or how and when?"

"Yes."

"Size, shape, color, age, religion, all irrelevant when that deep spiritual connection is made?"

"This was not a deep spiritual connection," Dr. Seymour said. "This was not love."

"And how do you know that?"

"It doesn't make sense."

"Love doesn't always make sense, does it?"

"I think it does when you're that old."

"Are you an expert on love as well, Doctor?"

"No," Dr. Seymour said with a smile, "And I don't know who is."

The spectators chuckled and the jury leaned back on their seats.

"Thank you," Bill said, sitting down, "No further questions."

I sprang up.

"Just a few questions, Your Honor."

"You learned during your review of the case, Dr. Seymour, that Mr. Everett never told anyone not even his sons about Ms. McCreedy's claim that she was his late wife's reincarnate?"

"Yes, Ms. McCreedy's deposition transcript stated that."

"What did that say to you?"

"It confirms what I have been saying. Mr. Everett couldn't hide that his new wife was twenty-four years old, but he didn't tell anyone the most important part . . . that she claimed to be carrying the soul of his late wife. If Mr. Everett was thinking along sound lines, and not in the grips of some sort of age-related dementia, transient or more pervasive, he would have told his children why he got married and what he believed. Hiding something as significant as that is an indicator of just how confused and unsure he was."

"No further questions," I said, returning to counsel's table and sitting down.

"A brief re-cross," Bill said, jumping up without waiting for the judge to respond.

"Dr. Seymour, it isn't unusual in our society to conceal things we may believe of a religious or spiritual nature, is it?"

"It depends on the things."

"Some people believe in guardian angels, but they don't go around talking about it?"

"I don't know."

"You're not an expert in guardian angels?"

That got some smiles in the jury box and titters in the gallery.

"No, I'm not."

"People keep secrets all the time, don't they? They avoid stepping on cracks or knock silently on wood without announcing to the world their superstitions?"

"This wasn't a superstition. This was a radical, transforming belief."

"Like finding God?" Bill asked.

"In a way."

"Most people keep their own counsel when it comes to their religious beliefs, wouldn't you say that Dr. Seymour."

"I don't know I've never made a study of it."

"Ben was a smart man," Bill continued, "and knew exactly how people would react to a statement that his new wife was a reincarnation of his former wife. Isn't the very fact that he didn't talk about it right away, but wanted to wait a while until his family got to know Susannah a little better compelling evidence of a reasoned and sound decision?"

"Or confusion . . . or pressure from his new, young wife."

"Just a few more questions," Bill said, looking up at the judge after she cleared her throat rather loudly.

"You don't consider people crazy based on their religious beliefs, do you Doctor?" Bill asked.

"It depends. If someone believes that he is God I would."

That got a few more laughs among the spectators.

"What about someone who believes in reincarnation, you wouldn't automatically think that they're crazy?"

"No."

"And that's because there are millions or better yet billions of people who do believe in reincarnation?"

"I don't know how many do," Dr. Seymour answered, "but I'm sure it's quite a lot."

"Thank you Doctor," Bill said, "no further questions."

"The witness is excused," the judge quickly said in case I had any ideas about another bite of re-direct.

"Call your next witness counselor?"

I stood up and called Mitch Everett to the stand. As he was sworn in, Mitch's posture was perfect, he had a pleasant, but serious, look on his face; he was a natural. Of course, it's always easier when you don't have all that much to say and all you plan on doing is telling the truth.

After going through the introductory stuff, name, education, family and employment, I got right down to business.

"Tell us, Mr. Everett, about your mother Rose Everett."

"My mother was a wonderful woman. She was the best listener I've ever met, which is why everyone liked to talk to her, my father in particular. He wasn't a big talker, except when it came to my mom."

Mitch rubbed his ear with his finger, something I noticed that he sometimes did when he was nervous.

"She was a little old-fashioned the way she dressed and the fact that she didn't like to travel far from home. She loved to read and she used to write little comments inside the cover of the books after she finished them," Mitch said with a smile, "about the characters and the story.

"She was the first one there with a casserole when something bad happened to a neighbor because for her it was all about family and friends. She had a certain resolve when it came to my dad and my two brothers and me."

"What do you mean?"

"She watched over us all the time, every minute, picking lint off my sweaters before she let me leave for school, cutting off loose threads like she was afraid I might be the one to unravel if she didn't. She did everything for us, too much if you ask me now, but that's the way mothers were back then."

I thought I glimpsed a slight nod from juror number 1, Millie, who was about the same age as Mitch, and my Rose, alternate number 1.

"There was nothing more important to her than us . . . and nothing more important to the three of us growing up than her."

"How did she die?"

"Slowly and painfully from cancer," Mitch said. The tension in his face brought on by that memory was very evident and clearly sincere. "She died on November 22, 1982."

"How did your father handle it?"

"Not well, none of us did. He talked about her constantly. We were able to get on with our lives, it was easier for us since we had wives and families of our own; the way it should be with children. It was harder for him.

"My father had retired a few years earlier and they had just moved down to Florida when she got sick. He refused to date any of the women who started chasing him after she passed.

"We told him it was OK, we encouraged it. We thought it would be good for him to find someone – a contemporary - to hang out with, if only to go out to dinner and a movie, but he just couldn't bring himself to do it. He couldn't get over my mother.

He didn't want to. He had his one great love, he told me, and now it was all about his children and grandchildren . . . and great grandchildren, he was hoping to see a couple of those as well."

I stood silently for a few moments to let the emotions sink in.

"Did you ever talk with your father about his finances and his estate?"

"Sure," Mitch said, "He usually spoke to me about finances rather than Jeff or Peter. He used to joke that I was the only one who ever read the business section of the paper. My brothers spend a lot more time in the sports section."

"What did you talk about with your father?"

"He made sure that I knew where his accounts were. He talked about how he wanted his estate divided when he died–equally between the three of us, but with each of the grandchildren getting twenty-five thousand when they turned twenty-one."

"Was that in his will?"

"His original will–yes, just as he told me."

"Did he give you an executed copy of that will to hold?"

"Yes."

"You still have it."

"I do, I gave it to you."

I went back to counsel's table and picked it up.

"Is this it?"

"Yes."

"I offer it into evidence."

"No objection," Bill said, standing up.

"The prior will is now in evidence," the judge stated.

"May I pass it around for the jury to look at, Your Honor?"

"Go ahead."

I handed it to the bailiff who handed it to the jury forelady.

"Go on, counselor."

"What else did you and your father talk about with respect to his finances?"

"We talked about the investments he was making. He was pretty conservative, far more heavily invested in bonds than stocks. He used to call himself the turtle investor, slow and steady. He was always joking that his investment goal was to make sure his three sons had enough to retire the day he died. I think he wanted to make sure we got to spend a lot of those years with our wives, instead of working too long like he did, my mother died so soon after he retired."

"How was he with his money?" I asked.

"What do you mean?"

"Was he a spendthrift or was he careful?"

"Oh, he was pretty tight-fisted when it came to himself. He was driving a ten- year old Lincoln when he died. But he was always generous with us and the grandchildren."

I walked over toward the jury, stopping between Mitch and the jury box.

"How was your father's mental state the last few years of his life?"

"He was pretty good about most of the everyday things, a little forgetful sometimes, and he repeated himself a lot, but that was to be expected at his age. He'd slowed down considerably, I mean in the way he moved around. I wanted to get him to stop driving because his reaction time was getting a little scary, but he took one of those elderly driving courses when his license came up for renewal and they told him he was OK to drive. I'm sure he would have been able to avoid that tire five years earlier."

"How about emotionally?"

"Almost all of his close friends had died over the past five years, so that was a traumatic period, but things had been pretty quiet on the death and illness front by the time he meet Ms. McCreedy."

"How often did you and your father speak?"

"At least twice a week, usually more, but it was much less often after he married her."

"What did you speak about before the marriage?"

"The kids, the job, my mother, he liked to reminisce about her, how he was feeling, what he was doing, his accounts, the old women down there – they still chased after him--things like that."

"How did he sound during those calls?"

"Fine most of the time, a little lonely sometimes, I think he was running out of people to reminisce with. He looked forward to our visits down to Florida, especially from the grandchildren. It's got to be hard at that age. We wanted him to move up to New York to be closer to us, but he didn't like the cold."

"Did the telephone conversations change after the marriage?"

Mitch nodded slowly.

"You have to answer verbally," I said.

"I'm sorry, yes. They changed after the marriage."

"How?"

"Well, there were less of them for one thing and the conversations got shorter. He asked about the kids, but that was about it. He barely answered my questions and it sounded sometimes like he was being prompted, like someone was whispering in the background. But I didn't push him. What could I do, we didn't hear a word about what was going on until after he was already married. You can imagine what a surprise that was."

"By the way," I asked, "did he ever mention to you that he had his new wife sign a waiver of her right to one-third of his estate?"

"No, never."

I took a little stroll toward my seat to let that answer sink in. I could feel the camera at the back of the courtroom focused on me.

"When did you first hear about Ms. McCreedy?"

"Not her in particular, but I remember my father mentioning that Alma, the woman who had been cleaning his house for years, had to quit for a knee operation. I reminded him a couple of times to send her flowers, although I'm not sure if he ever did. He told me that a younger woman had replaced her, someone from the Midwest, that's all he said."

"Did he say anything more about her?"

"That's it, other than that she was much younger than Alma and didn't mind listening to his stories. I think he was happy to have a new ear."

"What stories?"

"About my mother mostly, it didn't take much to get him talking about her."

"When was the next time you heard about her?"

"After they were married," Mitch said.

"How did you learn about the marriage?"

"I called one day late in the evening to see how he was feeling since I was having these funny feelings after a couple of our recent calls like he wanted to get off the phone as quickly as possible, like there was something he wasn't telling me, like the doctor had told him something and he didn't want me to know. He just didn't sound like himself.

"So I called late one night, it had to be after nine, figuring he'd be relaxed watching TV or getting ready for bed and more willing to talk. It was really strange because a woman answered the telephone. For a moment I thought I had dialed the wrong number, but she said no and quickly put my father on the phone."

"Did she introduce herself?"

"No, she sounded a bit surprised that I called."

"I asked him who that was – I was a little nervous that something had happened he wasn't telling me about, maybe he'd fallen and had to have a night nurse. I asked him if he was all right and he said yes. So I asked him who that was and he told me her name, Susannah. That was the first time I'd heard her name. I asked him if she was a nurse. He said she was the woman who had been cleaning his house. I asked him why she was working there so late and he said that they'd just gotten married, just like that, as if he were telling me about the weather or the latest Yankee score."

"How did you respond?"

"I didn't. I was dumbfounded. I didn't know what to say at first."

"So what did you say?"

"The maid, I said, you married the maid. He didn't respond. I know that was a stupid thing to say, but I really wasn't thinking. I was in shock so I asked him how old she was."

"How did he respond to that?"

"He got annoyed. He told me her age didn't matter and that she was much older than she looked. Then he said he had to go because they had just gotten back from dinner and hung up."

"What did you do?"

"I called my brothers."

"Then what?"

"I called him back the next morning."

"How did that conversation go?"

"He wasn't very talkative. He said that he was tired of being alone."

"Had he complained about being alone before?"

"Not really, not much, I'm sure he was lonely, who wouldn't be after all those years, but he never talked much about it. It was his choice over the years not to date or remarry. I know he missed my mom, but the only time he ever really complained was after the grandchildren had visited and the house got quiet again."

"I know I just asked about this, but did he mention the alleged waiver of her spousal right to one-third of his estate in that first call or any call thereafter?"

"No, never."

"What were your concerns?"

"Well, aside from his health, I was suspicious, concerned that she'd try to loot his life savings and leave him penniless. You read about things like that all the time."

"Objection," Bill said.

"The jury will ignore that last remark," the judge said.

"How did he sound when you called over the next couple of days?"

"OK in terms of the words he used, but he clearly didn't want to talk about it or to me, not the way he normally did. He sounded sort of flat, his answers were, I don't know how to put it, certainly not what you'd expect from a happy newlywed. I told him that I wanted to come down for a visit."

"What did he say?"

"Not right now, he said, since they were thinking of taking a little honeymoon cruise."

"Did you eventually go down?"

"About two weeks later."

"Where did you stay?"

"Usually I stayed with him, but this time I stayed in a nearby hotel. He suggested it. I wasn't going to argue, I mean I hadn't even met her yet . . . and she was young enough to be my daughter."

"Can you describe that first meeting?"

"I came over for lunch. The table was set; it was very formal. She was pleasant enough, hovering behind my father like my mother used to."

I had to bite my tongue when he said that.

"She was filling up his plate, waiting on him hand and foot. She was clearly trying to impress me."

"Did he or she say anything about your mother or reincarnation?" I quickly asked.

"No, not one word, the first time I heard the word reincarnation was when we filed this lawsuit to try to stop her from getting everything under this supposedly new will."

He said supposedly with as much disdain as he could muster.

"What was discussed at that lunch?"

"Not much, I didn't want to be confrontational, not in front of her. We discussed the kids, the weather, the Yankees, nothing significant. I was waiting until I could get my father alone."

"Were you able to get him alone?"

"Not on that trip. Really, I was never alone with my father again, and I came down three other times. She was always there. The only time I got to speak with him alone was on the telephone and it always felt like she was standing behind him while we talked."

"What makes you say that?"

"Because the conversations were different, they were very short, and sometimes I heard whispering in the background. He gave mostly one word answers to my questions, fine to just about everything. He still asked about the kids, but getting him to respond in any kind of detail about what was going on with him was like pulling teeth."

"Did he talk about his finances after the marriage, the way he used to?"

"No."

"Did you ask?"

"I asked him what was happening with his investments and what he was doing with respect to her."

He stared at Susannah when he said that. She just sat there smiling sweetly like she didn't have a care in the world.

"How did he respond?"

"He said not to worry about it that he had everything under control."

"Were you worried?"

"Of course I was worried, we all were. Here was this young woman who came out of nowhere. He married her, what . . . a month after meeting her, but what could we do? We weren't going to try to get him committed or anything like that. He still made sense on the telephone and he was certainly old enough to make his own decisions."

"You believed that then," I said, "Do you believe that now?"

"No I don't, now that I know the line she was handing him about being a reincarnation of my mother. I know my father, I've known him my whole life; he would never give away everything he'd spent a lifetime accumulating, which he had been saving for years for his children and grandchildren. He wouldn't do that to his family, reincarnation or no reincarnation, it wouldn't matter. And I know my mother, she'd never ask, she'd never want the money to go anywhere but to her children."

Mitch shifted uncomfortably in his seat and stared right at Susannah.

"All you have to do is look at her to know she's not my mother."

"Objection."

"Sustained, Mr. Everett, please confine your answers to the questions."

"Sorry, Your Honor."

I walked slowly back to counsel's table. I had more questions to ask, but I wasn't sure it was necessary at this point. I liked the way it would end if I stopped now and I figured I could make up anything I missed on re-direct.

"Mr. Clasen?" the judge said, "we need a question."

What more could Mitch really say, I wondered.

"No further questions, Your Honor."

"Counselor, your witness."

Bill started gathering up his papers, caught no doubt by surprise by my sudden ending. All eyes were on him as he stood up still flipping through his notepad and walked toward the podium.

"Mr. Everett, your mother never talked about her sister Eva, did she?"

"Not to me, not until the very end."

"She spent most of her life at Pilgrim State Hospital, a mental institution?"

"That's my understanding."

"Did you ever hear anyone talk about her?"

"Only my mother shortly before she died."

"She felt guilty about not visiting her, isn't that correct?"

"Correct."

"Yet Ms. McCreedy knew all about Eva and your mother's feelings of guilt, didn't she?"

"Yes."

"How do you explain that?"

"My father."

"Did you ever hear your father talk about it with anyone?"

"No."

"He didn't even talk about it with you during the twenty-five years after your mother died, did he?"

"No, but if she convinced him she was my mother's reincarnation, he wouldn't have thought he was telling her anything she didn't already know."

Good answer, I thought, exactly the way we had discussed it.

Bill put his hand to his chin. I knew where he was going I hoped Mitch did as well.

"So if I follow what you just said, you're saying that your father must have believed that Ms. McCreedy was a reincarnate."

"I suppose so, I'm sure she convinced him of that."

"Otherwise he wouldn't have talked with her about Eva."

"That's right."

"Do you believe Susannah is a reincarnate of your mother?"

"Of course not."

"So you don't believe it's possible that she knew about Eva from seeing into her past life?"

"I certainly do not."

"But you have no way of knowing for sure whether it's actually true or not."

"I don't believe there's an ounce of truth to what that woman is claiming."

"And that's your sincere belief?"

"Yes."

"And if someone holds a belief different from yours, does that mean that their mind is unsound?"

"If it's about her being my mother's reincarnate absolutely."

"Does that apply to the billions of people around the world who believe that they are reincarnates as well?"

"I don't think any of those billions claim to know who they were in a prior life. I'm talking about this one twenty-four year old woman who claims she was once my mother."

Bill nodded slowly, his chin resting on his hand.

"Do you know whether Susannah sincerely believes it?"

"I doubt it," Mitch said.

"But you don't know, do you? That's what the jury will have to decide."

"Objection," I said.

"Sustained," the judge said. "Ladies and gentlemen of the jury, I will frame the issues that you have to decide, not counsel."

"Sorry, Your Honor," Bill said, backing away from Mitch and looking down at his notes. "Do you know Mr. Everett whether there is a soul and an afterlife?"

When Mitch didn't answer right away, Bill added, "What I mean is you don't claim to have the definitive answer to that question-a question that has baffled mankind for millenniums, do you?"

"No."

"You don't know for sure one way or another."

"I know what I believe."

"Exactly Mr. Everett, it's all a question of belief, isn't it?"

"I suppose . . . when it comes to that."

Bill looked over at the jury.

"Just a few more questions," Bill said. "During Susannah's deposition, as well as during her testimony here, did she say anything about your mother that was incorrect? Did she get a date wrong, or a name wrong, or an event wrong?"

"Not that I can recall."

"In fact everything she said about Rose's life was completely on target, wasn't it?"

"More or less."

"From the chamomile tea that she liked to drink to her feelings of guilt about her sister, Eva?"

"She had a lot of time to study."

Bill smiled without rising to the bait.

"Let me ask you Mr. Everett, did you ever feel déjà vu, feel like you've been someplace before although you can't remember being there?"

"Who hasn't?"

"Do you believe that could have some basis in fact? Perhaps offering some evidence of reincarnation?"

"No."

"Do you believe that people who do believe that are crazy?"

"No."

"So if your father came to believe it that wouldn't make him crazy, would it?"

"If he believed in reincarnation . . . no . . . but if he believed that this woman was once my mother I'd say he was crazy."

"No further questions," Bill said walking slowly over to counsel's table and sitting down.

"A brief re-direct," I said, shooting up and walking toward Mitch.

"After the marriage, who answered the phone when you called?"

"She did."

"Did your father ever answer it first?"

"It was always her."

I looked over at the jurors, a solemn bunch, even jurors 4 and 5, Matt and Ira, only my favorite, alternate 1, Rose, my 74-year old widow, made eye contact. I couldn't resist offering another short prayer for either 4 or 5 to take sick, nothing life threatening, maybe an appendicitis attack or a mild case of pneumonia, just enough to excuse them from the jury.

"Did she ever talk to you on the telephone when she answered?"

"Not much more than hello and I'll go get him."

"Doesn't that seem a little strange for someone who thought she had your mother's soul? Wouldn't you think that she'd want to talk a bit with her son from a prior life?"

"Objection."

"Sustained."

"Did she ever ask you about your brothers or your children, her grandchildren from her supposed prior life?"

"She did not."

I turned around and looked at Susannah. She smiled back at me.

"No further questions," I said.

"You can step down," the judge said before Bill could think of any re-cross. "Call your next witness."

"We call Shelly Burger."

That got Bill's attention; a surprise fact witness will do that. Susannah hardly looked up from her hands, as she studied her nails the way people often do when they need a different focal point to escape from the moment.

The courtroom deputy brought Ms. Burger in from the witness room. She wore thick glasses and a frown, like it was all she ever wore, something she put on the first thing every morning and didn't take off until it was time for bed.

"Ms. Burger, are you aware what this case is about?"

"Yes, I've read the newspapers."

"Four months ago, on February 12th, your parents were supposed to have witnessed a new will signed by Ben Everett."

"That's what I understand."

"When did you parents die?"

"About two months later on April 8th and April 11th, my mother first, then my father; they went three days apart."

"What did they die of?"

"They were both in their late nineties, neither of them in good health." She spoke with very little emotion. She sounded more tired than sad. "Their hearts just gave out."

"What was their last year like?"

"It was hard. The last ten years were hard. They needed a lot of help. I was there almost every day."

"What was their eyesight like the last few years?" I asked.

"They were both almost completely blind. They could see the shape of things that were in front of their faces if the light was good, even then they couldn't see very clearly."

"How about their hearing?"

"Pretty bad as well, you had to shout, although they seemed to hear me well enough. The doctors said that was common."

"What was common?"

"That they could hear their own child better than anyone else; I guess that comes from listening to my voice for so long."

"Were they able to recognize people from a distance?"

"No, not from a distance, not even in the same room; I brought a cousin over on one occasion and it took forever for me to get them to realize who she was."

"Did they know any of the neighbors?"

"They used to, they lived there for over thirty years, but the neighbors they knew had all changed; died or moved into nursing homes. My parents refused to leave. They outlived everyone who was there when they first moved in, so they really didn't know anyone at the end."

"Do you know whether or not they knew Ben Everett?"

"I'd never heard the name mentioned before and I don't recall ever meeting him, and I've spent quite a lot of time there over the past few years, every afternoon actually after work. Of course, I spent my time in the house with them and around the corner in that community can be like five miles."

Ms. Burger looked over at the jury and sighed, some of the jurors, the female ones, seemed to sigh along with her.

"Do you think they were capable of recognizing Ben Everett and witnessing his signature in February?"

"Objection," Bill said, rising quickly to his feet.

"Sustained," the judge said after a moment's hesitation.

"Would your parents have been able to see Mr. Everett?"

"I don't see how."

"Would they have been likely to open the door to Mr. Everett and Ms. McCreedy if they came knocking?"

"If they could hear them knocking. They liked visitors and they would have been happy to help. They'd be happy to do anything for the company. If they were asked to sign their names to a car loan I'm sure that they would have."

"So you were concerned that they'd sign just about anything?"

"Yes, that's why I put a non-solicitation sign on the door."

"Would they have asked for some identification from the man whose signature they were supposed to be witnessing to verify that he was indeed Ben Everett?"

Ms. Berger's lips turned up, not quite a smile, but as near as her face would allow.

"They were like little children at that point. They would do pretty much anything you asked them to do."

I walked over with a copy of the will.

"Let me show you the will and the witness page," I said, "Can you identify your parents' signatures?"

"Their handwriting had become almost illegible over the past five years," she said. "I got a power of attorney a few years back so I could do all their banking and pay their bills."

She studied the signature page.

"Of course, it looks very different than it used to. They used to have such good penmanship. My mother was a second grade teacher and believed in large rounded letters."

She held the page up to the light.

"I can't be sure. It looks a little like the way they wrote, although they hadn't signed their name for me in quite a while, not since I got the power of attorney."

"So you can't say for sure either way?"

"No, I'm just not sure."

"Have you ever seen Ms. McCreedy before?" I asked.

She leaned around me to get a better view and I stepped aside.

"No, I don't believe so."

"Have you ever spoken to her?"

"No."

"How about me," I asked, "Is this the first time we have met or spoken?"

"Other than earlier this morning."

"One last question, are you being paid for your testimony today?"

"I'm not getting paid, but I am being reimbursed for my flight up here, the hotel room and my food."

"Thank you," I said turning to Bill, "your witness."

Bill whispered something to Susannah who whispered something back and then stood up.

"Ms. Burger, were your parents pretty well known in the community?"

"I'd say so. They were the first to move in after it was built and the only one of the original buyers still there. My mother was the first President of the condominium association and my father was the treasurer."

"Everyone knew that they were quite old, not in very good health, and rarely left their home?"

"I suppose so."

"Did everyone know about their hearing difficulties and eye problems?"

"I don't know."

"You could make yourself understood to your parents with a little effort and patience, couldn't you Ms. Burger?"

"Yes."

"There was nothing wrong with their minds, was there?"

"No, other than being a little stubborn."

There got a little smile from my alternate number 1, Rose.

"We all know what parents can be like sometimes," Bill said. "Did your parents say anything about having visitors on February twelfth?"

"I don't remember. When I came over after school I was mainly concerned with getting them dinner and getting them set for the night. There were people who came in during the morning to help them with breakfast and lunch, straighten up a bit, make sure they took their meds; visiting nurses, homecare aides, people like that. My mother would sometimes talk about who was there, but I was usually pretty busy getting things squared away."

"Those visitors you refer to who came in during the day could make themselves understood to your parents?"

"I hope so."

"They had hearing and vision problems, but they weren't completely deaf and blind, were they?"

"No, almost, but not totally."

"No further questions," Bill said.

"Just a few on re-direct, Your Honor," I said, standing up and looking at the jury to make sure I had their attention.

"Tell me Ms. Burger, did those visiting nurses and other scheduled visitors have a key to your parents' front door?"

"Yes."

"Why is that?"

"Because they weren't likely to hear the doorbell ring or a knock on the door."

"Any other reason?"

"I didn't want either one of them to have to get up to answer the door, they were both unsteady on their feet and their eye problems made it hard to maneuver. I was afraid they might fall."

"Did you ever leave the door unlocked for visitors?"

"Of course not, either they had a key or I tried to arrange to be there."

"Did you remind your parents in advance who was coming so they would know who to expect?"

"Yes."

"No further questions," I said, sitting back down.

Bill jumped up.

"Just a couple more, Your Honor?"

The judge nodded.

"People in that community get unannounced visitors all the time, don't they Ms. Burger?"

"I suppose so, I don't live there."

"You were there often, weren't you?"

"Yes."

"Pretty much every afternoon?"

"Yes."

"Were there ever any unexpected visitors while you were there?"

"On occasion."

"Workmen from the various cable and utility companies, neighbors with petitions to sign, lawn maintenance men with questions, or grandchildren in tow trying to sell girl-scout cookies, people like that?"

"Yes, from time to time."

"And your parents were ambulatory, weren't they?" When she didn't answer right away Bill added, "A bit unsteady on their feet, but ambulatory?"

"Yes."

"They just moved slowly and carefully."

"Very slowly."

"Could they open the door?"

"I suppose if they heard someone knocking. I don't recall seeing them open the door in years."

"Because when you were there, you would do it for them, isn't that a fair statement?"

"I suppose."

"And they could be made to understand what their visitors had to say to them, if it was said loud enough and close enough?"

"Sometimes, not always."

"Which was worse their sight or their hearing?" Bill asked.

"Their sight."

"Your parents were happy to have company, weren't they?"

"Who isn't at that age? They really couldn't talk on the telephone, so they liked it when I was around."

"Or one of the homecare aides?"

"Yes."

"Did they walk around the house from time to time to the kitchen or to the bathroom?"

"Yes."

"Did they sometimes sit by the window to watch what was happening outside, the way a lot of older people do?"

"Yes, but they couldn't see very far."

"They could see the light and the shadows, say from the clouds, cars and trucks passing by?"

"I guess so."

"Did you ever find them sitting by the window in the afternoon when they were expecting you to come by after work?"

"Yes, my father always knew what time it was, he had that knack even when I was growing up, like an inner clock, so he always knew when it was about four."

"So if Mr. and Mrs. Everett came at around three that day to have the will witnessed he could have been sitting by the window near the door?"

"He could have."

"Ms. Burger, you have no idea one way or the other whether your parents witnessed Ben Everett sign his will?"

"I do not."

"All you know for sure is that they would have been home on that date and that this at least resembles their signature."

"It could be their signature," she said, "I can't say for sure. They hadn't signed anything in quite some time."

"No further questions," Bill said.

The judge quickly excused the witness and then she excused the jury for lunch, having Bill and I stay behind to discuss what remained to be done.

"How many more witnesses do you have left Mr. Clasen?"

"All I have is my reincarnation expert."

"And who do you have on your rebuttal case, Mr. Lustenberger?"

"My client and there may be one other witness, I'm not sure yet."

"May I ask who?" I said.

"A childhood friend of Ms. McCreedy."

"What will she be testifying to?" I asked.

"You'll get to hear that when everyone else does," Bill said.

I'm not entitled to a preview of a fact witness, but Bill looked a bit too defensive if you asked me, almost as if he wasn't sure himself what the witness would say and was battling with his own client to keep her off the stand.

"I would ask for an offer of proof, Your Honor, if he decides to call this mystery witness, since I'm concerned about hearsay and relevance."

"She's a rebuttal witness, Your Honor," Bill said, "And I don't know at this point whether we will call her."

The judge frowned.

"You can object to her testimony when and if he calls her. It is a she I take it, Mr. Lustenberger?"

"Yes, Your Honor."

"Two pm sharp," she said, standing up and walking off the bench.

"A surprise witness," I whispered to Bill as we walked out of the courtroom.

"A surprise to me as well," he said.

We parted in the hallway, Bill to his client in their witness room and me to our witness room where I knew My Three Sons would be waiting with their sandwiches.

"So what did you think?" I asked taking the tuna sandwich I had made last night out of my bag.

"That she looked for a couple of witnesses who wouldn't know what the hell they were witnessing or who they were witnessing. The only people she could be sure would die before my father," Jeff said.

"She could have brought anyone along pretending to him," Peter said. "How would they have known the difference?"

"Exactly," I said, "I'm sure the jury got the point. If not, they'll get it again during my summation."

We ate a while in silence.

"But it does look like his signature," Mitch said.

"He could have signed it days earlier," Jeff said, "Thinking it was a Medicare form. Who knows what she told him."

I nodded my mouth full of stale bread and dry tuna fish. I had run out of mayonnaise.

"I don't see why Jeff and I can't testify?" Peter said.

"You can," I said, "But what's the point. What can either of you add to what Mitch already said? Neither the judge nor the jurors are going to like it if we just pile it on. It's too hot in the courtroom to be repeating ourselves."

Just then there was a knock on the door and Murray walked in. My Three Sons, who were none too enamored with Murray and his big bills, walked out to grab some coffee.

"Burger was worth the trip," he said. "No dog in the fight; had to get the jury wondering why our young reincarnate hadn't been more upfront about their problems."

"I'll be hammering her on that when he recalls her on rebuttal," I said.

"Well, don't hold anything back counselor," Murray said, sitting down and staring down at the remains of my sandwich. "This isn't the slam dunk you thought it would be?"

"Because she's good," I said.

"Best damn actress I ever saw."

I nodded while I tossed my sandwich in the garbage.

"He may have a surprise witness," I said. "He hasn't identified her, except as some childhood friend."

"Has to be someone from her father's barnyard church," Murray said, rubbing his chin, "Because I checked around town and none of the locals had anything to do with any of them."

"What could she have to say?" I wondered out loud.

"Let me see what I can find out," Murray said, pushing up slowly from the chair.

"There's no time for you to go out there."

"I always sprinkle around enough cash to leave a few deputies around. I'll make a few calls. Let's see if anyone has recently booked a flight east from the northern heartland.

"And I'm still checking to see if our grieving widow has spent any dough to set up a new Church of the Reincarnate."

With that Murray walked out and I went over my witness outline for Dr. Somnigupta. I left a few minutes early to step outside for some fresh air. However still and humid it was outside, it still felt better than the dead air in the courthouse. The crowds outside were smaller and quieter today, worn down by the heat and humidity.

I lit up a cigarette, my first in about six months, and leaned against one of the pillars of justice. I wondered why Susannah chose reincarnation instead of straight out love. Of course, if she had it wouldn't have gotten beyond a blurb in back of the local paper.

I saw Dr. Vasily Somnigupta climbing up the courthouse steps and went over to greet him and walk him to the witness room. He looked uncomfortable. While he was used to lecturing to an auditorium filled with students, believers and non-believers alike, this was his first foray into a court of law. Not much call to date for reincarnation experts in our legal system.

The jury looked in no mood to continue in this heat; they were red-faced and dripping with sweat.

"Call Dr. Somnigupta to the stand," the judge told the court clerk and he quickly appeared to take the oath. He affirmed rather than swore to tell the truth, as swearing was contrary to his religious beliefs, and of course he didn't use the bible. I ran quickly through his CV and Bill had no objection to accepting him as an expert in reincarnation and far eastern religions.

I planned on starting off with some questions guaranteed to get everyone's attention, while at the same time taking away some of Bill's thunder.

"Dr. Somnigupta, do you believe in reincarnation?"

"I certainly do."

"What religion to you practice?"

"Hinduism."

"How does reincarnation compare with the beliefs of other popular religions like Christianity, Judaism and the Moslem religion?"

"It's not that different when you analyze it. They all believe in a soul – life after death – it's more a question of what happens with the eternity that follows. Is it spent entirely in heaven with the Creator or are there occasions when a soul returns to earth for another go at it."

"Did the original Christians believe in reincarnation?"

"They did. They believed that certain souls returned as part of the learning process that helped bring them closer to God. The church turned away from that belief during the Middle Ages."

I turned to look at the jury and walked closer to the jury box.

"Dr. Somnigupta, do you personally know anything about your past lives?"

"I do not," he said. "In the course of a millennium you could probably count on one hand those who do. The soul's memory is impenetrable in this life."

"But there are exceptions?"

"Very, very rare, it would defeat the whole purpose of returning."

"How rare is it?"

"I don't think that there have been more than a half-dozen true revealed reincarnates in recorded history. And I use revealed reincarnate to mean someone who is legitimately aware of who they once were. Of course, there have been a lot of pretenders over the years. There are always people out there desperately looking for proof and who are very willing to believe anyone."

"Have you studied a lot of people who claimed to be revealed reincarnates?"

"I have met some who claimed to be and read just about everything that has ever been written over the past thousand years about others."

"Do you believe that Ms. McCreedy is a reincarnation of Ben Everett's wife, Rose?"

I glanced back at Bill expecting an objection, but he just sat there. I suppose it didn't matter at this point. Besides, once the question was out, even if the judge prevented the doctor from answering, everyone knew what his answer would be.

"I do not."

"Why is that?"

"First of all, reincarnation is all about time, time after death and time before life. Souls need time to evaluate and understand a life, what it meant and what was learned. Souls do not return that quickly, certainly not quickly enough to meet anyone they might have known in a prior life. It would defeat the whole purpose of experiencing different lives, and blur the distinctions, as well as the borders.

"Even where a soul is torn away by a particularly violent and horrible circumstance, it is compensated so to speak by a longer interval in the ether with the Creator. An illness is not the same thing since it's an act of God, unlike violence which is an act of man."

"Any other reasons for your opinion?"

"Yes, a reincarnate that has the gift of past sight, also has the gift of understanding what responsibility that awareness brings."

"Which is?"

"Never interfere with other lives and never use it to gain advantage."

"Which means what Doctor?"

"That this woman . . . ."

"Ms. McCreedy."

"Yes, thank you, that Ms. McCreedy, if she had truly opened the door to her soul would never have agreed to marry Mr. Everett or to take money intended for her former children. If indeed she was a reincarnation of their mother, she wouldn't be in this courtroom fighting for it. A true reincarnate would never want to intrude on the life left behind, not like this."

"Did you have an opportunity to interview Ms. McCreedy?"

"I requested an interview, but her counsel wouldn't allow it."

"What did you do instead?"

"I reviewed her deposition before the trial, as well as her trial testimony."

"Is there anything that you discovered in her testimony which reinforces your opinion that Ms. McCreedy is not a reincarnate of Rose Everett?"

"Yes."

"What is it?"

"Besides coming back too quickly, only one life has supposedly been revealed to her. Once the door to the soul opens, many lives become visible at once, not just one. Also, the fact that she kept it a secret from her alleged children and everyone else for that matter other than her new husband is unheard of."

"Why is that?" I asked.

"Because every other revealed reincarnate I've researched throughout recorded history, the likely pretenders, as well as the credible ones, were always very open about letting people know who they were and what it was they saw inside their soul. It's not something they could keep secret or needed to for that matter.

"It's very uplifting, it's the kind of thing they stand on a soapbox to shout about. Really, it's nothing short of a miracle. The fact that Ms. McCreedy told no one other than Mr. Everett suggests to me that it was not something she really believes or believed in."

"Objection," Bill said.

"Sustained," the judge ruled, "The jury will disregard that last remark. This witness is not here to testify concerning Ms. McCreedy's or Mr. Everett's state of mind nor is he qualified to do so. He is only here to talk about his studies, and the philosophy and religious practices that make up reincarnation."

"I'm sorry Your Honor," Dr. Somnigupta said.

I walked slowly back to counsel's table, my hand rubbing my chin as I thought about whether or not there was anything else I really needed to ask. Of course, the first attorney I worked for always said - when in doubt, summarize and conclude.

"You have pointed to the secrecy, the interference with a recent prior life, the fact that she claims to have seen only one life, and the unusually quick return as factors that suggest to you as an expert in the tenets of reincarnation that Ms. McCreedy is not a revealed reincarnate, is that correct?"

"Yes."

"Is there anything else?"

"A revealed reincarnate by definition gives comfort to the heart of man and cares nothing for this life. I am paraphrasing a line from Aristotle's Endemus."

That was a new one for me, as Doctor Somnigupta had not raised it before during our preparation session. I didn't like the part about giving comfort to the heart of man.

"Which means what with respect to Ben Everett's money?"

"She wouldn't want it and wouldn't take it."

I walked slowly back to my chair.

"In your opinion, Doctor, is Ms. McCreedy a revealed reincarnate?"

"No."

"Do you have any doubt about that?"

"I do not."

I stood in front of my chair, ready to sit down.

"Have you ever testified in court before as an expert, Dr. Somnigupta?"

"No, there's not been much call for this kind of thing."

That got smiles across the board from the jurors, as well as the judge.

"How much are you being paid for today's testimony?"

"$1,500 plus expenses."

"No further questions," I said as I sat down.

Bill stood up and walked slowly toward the witness.

"Good afternoon, Doctor."

"Good afternoon."

"You have no doubt Doctor that we have souls and that most of those souls are reincarnated, is that correct?"

"Correct."

"You would say that you yourself are a reincarnate - you just don't know anything about your prior lives."

"Not consciously no."

"Subconsciously?"

"There's déjà vu and dreams."

"Those rare individuals who can consciously see into their prior lives you call them revealed reincarnates?"

"Yes."

"How many revealed reincarnates have you met in your career?"

"Real or pretenders?"

"Let's break it down. How many pretenders?"

"At least four dozen."

"And were the reasons you were convinced that they were not real revealed reincarnates similar to the reasons you've given here today?"

"In some cases, in some cases they had the facts about the past or their prior lives so mixed up it left their credibility in doubt."

"Names, dates, places, likes, dislikes, things like that?"

"Yes."

"In other words, they got the facts wrong."

"That's correct."

"Would you say that was one of the principal techniques used over the years to disprove the credibility of a revealed reincarnation?"

"I would say it's one of the most common techniques."

"Have you looked into the facts that Ms. McCreedy has talked about with respect to Rose's life?"

"Somewhat."

"How did you do that?"

"By reviewing her deposition testimony and talking to Rose Everett's three sons."

"And the facts that she remembered about her prior life turned out to be pretty accurate, didn't they?"

"Yes."

"In fact, they've turned out to be completely accurate?"

"Yes, but you have to remember she lived with Mr. Everett almost a year and recent facts are easier to find in today's internet world. If she claimed to have lived before, say during the Revolutionary War, than having her facts correct would have been of more significance."

"Is it your testimony that a person's favorite tea can be found on the internet?" Bill asked.

"Nothing is secret anymore."

"But she died over twenty-five years ago, long before the internet."

"She could have learned that from her husband."

Bill took a short walk around the room.

"Ok, but to be clear . . . fact discrepancies is not on your list of reasons for doubting that Susannah is a reincarnate of Rose Everett?"

"That's correct."

"Because there was not one single fact discrepancy that you were made aware of, was there?"

"Not based upon the limited number of facts available in her deposition transcript and testimony."

"There were quite a number of facts available in her deposition and testimony, weren't there Doctor?"

"I'm not sure what quite a number means."

"There was testimony about what Rose liked to eat and wear, what she liked to read, the kind of person she was, about her friends, her childhood and some intimate facts about her relationship with her sister, her husband and her children?"

"There were facts of that nature, yes."

Bill flipped to the next page of his notepad.

"What about genuine revealed reincarnates, how many of those have you personally come across?"

"None."

"Did you say none?"

"Yes."

"Then how is it that you still believe so strongly in reincarnation?" Bill asked.

"Belief is not a question of proof. It's not based on something you can see. It's more something you feel."

"So you would call belief more intuitive?"

"I think that's fair."

Bill looked at the jury and nodded.

"And you believe in reincarnation?"

"I do."

"Despite the fact that you haven't, in your opinion, ever met a true revealed reincarnate."

"That's right."

"And despite the fact that very few people in this country believe in reincarnation?"

"Yes."

"And Ms. McCreedy, who was also raised believing in reincarnation, believes just as you do."

"I don't know what she really believes."

"You have no reason to doubt her belief, do you?"

"I do, based on her behavior with respect to her second husband and his estate. That's not the behavior of a true revealed reincarnate."

Nice bit about the second husband, I thought.

"Assuming for a moment Doctor Somnigupta that she really does believe, just as you really believe . . . by the way, that wouldn't be strange--in your opinion – her believing in reincarnation?"

"No."

"Or her husband, Ben Everett, coming to believe in it as well?"

"Conceptually no - however if he believed in it because she convinced him that she was a reincarnate of his late wife then my answer would be yes."

Bill put his hand to his chin and nodded.

"Because you don't believe it's likely to be true for the reasons you gave to Mr. Clasen during your direct examination?"

"Correct."

"But if Ben Everett had that intuitive feeling, that feeling which you call belief, that wouldn't make him crazy would it?"

"Objection," I said, pushing my chair back and standing up.

"Sustained."

"Your testimony about a revealed reincarnate not coming back that quickly or interfering with a prior life, or keeping who she once was a secret is based on how you believe reincarnation operates, isn't it Dr. Somnigupta?"

"It's based on an academic career studying everything written about reincarnation and reincarnates."

"But everything that's written is based on belief, isn't it? There's no scientific proof is there? There are no rule books or guidelines for reincarnation, are there doctor?"

"There are writings by people considered to be holy, much like Christianity, Judaism and Islam."

"But there are no rules, for example, that state what a revealed reincarnate can and cannot due . . . sort of like the Ten Commandments?"

"No."

"So the rules you posit are what you believe based on your extensive reading?"

"And research and studies over the course of my entire career, as well as my writings."

"And the same applies when you testified on direct that a revealed reincarnated should normally see more than one prior life. That statement was based on your years of study and research, and your interpretation of those holy writings? Yes or no if you can please, Doctor."

"Yes."

"It's not based on meeting any revealed reincarnated, because you have never met one?"

"That's correct."

"Your expertise is based in part on what you have read and how you interpret what you have read? Again, yes or no if you can."

"Yes."

Bill walked over to the table and picked up a document then he walked over toward the jury.

"I'm looking at an article you wrote in 2006 Dr. Somnigupta entitled 'Recycling Life' that appeared in *The Far Eastern Religious Quarterly* put out by the University of Bangalore in India, do you remember writing that article?"

"I do."

Bill held the journal up for everyone on the jury to see and then opened it.

"Do you remember writing 'There is a distinction between one's mere appearance and personality and the deeper self and that by means of metempsychosis and karma we are all involved in a process of spiritual evolution that might be compared to natural evolution."

"I do."

"And by that you meant, in part, that what Ms. McCreedy looks like in this life, as well as her current personality is distinct from her deeper self . . . her reincarnated soul?"

"Yes."

"So her soul could be the same as the soul of Rose Everett or Joan of Arc for that matter, even if she looks and acts very differently from both of them?"

"Yes, the soul is very distinct. It does not necessarily control personality or behavior, although in this case I don't believe it's the same as Rose Everett's soul."

"I understand that doctor, you've made your opinion perfectly clear. What I'm asking is more a conceptual question. Ms. McCreedy could have the same soul as Rose Everett even though she might look very different and have a very different personality?"

"Conceptually, yes."

"In fact, that's what you wrote, isn't it?"

"Yes."

"Is it fair to say Doctor that while you believe Ms. McCreedy shares a soul with someone who lived before, you just don't believe that it's Rose Everett's soul?"

"That's correct."

"Do you have any idea who that other soul might be . . . the prior life she once lived?"

"Of course not."

"You just believe you know who it can't be, is that it?"

"I'm just saying in my opinion it's not the person who she is claiming that it is."

"Based on the various factors you've already discussed, the timing, the interference?"

"And the silence," Doctor Somnigupta replied. "Yes."

"Can you tell me the gender of the soul that Ms. McCreedy has?"

"Souls have no gender."

"Did you write in this article doctor that –quote - Souls have a tendency to migrate together and meet time and time again when they are reborn – unquote."

"I did."

"Which means the fact that Ms. McCreedy, Susannah, came into Ben Everett's life, whether it was to clean his house or to marry him, makes it likely that her soul once shared a prior life with him?"

"Yes, but that doesn't mean it's likely that she shared the very life he was living twenty-five years earlier. It is much more likely that it was a life 200 years earlier . . . or it could be a new meeting; that's part of the learning process as well."

"I'm not talking about two souls who become neighbors or meet at work. I'm talking about two souls who marry as Susannah did with Ben. Didn't you write that a familial relationship like that is a strong indicator of a close connection in a recent prior life?"

"It indicates a strong possibility, nothing more."

"Well, let's read exactly what you did write. 'Where the connection is familial in nature the likelihood of having been closely entwined in a recent prior existence is almost a certainty.'"

"I was referring to children, a familial relationship, not an artificial one such as a marriage."

"You don't believe that a husband and wife are a family?"

"I was using familial in the sense of a blood relationship."

"Are you suggesting that love and marriage is a bond that's less strong than a blood relationship; that it doesn't reach down as deeply into the soul?"

"No, I'm not, it certainly can, but it can also be very superficial in today's society, the result of hormones and appearances more than anything spiritual, which I suppose is why there are so many divorces."

"So a good marriage would be a better indicator that two partners were together in a recent prior life than a bad marriage?"

"A blood relationship would be a better indicator."

"Do you know anything about Susannah and Ben's marriage?"

"Nothing other than the enormous age difference."

"Can there be true spiritual love between people of different ages?"

"Certainly."

Bill looked down at his pad.

The problem with academics, I thought, is that they write so much over the years and care not a whit about consistency.

"I suppose you would agree doctor that God's ways are mysterious?"

"I'm not sure what you're getting at."

"That we can't always be expected to understand what God does and why?"

"Yes."

"Do you believe that God is limited by the rules you've suggested about secrecy, non-interference and the number of years that must pass before a soul is allowed to return to earth?"

"No, but I think God sets up certain procedures that run on their own, like the laws of nature, like gravity."

"But God can make exceptions, would you agree with that? He can make a bird fly and flowers bloom even in the heart of winter?"

"Yes."

"So sitting here today you don't know for certain whether Ms. McCreedy is one of those exceptions?"

"I don't, I just don't believe it to be the case."

Bill put his hands in his pocket and strolled around the room, his head down, like he was deep in thought.

"There's that word belief again," Bill said, stopping in front of the witness. "You don't believe that she is, but you wouldn't say that someone else who believes that she is, like Ben Everett for example, was wrong or misguided, any more than you would say someone who believes in Jesus is wrong or misguided?"

"Objection," I said.

The judge thought it over.

"Sustained."

Still, the point was made.

"You said during direct that you wanted to speak to Ms. McCreedy, but I wouldn't allow it, do you recall saying that?"

"Yes."

"Did you ever ask me to speak to her?"

"No."

"Who did you ask?"

"I asked Mr. Clasen."

"Do you know whether he asked me, or did he say not to bother since I would be likely to say no?"

"I don't recall, I think he said it was too late. I thought that had come from you."

Bill backed away slowly toward the jury box.

"Doctor I'd like to change the subject a moment. Did you ever hear of the poet Goethe?"

"Of course."

"Did he claim to be a revealed reincarnate, who lived before during the time of the Roman Emperor Hadrian?"

"Yes."

"Was he pretending or real?"

"I haven't studied it enough to form an opinion."

"How about Napoleon Bonaparte," Bill said, "Did he claim to a reincarnate of Charlemagne."

"I've heard that."

"Never studied it closely?"

"No."

"Henry David Thoreau, Ralph Waldo Emerson, Walt Whitman, Herman Melville, Arthur Conan Doyle, all believed that they could see into their prior lives, is that correct?"

"All believers in reincarnation," Dr. Somnigupta answered. "I don't recall whether or not they actually saw their prior lives."

"Henry Ford, Rudyard Kipling, Yeats, James Joyce, Sir Winston Churchill, Robert Frost, Henry Miller, Charles Lindbergh, all claimed to have seen some aspects of a prior life, didn't they?"

"I believe they were talking in general terms, reinforcing their belief in reincarnation, not claiming to be true revealed reincarnates."

"The Old and New Testament is filed with references that appear to deal with reincarnation or at least that was the interpretation during the early years of the Christian Church, isn't that correct Doctor?"

"Yes."

"Luke 20:35-36 for example where Jesus says: 'They who are accounted worthy to obtain that world . . . neither can they die anymore.' Is that one such example?"

"Yes."

"Because it suggests that you can die more than once?"

"Correct."

"Just a few more questions Doctor. You have no opinion as to what Ben Everett believed about reincarnation or about the connection between his soul and Ms. McCreedy's soul?"

"I do not."

"Although the fact that he gave her his house and changed his will to make her his beneficiary is a pretty good indicator of what he believed."

"Objection."

"Sustained," the judge said, giving Bill a dirty look. "Ladies and gentlemen of the jury, that is the decision you have to make, no expert can decide what Mr. Everett believed or didn't believe."

Bill hung his head down for a moment of contrition, but I'm sure he would ask the same question again if given the opportunity.

"By the way Doctor, you testified during direct concerning a line from Aristotle about one purpose of a revealed reincarnate was to," Bill flipped a few pages back in his pad, "give comfort to the heart of man. Do you remember that?"

"Yes."

"Don't you think that Ms. McCreedy would have brought great comfort to the aged heart of Ben Everett?"

"Yes, but his need for comfort was probably one of the things that made him so susceptible to a story like that."

"No further questions," Bill said, turning his back on the witness and walking slowly to his chair.

"No redirect, Your Honor," I said, rising from my seat.

I thought it went well enough and I didn't want to give Bill another bite of the apple on recross. Besides, this whole line of questioning was getting a little too weird for me.

"Any other witnesses?" the judge asked me.

"No, Your Honor, we rest."

"Then we'll break for the day here," Judge Shanawit said to the jury. "We will reconvene at 9 am tomorrow."

We all stood up while the jury filed out.

"Who are you calling on rebuttal Mr. Lustenberger?"

"I'm going to recall my client, Your Honor."

"And after that?"

"It's still up in the air."

"Well you have tonight to decide, because it looks pretty clear to me that we will be finishing tomorrow. Be ready with your summations," the judge said, standing up and stepping down from the bench.

Murray was waiting for me when I opened the door to my office. He sat there examining his nails while I got organized. Finally, I collapsed down on the chair behind my desk.

"You're not going to like this," he said.

"The mystery witness?"

He nodded and pulled his chair closer to my desk, which wasn't all that easy for him to do.

"Another reincarnate?" I said.

"No, that wouldn't bother me, unless it was my first wife, then I'd be worried about a knife in the back. No, she's another twenty-four year old who grew up attending her father's church."

"A friend?"

"You could say that."

"I've had enough challenges for one day," I said, taking a bottle of single malt scotch out of the drawer. "I'm not in the mood to play twenty questions."

"Her name is Jenny," Murray said, "And she never testified like Susannah, never claimed to recall a prior life, but she was there that day Susannah cried out Rose. Her family came down about once a month from over the border in Canada and camped out behind the barn . . . although she always slept in Susannah's room."

"What does she do now?" I asked.

"Nothing, she still lives at home, she's what they call intellectually challenged these days, and we used to call as dumb as a stone."

I sighed and poured myself a shot of scotch. I poured one for Murray as well.

"Single malt?" he asked and I nodded.

He drank it down like water.

"I had someone speak with her parents. They wouldn't talk at first, so it cost your boys a few bucks, but Jenny says that our girl was talking in her sleep that night - after calling out Rose's name."

"Let me guess," I said, sipping my scotch and letting it roll slowly around my mouth, "she called out Rose's last name . . . Everett."

"Pretty good counselor," Murray said, pushing his empty glass back at me, "But it was just Ben, good old Ben."

I pour him another drink, which he downed in a gulp.

"Maybe she had an Uncle Ben?" I said.

"The rice king, no such luck."

Murray pointed down at his glass, but I ignored him.

"So she's lying to help her out," I said. "Who's going to believe her childhood buddy?"

"The funny thing about juries," Murray said, "The dumber they are, the more believable they seem."

I nodded slowly while I finished my drink and poured both of us another shot.

"OK, so I need something else to impeach her with besides her obvious prejudice," I said. "What else have you got?"

Murray tilted his head back and poured the scotch down his throat.

"This is good stuff," he said.

I didn't see how it could linger on his tongue long enough for him to taste anything.

"What else have you got?" I asked again.

"It's a little tricky."

"What?"

"She's not only as dumb as a stone she's as queer as a three-dollar bill."

"What's that supposed to mean?"

"Her parents quit the barnyard church when she was sixteen. It seems that Jenny was still sleeping in Susannah's room, except they weren't doing much sleeping."

"Lesbians?"

"Fruitcakes," Murray said with a laugh, sliding his glass over for another shot when he saw me pick up the cap, "The original Republican sin."

I wasn't interested in cross-examining Susannah on her early sexuality or preference. No one was ever going to argue that her marriage was based on some maddening chemical attraction to Ben, but maybe I could use it to impeach her friend.

Jenny would surely have been following Susannah's exploits in the news, and might be eager to lie for her former love, a simple one word lie – Ben - at least that's what I can argue if she takes the stand, although I'd have to be careful going after a simple girl like that in front of a jury with mothers.

Of course, I could also argue in summation that why else would a gay Susannah marry old Ben, except for the money. Perhaps the challenge she'd been given in Susannah's life was to deal with homosexuality and obesity, differences she didn't have to face as Rose; it made me uncomfortable thinking along those lines, as if Susannah were actually telling the truth.

I poured us each another finger.

"If you ask me," Murray said, after throwing back the scotch and rising slowly to his feet, "I'd use it on little Jenny, bash her with it, the jury's got no emotions vested in her, but I'd be careful when it comes to our wandering soul. You never know how that kind of stuff is going to play these days. The juror questionnaire doesn't leave any blanks for sexual experience."

"I supposed that's why Bill was so unsure about using her. It introduces a whole new element. I can always argue that she picked reincarnation because she didn't want to rely on love in case the truth came out."

Murray got up to leave, which was always a slow process.

'This doesn't give you any doubts, does it?" I asked.

Murray looked down at me, the scotch having made all his tension disappear.

"I'd lay off the booze if I were you," he said, "A scam is a scam is a scam."

With that Murray left and promised to contact me with anything else he could find out.

I took out my notes on Susannah and started roughing out some points to hit on my second bite of the apple. I stared at the phone from time to time, but it sat there mutely, at least until I closed the door to my office and stuck the key in the lock. I thought about letting it ring, but perhaps it was Bill with a last minute settlement offer, or one of the sons.

Of course, I knew who I hoped it was.

"I was about to hang up," Aurora said.

"I would have thought that someone like you could sense I was coming back to answer the phone."

"I'm not that kind of psychic."

"Right, so did you speak to our good friend Eva last night?"

"I didn't hear from Eva until a little while ago. That's why I'm calling so late."

"You make it sound like she calls on the telephone," I said.

"A spiritualist can't control the where and when."

"So what was it, a voice over the television or out of the toaster?"

Aurora laughed.

"It's always in a dream for me. I fell asleep on the couch before."

"You're lucky," I said, "I'm usually falling off cliffs in my dreams or out of windows."

"That's too bad."

"Why, what does it mean?"

"My specialty is communicating with the dead, not interpreting dreams."

"Give me your best educated guess," I said, having been troubled over the past year about how frequently I've been having those dreams.

"It represents feelings of inadequacy and helplessness," she said. "Your subconscious is feeling heavy and unsupported . . . worried."

"About this case?"

"No, not the case, it's something much more elemental, something about your life that's not satisfying you, something that's missing."

I didn't need a psychic to figure that out.

"Who doesn't have something missing?" I said.

Of course, I was missing some of the more obvious things, like a companion and a belief in anything more than myself and the rule of law.

"Falling represents the feeling that you're in a downward spiral," she added.

"And if I hit bottom in my dream I die, right?"

"Wrong, that's a whole lot of nonsense, an old fish wife's tale. What your dream is trying to tell you is that you need to find a way to feel lighter and freer, you need to make a change in your life, to try something different."

"It's called retirement."

"That's my five-cent interpretation. Take it for what it's worth."

Of course, I didn't tell her that I've been thinking hard about quitting the law and trying something else for quite some time, perhaps moving for a year to a Greek island like Santorini to write and paint.

"Are you still there?" she asked after a long moment of silence.

"I owe you five cents."

"And I intend to collect."

The only sound for a while after that was our breathing. I interrupted the silence by blurting out, "I was just on my way home if you want to tell me in person."

I could almost hear her thinking over the phone.

"You sure that's a good idea?" she said.

"It's OK with me, if it's OK with you."

I felt like a fool. I hadn't done this kind of thing in years.
"OK."

I gave her my address and home telephone number.

"I'll leave the garage open, would you mind pulling in?" I said.

"If you're worried about the neighbors," she said, "Don't, there's no sign on the side of my car."

"I know it's not that, I've noticed a strange car parked across the street a couple of evenings. I'm sure it's the one of the reporters."

"And you don't want them to think that you're consulting a spiritualist as part of the case."

"Exactly."

At home I showered, put on fresh clothes, and straightened up a bit putting my dirty laundry in the back of my closet.

As soon as I heard her pull into the garage, I pressed the button to close the door.

"I feel a little like a spy," she said.

I followed her into the house. She had a lovely neck and her shoulders, the part that was left uncovered by the scoop neck of her blouse appeared much younger than the rest of her.

"I made some coffee," I said.

"I'd rather have some wine."

"I don't have wine, just scotch."

"That'll do."

She wore no make-up and loose fitting clothes that looked as comfortable as they did stylish.

"Aurora . . . ."

"I prefer Betsy," she said.

"You're off duty?"

"I'm sitting in your home drinking scotch."

I smiled.

"Ok, Betsy, tell me Eva's latest revelation."

"First, I wanted to say that I watched everything today on TV and I think you're doing well, although I don't think that doctor knows what he's talking about."

"Why do you say that?"

"Because souls can come back anytime, an hour, a day, a week, a month later; time is not the same when it comes to souls."

"Then I'm glad Bill is not calling you as a rebuttal witness," I said with a chuckle.

Betsy laughed as well. She had a sweet, very natural laugh.

"Were you ever married Joe?"

"No, I didn't like what I saw growing up."

She nodded slowly and sat there quietly.

"How about you?"

"No, never."

I waited for her to tell me the reason, but when she didn't volunteer it I asked.

"Similar reason?" I asked.

"No, my parents were quite happy and I had my opportunities. I've been asked a number of times and always said no."

"Why."

"You're going to think the reason is strange, as strange as what I do."

"Try me."

"I only get the dreams when I sleep alone. That's the only time I seem to be able to make the spiritual connection."

"The spirits don't go for threesomes?" I said.

Betsy only smiled this time.

"Sorry, bad joke?"

"No, I've heard it before."

This time I smiled

"I don't know why it works that way with me," she said, "but it does."

She took a sip of scotch.

"Although lately," she said, "I've been thinking I've had enough of it. I'm tired of hearing from the dead. I'll be with them soon enough."

She looked so vulnerable; I wanted to put my arm around her.

"You don't know when you're going to . . . ."

"No," she said, taking another sip of scotch.

"I know how you feel," I said. "I've felt the same way about the law for quite a while."

She raised her glass and we clinked a silent toast. It can't be easy I realized communicating with the dead or at least believing that you do.

"First things first," she said.

"Right, what's Eva's message today?"

"She said the door is shut."

"What does that mean?"

"The door to her soul, Susannah can no longer see into her past life. She knows what she remembers seeing and speaking about before it closed, but she can't see anything new now about Rose's life."

"How do I know what she doesn't know?"

"I don't know Joe, I'm just the messenger. Is there anything significant that hasn't come up yet?"

I wondered for an instant if Aurora wasn't actually a plant from Susannah McCreedy trying to steer me in the wrong direction, but I waved that thought off.

"I'll keep that in mind during her re-cross," I said.

"That's all she wanted me to pass along," Betsy said, as if she were thinking that meant she should leave.

As tired as I was, the thought of that must have drained the blood from my face.

"You need to get some rest," Betsy said.

She had big beautiful, sky-blue eyes.

"You could stay the night if you'd like," I said.

I felt like a little boy who didn't want to be left alone in the dark. I smiled at Betsy and was relieved when she smiled back.

"I have an overnight bag in the car, I'll go get it."

We got ready for bed, like an old married couple, sharing the bathroom as we brushed our teeth. There was something so comfortable about her. I didn't feel the least bit self-conscious. I smiled at the thought of Susannah calling us soul mates.

"I haven't done this in a while," I said, "quite a while."

"Nor have I, but it's not something you forget how to do."

"And I'm going to have to jump up and run out early in the morning."

"I understand."

We both wore pajamas to bed, but they didn't stay on for long. I knew I'd be a little tired tomorrow, but I didn't care.

She smelled wonderful, a bit like lavender, and just brushing my lips against her neck released all the tension in my shoulders. Her eyes were moist and filled with kindness. I could have spent the night kissing her eyelids and it felt as if I spent a good part of our loving making doing just that. Touching and kissing her, being touched and kissed, so slowly and tenderly, almost as if it were our first time, not just with each other, but with anyone – and perhaps it was at this stage of our lives. It felt like a commitment of sorts, a promise of trust and a declaration that it was never too late to dream.

She fell asleep before I did and I lay in bed staring at the ceiling thinking that it was more satisfying than it had ever been before. When I finally did fall asleep I slept soundly until the morning and if I had the falling dream again I didn't remember it.

Chapter 13 – The Final Witness

"Reincarnation is a way for God to improve his earlier works."
— Norman Mailer

The heat wave broke during the night and the temperature dropped almost twenty-five degrees so the morning felt chilly. A new front had rolled in blanketed with deep, dark clouds that seemed intent on suffocating everyone and everything around the courthouse.

Bill and I met at the top of the steps.

"Looks like we'll go to the jury today," he said, holding the door open for me.

"Does that mean you're done after Susannah?" I asked.

"Don't know. But if I have another witness she'll be quick."

"So it depends on how Susannah does on cross?"

"On what she decides, it's her call."

"Want to give me a name?"

"As if Murray hasn't already told you," Bill said, as he headed over to his witness room.

My Three Sons were sitting in our witness room squeezing their cups of coffee so tight that it made the veins pop out in their necks. They quizzed me on how I thought it was going and I sounded more confident than I felt. Then there was a knock on the door and the courtroom deputy said that the judge wanted to see counsel in chambers.

"Any idea what this is about?" I asked Bill in the hall.

He shook his head.

"Come in gentlemen," Judge Shanawit said. She was not yet in her robes, just an ordinary middle-age woman with crow's feet and frown lines sipping her morning coffee, the paper opened up in front of her.

"Juror number 2 has a family illness and has to be excused."

Ellen, the elementary school teacher, I really liked her, but that brought up Alternate 1, Rose, my 74-year old widow, the one who had been looking kindly in my direction for most of the trial, almost like I reminded her of one of her late husband. I would have preferred that jurors 4 or 6, Matt or Ira, dropped off, or even juror 3, Frank, the postman, but I definitely thought of Rose as a trade up.

"Why don't we adjourn until tomorrow and give her another day?" Bill said. "We don't have much more to go."

"I thought about that," the judge said, "Except it sounded like something that would keep her out for more than a day so I've already excused her."

With that Bill looked down at his shoes. It's not that he liked Ellen I think he was more afraid of Rose.

"It's probably a wash," I said to him on the way out.

"Probably," Bill responded and something in the tone of his voice told me that the surprise witness was much more likely now.

We resumed a bit late with Susannah called back to the stand. She sat down and began smoothing down her dress the way I remembered my mother doing, brushing off imaginary crumbs and pressing out invisible wrinkles before looking up again at the jurors and smiling. My heart skipped a beat when I noticed Rose smiling back, along with Matt and Ira. I've been wrong before with jurors, but could I be that wrong? Maybe she was just happy to move up to the regular jury.

"Good morning," Bill said.

"Good morning."

"I've called you back to the stand Ms. McCreedy to address a few points that came up after you testified. First, let me ask you what name you use when you're not in court."

"I go by Susannah Everett."

"Has that been since the marriage?"

"Yes."

"How is it that you have been going by the name McCreedy during the trial?"

"It was my own choice. I didn't want to make things too uncomfortable for the family or confusing for the jury."

I thought about objecting, but to what purpose.

"Now do you remember the testimony given by Ms. Burger concerning her parents?"

"I do."

"They were the ones who witnessed Ben signing his new will?"

"Yes."

"Can you describe in more detail what happened that day?"

"When we came to the door they were both sitting by the window, which I'd seen them do often when Ben and I went for our walks around the neighborhood. A lot of the older people do. It's more interesting if you ask me than sitting around all day watching the same shows on television."

I thought I noticed Rose nod slightly.

"So I waved at them and we went to the door. I didn't have to knock, because Mr. Burger got up to open it."

"I understand that their eyesight wasn't good," Bill said.

"It certainly didn't appear to be and I'm sure they couldn't see our faces clearly, but it certainly seemed good enough to see things outside and at a distance - why else sit by the window? Besides, they were both wearing glasses. Why would you do that if it didn't help? And they had no trouble walking to the kitchen table where the will was signed . . . slowly, but they didn't need any help."

"What happened next?"

"After we exchanged some pleasantries, I explained to them why we had come. It took a little while because they had hearing problems as well, but they definitely got it. They were old with hearing and vision problems, but they weren't dumb. They understood exactly what we were asking."

"Why didn't you mention anything about the extent of their hearing and vision problems when you testified before?"

"I wasn't asked and it didn't seem that unusual. A lot of people down there have hearing and vision problems."

"Did you actually see them both sign on the witness lines?"

"Absolutely, they took a pen out of a kitchen drawer and signed at the kitchen table."

"You heard the testimony of Mr. Everett?"

"Mitch?" she asked, like she was calling out to her son.

"I'm sorry Mitch Everett."

"I did."

"Did you generally answer the phone after you married Ben?"

"Almost always."

"Why was that?"

"Ben moved pretty well for an eighty-eight year old, but he was still eighty-eight and I could usually get to the phone a lot quicker than he could."

"Would he answer the telephone if he was next to it?"

"Sure."

"Did that ever happen when Mitch called?"

"I can't remember every instance," she said. "I'm sure it did on occasion. The boys called frequently."

I could feel Mitch's muscles tighten.

"They generally called in the early evenings when Ben was sitting in his recliner watching the news. He didn't like to move once he was there, so I usually answered the phone."

"Did you consciously try to avoid speaking to anyone in Ben's family?"

"No, of course not, I loved hearing their voices–it gave me the shivers just to hear them–but it was clear that they didn't want to speak with me and I didn't want to press it or make anyone feel uncomfortable. I knew how this must have looked to them."

"Did you try to prevent Ben from speaking with anyone or going out alone with anyone?"

"If you knew Ben, you'd know there was no chance of that. He was pretty stubborn and he did what he wanted." Susannah sighed. "No, I usually left the room when they were on the telephone, unless we were in the kitchen or someplace like that to give him some privacy, and Ben went out on his own frequently to the library and to get gas or pick up milk, things like that. It was important for him to get around on his own. He'd been doing that for the past twenty-five years and there's a comfort in those little consistencies in life. Sometimes he went to the clubhouse to exercise. You can probably guess that's not something I generally like to do."

Why no mention of his stamina in the bedroom, I wondered.

"And I would have done the same when Mitch came to the house for a visit if it was OK with Ben. You know, leave them alone, but Ben didn't want me to leave. He wanted me around, he said, because it kept the conversation from getting too heavy."

Bill nodded at Susannah to go on. A bit too rehearsed if you asked me. I hoped that the jury noticed.

"Ben avoided having lunch alone with Mitch, because he knew that it would be all about me. I'm not sure he was ready to discuss it yet, particularly the reincarnation part. He would have eventually-- we both would have--as hard as they might have found it to believe, but that unbelievable accident took care of that."

Susannah wiped a real tear from her eye. She was beyond good. Bill stood there a moment looking at his notes.

"Counselor?" the judge said, snapping Bill out of his reverie.

"Ms. McCreedy, would you have liked to meet with Dr. Somnigupta before the trial?"

"I think that would have been fun . . . and very interesting."

"Why didn't you?"

"No one asked."

"You heard the testimony by Dr. Seymour about older people having selective dementia?"

"I did."

"During the time you were married, did Ben ever exhibit anything that gave you concern about his ability to make a decision or process information?"

Susannah looked up at the ceiling while she thought about it.

"Oh he certainly forgot things like most people his age. You know, names, dates, what we had for lunch the day before, but they were never really anything significant. He still spent time talking to his broker and watching the news, reading and talking about the future. No, I'd have to say that Ben was sharper than a lot of men half his age."

"What do you mean when you say talking about the future?"

"Ben wanted us to visit England," she said. "He'd spent some time there during the war and he wanted to see it again, particularly the Sheffield area where he was stationed. We were also making plans for one of those cruises to Alaska in the spring."

"No further questions," Bill said, surprising everyone but me with the brevity of his questioning. He certainly didn't want her up there again for too long.

"Counselor," the judge asked, "any cross?"

"Just a bit, Your Honor."

I drew close to Susannah.

"Did you and Mr. Everett have a cordless telephone in the house Ms. McCreedy?"

"Yes."

"How many cordless telephones were there?"

"Two, one in the kitchen and one in the den; the one in the bedroom had a cord."

"But the other two could be taken off their cradles and carried around the house?"

"Yes."

Of course, I knew all this from Murray.

"So Ben was never far from a telephone."

"He never took it with him when he sat down to watch the news if that's what you're asking. He was sort of old-fashioned that way. I guess because we . . . he had grown up with the cord phones."

I glanced at the jury.

"Of course, I told him to take it with him when he sat down on his recliner, but he refused. He said he wouldn't walk around holding a phone like it was some kind of life preserver."

Rose, my beloved alternate juror, now juror number 3, was looking at Susannah without any trace of skepticism or doubt, almost as if she were listening to an old friend.

"So you answered the telephone all the time for Ben's convenience?"

"Most of the time."

I picked up the will.

"With respect to the Burgers, your testimony is that you didn't mention the extent of their hearing and vision problems the first time you testified because no one asked, is that correct?"

"Yes, as well as the fact that it didn't seem all that unusual, you have to remember it was a community of old people. They all have hearing and vision problems."

"But theirs was a lot worse than most of the people in the community, wouldn't you say?"

"Yes, they seemed worse, a lot worse I can't say."

"The fact that they were sitting by the window and saw you coming so you didn't have to knock didn't seem relevant to the story when you first testified about it the other day?"

"I thought the important part was the witnessing of the will, not how we got inside the house. I sort of took that for granted, either you knock or someone sees you coming and opens the door."

"Did you have to speak loudly to make yourself understood?"

"Yes."

"And you didn't think that was important enough to mention."

"I don't believe I was asked about it."

"You heard their daughter testify about how serious their hearing and vision problems were, didn't you?"

"Yes."

"You were here in the courtroom?"

"I was."

"And after hearing her testimony, you decided you had to take the stand again and tell the jury the details that you left out the other day, why is that?"

"Objection," Bill said.

"Overruled."

"I wanted to make it clear that I wasn't hiding anything and that I didn't disagree with her. It was clear to me that the Burgers had hearing issues, more serious I think than their vision problems, but they were still able to understand what they were doing and witness the will. They were elderly, but they weren't senile. I wasn't sure that came out clearly enough in Ms. Burger's testimony."

"How do you know that the Burgers understood it was a will that they were witnessing?"

"Because I told them so and they nodded when I did."

"Did they recognize Ben? Withdraw that - let me first ask you, did the Burgers know Ben?"

"I'm pretty certain that they did. He certainly knew them."

"If they didn't know him or recognize him, how would the Burgers have known that it was actually Ben signing the will and not someone else, another man you had brought along pretending to be Ben?"

"Another eighty-eight-year old man?" she said, answering my question with another question.

"Did you show them Ben's driver's license?"

"No."

"Did you introduce him?"

"I'm sure we introduced ourselves that would be common courtesy."

"So they had no way of knowing whether the man in their living room was really Ben Everett?"

"I'm sure they would have known the difference between one of their neighbors and a total stranger."

"And that would that been how - by sight or sound?"

"They weren't stupid, they were old." Susannah said, a little perturbed for the first time. "Besides, I was there and I saw Ben sign it. It was Ben, not a stranger, and the signature bears that out."

I raised the will over my head and shook it.

"You mean this illegible scribble on the line above his name?"

"That was Ben's signature. It has been like that for quite some time. Hands get a little unsteady as you get older, you'll find that out soon enough."

I put the will back down on the table. I had finally gotten Susannah a bit upset, unless this was also an act to get some sympathy from the women on the jury – you know the evil attorney browbeating the poor defenseless widow.

I took a little walk back to counsel table.

"I want to change subjects again, Ms. McCreedy. I'm curious, can you look inside yourself as you sit here now and see into Rose's life. So that if I asked you a question about something from her past, you'd be able to see it and answer me correctly?"

"Objection," Bill said, "beyond the scope of cross."

"I'll allow it." The judge turned to Susannah and said, "You may answer."

"It doesn't work like that."

"The vision comes and goes."

"You could say that."

"And it's not here now? Is the open door into Rose's soul closed at the moment?"

"I wouldn't say that sitting here in Court is conducive to looking into one's soul. Besides, it's more like a mountain in the far off distance that's obscured most of the time by clouds than a door to a room you can open whenever your feel like it and walk right in . . . and like a mountain in the distance you can see the big picture a lot better than you can the small details."

"So even if you could look into your soul now, into your past life, into Rose's life, you'd know some of her history, the broad picture so to speak, but not all the details."

"Not all the details, no."

"That's convenient," I said.

"Objection," Bill said.

"Sustained."

"Who of us remembers the entire history of our own lives even while we live it," Susannah added.

My alternate juror of the same name, Rose, nodded slightly in response. I could have kicked myself for making such a stupid comment.

"But it's definitely cloudy now so you couldn't see clearly enough to answer any new questions about Rose's life?" I said, keeping the sarcasm in my voice below an objectionable level.

This was about as far as I was willing to go. I could see Bill holding himself back from jumping up with an objection.

"That's right, nothing more than I already know," she said, "which is quite a lot."

"I'm sure it is quite a lot," I said, "After all you had almost a year with Ben to talk about his life with Rose, didn't you?"

"Ten months."

The jury looked tired and disinterested in this line of questioning.

"How much more do you have counselor?" Judge Shanawit asked.

"Not much, Your Honor, just one final subject area."

I walked back and leaned against counsel's table.

"Ms. McCreedy, do you remember telling the jury that Ben wanted you to have his money so you could give it to his grandchildren over time and in this way avoid taxes?"

"Yes."

"How many grandchildren are there?"

"Nine."

"Let's see $50 million divided by 9 is about 5 and ½ each. Did Ben want you to give anything to his sons?"

"Of course."

"So that's 3 sons and 9 grandchildren, 12 people, that's about 4 million each . . . that would certainly give Ben's grandchildren a good start in life and help his sons with their retirement, wouldn't it?"

"Certainly."

"And you said that's what you intended to do?"

"Yes and give away some to charity."

"And Ben would expect you to do no less since he believed that you were the reincarnation of Rose?"

'Because he knew who I was . . . his kindred soul."

"And he realized that after ten months?"

"More like ten days," Susannah said, still a little testy.

I took a moment to stroll around the courtroom, forcing the jurors to focus on me.

"Did you leave out anything else when you testified the other day about what you planned to do with the money?"

"Cover my living expenses of course."

"Anything else?"

"And charity to help fight cancer, I said that the other day as well."

"Anything else?"

"Not at the moment."

"The children, the grandchildren, your living expenses and a cancer charity – that's about it?"

"Yes," she said, "more or less."

I walked slowly toward the jury box, their eyes were bouncing back and forth now between Susannah and me like they were watching a tennis match.

"Ms. McCreedy, did you ever hear of the Reincarnation Institute?"

"Oh yes, I understand now what you're getting at."

"I'm not getting at anything Ms. McCreedy, I'm just asking you a simple question that requires a simple yes or no. Did you ever hear of the Reincarnation Institute?"

"Yes, it's another charity."

"It's a corporation that was founded by your father over thirty-five years ago, wasn't it? Again a simple yes or no will suffice."

"Yes."

I glanced over at Bill. His expression hadn't changed, but I could tell by the way he sat back in his chair that this was catching him by surprise.

"And it's been moribund since his death?"

"Moribund?"

"Inactive."

"Yes."

"But you have resurrected it so to speak, haven't you."

"I have. I think it's important for people to understand reincarnation and what it means in terms of life, death and God, particularly in light of what has happened to me. That's one of the charitable activities I had in mind."

"But it's a for-profit corporation, isn't it?"

"I don't know. It was set up so long ago by my father. Perhaps they did things differently back then. I would have thought it was not-for-profit."

I pulled out the corporate filing from the Minnesota Secretary of State.

"Ms. McCreedy, I'm looking at the 1976 filing in Minnesota by your father and the box next to for-profit corporation is checked."

I walked up to the stand and showed it to her.

"Does that refresh you recollection as to whether it's a for-profit corporation?"

"It does not. I know it existed because my father talked about it during his sermons because he wanted to spread the word about reincarnation, but I don't know anything about how he set it up or the legal niceties."

"But you have recently filed the necessary documents and paid the necessary fees to restore it as an active corporation in good standing, haven't you?"

"I asked an attorney in Minnesota to do that because I can't keep what I have seen and felt to myself. It's an act of charity as well . . . spreading the word. "

"About reincarnation?"

"Yes, about the wonderful things awaiting all of us after we leave our earthly bodies."

Keep talking crazy to me, I thought, because this is exactly who I want the jury to see.

"And how is this corporation going to be funded?"

"From donations."

"And Ben Everett's money, isn't that correct?"

"Yes, to get it started. Ben was all for it. In fact, we talked about starting it up again . . . shortly before the accident."

"You have nothing in writing to confirm that, do you Ms. McCreedy?"

"No."

"It's not mentioned in the will?"

"No, it was just pillow talk."

"Something you neglected to mention when you testified the other day."

"It's a charity, it's just seed money."

"How much is this seed money going to be Ms. McCreedy, a thousand, a hundred thousand . . . a million?"

"My goodness no," Susannah said, putting her hand to her chest like the very thought of it was giving her indigestion, "Something small, like ten thousand dollars."

"And if it doesn't take with the first ten thousand dollars, will you add another?"

"I don't know, but it will take. People are hungry for answers." She sounded like the old notions salesman selling the elixir that can cure everything that ails you for a measly dollar.

"And if this will is probated and you receive Ben's $50 million is there anything to prevent you from putting a million dollars or more into the Reincarnation Institute?"

"Just my integrity and my promise to Ben to do the right thing."

I walked slowly back to my seat.

"And you also forgot to tell us about the Reincarnation Institute when you testified the other day?"

"Because it's a charity and I said charities."

"No further questions," I said, sitting down.

Bill jumped up and walked over to Susannah.

"Ms. McCreedy, did you ever say in your direct testimony the other day that you intended to give every cent to Ben's children and grandchildren?"

"No, I would never have said that. The boys don't need all that much, they've done very well for themselves and we talked about making sure the grandchildren got a head start. There is plenty of money for that, but Ben knew there would be a lot left over to help others – for causes that were dear to us – breast cancer for one . . . and reincarnation."

"No further questions," Bill said.

The judge looked over at me and I shook my head from side to side. With that, the judge excused Susannah and took a short recess to give Bill a few minutes to decide if he really wanted to call his surprise witness.

You could see the expectation on the faces of the spectators, as well as the cameraman when we returned from the break. They were expecting Bill to rest and the case go to the jury. The only news of interest at this point was the verdict.

"Mr. Lustenberger, do you have any additional witnesses?"

"One more, Your Honor. We call Jenny Blaine to the stand."

All eyes went to the back of the courtroom.

Jenny was a little waif, so thin that the mothers on the jury couldn't avoid wincing.

Her dress didn't fit at all. It hung down from her shoulders like a sack, like something that had been passed down from a much larger sibling. As she walked slowly to the stand, a bit unsteady, her tiny feet and ankles were swallowed up by her sneakers. I could see why Bill was reluctant to use her. The reaction to a witness like that was too unpredictable.

The deputy guided her up the step to the witness box and she sat down.

"You have to stand up to take the oath," he said.

It wasn't clear to me that she heard him because she didn't rise until the bailiff motioned for her to do so. She followed his lead as well in raising her right hand.

"Do you swear to tell the truth, the whole truth and nothing but the truth?" he asked.

"The truth," she said.

It sounded more like a guess at a multiple-choice question, although she said it with an exaggerated nod which satisfied the judge.

Bill asked permission to approach the bench. He explained that Jenny was a bit slow and requested permission to lead the witness. The judge agreed.

"Ms. Blaine can you tell the jury where you are from?"

"The farm," she said.

"Where is the farm?"

"Canada."

"Is it near Bemidji, Minnesota?"

A big smile spread across Jenny's face and she waved at Susannah.

"Yeah."

Bill walked over to Susannah and stood beside her.

"Do you know Susannah McCreedy?"

"Hi Sue," she said.

"How do you know her?"

"We used to go to her daddy's church until we stopped."

"The one that preached reincarnation?"

"The church of many lives – that's what my mom called it."

"Did your family come down from Canada for the services?"

"Once every month."

"How long was the drive?"

"Long."

"You'd spend the night, wouldn't you?"

"I stayed in Sue's room."

"Were you friends?"

"Best friends."

Bill took a deep breath.

"Jenny, you know the difference between the truth and a lie, don't you?"

"The truth is the gospel."

"And a lie?"

"A lie is the devil."

"Do you remember the Sunday that Susannah gave testimony?"

Jenny looked confused.

"When she saw her other life?"

Jenny nodded.

"Is that a yes?"

"Yeah, she was Rose."

"In her prior life?"

"Yeah."

"Did you ever testify in church?"

Jenny didn't respond.

"Did you ever see a prior life?"

"No, but I still look."

"Can you tell us what happened that night after Susannah called out the name of Rose?"

"Her Daddy was so happy we had ice cream and didn't go to sleep until really late."

"What do you remember about that night, after you went to sleep?"

"Sue fell right asleep, she was really, really tired."

"What else do you remember?"

Jenny shrugged.

"Do you remember whether she was talking in her sleep?"

"Oh yeah."

Jenny looked up at the judge.

"Sleeping is when we are closest to God," she said, "Almost like being dead."

The judge nodded. The jurors were riveted.

"What did she say?" Bill asked.

When she didn't respond, he added, "While she was sleeping."

"Another name."

"What name?"

"Ben."

"That's all?"

"She kept saying Ben."

"What did you do?"

"I woke her and said there's Jenny, but no Ben here."

"What did Susannah say?"

"She laughed, said I made it up."

"She didn't remember."

"No."

"You sure the name was Ben?" Bill asked.

"Ben."

"Did you tell anyone?"

"Her Daddy."

"What did he say?"

"Objection," I said.

"Sustained."

Bill knew it was hearsay, but he obviously wanted the jury to speculate on his response.

"No further questions."

I remained seated a moment while scribbling some notes in my pad and thinking about the best way to approach her on cross. I didn't want the jury angry with me for giving Jenny too hard a time or making her cry, but I couldn't let it go without some tough questioning.

"Hello Jenny, my name is Joe Clasen and I am an attorney also."

"Hello."

"We have never met, have we?"

"No, I'd remember meeting you," she said with a big smile.

"Do you know what this case is about?"

"Sue needs money."

"Who told you that?"

"My Daddy," she said.

"Did you speak to Susannah about it?"

"No, he said I can't, not until after."

"What else did your Daddy say?"

"Sue needed my help."

"And you would do anything to help her, wouldn't you?"

"Yes, anything," she said her eyes wide open and somewhat teary as she stared over at the grieving widow.

"You love Sue, don't you?"

"She's my best friend."

"When did you see her last . . . before today?"

"I don't know. A long time ago, we stopped going to church when I was sixteen."

"Was that the last time?"

"Yeah."

"How come you stopped going?"

Jenny got choked up and just shook her head from side to side.

"Did something happen between you and Sue?"

She nodded.

"Yes?"

She nodded again.

I decided not to press for any of the details. I wouldn't score any points with the jury by reducing her to tears. Let the jurors imagine what happened. It couldn't be that difficult.

"You said that Sue's father was very excited when she testified and called out Rose's name."

She didn't respond.

"Is that right Jenny, Sue's father was very happy?"

"Yeah."

"And you said you stayed up late that night because her father was so happy. Her father had really wanted Sue to see a past life, hadn't he?"

"Sure, who wouldn't?"

"Tell me Jenny, did Sue ever mention any other names?"

"Yeah."

"A lot of different names."

"Yeah."

"Do you remember who they were?"

"No."

"Do you remember Sue's father's name?"

She thought about it a while and then shook her head no.

"How about her mother?"

"No."

"How is it your remember Ben's name."

"I just do."

She looked sheepishly over at Susannah when she said that.

"Did your father say that name– Ben--to you before you came here?"

Jenny thought about it.

"Maybe, I don't remember."

"Were you asleep when Sue started talking in her sleep?"

"I don't know, I think so, I don't remember."

"Do you know that Sue got married?"

"To Ben, like in the dream, but he died."

"Who told you that?"

"My Daddy."

"Did your father receive any money for you to come here?"

"Sue gets the money, not my father."

"Does he also get some money?"

"I don't know."

I thought about pressing the question, but the fact that Bill had to rely on Jenny at this stage of the trial had to signify to the jury just how desperate he was.

"No further questions."

"One question on redirect, Your Honor," Bill said.

The judge nodded.

"Are you sure Jenny that Sue called out the name Ben in her sleep that night after she testified about Rose in church?"

Jenny sat quietly a moment.

"Ben," she said.

It sounded anything but definite to my ear, but you hear things the way you want to hear them at times like this.

"Thank you Ms. Blaine," the judge said, "You may go."

Jenny stood up and walked out just as slowly as she had walked in, trailed by dozens of eyes, a television audience of an indeterminate size and the hollow sound her tiny feet made on the courtroom's worn granite floor.

"Do both sides rest?" the Judge asked.

Both Bill and I confirmed that we did.

"Let's proceed with the summations," she said.

I looked at my watch. It was 11:30. The judge knew what I was thinking, but she wasn't going to break early. She had told us this morning that she was limiting summations to 30 minutes and she clearly wanted to squeeze them in before lunch.

As the challenger to Susannah's petition to probate the will, I had to go first, and before I stood up I took a few quiet breaths to quiet my heart, which was beating so loudly in my ears that it sounded like thunder.

Chapter 14 – Summations

"Souls are poured from one into another of different kinds of bodies of the world."
— Jesus Christ

"Ladies and Gentlemen of the jury," I said very slowly to fill up some time while I continued to organize my thoughts. "My clients and I appreciate the attention that each of you have given to the evidence presented in this matter, particularly considering how warm it's been in the courtroom the past few days.

"As you surely know, this is very important to Mitch, Peter and Jeff Everett, as well as to their wives and children, the grandchildren of Rose and Ben Everett. You and you alone will decide whether the money that Rose and Ben Everett worked so hard and long to accumulate will go to their children and grandchildren or to Ms. McCreedy.

"And we can't forget that it's much more than just money, since according to this new supposed will Ms. McCreedy gets everything . . . every keepsake, every photograph album, the old silver candlesticks brought over from the old country, the Mother's Day and Father's Day gifts, even Ben's watch handed down from his father and promised to Mitch.

"It would include every stick of furniture, every book, every picture hanging on the wall, even if it were something done by one of the grandchildren, and anything that may have been passed down from Rose and Ben's parents. Is it really believable that Ben would knowingly execute a new will without carving out some of these keepsakes for his children and grandchildren? The question is whether you will give it all to her based on this highly questionable document."

I held up the will for them to see.

"And under such highly questionable and unusual circumstances."

I looked over at Susannah and waited for the jurors' eyes to follow mine.

"The first question you have to answer and perhaps the easiest one is whether in fact this is Ben's signature and whether his signing was actually witnessed by two people who understood what they were witnessing, as required by Florida law. Ms. McCreedy tried to brush over it the first time she testified swearing that she and Ben went to the Burgers, explained who they were and what they needed, signed before them and they signed below as knowing witnesses. Simple, neat and clean - end of story."

I turned around for a moment and looked at the empty witness chair.

"But it wasn't the end of the story as we later learned from the daughter of the Burgers, who is what the law calls a disinterested witness, the most trustworthy of all witnesses, because she has nothing to gain by the outcome.

"We learned from her what Ms. McCreedy had neglected to tell us the first time around, that her parents were nearly deaf and blind. Funny that she didn't think it worth bringing up until Ms. Burger told us. Her parents were so deaf and so blind that Ms. McCreedy could have come with just about anyone and gotten them to sign just about anything. Just take a look at Ben's signature on the will. It's hardly legible. It looks like the scribble of a 5-year old.

"Or perhaps Ben did sign it at home unaware of the significance of what he was signing. Look at where his signature is. It's on the last page with only two lines of meaningless text above it; a page that curiously has an extra staple hole as if it was detached and added back. Perhaps Ms. McCreedy detached the last page and asked Ben to sign it telling him that it had something to do with changing her residence for her new license and then reattached it, forgetting for a moment to carefully align the staple holes. Look at it yourself, you can ask to see it. Take it back into the jury room.

"Perhaps she took it with someone else or even alone to get the Burger's to sign as witnesses. They were very elderly and infirm, as Ms. McCreedy forgot to mention on her direct, and of course they're not here to tell us who was there, what was said or what they understood they were signing. What we do know from their daughter was that because of their hearing and vision difficulties it would have been almost impossible to make that clear."

I walked along the jury rail, my eyes jumping from one juror to another.

"Can you bless a new will as fraught with doubts as this one . . . that disinherits an entire family and enriches a twenty-four year old woman who came ten months earlier to clean an old man's house? That's the initial question you have to answer - was this will properly executed and witnessed? If the answer is no, then you need not address any of the other issues . . . you need go no further. If you're still not sure, there's a second question, which I call the elephant in the room. It's the reason why we've had so much interest by the press in the outcome."

I looked at my watch to see how much time I had left and looked for a moment into the camera. I didn't know if I was looking for myself in the reflection or for Betsy at the other end.

I took a deep breath and walked down the jury rail, nodding as I went along, my eyes unblinking and my lips snapped shut. I let the silence roll over the jurors and fill the room.

"The second question is whether Ben himself understood what it was he was signing and what he was doing or whether it came about as the result of what the law calls undue influence.

"The judge will tell you how the law defines undue influence, but it will be up to you to determine how the facts here fit that definition. Did Ben Everett really know and understand what he was doing when he supposedly gave everything he had accumulated over a lifetime to a twenty-four year old woman he had just met, as opposed to his children and grandchildren?"

I backed up until I stood beside Mitch.

"If Ms. McCreedy had been claiming true love, you know, that rare May-December romance that you see from time to time in the movies then we could weigh the facts surrounding their meeting, consider their compatibility and attraction, and determine the likelihood of love. We all know love or at least we have our own experiences and opinions about it.

"But the story Ms. McCreedy tells goes in a very different direction – perhaps because she knew love wouldn't make much sense here--creating instead a different kind of fiction, a miraculous, divine inspiration that Ms. McCreedy well knows can never be proven or disproven."

I put a hand on Mitch's shoulder.

"I suggest to you that her story is too preposterous to be believed, regardless of whether you believe or don't believe in the soul and an afterlife. The conclusion is inescapable--Ben Everett was duped by a very young, very persuasive, and very articulate woman, who in the span of ten months alienated him from his family . . . and his money."

I lifted up my hand, picked up the will and stepped before the jury.

"The clearest evidence of Ben's fragility and the unsoundness of his decision is the fact that this woman claims to have convinced him after two or three times cleaning his house that she was the reincarnation of his late wife, Rose. The woman he had loved for most of his life, the woman he could never replace and didn't even try for twenty-five years after her death.

"Rather than claim that Ben fell in love with her, as you might expect if this were a television soap opera, or a typical scam, she has the temerity to claim that Ben wanted to marry her and give her everything he had because he was convinced that she was really Rose come back to be with him at the end.

"Ladies and gentlemen of the jury, if he did fall for that story, which he apparently did than that should be the end of your deliberations, because that is the essence of undue influence. She is not Rose any more than I am George Washington or you are Abraham Lincoln. We may have eternal souls, but those souls come to us as babies, as the great philosophers used to say as a 'tabula rasa' – a clean slate for us to write on with all the experiences and loves we will have in this life.

"Even if they are recycled or reincarnated, they are purified and cleansed according to every precept of every far eastern religion that ever lived, so that each of us gets to make our own mistakes and learn from our own experiences. You don't get to trade in memories from a prior life for riches in this one."

I put down the exhibits and stood staring at the jury for a moment with my arms folded defiantly across my chest. Then I took a deep breath and walked to the witness stand and stopped before the empty seat.

"Now I don't pretend to know what eternity is or what awaits us, and I'm not going to stand here and tell you I know what the human soul is or isn't, or what's inside it in terms of memories and lifetimes. This isn't the place or the time to decide that. This case isn't about God or the afterlife. It's about this life and this woman.

"Of course, what I say to you now is simply argument, as the judge has explained to you, it's not evidence. What you have to look at as jurors is the evidence from the witnesses' testimony, the documents in evidence and the very circumstances that led to the alleged disinheritance.

"Let's first examine what's not in dispute – first, that Ben was devoted to his late wife Rose and remained in love with her for twenty-five years after her death, keeping to himself, and away from all the single, older women in Florida who would have loved to make Ben their companion.

"We know how much he liked to talk about her from Alma Brown, the woman who cleaned his house for so many years, as well as from his son Mitch. Imagine all the things he told Ms. Brown over the many years she worked for him.

"We also know that Ms. McCreedy grew up attending services run by her father from a barn, a fringe religious group that believed everyone could see into their past lives if only they tried hard enough. We know that he wanted her to testify, to find a past life, and what daughter wouldn't want to please her father. So one day she stood up and called out the name Rose, nothing more, nothing about who that Rose was or how she lived, just a name, something to satisfy her father, a name coincidentally that belonged to his mother, her grandmother.

"Third, we know that she lived for a while in Las Vegas working at one of those marriage mills and was married there to another older, sickly man, who unfortunately had no real monetary assets when he died, but did have a car which she used to travel to Florida.

"Fourth, we know that Ms. McCreedy had very little money when she arrived in Florida and quickly found a job cleaning houses, taking over for Alma Brown who was about to have knee surgery. She met with Ms. Brown before starting and we know that Alma told her all about Ben and Rose; when she died, how old Ben was, and how devoted he was to her . . . undoubtedly telling her some of the Rose stories she had heard during the almost fifteen years she worked for him . . . enough for Ms. McCreedy to make quite an impression on Ben Everett."

I walked over to the jury and leaned against the jury rail.

"I'll tell you something else that common sense tells us. This young woman, Susannah McCreedy, is sharp. She heard the name Rose and when she realized that she had died a year or two before she was born, and just how fixated Ben was on her after all these years, a light went on in her head.

"She hadn't forgotten that newspaper article eight years earlier, because she carried it with her. And she realized she might get more than a car this time; perhaps if she got lucky she might wind up with a place to live and some money. And she got that and we might not be here today if she hadn't gotten greedy and set her sights on more . . . on the $50 million jackpot."

I pantomimed the pulling of a lever on a slot machine as I said that.

"Ben didn't stand a chance. He was eighty-eight years old, slowing down every day, far away from his family, undoubtedly lonely, when into his life replacing his old cleaning woman appeared a younger woman who laughed at his jokes and seemed so very interested in everything he had to say, particularly the stories about his wife Rose.

"She remembered the stories Alma Brown told her, studied the pictures of Rose in his house, looked at the albums, asked questions and after a week or two was able to tell him all kinds of things about Rose. Perhaps repeating stories Ben had told her the week before. You heard how forgetful Ben had become, so when she threw them back at him a week or two later, he was amazed and dumbfounded.

"What she offered was better than a séance. Susannah McCreedy was a medium of sorts who offered Rose herself... reincarnated. How could Ben resist."

I backed up until I was standing across from Susannah, who I refused to look at, although out of the corner of my eye I could see her sitting there with her hands folded on the table, as if she were as bored by all of this as the judge.

I walked slowly back to the jury and lowered my voice.

"But her plan went better than expected. He agreed to keep the reasons for their marriage secret. She kept him away from the clubhouse and never left him alone with his sons when they called or came down for a visit."

I glanced at my watch. I knew Judge Shanawit would be somewhat lenient about the 30 minutes, particularly with the whole world watching, at least the cable world. And I would love to have taken it to lunchtime so that the jury would break with only my words ringing in their ears.

I stepped back and raised my voice.

"This isn't a verdict on reincarnation or God or the afterlife. It's a vote on the credibility of Ms. McCreedy's story and the soundness of Ben's intentions."

I explained how easy it would have been for Ben to set up trusts in his will to make sure his children and grandchildren received something and I reminded them how Ms. McCreedy changed her story when confronted with her investment in the Reincarnation Institute. I also reminded them about Dr.

Seymour's testimony and the difference between talking to your broker over the telephone and to a twenty-four year old woman who claims to be the embodiment of your late spouse.

"Of course," I said, "Ms. McCreedy is no fool, so to make Ben sound like he was thinking soundly when they got married she testified that he had in fact made her sign a waiver of her spousal right of inheritance."

I sighed loudly and looked over at Susannah and then back at the jury.

"But where is it," I said quietly.

"Where is it," I said much louder this time. "It can't be found. It's not in any of his important papers or in any of his drawers. The lawyer doesn't have it, neither does Mr. Milstein . . . because it never existed. She made it up just as she made up her life as Rose."

Throwing it away made no sense, I explained, since if Ben came to doubt this woman and decided to change his alleged will back to the way it was he'd need that waiver to prevent her from still getting one-third, and one-third of $50 million is quite a haul.

"Undue influence is the only conclusion as to why Ben married so quickly and deeded ownership of his home to her, along with a sizeable bank account, a gift, which he could not reverse. Undue influence is the only conclusion that would explain how she convinced Ben to keep it all a secret from his family - the reincarnation, the deed and the bank account . . . and eventually the new will. Undue influence is the only conclusion as to why Ben would give away everything he owned from his father's old watch to his photographs without so much as a word to his children or grandchildren."

I looked over at my three clients and sort of wished I had given in to their requests and allowed them to bring the grandchildren to court.

"Now Ms. McCreedy's counsel gets the last word because that is the rule in this court, since she is the party seeking to probate the will and we are the parties seeking to stop her. And we also have the burden of proof, as the judge will explain to you, the presumption normally being that a signed and witnessed will reflects the true intention of the testator. A burden, which I suggest to you we have met a hundred fold.

"Of course, I don't know exactly what Mr. Lustenberger will say, but I'm sure he will try to make your decision sound like a referendum on God and the existence of the human soul. Does the soul migrate from one body to the next, no one knows, so by what right, he might say, do you or anyone else have to disbelieve two people who believe that and act accordingly?

"Perhaps he'd have a point provided Ms. McCreedy truly believed she was the reincarnation of Ben's wife, and, more importantly, Ben did as well, based on real facts, not trickery and fraud. Perhaps he'd have a point if he wasn't eighty-eight and there wasn't fifty million changing hands as a result of this supposed belief.

"We all believe different things, he may say, and we are each entitled to our beliefs and to act on our beliefs, which is true. I don't disagree with that for one moment, but we are not entitled to take our beliefs – real or contrived-- and brainwash a weak, susceptible individual, whether it's an elderly man, a recent widow or a young child to take advantage of them.

"Would it have been any different, he may say if he had given all of his money to fight breast cancer, instead of his three sons and nine grandchildren? Would they be here challenging the will if that were the case?"

I took a breath and stepped up to the railing. I reduced my voice to a whisper so that the jurors would all lean forward in their seats.

"Maybe not, but that's not the case here, not by a long shot. Ms. McCreedy is not a charity and the only one who will benefit from this money is her."

I paused and when I spoke again I could hear my voice ringing out like a bell, "What I would remind you if I had the opportunity to talk to you again afterward is that Ben didn't give his fortune to charity. He didn't give it to his church or a long-suffering companion who stood beside him for twenty-five years after his wife died. He gave it to a twenty-four year old drifter from Minnesota by way of Las Vegas, who had already buried one older husband and wound up with his car. He gave it to someone he met a month before marrying her and less than a year before he died, who knew Ben's weak spot–Rose–and went right for it."

I took a deep breath and wiped my brow. Then I walked slowly back to my seat.

"Ben was the perfect victim, susceptible to a siren who whispered his beloved's name."

With that I thanked the jury and sat down. I looked at my watch, so did the judge – 35 minutes.

Bill immediately stood up, put his hands in his pants pockets in a very folksy way and remained standing beside Susannah, who looked as calm as ever. I bit down on my tongue as soon as it dawned on me that I had completely forgotten to say anything about Jenny. Of course, the weakness of her testimony was obvious enough, although I would have liked to point that out.

"Two people can stare at the same colorful sunset and see two different things," Bill said. "One person may see it as a gift from God, proof of the divine and eternal, and another may look at it as phenomenon of nature, something that happens to light when it passes through the curve of the horizon and hits droplets of moisture in the air. We each have our own feelings as to what it may represent, but I don't know how any one of us could say one person is right and the other is wrong. We are each, as my colleague just told you, entitled to our own beliefs."

Bill rested his hand gently on Susannah's shoulder for a moment before approaching the jury box.

"Now some people don't believe in God, although I suspect many more do, and those of us who do believe that there is more to a person than the body. Call it the spirit or the soul, the eternal or the spark of divinity - call it what you will - but we believe that it is an essence that survives after the blood has ceased to flow. There is not a religion in the world that doesn't believe that. It's something that we all share in common.

"What happens to that soul, that essence, after we cease to breathe has been debated for millenniums by people a lot wiser and closer to God than you and I. It ranges from heaven to hell to a thousand places in between. The belief that the soul, that essence of the divine, is born again, reincarnated in another life, is one of those beliefs.

"It's a belief that is found throughout the world and throughout history. It is so widespread as to count its adherents in the billions. It can be found in the bible, in the early teachings of the church and as a basic precept in two of the four major religions on the earth."

Bill leaned against the railing.

"Now if my client, if Susannah McCreedy, had never believed in reincarnation before and brought it up for the first time when she met Ben, I would agree that it might sound like someone with a more sinister motive, someone without a true and sincere belief. Understandably, a situation like that would be filled with doubt and suspicion. But that's not the case here, not by any stretch of the imagination.

"Susannah grew up, as much of the world has, believing that our souls go to God after we die and are reincarnated again – returned to earth as part of a learning and maturation process. Growing up, she witnessed people reach inside for a glimpse of their past life, pieces of memory that some might call déjà vu, and indeed as a young girl of 16 she caught a glimpse of hers as well, standing up before the congregation and calling out the name she saw in her soul . . . Rose.

"There is no question that occurred over eight years before she met Ben because there were witnesses, including a reporter from the local newspaper who wrote it down, and we have that article," he said holding it in front of him for the jury to see, "but you know that, and it's not in dispute. Nor can anyone really doubt the sincerity and truthfulness of that simple young woman, Jenny, who recalled Susannah calling out the name Ben that very same night . . . Ben," Bill repeated softly, backing slowly away from the jury.

He gave the word some time to sink in.

"To think that Susannah's belief is not sincere, but something she concocted while sitting down with Alma getting ready for her new job is what's preposterous, not her belief in reincarnation. To think that it is anything less than genuine does a disservice to her, her family and the billions around the world who hold that very same belief.

"Perhaps even some of you do. Who of us hasn't met someone who reminds us of a long departed friend or relative and felt the similarities, not just in looks, but in personality and spirit? This entire case starts and finishes with the sincerity of Susannah's belief. There can be no undue influence when there is sincere belief."

Bill looked for a moment at Susannah before turning back to the jury.

"I see no evidence, circumstantial or otherwise, that has come out at this trial that would make anyone doubt that sincerity. It is her sincere belief - as true as any other - which is the basis for all that came afterward . . . the love and marriage, the gift of the house and the account . . . and the will."

Bill walked over to Susannah and I could swear that she was illuminated for a moment by a ray of sunlight that found its way through the trees outside. I've seen enough coincidences in my life to dismiss that one as well, but I still didn't like it. I glanced at the jury to see if they had noticed. There was no surprise registered on any of their faces. Indeed, there was no emotion of any kind.

"Now I know that Ben's sons have the burden in this case because they are trying to overturn Ben's expressed wishes, but we'll gladly take on that burden. If you don't believe Susannah sincerely and truly believes she is a reincarnate than don't go any further. But if you do, if you accept her belief as genuine as your own, than you have to ask yourself one final question . . . could Ben have come to believe it as well."

Bill walked behind Susannah. Fortunately, the sun disappeared behind a cloud.

"Of course, we don't have Ben here to answer that question, but he did answer it for us in a number of very significant and meaningful ways. He answered it by marrying Susannah – still a little uncertain, but a mark of his intelligence and awareness, he had her sign a waiver of her statutory right to one-third of his estate, so that if he was wrong, if he came to disbelieve it, he didn't have to worry about her taking a third of his estate. But those doubts began to melt away as he got to know Susannah better, and he decided to make sure she had a house to live in and money to live on when he was gone.

"Those are two very clear answers to the question – indicating yes, Ben did come to believe in Susannah's sincerity and spiritual connection to his late wife. Then he answered it again for a third time – evidencing what he sincerely came to believe many months later when he changed his will to give Susannah his estate to distribute - in large part to their children and grandchildren and to use the rest as she saw fit, including furthering the belief that she so strongly held and he had come to share – that the soul goes on after death to be reborn."

Bill glanced down at the pad on his desk.

He talked about what Susannah felt at 16 when she called out Rose's name and Ben's – in her sleep – and all the small details that she knew about Rose's likes and life.

"You heard her speak," Bill said, "You saw her on the stand. Do you have any doubt that Susannah was speaking from the heart? Could a 24-year old woman be that calm and serene if she weren't? And what she knew about Rose was remarkable.

"The happiness that this discovery – this belief - brought to Ben and Susannah in the course of one year was priceless. It's not something that can be measured in days or dollars, only in spirit and contentment. Yes, it ended prematurely due to an unfortunate accident, but where is it written that a love must last five years to be meaningful? Ben decided what he wanted to do and he did it. He had that right."

Bill walked slowly toward the jury and lowered his voice.

"If Ben's fortune had consisted of his house and fifty thousand dollars would we be here today? I don't think so. How about a house and one hundred thousand dollars? I would say no. Does the sincerity of Susannah and Ben's belief and Ben's freedom to decide what to do with his worldly assets become voidable just because the amount is in the millions instead of the thousands? Don't let the size divert you from the task at hand.

"The question is whether Ben's actions over the course of a year of marriage confirm that he came to believe in Susannah's vision as much as she did and that he signed a new will because in his heart it was what he wanted to do."

Bill went on and on about how Ben came to believe in Susannah and her spirit and gave her something much more valuable than his money, he gave her his trust.

"Undue influence," Bill said, raising his voice, "is when people approach senior citizens with lies about their children being sick or relatives in trouble and ask for money. Undue influence is when they approach the elderly with lies about what they owe the government and the need for immediate costly roof repairs. They are simply con men and frauds.

"A woman who believes in God and the soul, who feels touched by the divine, and shares what she feels, who brings happiness and contentment to someone who will in not too many years take leave of his body has not used undue influence any more than the priests, ministers and rabbis do when they tell us how God expects us to behave and live and die . . . and tithe to the church."

Bill cleared his throat and walked back to Susannah. She didn't smile. She just sat there gazing at the jurors, an understanding and grandmotherly look on her face, like they were disobedient children who she could never stop loving, no matter what they decided. It was almost as if she were letting them know in advance that she would forgive them if they decided against her. She must have spent untold hours, I thought, perfecting that wise and mature look.

"And yes there are experts like Dr. Seymour who can talk in generalities about old people, but he can't tell you how that applies to any one individual and especially not to Ben, who he never met. Everyone, including Ben's own son, confirmed just how sprite and lively Ben was and how aware and intelligent. Does intelligence suddenly stop short like that when it comes to what you believe?

"Was Ben somehow rendered incapable of judging what he thought about God and the soul because of Susannah's belief? Did her beauty dazzle him?"

Bill walked behind Susannah and put his hand on her shoulder.

"And don't forget Jenny. She's a simple soul and I don't think that there is anyone in this courtroom who believes her capable of lying. She remembers well that night that Susannah called out Rose's name and she remembers that night when she called out yet another name . . . Ben."

Bill lifted his hand almost as if he were about to give a benediction and walked slowly toward from the jury.

"She called out the name Ben," he said, raising his voice and sighing loudly enough for everyone to hear.

"If you believe Jenny incapable of telling a lie than your decision is clear. The sincerity of Susannah's belief is beyond question and Ben was free to believe as well."

Bill leaned against the jury box and dropped his voice to a whisper, so that the court reporter, the judge and everyone else in the courtroom had to lean forward to hear him.

"We don't know what God has waiting for us after we die, but you certainly cannot deny that it could very well be what Susannah has experienced . . . and Ben. It's a wonderful thing to find someone who you think you have lost. We do it sometimes in life when it comes to great distances, why not in time as well?"

Bill looked up at the ceiling and his voice rose with his gaze.

"A belief in the soul and a vision of what may lay before us is not undue influence. A belief that you may have found the love of your life deep inside another person who carries the same spark of divinity is not undue influence. A decision to give away material things to someone who has answered a question that has troubled you for most of your adult life and brought you contentment at a time when you needed it most is not undue influence. It's called faith and love . . . and there is no wrong or right when it comes to faith and love. It's what makes people like Ben do the unexpected and take a different path."

Bill backed away and looked at me.

"I'm a big believer in common sense just as my colleague is, but common sense doesn't hold all the answers. It doesn't hold the answers when it comes to the mystery of the soul. There's no substitute for common sense when it comes to most of our day to day activities, but when it comes to God and eternity it's the uncommon sense we need . . . the uncommon sense of spirit and belief, of faith and courage to follow our own path. I think that's what makes the human race so unique and special. Don't deny Ben his belief and his right to do what he thought appropriate at the end of his life just because you have a different belief or find it hard to believe in what he came to believe.

"He was confident that Susannah would do the right thing because of what he saw in her heart and soul, and if he didn't always see his late wife, he saw parts of her there, and he recognized the same intrinsic divinity. His actions confirm that, they shout it out loud and clear."

Bill walked back to his chair and glanced at his watch. He still had a few more minutes left.

"Who are we to deny Ben his free will and the different path he chose with it?"

With that Bill thanked the jury and sat down. I had to admit it was a good summation. It was more emotional in a way. Of course, it's always good to get in the last word, I thought, still kicking myself about not mentioning Jenny.

The judge thanked both sides and turned to the jury.

"Ladies and Gentlemen of the jury, I am going to excuse the remaining alternates at this time and thank them for their time and attention. If you have anything in the jury room, please go with the deputy now and take it out. You are free to talk to anyone about this case, but I would ask you not to, particularly not to any reporters, at least not until the verdict has been announced."

With that the alternates left. They looked disappointed, as if they had to leave the party early. I'm sure they were looking forward to their fifteen minutes of fame, to be the center of national attention for one time in their lives, but that would belong to the first six jurors who would actually participate in the deliberations. Normally I would have had my secretary waiting outside to speak with the excused alternates, but the judge had directed Bill and me not to speak to them until the verdict had been reached.

"I'm going to ask the remaining jurors to adjourn to the jury room while I prepare the charge. You can have your lunch and relax a bit. After lunch I will read the charge to you, which are the instructions about the law that you must follow in deciding the case. I would remind you again not discuss anything about the case among yourselves until after you have heard the charge. At that point you can begin your deliberations."

With that the other deputy escorted the seated jurors back to the jury room.

"I have counsel's requests to charge," Judge Shanawit said, "Which I will consider during lunch. Let's meet back in chambers at two for the charging conference."

With that the judge left the bench and I went back to the witness room to discuss things over with My Three Sons.

"I wonder if Dad really knew what he was doing," Mitch said. "What if he really believed it? Hey, we've all done some stupid things with money, why not him?"

"Bullshit," Peter said.

"You mean brainwashed," Jeff said.

"I don't think your father had a chance," I said.

"Wouldn't it be something if it were true," Mitch said, and both Peter and Jeff made fish faces.

We all sat there a while staring at the center of the table, as if we expected something important to materialize there. It's normal to have doubts at the end. No one would ever go to trial if the outcome was always a forgone conclusion. We all knew her story was nonsense, everyone in the courtroom did, but who wouldn't want to find some reason to doubt, who wouldn't want to believe some of it. And what deep-seated prejudices were there among the jurors against a rich and good-looking family like the Everetts?

"She'll still have the house," Jeff said, "and the bank account."

"And don't think the jury won't remember that," I said. "But you can go after that if we win, if you really want to. If it was undue influence with the will than it's the same with the house and bank account."

"Let her have the house," Mitch said.

"Over my dead body," Jeff said, although I doubted he'd have the stomach to do it all over again in Florida.

"So you're pretty confident we're going to win?" Peter asked.

I nodded. I would have answered that way even if I wasn't--you have to as an attorney, especially after trial, better to be shocked by the result than fill the room with doubt.

We went out to lunch together and spent the entire time dissecting the witnesses and the body language of the jury until I had to leave to attend the charging conference.

It was a straightforward, fair charge, putting the burden on My Three Sons to prove by a preponderance of the evidence either that the will was not properly executed or, if it was, that Ben signed it as the result of undue influence.

"This has been a strange one," the judge said, as she put on her robe. "I appreciate how counsel tried to keep us earthbound for most of it."

We both laughed, forced laughs, but what choice did we have.

"What do you think?" I asked Bill, as we walked back to the courtroom.

"That the only one who doesn't care about the outcome is my client," he said. "She is a strange one."

"Because she's already won a prize and now it's just a question of running up the score."

"Maybe and maybe not."

Responses like that always leave me feeling like I've been talking to myself.

It took the judge about thirty minutes to read the charge, at which point the jury retired to the jury room to begin their deliberations. A marshal, his arms folded across his chest, was posted in front of the door in case anyone had any ideas of listening in.

"Don't wander too far," the judge said to Bill and me.

We both headed back to our offices, which were in opposite directions about a block from the courthouse.

"Don't think it will be quick," I told My Three Sons before I left. "The jurors are going to want to take their time. They owe it to the parties, to the issues and especially to the press. Besides, they're going to enjoy knowing that the whole world is waiting and watching, at least the Court TV world."

Of course, a quick decision would be in our favor, the more time they spent deliberating meant the more likely there was more than one dissenter.

The crowds outside were quiet, sitting around dosing in the sun. The reporters who found the energy to walk alongside me to my office got the same answer to their questions that I assume Bill gave them.

"I'll have no comment until after the jury's verdict."

Chapter 15 – The Verdict

"So as through a glass and darkly, the age long strife I see where I fought in many guises, many names, but always me."
– General George S. Patton

"We took a secret ballot as soon as we got back to the jury room," Rose told the reporters the next evening after a day and a half of deliberations, "just to get a sense of where we stood." Her hands were very animated as she spoke. She sounded nothing like the quiet, older widow I saw sitting solemnly in the jury box.

"The judge said it had to be a 5-1 vote and the first vote was 4-2. I was surprised by that, really surprised. I was sure we'd be 6-0 right from the start. I mean one more for that woman and we'd have been evenly split, and maybe it could have gone the other way because we all agreed that we weren't leaving without a verdict."

I already knew who the two holdouts were from my conversations with Millie, the forewoman, who refused to speak to the press, but didn't mind speaking to me. They were Frank, the angry postal worker, and, somewhat of a surprise, juror 5, Lauren, the single mid-30s business owner.

"Do you think she saw herself in the same position someday, marrying an older rich widower?" I asked.

Millie sounded confused by the question.

"How would I know that?"

"Did she give a reason?"

"She believed her."

"She believed in reincarnation?"

"I don't know, we didn't get that personal. She believed that Susannah did and Ben as well," Millie said. "Her point was that if Ben could have given all his money away to charity while he was alive, why couldn't he give it to her if he came to believe in reincarnation. It was his money."

"And you?" I asked.

"My mother lost it in her late seventies. She didn't even recognize me. He couldn't have been thinking straight at his age."

Frank, the postal worker, bought Bill's argument that if it was OK with five thousand dollars then it should be no different with fifty million dollars. Besides, he argued, there was no proof that that old man didn't know what he was doing. Being eighty-eight, Frank said, doesn't make you an imbecile.

"I think all six of us were pretty religious in our own way," Rose said when she was interviewed on the Today Show, "But most of us – the four of us - just didn't believe her. God may act in mysterious ways, but not ridiculous ways. It was way too cute if you ask me. Here she comes fresh from burying her first older husband, flat broke, hears about Ben and Rose, and the next thing you know she's married again to a rich man. Why would God waste a miracle on someone like that?"

Matt only spoke to the press once immediately after the verdict. He admitted that he believed in spiritual rebirth, which is what he called it, although he didn't believe in Susannah.

"If she were really Rose," he said, "She'd have renounced the will and been content with the house and the bank account. She wouldn't fight with her former sons. She was pretty good acting out the old woman, I'll give her that, but she was entirely too greedy for someone supposedly connected to the cosmos like that."

Ira was happy to talk to anyone, anywhere, anytime, but the press quickly got tired of listening to him. He talked too fast and too loud and he sang a one-note tune. He said that he knew Susannah was a crook from the first day. He could smell a scheme like that a mile away. Love or reincarnation, he said, it didn't much matter; it was always the same story, a twenty-four year old loser looking for the big score.

After that first 4-2 vote, Rose said, they argued back and forth for the rest of the afternoon until the judge sent them back to the hotel for the night. It seemed pretty clear at that point, Millie told me, that Frank and Lauren were prepared to stick by their positions and the four of them were worried about a hung jury.

"We didn't want to give her the satisfaction," she told me.

The next morning Lauren pressed her point. It didn't matter she said if Susannah thought she was Rose or Joan of Arc because all that really mattered was that she truly believed she was a reincarnate.

"Susannah believed it," Lauren said, "and look how calm and content that's made her? So why couldn't Ben fall in love with her just for that."

Frank believed in freedom of choice and said that nothing he'd heard convinced him that Ben was too far gone to make up his own mind.

"As stupid as the decision may seem looking back on it now," Frank said, "It was his money to do with as he pleased."

Rose started working on Lauren because she knew she wasn't going to reach Frank. It was clear that no one could. So Rose had the court reporter read back Susannah's testimony, as well as Dr. Seymour's so they could go over it again with Lauren, and in the end Lauren agreed to change her vote, especially when it was getting late on Friday and the judge made it clear that she'd make them deliberate all weekend if necessary.

She changed her vote, she said, although not her mind. She still believed love didn't have to answer to reason or common sense and was entitled to make its own mistakes, but she agreed to throw out the will because in the end Ben was an old man and was probably more susceptible then he'd normally have been, and it left the parties pretty much where they would have been if the will hadn't been changed - the family would get the money and the keepsakes and Susannah would get the house and the bank account. It seemed like a fair compromise to her.

Bill said that Susannah was not planning to appeal, which was no great concession since she didn't have anything to appeal from. The judge didn't make any erroneous rulings and her charge was straight by the books. I couldn't give him the same assurances with respect to the house and the account because the brothers were bickering like a couple of twelve year olds about whether or not to go after her in Florida for that.

My advice was to let it go. It would be another media circus and in the end they were entitled to all of Ben and Rose's personal effects anyway, as well as all the furniture, since the deed to the house didn't include the furnishings. They stripped the house bare within a week.

The reporters lingered around for a couple of days, but within a week it was back to normal. Once again I was trudging alone up the courthouse stairs to yet another preliminary conference about some slip and fall case, the park now completely deserted except for one or two religious pamphlets missed by the cleaning crew lying under a bench and more birds than usual picking over the crumbs left from the occupation.

I spoke almost every night with Madame Aurora after the verdict, which is how I thought of her when I wasn't with her, and other than her congratulating me on the outcome and me thanking her for her well-intentioned assistance, we didn't speak about the case. Instead, we spoke about ourselves and our pasts, like a couple of high school kids who had just met a school dance.

We both agreed that it would be better not to see each other for a week or so, until the news settled down and the latest crime of passion pushed Susannah out of the public's memory. I still didn't want Betsy remotely connected with the case, which is what I told her, although what I was really concerned about was tainting my efforts and reputation with rumors of my legal consultation with the occult.

A week after the verdict Murray popped into the office to congratulate me and drop off his last bill, which was sure to pop out the eyes of My Three Sons.

"It was really a slam dunk when you think about it," he said, "once we had the information about Alma and the first husband."

Murray was not shy about claiming credit.

"Any chance we can get the DA in Florida to go after her criminally?" I asked in response to questions from Peter and Jeff.

Murray laughed.

"They're too busy chasing drug dealers to worry about the bona fides of the latest prophet."

Prophet, I suppose, was the right word, since Murray had heard that Susannah had put the Florida house on the market and contributed a big chunk of the money in the account set up for her living expenses to the Reincarnation Institute. He'd also heard talk about her traveling the lecture circuit in the fall.

It was the Friday night after Murray's visit that Betsy came for the weekend. We didn't leave the house. I'd stocked up with some really nice wine and food and it felt like we were a couple of teenagers with our parents out of town.

We were lying in bed Sunday morning at about 10am, late for me, as I rarely stayed in bed past 7:30. Her head was resting on my shoulder and each of us was staring up at the ceiling, perhaps into our own imagined futures . . . futures that I hoped looked very similar. I couldn't decide whether I was sleepy again or aroused when Betsy broke the silence.

"I had another dream," she said.

"Another communication from Eva?"

I could feel her nodding.

"I thought you only got them when you sleep alone," I said, feeling a little anxious.

"That's true," she said, turning to look into my eyes. "I've had the best sleep this weekend, better than I can ever remember."

"I'm confused."

"It was Thursday night."

"Why didn't you say something earlier?"

"I was waiting for the right moment."

I didn't think this was the right moment. I didn't think there would ever be the right moment for something like this, but I just lay there without saying a word.

"Eva came to say goodbye."

"What does that mean?"

"She's being reincarnated."

I couldn't help a little sigh.

"Don't you even have a small doubt at this point about your soul?" she asked.

"Not the slightest. The light shuts off, it all goes dark; no fantasy is going to change that."

"How can you be so sure?" she asked.

"I just am. It's something I know . . . I believe and we both know that belief requires no proof."

"It must be tough for you to fall asleep."

"Sometimes . . . not with you here."

"Susannah wasn't lying," she said, rolling off my shoulder and turning toward me on the pillow so we were face to face.

"I'm glad you weren't on the jury."

"I still wouldn't have given her the money. She shouldn't have tried to interfere like that."

"Is that all Eva had to say," I said, "Goodbye?"

"No."

I could hear the hesitation in her breathing.

"Go ahead," I said, "I won't laugh."

"She said that the whole thing with Susannah was a mistake."

"What whole thing?"

"Her being able to see her past life."

"Like a tear in the space time continuum," I said, quoting a line I remembered from a Star Trek show.

Betsy smiled. "No, but it wasn't part of some greater plan, it didn't happen on purpose, it was just a mistake; the cosmos have unforeseen events as well."

"She said that?"

Betsy answered me with a look.

"OK, I get it, it was a mistake."

"A mistake that's about to be corrected," she said.

"Does that mean what I think it means?" I asked.

She answered again with her eyes.

The sigh I let out this time was much louder. We climbed out of bed, got dressed and went out on the back porch to drink our coffee.

"Can we put this behind us for a while," I said. "I need some time to put things in perspective. I need to go cold turkey . . . no talk about the soul or the afterlife."

"Sure," she said, stroking my arm.

"We can agree to disagree," I said, "and leave it at that."

"I'm used to the skepticism," she said, staring up at the clear, blue, summer sky.

A week later, Betsy turned out to be right. Susannah died in her sleep. Her heart simply gave out, according to the coroner, probably because of her weight or her sadness at the rejection by the jury and the loss of Ben, at least according to the *National Enquirer*. Just as she had promised, her will named Mitch, Peter and Jeff as beneficiaries.

They got the house which had not yet been sold, although almost all of the money in her expense account had already been transferred to the Reincarnation Institute, as if she knew what was about to happen. I'm sure there are drugs you can take to make a death like that appear natural.

A few days later the letter came. It was in an unmarked envelope, by that I mean there was no return address and no postmark, as if the letter had been delivered without going through the normal postal channels. When I first saw it on my desk I thought it might be another resume, which I had suddenly started receiving as the result of my Court TV fame, or another solicitation for a donation, which had also increased exponentially since the trial.

It sat unopened for most of the day. After my secretary left and I was getting ready to leave for the night I noticed it again and almost threw the letter away without opening it, but something stopped me. Maybe it was the handwriting, which looked vaguely familiar or the way it had sat there all day in the exact same spot, refusing to budge.

Dear Joe,

Attached is the waiver you were looking for. I found it in the freezer. I should have known to look there since that was a favorite hiding place for Rose, which is why I'm sure Ben put it there. She used to hide her jewelry there whenever she went on vacation.

By the time you get this Joe I will certainly have finished with this body. You should have no feelings of regret or blame since it's not your fault and I look forward to it. None of this feels right. When you see as far back as I have it weighs heavily on your heart, certainly when you see some things you'd rather not.

I decided after the trial that it couldn't have been intended. It had to be a mistake, a spiritual birth defect. It leaves me feeling like a freak —inside and out, even though it gives me great comfort at the same time. Still I can feel the rectification coming. The cosmos balance things out eventually, rather quickly really.

It's a natural death I see coming Joe. I can see and feel it as surely as I do Rose's pain and anguish at the end of her life. Still, the time has not been wasted. I have learned a great deal about the importance of not limiting possibilities . . . doubt is a good thing, a far better thing I think than certainty. Certainty is too smug and can often be wrong. Doubt is never wrong since it always allows for redemption and hope.

The heart doesn't have all the answers any more than the head does, Joe. There is a third part to human nature—call it the spirit or faith— which is as important for us to nurture as intelligence and love.

I know you do not believe in much beyond what you can see and feel, but I know you want to, everyone does, and I want to help you. I thought about the best way to do that and have come up with this. I know all about the call Rose got as a young girl when she knew her father had died before answering it. I know about her guilt for not visiting Eva after she was institutionalized and how painful that was at the end of her life. I know these things because I saw them in my soul, which sits below and behind my heart like a photo album.

I also know things about Mitch, Peter and Jeff that you do not, that was never mentioned, that not even Ben knew. That Mitch was with another man for some point in college, something he told Rose and made her promise never to tell Ben, who would never have understood. Ben was a good man, but a big believer in mind over body, and intolerant of things that men tended to be intolerant of back then. It was a promise Rose kept.

I also know that Jeff made a girl pregnant his first year in college and came to Rose for help. Ben did not easily tolerate errors in judgment from himself or from his sons. That remained a secret between Rose and Jeff as well. Boys tell their mother's things because they know they'll be safe and never thrown back at them. Men are not always that compassionate.

We will meet again Joe, you can trust in that, because we are souls that have met before.

Kindly,
Susannah.

I never asked Mitch or Jeff about what she wrote because I somehow knew that they were true, particularly after the notary, a local Florida pharmacist, confirmed Ben's signature on the waiver. I showed the letter to Betsy who, keeping with our agreement, nodded her head, but said nothing. Of course, she didn't have to.

I found myself falling asleep easily after Susannah's letter, without the aid of sleeping pills, with or without Betsy, and waking up more refreshed than I have since I was in my twenties when there never seemed to be an end in sight. And strangely enough the falling dreams have stopped.

Perhaps that was part of Susannah's purpose in life--to end Ben's doubts and resurrect mine. It's a lot easier sometimes to live with doubt, than it is with certainty.

###

Sample: *The Year of Soup*

The Preamble – Two Soup Lovers

I decided to open a restaurant on my 30th birthday after three different lovers and the same number of careers. I started after college as a beat reporter for a local newspaper on the New York side of Lake Champlain in Plattsburgh. That lasted for three years. I then became an art teacher at a private school in rural Vermont for another three years, followed by a stint as an assistant to a fashion photographer in San Francisco. It shouldn't be too difficult to figure out how long I lasted in that job—three years. Everything in my life seemed based on threes, including my cycle, which is closer to three weeks than four.

I decided to open a restaurant to break that numerical jinx because I read that it takes at least three years for a restaurant to start making money and with a ten year bank loan I had no choice but to stick with it. Besides, cooking and eating have always been the easiest way for me to forget and move on. I'm not referring to rich, chocolaty desserts or fried foods like homemade potato chips, although both, especially when combined with an old late-night movie, can be a wonderful amnesiac in the aftermath of a break-up, especially when it seems as if you're running out of time. For me, it's always been about soups. I suppose because my great-grandmother was famous for them, as was my grandmother and mother. When my mother died way too young, the victim of a smoking habit she couldn't shake, she left me the family notebook filled with hundreds of handwritten soup recipes that went back across the Atlantic to my great-grandmother's mother and her grandmother.

On those days when I feel singled out and alone, ready to weep if I see one more dark cloud, which has become more and more frequent as my success with relationships has failed to come close to matching my expectations, it's always soup I turn to. It's soup that helps me pull the emotional plug so those feelings can run out my mental drain, and it's more than just the soup—it's the preparation as well that helps make the bitter a bit sweeter.

Take potato leek soup, for example, a basic and simple soup with what seems sometimes like a heavenly reward. First, there's the steady, rhythmic chopping of the potatoes, the leeks, the celery and the onions. The sound of the knife against the cutting board, that old, familiar cutting board given to me by mother as a housewarming gift when I moved into my first apartment, cut and bruised by more emotional mishaps than it deserved, provides a soothing counterpoint to the sharp beating of my sad heart. The focus and concentration that it takes to slice the garlic thin enough to crackle and disappear when sautéed in butter, and it has to be 100 percent butter—margarine can be no substitute at a time like this—always manages to turn those moments of preparation into the only reality.

Browning the ingredients brings an amazing auditory and olfactory comfort. The smell of sautéing onions and leeks, a staple in my mother's kitchen, is like reconnecting with an old acquaintance who remembers me at my best or hearing from a favorite aunt who still holds me up high on a pedestal, regardless of how low I may feel my life has sunk. The onions brown, seemingly alive as they yellow and shrivel with time, always drawing my undivided attention, almost whispering as they simmer, as if to remind me that there is a life force that lives on even when my expectations are lower than they've ever been before. It's a scent that reaches back to my childhood and further connects with my ancestors like some kind of culinary DNA. It's a scent that always helps me empty myself of some of the heartache, at least for a little while, like a narcotic whose high is instantaneous and which takes it time dissolving so the trip back down to earth is slow - the same way the smell of sautéing onion and leeks lingers throughout the house long after the soup has been eaten and put away.

When everything is evenly browned, it's time to add the chicken stock. Now, if I can see the ugliness coming, and often I do, even if it's only subconsciously, I will put up some homemade stock in anticipation. However, when I'm blindsided, as I was in my last relationship, abandoned in complete surprise, and forced to move again this time from San Francisco, then it's canned or out of a box, passable but not nearly as good. The canned soup is always missing something, whether it is patience or passion, it just doesn't offer the same resistance. Good home-cooked stock can make the difference between a long season filled with regret or moving quickly on to forgiveness.

Unfortunately, cooks have to make do with what they have available, as do each of us in life when we are plagued with poor choices. When it came to poor choices I had Nick, Jack and Jolene, and I wasn't planning to make any more.

Now, I've always thought that there is a certain satisfaction that comes with bitterness, which is why we hold on to it as long as we do, even why you sometimes like the taste of it, which probably explains why I like the simmering part most of all. It tames the bitterness so that even the worse memories become more palatable. It goes on for hours making promise after promise which, in the case of soup as opposed to people, it usually delivers on.

When the simmering is done, about two-thirds of the soup gets liquefied in the blender and returned to the pot with a drop of cream—heavy for major disappointments, light for the others. The soup then has to cool a bit so it can be served warm, not hot, because you can't distinguish all the flavors when it's too hot, and without all the flavors it will never be able to take hold of my despondency and anxiety as I sip it down.

In my experience, good soup is defiant of every mood and always manages to release somewhat that tight grip time and recent memories may have around my heart. It turns wherever I am - the kitchen or the small dining area in my new restaurant - into a place where those veils of troubling thoughts and confusion about who I am and what I want are not quite as suffocating as they often tend to be.

Of course, it helps to be accompanied by a good red wine and the appropriate bread which, in this case, would be sourdough that I always keep frozen at home and have delivered fresh every day at the restaurant. I named it Circa for the last nine years of my life that I'd just as soon forget – especially the two men and one woman who inspired me to disavow any future that might involve romance and to keep the rest of humanity at a safe distance.

Instead of just cooking for my own memories, I decided to open a restaurant to see if I could help others forget and let go, if only during the course of a meal. What better way to do it than with a restaurant where soups are the only course, hearty bowls and warm, crusty bread. I figured that I couldn't be the only one out there susceptible to soup's medicinal qualities and I was right, although I'm getting a bit off track since this story isn't about soup, it's about me and one of my first customers, my favorite customer actually, an old man named Roger Peckinpaw Beanstock, known as Professor Beany, Professor Emeritus of English at Smith College. He walked in the first week I opened—Thursday night—as he would every Thursday night for a year, until my soup could no longer drown out the voices in his head.

About the Author

The Laws of Attraction is Howard Reiss' third novel.

Howard Reiss' second novel, *The Year of Soup* was inspired by a dinner at a small restaurant in Northampton, Mass. when an old professorial looking gentlemen with a bottle of wine in a paper bag sat down at a table in the corner and was immediately joined by the young, female proprietor and chef. Although he couldn't hear their conversation, he tried to imagine it and their stories as well. This novel received the Silver Medal for Best Fiction in the North-East Region at the Independent Publisher Book Awards in 2013.

Howard Reiss' first novel, *A Family Institution,* published in 2011, was based on a true incident involving the discovery of an aunt hidden from the family who spent most of her life in Pilgrim State Hospital. The main character's quest for the truth about what happened takes him to Pilgrim State where he takes a job in the records department, learns a lot about how the mentally ill and, in particular, his aunt was treated in the 1950s, and in the process turns his life and family upside down. It's a serious subject approached with a strong comic touch and has been a growing favorite of book clubs around the country.

Connect with Me Online

Website: http://www.HowardReiss.com

Facebook: http://www.facebook.com/HowardReissAuthor

Twitter: @HoRoRe

Lightning Source UK Ltd.
Milton Keynes UK
UKHW022025241121
394516UK00010B/598